A Man
of
Insignificance

by

K.C. Dowling

Grosvenor House
Publishing Limited

The right of K.C. Dowling to be identified as the author of this
work has been asserted by him in accordance with Section 78
of the Copyright, Designs and Patents Act 1988

Edited by Jon Twigge
Cover illustration and design by Luciano Braga
The book cover picture is copyright to K.C. Dowling

This book is published by
Grosvenor House Publishing Ltd
28-30 High Street, Guildford, Surrey, GU1 3EL.
www.grosvenorhousepublishing.co.uk

A CIP record for this book
is available from the British Library

ISBN 978-1-78148-326-8

Contents

Acknowledgements

I would like to thank in general everybody who contributed to the creation of this book. In particular I would like to thank my editor Jon Twigge and my cover designer Luciano Braga as well as Carol Saunders, Debbie Appleton and many of the guests at The Springfield Hotel, Marple.

As with virtually everything I do, I would have been unable to do it without the support, tolerance, patience and understanding of my wife Elaine. So a special thanks to her.

Chapter 1

Number One, Gaol Street

Upon first consideration number one, Gaol Street, Beaumaris, Anglesey, Wales, is not a particularly evocative address. Upon reconsideration this is just not true, for as an address, Gaol Street is extremely evocative. It is just that the name itself brings to mind an image that is the exact opposite of what that description actually represents, which is a pretty little terraced cottage in that tiny Welsh, tidal-waterway town that finds itself at the eastern ingress of the Menai Strait.

He had been away in Beaumaris for a long weekend where he owned the small cottage in Gaol Street. The house itself was just on the edge of town which was exactly where he found himself to be in life. Not in the centre, not completely outside of it, but just on the edge. The little house was where he had been staying over the last four days. He had bought it on impulse nine years ago when his finances had been in better shape. Amazingly, Charlotte had actually allowed him to keep it after the divorce. That part of the settlement had always puzzled him as she hadn't shown the same generosity with anything else. He put it down to the fact that the place wasn't actually worth that much, particularly in these straitened times and if she had wanted to take it for herself, she would have had no use for it and it would have only been to sell on and in order to do that she would have had to spend some time and money and Charlotte wasn't enthusiastic about spending time nor money, unless of course it was on herself.

The house had been a bit run down initially and probably would still seem that way to some but as far as he was concerned it was now very comfortable. Total refurbishment had never even crossed his mind, so the imperfect condition that he had found it in wasn't serious to him, it was just superficial: decoration throughout, the obligatory leak in the roof, no gutters to speak of, the timber front door was rotten, two rotten window frames and the glass in the cellar skylight had disappeared. Along with some other miscellaneous bits and the back wall, these were the totally identified defects. The back wall was the biggest job, it was leaning and defying gravity by still being there at all. He had employed local tradesmen to rebuild the wall and fix the roof, replace the gutters and the windows and the door, the other bits he'd done himself and the decorating he believed was work in progress but the truth was that he had just ignored it. Anyway, what was wrong with red and green flowered wallpaper he asked himself, it all comes back into fashion eventually, what indeed? The plumbing still seemed to have a mind of its own and couldn't be relied upon on all the time but he knew that so did he and he also knew that he couldn't be totally relied upon either, so in that sense the little house and himself were somewhat harmonized.

The little cottage was on the same street as the old Beaumaris Gaol, hence the name of the street. By a strange quirk, the Gaol building itself had been designed by one Joseph Aloysius Hansom, the same man who had designed the once ever present and eponymous Hansom Cab. To the critical friend it may have seemed perverse that whilst one of Joseph Aloysius's designs gifted a person the facility to travel in comparative freedom and comfort, another one did the opposite and curtailed or even prevented anything that resembled either of those two human requirements.

Every time he stepped outside the front door of his house there was this gaol looming, large, grey, grim and formidable with its high walls and huge, clanging iron doors intruding unapologetically into view. It had been there since 1829 and it seemed to be very well settled on that particular site.

The gaol itself had not actually reigned very long as a gaol, after which it had been used as a police station and strangely enough a children's clinic during the 1960's. In 1862 there had actually been two public hangings within its walls but all those histrionics were long since gone and it was now completely empty of all prisoners and gaolers. After nearly one hundred and fifty years of existence it had been converted in 1974 to a heritage museum and since then had been firmly established as such. It now receives around thirty thousand visitors a year. They all pay five pounds to the nice but sometimes disinterested lady behind the counter and each and every one of these visitors, in contradiction to the previous tenants, can come and go as they wish. He'd visited it once with his son and daughter and had been struck by the irony of walking around it in total freedom.

Charlotte may not have cared for the little house but for all its shortcomings he did. Apart from a new settee and some new beds and bedding he'd furnished and kitted it out from the island's charity shops and to him it felt lived in, which was exactly what it was. He felt comfortable there, safe, and he escaped to it whenever he could. There was another big plus for the little house, which he hadn't known when he'd bought it, well he didn't ask and nobody ventured forth with the information, for some technical reason to do with the Gaol building there was no telephone reception in the house and therefore when he was inside the house, as far as telephone contact was concerned, he was completely out of reach.

There was probably another reason for Charlotte not contesting his ownership of the little house and that was because when they were both actually in Beaumaris itself and they were surrounded by all that beautiful scenery and clean fresh air, all he'd managed to do was set up camp in either Ye Olde Bull's Head, the White Lion or the Liverpool Arms and drink either large glasses of red wine or pints of local beer, sometimes both and often, until he could drink no more. It wasn't that she didn't enjoy a drink herself, although he had to admit her consumption by any stretch of the imagination could only be considered social and moderate, whereas his by the same stretch of imagination would be considered not. She used to complain to him about it and assuming her best head teacher's voice would say, 'have we come all the way here to have to walk backwards and forwards past that Gaol, just for you to be able to sit in the pub, we may just as well have stayed at home!'

3

So, in fairness, he thought that the cottage probably represented a negative memory for her so why would she want to spend time and money on a negative memory?

Anyway, she had done alright financially out of everything else. She wasn't exactly destitute so why should she have his little house as well? She certainly wasn't short of money, she had always earned much more than he ever had. Then there was the significant legacy from her late mother that he'd never seen a penny of and she'd kept the main house and virtually everything else that she could think of. Throughout the divorce proceedings he'd made no financial claim against Charlotte, even though his lawyer, Nicholas Sipe, had repeatedly urged him to. Lawyers though, he knew all about them only too well, they tried to cause and create conflict in order to protract and complicate situations that were often quite simple. They pretended that it was in their client's own interest, but lawyers were only interested in one thing, money, and as far as that was concerned they worked in the interest of one person only, the lawyer. If they discovered that you actually had any money then they weren't content until they had wrested it from you, under the pseudonym of a fee, and shared it amongst themselves. So with this in mind he had ignored most of Sipe's advice, he'd only hired him as a token anyway and that had cost him enough and he was determined that his divorce would be as acrimony free as it was possible to be. He might be divorcing his wife but his children were still his children and Charlotte was still their mother and this situation would exist for the rest of his life, certainly long after he'd paid his lawyers fee. He wasn't going to make any attempt whatsoever to strain relations even more with Charlotte and his children just for the sake of money and just so lawyer Sipe's family could be financially advantaged at the cost of his own being financially disadvantaged.

It was also common knowledge that Archie, Charlotte's father, was *old money* and there was only her and her sister for it to go around when that time came. So all in all, Charlotte's financial security was assured, which was the exact opposite of what could be said of his, with an ever dwindling divorce settlement, two little houses, one in Beaumaris and one in Winton

Kiss and a meagre councillor's allowance being his only sources of income and equity.

Over the years little had altered with his activities in Beaumaris. Obviously Charlotte had long since gone out of his life although not entirely. She did show up now and again, usually with issues to do with the children, but even these appearances were becoming less frequent, particularly now with both children being away at university, but The Liverpool Arms, Ye Olde Bull's Head, the red wine and the local bitter et al. were still there. His recent brief holiday had been firm testament to this and it flashed through his mind that he may have gained a little house but he'd lost a wife. Was it worth it he asked himself? It wasn't that he didn't care but he couldn't come up with an answer in the time that he had, plus the fact that he'd pondered on this conundrum for many hours throughout a multitude of previous occasions and had still not resolved the question, so he wasn't going to dwell upon the subject now.

He'd woken up in the little house earlier this Monday morning at about 10:00am after a seamless afternoon and evening in the White Lion. Now he sat at the kitchen table with a mug of tea and some toast and Marmite. He considered staying in Beaumaris another day. That would most certainly have been his preference but then he vaguely remembered that he had some routine meeting to attend on the Wednesday and in advance of it he had to get through an absolute mountain of reading. These meetings were always the same, it was all reading and when it wasn't, it was all writing. These tasks were always ever present before the inevitable meeting and the inevitable conclusion of all these inevitable meetings, whatever the subject, whosoever attended, was always that there would be *another* meeting. No matter what anybody did or said there was no way out of this vexation. Anyway, he would have to do his reading tomorrow, on the Tuesday, which really meant that he would have to return today. After some brief mental dither his mind was made up, he would head home today.

He felt a little groggy so he strolled around Beaumaris town in the open air for a while until his head cleared. He meandered from his little house, passing the gaol, there was no escaping it he thought. He pardoned his own accidental but spontaneous mental pun.

As he walked down Castle Street he stopped to draw some cash from the hole in the wall at the bank, but why was it he thought that whenever he went to these holes in the wall, that no matter where the hole was or even where the wall was, that the person in front of him was always the carer for half the elderly population in town and was withdrawing all their different pensions in cash in one clean go, and so it was today. So he stood there second in a queue of two for almost a full ten minutes.

Finally he strolled along the front and down the short pier and back again. The sun was out and he looked up at clear blue skies. The day had the beginnings of a fine day. The day-trippers were queuing up in their shorts and T-shirts with their kids and their rucksacks and their plastic bottles of water to take the short boat trip to Puffin Island. All the years he'd been coming to Beaumaris and he'd never even considered taking that trip. His eyes swept along the slightly crumbling, but still very elegant, Georgian terrace at the east end of Alma Street, then he walked through the gap and passed the White Lion. As he did he gave a sidelong glance through the window, half expecting to see himself still sitting there alone and disconsolate at the table with an empty glass in front of him just like that L.S. Lowry painting, or was it Van Gogh, he wasn't quite sure, but the room in the White Lion was half dark inside and completely empty, so he concluded that he wasn't there.

Overall he decided that Beaumaris found itself in a state of slow but gentle, lazy decay and he found that interesting. He found himself at the castle end of Castle Street whereupon he went into the Castle Cafe for his customary filtered black coffee and a quick flick of the cafe's newspaper.

Two cups later, another walk past the Gaol, a quick check on his tiny house and he was in his car ready for the off. Then, that was it, he was gone. Goodbye to Gaol St and Beaumaris, until the next time!

He took the drive back at a leisurely pace. It had taken him just under three hours, which for 107 miles door-to-door with a halfway stop wasn't bad, taking into account the slight presence of holiday traffic. Now he stood outside his own front door in the village of Winton Kiss and in the sunshine with his bag of Beaumaris dirty laundry in one hand and his front door key in the other. It occurred to him that recently his life had been spent between these two places, Winton Kiss and Beaumaris.

Winton Kiss is a small town or large village depending upon your own perspective. He had always thought of it as a village. It has approximately three and a half thousand inhabitants. It sits at the start of the Peak District National Park foothills and you can view a distant Kinder Scout, the Peak District's highest mountain, from some Winton Kiss streets. The Winton river runs just along the edge of the village centre, poetically kissing it slightly, hence the name. Chasing the river and running alongside it in parallel is the village's main street, appropriately named, River Street.

River Street is probably no longer than two hundred metres and is just wide enough for two cars to pass each other side-by-side. Nevertheless, River Street has: three pubs, three trendy wine-bar-cafe-type places, a post office cum general store, an estate agents, a bakers, three hairdressers, a bridal gown shop, a bookshop, a fireplace shop, a beauty therapist, a chiropodist, a chemist, a fish and chip shop, two or three other shops that keep changing what they have to offer, a dentist's practice and a doctor's surgery. Winton Kiss is in the political ward of Malton, which in turn is in the metropolitan borough of Norford, a nearby larger town. Winton Kiss sits on the main Manchester to Sheffield rail line and is a minute or two over twenty minutes by train from and to Manchester and around a minute or two less than an hour by train from and to Sheffield.

Many years ago the village had been in the parish of High Peak, Derbyshire and the Winton Kiss residents were pleased with that. Then, because of the never-ending boundary changes, which are usually drawn and redrawn for political motivation, it found itself in Cheshire. The residents didn't appreciate that as much as High Peak, but it was marginal in their eyes and they soon got used to it. Latterly though, a major travesty had taken place and Winton Kiss had changed its address yet again, it had become part of the Metropolitan Borough of Norford. There was even worse to come for it was now addressed as Winton Kiss, Malton, Norford, Greater Manchester. It was the word *Manchester* that was the problem. Residents did not appreciate that at all. They were haughty and disdainful about any associations with Manchester itself. There was an element of hypocrisy in this stance as many of these residents originated from this city themselves and a significant number of them earned their living there, commuting on a daily basis.

Even though most of the residents were too young to remember when Winton Kiss had been in Cheshire, and none of them that remembered it being in High Peak were still alive, they still complained in the bars and cafes about its now *Manchester* address. Some of them still stubbornly referred on any correspondence to 'Winton Kiss, Cheshire' and a few still referred to it as being 'Winton Kiss, High Peak.' In support of this denial a small number of them even had specially printed letterheads and business cards to prove it. The village may well be only a short train journey to Manchester city centre but to the residents of Winton Kiss that industrially-revolutionised Metropolis, which surely now had become England's second city after London, was considered a whole world-and-a-half away from their town or village.

There were young families in Winton Kiss. To educate the children it contained two primary schools and the larger town of Malton had two Secondary schools. Originally Winton Kiss had been an Anglo-Saxon settlement before it had trundled its way meekly through English history until it arrived as a canal village. Later it was a Victorian mill village but its growth since the 1960's owed much to its previously mentioned location along the main Sheffield to Manchester rail line. However, many of the residents seemed to be of a certain age and he'd read somewhere that fifty-four per cent of the residents of the whole of Winton Kiss were over fifty-five years of age.

Apart from the carousing of a few drunks on entering and leaving the bars on weekend nights, it was a quiet place where there was little that was happening and little that was going to happen.

He had lived there for twenty-two years since he had come out of the army whereupon he had married Charlotte. His army career had been cut short. He had joined up four years before he had met her and after they had both realised their depth of feeling for each other she had told him that being a First Lieutenant in the King's Rifles was not conducive to her idea of married life and that she was certainly not going to become an army wife. She had pressed the ultimatum upon him of either her or the army, and after some brief indecision he had resigned his commission and sought his early discharge. Save an old platoon photograph and a medal for *best marksman,* both hidden away in some long forgotten drawer and which he accidentally came across every few years, his military days were now a long ago distant memory.

Charlotte had lived in Winton Kiss even before him but she'd since moved out, after the divorce. He had stayed, well he had nowhere else to go for one thing and for another, for the last fourteen years he'd been the locally elected councillor and as such was expected to live in his own political ward and more than anywhere, even more than the little house in Beaumaris, he now thought of it as home.

He stuck his key in the front door lock and with his now free hand he checked his outside mailbox. It was a one-foot-square black metal box with *Post* written on it and a red rose engraved on the front. His mother had bought it from the boy scouts jumble sale some years ago and every time she saw it she would regale anyone in earshot with how she had cleverly bartered down the price, with a twelve-year-old boy scout mind you, but she often left that bit out, to seventy-five pence.

'These are thirty pounds in Malton Garden Centre,' she'd say triumphantly, 'and I paid pennies for it.'

You could lock the outside mailbox if you wanted to but he didn't lock it. In fact he left the key in it all the time so he didn't lose it. Nobody had ever stolen any of his mail, he didn't expect them to and if somebody decided that they wanted to, they could have it with his permission. There was never anything interesting in it anyway and even less by the way of cheeriness. He considered that his mail fell into two categories, it was either somebody complaining about something *to* him or somebody demanding something *from* him.

He lifted the mailbox flap and fished out a solitary, white envelope. It was, unusually, handwritten. He held it up in the sunlight and studied it. It was handwriting that he recognised, not the actual hand itself but the style, it was a style that his father had used and now seemed out of fashion. This style was favoured by older people with grammar school educations, he remembered it was called Copperplate. He didn't get many handwritten envelopes, he thought back unsuccessfully to when he had last had one. It was addressed to him in his official capacity as the locally elected member, *'Councillor Danny Senetti.'*

In this capacity he received lots of communications, some letters but mostly emails, and less than ten per cent of them were worth reading and about ten per cent of that ten per cent were worthy of a response. Phone texts, he got a lot of them too, although he didn't respond to any of them and approximately the same mathematical equation that applied to reading the emails applied to reading the texts. He thought again that it was quite a while since he had actually received a handwritten envelope.

His eyes focussed as he tried to see through the envelope like an X-ray. It struck him that in this aspect he was turning into his own mother. That's exactly the sort of thing that that she would have done. He could just see her now in his mind's eye, holding a letter aloft in front of the electric light, as if somehow the ray of the light would shine through the paper and reveal the letter's contents and the name and address of the sender.

'Now who can this be from? I don't know anybody who writes that way, I don't know anybody in Sheffield, I've never even been there,' she'd say studying the postmark.

Then she'd launch into a question and answer session with herself as she tried to identify the letter writer. 'Is it a man or a woman's hand? I think it's a man's, it looks to be a man's to me, it looks similar to your Uncle Ken's writing. Oh, it can't be from him can it? He's dead,' she'd announce. Eventually she'd open the envelope.

It wouldn't end there and once the author had been identified there would be a supplementary monologue. 'Oh it's from her, it's not a man at all, I knew it wasn't, what is she writing to me about? I've only met her a couple of times and I hardly know her.'

So it would go on, she'd put the letter behind the clock on the mantelpiece, always in the same place. Then she'd say, 'I'll read it properly later, with a cup of tea when I'm more relaxed.'

He opened his front door and saw the last few days' newspapers piled in the mat well. Naturally he'd forgotten to cancel them during his Beaumaris trip, he ignored them as he bowled the wash bag softly up the long, narrow lobby. It skittered along the polished floor and nestled snugly next to his old, battered, briefcase.

He looked once more at the white envelope that he still held in his hand. Today was Bank Holiday Monday and the sun was actually shining. This was a rare combination! Rare? No, in fact it was a unique one, in England anyway, sunshine on a bank holiday – never been known! He didn't really know what bank holidays were for any more, especially now that his two children had grown up and now that Charlotte wasn't around, they seemed to have lost any meaning without family.

What he did know was what bank holidays were not for and that was they were not for opening letters, even ones that were handwritten in an elegant copperplate style and presented in a crisp white envelope. The letter could wait until tomorrow he thought to himself. Without even crossing his own doorstep he placed the unopened envelope on the small hall table, pulled his front door shut, walked down his short garden path, out of his gate and began the slow descent, down the long hill towards the Black Swan.

Chapter 2

Maxine Wells and Helen Day

It was Tuesday and it was early evening, the day after the bank holiday and by now most people had eased themselves back into their normal life routines.

Dr Maxine Wells checked her surgery computer for the last time today. It had been an ordinary, typical, routine surgery with the usual procession of ills, ailments, complaints and neuroses, many of them real, many of them exaggerated and some of them imagined altogether. Why then at the end of it was she sat there, her long, slim hands joined together under her chin as if in prayer but in reality in concentration and obviously perplexed and seemingly concerned about something?

The source of her concern and perplexity was one of her patients, Helen Day. Helen had not turned up for her 4:15pm appointment. Helen had been a patient of the doctor since Maxine had first taken over the Winton Kiss practice from her father, seven years ago. Since then Helen had taken numerous appointments. In fact, Dr Wells thought that these appointments often seemed to be about the most trivial of concerns. She thought sometimes that Helen really just came in for a chat and that any ills referred to were inconsequential and just gave her an excuse to do exactly that. Of course the doctor would never suggest that to a patient and even if it were true, that was what she was there for, to make people feel better, and if coming in for a chat made you feel better then where was the harm? So she always listened and sometimes she advised and sometimes she even gave Helen a prescription that she suspected Helen rarely converted.

The point was though, that without exception Helen Day always attended these appointments, every single one of them, except the one today and the one today was certainly not a trivial issue. Maxine had received the test results back from the hospital and as she had suspected there was an issue and she needed to speak to Helen straight away. In fact, every ticking minute until that conversation took place was potentially worsening the situation for her patient.

The doctor checked again at reception to see if there had been any last minute messages from Helen but Paula the receptionist informed her that there had not. Patients of course did miss appointments. Some missed more than they kept and seemingly as a matter of routine. Missed appointments were in fact a consideration for the practice and the matter had been discussed at the last practice meeting, there was actually a notice in reception about missed appointments.

Helen was aware that the doctor was waiting for test results and that there was some sense of urgency about the situation. Maxine Wells mulled things over in her mind for a minute. Perhaps she should call Helen, was she being intrusive? Was this part of the doctor patient relationship? Should she be chasing patients to keep their own appointments? She asked herself all these questions in her head. She thought about them all for a moment and decided that she wasn't, sometimes it was and in this case she should. She picked up her phone and dialled Helen's number. It rang three times and when the answering machine responded, she left a brief message.

'Hello Ms Day, Dr Wells here, you didn't keep your appointment at the surgery today, perhaps you'd care to call the surgery on this number,' she recited her surgery number, 'and we can rearrange.'

She was deliberate and took care to speak clearly and slowly as the answering machine had requested. She didn't say anything about any urgency, patients get anxious when you use that word and she didn't want to set any hares of any kind running just yet, if at all.

That would have been it for most people, they would have left it at that, at least until tomorrow, but not Doctor Maxine Wells.

Helen's house was on her way home and Maxine thought that she might just visit her on the journey. She didn't really know why but she had a sense of some harm befalling. It wasn't logical, it wasn't rational, but she couldn't deny that the feeling was definitely there.

Doctor Wells left her surgery at precisely 7.30pm as she did most evenings. The weather had changed for the worse, instead of the bright May sunshine and clear blue skies that had overlooked her when she had signed in at 3:00pm, she now encountered the usual sky of wan, the colourless North West of England blanket, and as if by cue, soft rain was starting to fall. She climbed into her newly purchased silver Mercedes convertible, shut the door and made herself comfortable and safe. She edged cautiously out of the surgery car park and headed slowly up the lane towards Helen Day's house.

In the village Helen's house was known as the *White House*. This was because it stood at the end of a terraced row of cottages and whereas the others were all stone presented, the outside walls of the White House were painted completely white.

During the short, five-minute drive Maxine Wells allowed herself to ponder upon the enigma that was Helen Day. Helen was a little bit of a mystery, she had had arrived in Winton Kiss about ten years ago. At that time Maxine was at medical school in Dublin. Helen didn't visit the surgery at all then, in fact she wasn't even registered as a patient, she registered shortly after Maxine had joined the practice. She was a well-spoken, seemingly educated woman, elegant in appearance, thin and tall, at least for her generation, about five feet eight. She was very upright and walked as if she was balancing something on her head. Her hair was neatly cut and combed and still blonde, even at the age of seventy, although Maxine thought that she probably had some assistance with the colour from one of the local hairdressers.

Nobody in the village knew much about Helen. She didn't give out a lot and apart from going to church on Sunday she didn't go out much either. Even in church she sat at the back on her own. She didn't socialize in any conventional way. She avoided question and answer conversation, you could talk with her for half an hour, not that anybody ever engaged her for that long, and you would know no more about her at the end of the thirty minutes than you did at the beginning of them. For Helen it was as if information avoidance was an art and she had mastered it.

Someone passed it around that she was now retired but that she'd worked as both a teacher and a social worker. None of this though had ever been substantiated. It was known that Helen had once acted in some official social work capacity for Theresa Rafferty but Theresa's lips were sealed on a matter that Theresa herself described as being confidential. Someone also passed it around that Helen had been born in London but she'd lived and worked in America for a lot of her adult life but Helen herself had never made any reference to this and nobody really had the presumption to ask her outright.

Given this claim by persons unknown, if it were true then it was strange that she had not the merest trace of an American accent and according to Tom De Stefano, the village's resident Texan, 'If she's ever set foot in the place then I'm a Mexican,' and he clearly wasn't, although Tom was prone to making statements of that kind about a lot of things and over the years he'd also assumed, amongst other identities, an Aborigine, a Russian monk, a Chinese mandarin, the Lord Jesus Christ and his own particular favourite, a one-eyed son-of-a-gun. He clearly wasn't any of those either so his view really didn't carry much in the way of credibility.

In point of fact Helen spoke in a precise, clipped way, with a type of received pronunciation, as if she'd had some kind of elocution lessons. Her accent reminded Maxine of Sally Watkins, an old friend from medical school, and Sally had received elocution lessons. Helen's received pronunciation also had the merest trace of a very slight accent, it wasn't there all the time just the odd word, but the doctor wasn't very good on accents and she couldn't really place it.

Not long after Helen had arrived in the village a young French woman had called into the post office looking for directions. The young woman had no English and Helen was in the shop at the time. She engaged the woman in her native French tongue both easily and fluently, so within the hour it was common knowledge in Winton Kiss that Helen Day spoke fluent French. Naturally this only served to enhance the air of mystique around her and foster even more stories, this time about her French connection.

Helen wasn't hostile or unfriendly, in fact the opposite was true, she was well mannered and polite in general interaction and in the conduct of day-to-day life, but if anybody asked her anything that facilitated her giving some background information about herself she would just smile and respond with no response, at least no verbal response. On rare occasions she could be brusque and there was a story that circulated the village whereupon she had entered a local hairdressers and when the young stylist had asked her 'how do you want your hair doing today?' Helen had responded by saying curtly, 'in silence please.' On the whole though she would listen attentively to others as they rattled on about their day-to-day comings and goings but if any of them asked her directly about her own activities or plans she would give answers such as 'only business' or 'some tedious but necessary journey'.

About six times a year Helen took the train from Winton Kiss train station to Manchester Piccadilly but nobody knew what she did when she arrived there. Many yearned to but none dare ask. Tom O'Keefe, the stationmaster, had reported to the people of Winton Kiss that when she returned she had no bags with her so it obviously wasn't shopping. Over the years, on two separate occasions, she had been seen by two separate *Kissites* in Manchester, once when she was coming out of a bank and on the other occasion she was seen in Manchester Town Hall. It was Becky Morton the barmaid from The Black Swan who had seen her at the town hall, Becky worked there as part of her day job. Maxine mused that Helen was probably making some mundane council enquiry or carrying out some other routine errand but many in the village saw it as an opportunity for further speculation, so that's what they did, they speculated.

Helen certainly had no close friends in the village and she made no mention of any family or friends outside of it. Apart from three people nobody could ever recall her having any visitors at her house. Apart from her trips to Manchester she rarely, if ever, went further than the village or the neighbouring town of Malton. A lot of the residents were intrigued by her but in Winton Kiss there were those who were intrigued by anybody whose business, family history and life story they didn't know all about. In fact some made it *their* business to find out all about *your* business. However in Helen's case they'd been unsuccessful.

For all her reclusiveness Helen Day wasn't unpopular. Most local folk just looked upon her as being a harmless eccentric, and there were a few of them in the village besides her, so really no revelations there! In fact, Maxine mused that you would be hard pressed to find a good number in Winton Kiss that couldn't be defined as eccentric, it was that sort of place, and in any case what exactly was wrong with keeping yourself to yourself? Very little Maxine concluded.

Helen Day wasn't ostentatious but it was obvious and apparent to others that she wasn't without money. She wore little jewellery but her clothes were expensive and there were other signs, every year without fail she donated five hundred pounds to Paddy Considine's cancer-charity walk, although she never went on it herself and she didn't come to the Travellers Oak for the presentations, announcements or celebrations afterwards. When Guy Trousdale, a local aspiring artist, had an exhibition in Winton Kiss church hall she unflinchingly, there and then, paid seven hundred and fifty pounds for one of his exhibits.

It was also well known that she had paid cash for her house and that it was expensively furnished. Few had been in it to see any of the furniture but they had seen the posh liveried vans that had delivered it. In fact she paid cash for most things, rarely did she use anything else. She didn't have the abundant ever-present plastic cards that everybody else seemed to have. Although Helen never spoke of it and it really didn't show, Maxine knew that Helen was a drinker and when Maxine had routinely asked her about her consumption Helen had lied. There had never been any sightings of her in any of the local pubs and even though the royal wedding celebrations had been in the lane right outside her house and the day was blessed with reasonable weather Helen Day didn't put in an appearance.

Maxine paused outside The Travellers Oak pub to let an oncoming vehicle through as the lane was narrow at that section. She could see through the pub window and into the bar which was thronged with early-doors drinkers. She couldn't make out their faces though she recognised some of them from their silhouettes. She came to recognise body shapes even in silhouette, it came with practice and the fact that most of them came through her surgery door at one time or another. As the car passed the driver gave her a friendly wave in acknowledgment for her driving courtesy. The white and pink blossoms were out along the lane and the soft rain had brought out their sweet aroma.

There was one other thing to add to the mystique of Helen Day, this was not speculation it was tangible, and it came from Maxine's personal experience. Just about the time Maxine had joined the practice Helen had consulted her at the surgery. She couldn't recall Helen's actual complaint, only that it had been trivial. Helen had with her an expensive Jimmy Choo handbag and during the conversation the clasp came undone and some of the contents spilled onto the surgery floor. Helen, quick as light, got up from her seat, knelt down and hurriedly scooped them up. As she did the handbag gaped open momentarily and inside its silken folds Maxine was almost certain that she saw a small but deadly-looking, gunmetal coloured revolver. She didn't know whether it was real or a replica and if it was real, was it loaded? She wondered why Helen Day, or for that matter anybody at all, would want to walk the streets of Winton Kiss with a loaded gun in her handbag. There didn't seem to be anything to Maxine that warranted such a precaution, if indeed it was that. The gun sighting had unsettled Maxine a little, so much so that she'd mentioned it to her dad, Doctor Tom, but he'd dismissed it with one of his typical pointed philosophies by saying, 'If you looked into all the women's handbags in Winton Kiss half of them would have something in them that they wanted to hide and it's really none of our business.'

She didn't really know what he meant and her impulse was to disagree with him, this wasn't a letter from a lover that Helen was hiding away or a secret half bottle of gin, it was a deadly weapon.

Maxine thought about it for a moment and decided that there was nothing in her own handbag that she had to hide. Dad though was Dad and he was usually right about most things, especially anything to do with human nature and specifically human nature in Winton Kiss. She therefore put the image of the gun to the back of her mind and right up until now it had stayed there.

Helen Day, eccentric Maxine thought, perhaps, but harmless, Maxine thought, perhaps not. All things considered it was as if Helen Day was hiding herself away and trying to protect herself from something or someone. This might seem wild imaginings but during her years as a doctor Maxine had discovered that some people most certainly do have secrets to keep and things to hide. Virtually every day of her working life at least one patient would say, 'This is in the strictest confidence Doctor isn't it?' and why did they say that? They said it because they didn't want anybody else to know, that's why, and although she was not really curious herself to know exactly what Helen Day's secrets were, over the years this was the view that Doctor Maxine Wells came to form about Helen Day, that Helen most definitely had something that she thought she should hide and she was doing her utmost to hide it.

As Maxine pulled up outside Helen's cottage she thought that she'd caught a glimpse of the Reverend Bel disappearing into Mrs Ecclesbridge's across the road. As if to confirm her sighting she could see what she thought was the cleric's pedal cycle propped up against the gable end. Bel was the new energetic vicar and a relative newcomer to the village. She'd taken over All Saints Church from the late Reverend William Rice. She'd come immediately from some remote part of Wales but before that she had been in London and the talk was that she had been one of the first ever female clergy to be ordained. This was to be her last parish before retirement and when villagers had first heard of her appointment there had been a mixed response. However, Reverend Bel wasn't lacking energy and she was making quite a favourable impact in the village, particularly with her strong worded sermons on traditional family values. Despite Winton Kiss having more than its fair share of hills the new vicar cycled everywhere.

19

It seemed appropriate that the Reverend Bel should be around as Maxine was actually thinking of Helen, for the churchwoman was one of the *only three visitors* of Helen's that Maxine had been thinking about earlier. Maxine knew Bel to be in her late fifties yet she appeared ten or even fifteen years younger. She was extremely attractive and intelligent with dark Latin looks and had caused a bit of a stir with the men-folk when she'd first turned up in Winton Kiss. The excitement had been short lived and had quickly turned to disappointment when three weeks after her arrival she'd been joined by her equally attractive and much younger husband who in turn caused quite a stir with the womenfolk. He wasn't around the village much, he worked for some oil company in the Middle East and spent most of his time out there. In fact, Maxine thought that she'd only seen him once and she couldn't even recall his name.

Bel had brought about a little negative reaction from some of the older women in the village but that was because she was a woman and some people just couldn't accept that women and priests can go together. Bel seemed oblivious to all the fuss, Maxine thought that she'd no doubt experienced it before. She came over as a dynamic but kindly person who was preoccupied with her calling and making a good name for herself in her parish, which was exactly the way a new vicar should be. Maxine thought that in Winton Kiss there were just too many people of a certain age and attitude that had been around the village a long time and held the same out of time views. She saw the new vicar as an asset and she liked her. The Reverend Bel obviously visited Helen Day as part of her clerical administrations.

Maxine's mind turned to Helen's two other reported visitors, Theresa Rafferty and Danny Senetti. Theresa was the local foster mum, she was originally from Dublin. She was a single parent and she had three young daughters: one of her own, Jane, who was sixteen years of age and two younger girls, Nicola and Emma, who were fostered. The younger girls were both at the local Catholic primary school. Theresa herself was in her mid-thirties, the same age as Maxine, and Helen seemed genuinely fond of her. In fact she seemed the only person that Helen was genuinely fond of.

Senetti, Maxine thought, now he was a different proposition altogether. He was the local councillor who was well known in the village and had gained himself a bit of a reputation, mostly for all the wrong things. These things were not to do with his activities as a councillor, they were usually connected to either his personality or his conduct. He had once been described by a political opponent of his in the local newspaper, and to the amusement of all, as being an inveterate blackguard. The description had stuck and he was sometimes referred to by locals, behind his back of course and in humour, as *Danny the Blackguard* or *Inveterate Senetti*. The latter was really an indirect humorous reference to inebriate instead of *inveterate* and to his alleged heavy drinking habit. In pursuit of this habit he was often to be found giving forth in one of Winton Kiss's three local pubs.

Last year, and the year before, on several occasions he'd been espied in the early-morning hours stumbling out of the White House and into a waiting taxi. As was often the alleged case with Senetti, in those precise moments he seemed to be under the protection and influence of alcohol. Maxine couldn't quite figure out the connection between Senetti and Helen Day, they didn't really seem to go together and were an odd pairing. The prim and proper, reclusive, bespectacled spinster and the drunken, gregarious, inveterate, blackguard councillor.

Helen though hadn't always been quite the spinster that she portrayed herself to be or that she would have others believe she was. Maxine had superior knowledge as far as that was concerned, after all she had seen Helen's medical records. These records were a strange indication for they showed that before Helen came to Winton Kiss she had rarely sought medical advice for twenty years or more on any issue yet since she'd arrived there she'd sought medical advice on an almost regular monthly basis. One thing that they did show was that as a younger woman she'd had a pregnancy and given birth so she hadn't always been quite that spinster.

Following on from that during one of Helen's consultations Maxine had asked her about 'any family' and Helen had answered by saying that she didn't have any. When Maxine pressed the issue by making a reference to her pregnancy and Helen's relationship with the child Helen at first seemed to be going to engage on the subject, then as if she thought better of it she answered by saying, 'We lost touch many years ago and now we're completely estranged.' Maxine sensed that the comment was tinged with sadness but she didn't raise the issue again as it was obvious that Helen didn't want it to be raised.

Maxine thought back to Senetti. She had never actually met him. She'd never even had a conversation of any kind with him but she'd heard stories. She had seen him about occasionally but not that much. She knew that he was on her patients' register but she was fairly sure that he had never consulted her about anything. Apparently he had called into the surgery once, to pick up a prescription for his wife, but that was several years ago and that was the only occasion, he had never attended in his own right, although if he carried on drinking the way it was alleged he did it would probably only be a matter of time before he made an appearance.

She thought that he probably spent a lot of time in Norford Town Hall with his council business or out and about in his political ward whereas she spent most of hers in her Winton Kiss practice, usually confined to her surgery. When she wasn't there or doing home visits she was at home with Doctor Tom so her own and Senetti's waking and walking hours were not compatible to either of them being in the same place at the same time.

She had actually seen him last year. She remembered now it had been a couple of days before Christmas Eve at Winton Kiss train station. In fact she'd shared the same small station waiting room with him and a few others whilst they'd all sheltered in wait for the train to Manchester on that freezing-cold December morning.

He had sat there opposite her, one leg hung over the other, staring gormlessly at the wall. She had noticed how unkempt he looked. He was unshaven, his shoes were badly scuffed and he wore an old, faded black overcoat with a scarf that seemed to be draped everywhere but around his neck. His trouser bottoms had ridden up and she also noticed that he was wearing odd socks, one was green whilst the other was blue. His hair though tousled was still thick and raven black, there was no sign of any grey yet. She thought this unusual for a man of his age, which she put to be about middle to late forties, and she wondered if the colour was from a bottle. He'd obviously combed it that day with his hands. His coat was unfastened and she could see that there were only two buttons on it where clearly once there would have been three. Through his open coat she could see the onset of a beer gut that came to rest above his belt. Actually it was more than an onset, it was fairly well established. She was drawn to his hands which in paradox to the rest of him were scrupulously clean, his fingernails were perfectly cut and manicured. She thought that she'd never seen a man with neater nor cleaner fingernails. Somehow they didn't seem to go along with the rest of him. He wasn't dirty, no it wasn't that, yet his face seemed to match his clothing and demeanour whereas his hands did not. There now! She thought that she had it. Yes that was it, the overall impression exuded by Danny Senetti was one of being a bit crumpled and ragged around the edges. Yes, pleased with her own descriptive powers she thought that description aptly suited him.

They had sat a few feet apart and opposite each other in complete, mutual un-acknowledgement. She remembered that when the train bound for Manchester pulled into Winton Kiss station he checked his wristwatch, rose rather ponderously to his feet and walked past her to board it. He didn't once look at her and as he passed by her he paused and she recalled that he absolutely reeked of what was unmistakably – last night's drink.

She also remembered that a couple of years ago he had been involved in some scandal. She'd overheard her dad talking about it in the kitchen with Ben Goldstein, a councillor friend of his. She couldn't hear precisely what they were saying, and they were talking more about it being hushed up by the political manipulators at the town hall than what the actual scandal itself was, but she had heard a little bit and she was fairly certain that it was something to do with some kind of relationship that Senetti had been having with a schoolgirl. Doctor Tom and Councillor Goldstein were saying that he'd almost lost his council seat over it, but obviously in the end he hadn't.

Maxine decided that even if she couldn't be sure that Senetti wasn't a complete drunk or a child molester, he was most certainly a local politician and some would think that being one of those was probably worse than being either, or even both, of the other two.

Therefore, in her eyes he had three out of three chances of being a little unsavoury so it was best to keep your distance from him. Anyway, there was no particular reason why their paths should ever cross. If she needed something from the council she'd consult another councillor and if he did actually ever turn up at her surgery, well then, that would be a professional situation.

So that was it, as far as Doctor Maxine Wells and Councillor Danny Senetti were concerned, she didn't particularly take to him, in fact she took against him and she certainly wouldn't trust him with anything or anybody of even minimal value. When she boarded the train she made sure that she sat as far away from him as she could get, which on that particular day was to the rear of the third and last carriage as he sat to the front of the first one.

Her thoughts came back to Helen Day. Perhaps Helen and the blackguard councillor were in some kind of clandestine relationship. Surely not, even in his late forties Helen was still old enough to be his mother. Perhaps they were just drinking pals. Perhaps, Perhaps, Perhaps! Maxine had to admit that she'd come across much odder pairings, and certainly bigger age gaps, she mused on. Anyway, whatever there was between Helen Day and Danny Senetti must have stopped because the sightings had ceased and nobody in the village spoke about such incidents anymore.

The row of cottages with their stone walls, old slate roofs and diligently tended front gardens made a pretty sight in the soft summer evening. Even though it was drizzling rain there was still plenty of natural light left and the rain had benefitted the little gardens by perking the flowers up. The White House stood at the end of a terrace block of ten. Historically the White House had been the schoolhouse and the other nine houses had housed the teachers and staff. That of course was two hundred years ago. Now they were just a row of pretty cottages in a pretty Cheshire village.

Helen's cottage had those typical, leaded cottage windows and Maxine noticed that all the ground-floor front curtains were drawn shut. She could see the weak glow of some of the electric lamplights behind some of them. She looked up at the second-storey windows and noticed that the curtains were drawn also. She thought that before she trespassed, uninvited into Helen's boundaries she would just try the telephone one more time so she called her again but the answering machine kicked in just as before. She rang it yet again with the same result. She found herself outside the polished wood, front door and rang the bell. Somewhere inside the house she could hear the sound of Ravel's Bolero from the bell chime inside. She pushed gently on the door but it resisted and she could tell that it was locked shut.

She thought about scribbling a message on the back of one of her business cards and putting it through the letterbox and leaving the rest to Helen but she dispelled the idea almost as soon as it entered her head. No, she'd taken the time and trouble to come here so she may as well follow her actions through as far as she could. Opening the side gate she went around to the back of the house. The curtains were all drawn there too. Momentarily, Maxine looked across the valley at the rain-swept, breath taking view over the Cheshire plain. She thought how green and beautiful it looked. She walked over to the back door wondering if she should give it a push. She pushed gently as she had minutes earlier on the front door. This time it was unlocked and it opened up in front of her. As Maxine stepped in gingerly she spoke softly, 'Helen, it's Doctor Maxine Wells, forgive the intrusion, are you alright, you didn't keep your appointment today?'

There was no answer so she repeated herself, a little bit louder this time, as she progressed through the kitchen and opened the door to the dining room. Still no answer. She moved quietly through the dining room and opened the door to the lounge.

Maxine Wells was a trained physician, she had been so for nine years and prior to that she had trained at medical school with all the implications such training and practice has, but what she saw in Helen Day's lounge that evening shocked her. As Maxine entered the lounge she observed it was deceptively large. She saw

Helen straight away, she was sat in a chair in the corner close to the window but out of sight of it. She had two small head wounds, one in the forehead and one on the right side of the temple. Maxine had seen enough murdered corpses to know that Helen had been shot dead.

Maxine had spent twelve months on secondment with Dublin Garda detectives in the Pathology and Forensics Department and once during one single nightshift she'd been called to four separate crime scenes involving six murders. After a while doing that job you became dispassionate about murder victims, they were just part of life, they were just bodies or at least most of them were, it was always very different somehow if you knew the person who had been murdered. This had happened to Maxine twice before and you always felt that little something that you didn't feel for complete strangers. No matter how tenuous or remote the personal connection you could never view it in exactly the same dispassionate way as you viewed all the other corpses. It was probably something to do with the fact that you knew something about them before they were just a corpse.

There was no doubt about it Maxine thought, for that was exactly what Helen now was – a corpse!

There was the usual amount of blood around the room and Maxine knew that Helen had obviously been killed by a third party, unless she had found a way to shoot herself twice and even if she had, where was the gun? Maxine couldn't see one although she did see Helen's handbag. It was open but there was no sign of the gun that she had recalled seeing in her surgery some years ago. The bag though was full of the large amount of cash that Helen was reputed to carry around with her. She didn't touch the money but noticed that the wad seemed intact. It went through Maxine's mind that whoever killed Helen was obviously not interested in it, even as an unexpected or accidental bonus. In fact, with such a large amount of money still lying around she concluded that the killer seemed to have decided to deliberately not take it, so whatever else the motive was it certainly was not done for financial gain.

There was nothing in this whole composite picture of the corpse that shocked Doctor Wells, no, that wasn't it, she'd seen this type of scene many times before. However, what did shock her, in fact it made her shiver and freeze to the bone was the condition and sight of the lounge itself and it wasn't so much the visual picture as the chilling sense and feeling the room exuded. The room had been systematically desecrated and wrecked beyond understanding. Virtually every dormant thing had been broken and then broken again. Every piece of glassware, pottery, mirror and every stick of furniture had been hammered, hacked, chopped and cut until it could be desecrated no more. It was as if it had been done as part of some wild, ritualistic practice that to the murderer was just as important as the murder itself. In fact it was as if it had been more important. It was as if some terrible yet symbolic act was being carried out.

Helen Day would have died instantly but it would have taken quite some time to inflict such wanton wrecking on what was once somebody's living sanctuary. Maxine had once seen a revenge killing in Glasnevin, Dublin where the murder scene had been violated by a maniac but it was nothing to this. She looked up and stared at the white fireplace wall and the mirror above it. This mirror, for some reason, had escaped the vandalism and there was some writing on it that looked as if it had been daubed on in red lipstick or crayon. The writing was a little unclear and it seemed to comprise of one word and some numbers, she couldn't quite make either of them out. She delved into her handbag took out a pair of spectacles and put them on, they didn't improve the purpose much. She stared at the message on the mirror again. She thought that it read as a series of letters followed by a series of numbers specifically C-O-M-B-E-E-N and then the letters one, eight, four, eight. So it seemed to read:

COMBEEN 1848

She stared at the writing yet again, was it a message, was it a clue? Who had written it, Helen, the murderer? What did this message refer to? Who had it actually been written for? She had no idea, she'd never heard of 'Combeen' before. There was something else that caught her eye, it was stood erect at the dead woman's feet as if it had been placed there. It was a small, porcelain statuette about ten inches in height. Like the mirror it had survived the maniacal onslaught that the rest of the chattels had been put to. The statue was obviously old but though its colours were faded they could still be made out. It was a statue of a lady with her eyes closed in serenity and her arms outstretched with the palms of her hands open in a peaceful gesture. Her feet were bare and she wore a full-length, white gown, a pale blue shawl and a white hood. The effect of holiness that this figurine presented was further established by a gold cloak. Maxine had seen this type of statue before, it was typical of a Catholic household. She'd seen them virtually every day when she had worked in Dublin, it was a statue of the Virgin Mary. She thought it a little out of place as Maxine knew that Helen was not a Catholic, in fact she worshipped at Reverend Bel's C of E Church. Instinctively Maxine picked up the tiny figurine. At its base was a scroll and on the scroll was an inscription. The inscription was very faded with age and some of the letters had been erased through time. She tried to read it:

To a l n e en fr the S ers Oct 196

She turned it over to look at the underside, it also had an inscription, some of the letters were missing, once again she tried to read it, '...*DE IN NO...*' Was that a place she thought? Was it perhaps Latin? It sounded Latin, she knew that some of the Catholic Mass was said in Latin or at least it used to be. She knew some Latin but it wasn't her best subject.

She didn't quite know why she did it but she took her phone from her handbag and she began to take photographs. She took several shots around the room in general and in particular she took shots of the writing on the mirror and also of the little figurine ensuring that she got a close-up of the inscriptions on the scroll and on the underside.

Then the point of realisation hit her full in the face. She was standing in the middle of a crime scene and she was taking photographs and theorizing when none of it was actually any of her business. Her business as Helen Day's doctor was to keep her alive and as she was now dead, Maxine's responsibility had now ended. Furthermore, she was contaminating that very crime scene that she had just recognised that she was in. She took off her spectacles and put them back in her bag. She put the statue back exactly where she had found it, at the dead woman's feet. Keeping her phone in her hand she switched off the camera app and dialled 999. The operator answered quickly and asked her which service she required.

'Police please.'

A very short silence followed, then a female voice said, 'Police, can I help you?'

'Yes, I need to report a murder.'

'Where exactly is this?'

'It's at the White House in Winton Kiss.'

'Can I have your name please?'

'Yes, it's Wells, Doctor Maxine Wells.'

Almost as soon as she finished the call she heard the low scream of car sirens in the distance, gradually getting louder.

Chapter 3

The Irish Peasant Boy

Finbarr Joseph Breathnach did not know exactly what day of the week it was. Hunger did that to a person, it affected every part of you including your memory and Finbarr had been hungry for as long as he could remember and by now he'd forgotten how long that was. As if in contradiction of his memory lapse about the day, he knew the exact date, it was September 30, 1848, and it was his birthday, he was fourteen years old today.

On this day of usual celebration he sat there amongst the wreckage of his cottiers hut at the edge of his conacre plot. He was in despair and humiliation. Dawn was breaking and he had been sitting there in the same unmoved position all night. He had stayed in that position beneath the three trees since the Wreckers had left the night before and he'd just remained inert in the darkness. Any feelings he had had been numbed by the recent events in his young life and he was completely immune to the cold autumnal air. As the brown blackness descended, the leafless trees had screamed in the wind through the night all around him, like three demented banshees, but yet he hadn't stirred. He didn't have the strength in a way that a man needs strength to do anything else.

He had known all that day, yesterday, that they were coming. They'd arrived as soon as the darkness had, they always came in the dark. They came on their horses, six of them, with Padraig de Hay, the middleman at their head. Six of them Finbarr thought, it took six of them to take on one fourteen-year-old peasant boy starving with the hunger, dressed in rags and with what he could pick up off the ground as his only weapons. Finbarr hadn't tried to stop them, he was too weak for that. He didn't even make a token protest and if he had have done he would have received a broken head or worse for his efforts from one of the shillelaghs or the pistols that they all carried with them as a matter of routine. All that is except de Hay himself for he carried neither pistol nor shillelagh, why would he need them when he could get others to do his bidding for him?

To start with there wasn't that much to destroy and it didn't take them too long, maybe fifteen minutes at the most, but in that time they made sure that they had broken, smashed and cut everything that was visible to the human eye. After that they ripped off the roof of the hut and demolished the walls, then as a final parting shot, one of them on horseback had trampled all over his beloved mother's tiny wild flower garden. The only consolation for Finbarr was that his mother couldn't see the deed. She'd loved that little garden, it had been her salvation through the hunger, but she'd been dead these last three months.

They said that she'd died of the fever but he knew that what had really killed her was Ireland's twin disease of despair and hunger. The hunger that was endless and all prevailing and strangled the land with its un-openable vice-like hand and the despair that looked down upon everything, just the same as a vindictive, angered god. It wasn't just Finbarr's mother who was dead for all his family were too. They'd all died of the same twin disease. First his father, then his four sisters, one by one, and finally his beloved mother.

He was the youngest and now he was the only one left. Before the Wreckers left, de Hay had ridden over to the boy and looked down upon him, mighty on his big, black stallion whilst Finbarr grovelled on the ground. Finbarr didn't look up at him, he daren't, but he knew that if he had that de Hay's black eyes would not have shown a germ of pity or a grain of sympathy towards him. He spoke to Finbarr in that half speaking, half whispering, hissing serpent's voice of his and said:

'You have shown yourself to be a man of insignificance but even a man of insignificance should have something to remember himself by.'

Then he let fall to the ground the tiny wooden crucifix that had belonged to Finbarr's mother. It was a talisman that she had treasured and just before she died she had given it to Finbarr. After her death he'd hung it up in the hut. De Hay must have picked it up from amongst the rubble and seen even a simple, holy, wooden crucifix as an opportunity and an object to inflict even more cruelty on another human being.

Then de Hay made to ride off. The horse moved a few paces before the Middleman reined it to a halt, turned the animal around and hissed two more words in the peasant boy's direction, 'Dawn tomorrow!'

Finbarr knew the meaning of the words only too well. He knew that de Hay would already have new tenants lined up at an increased rent and he knew that 'dawn tomorrow,' was the deadline for being off the land for good, never to return to it.

Now dawn was upon the land once more and he knew that soon the Wreckers would be back. They would return to see if he had complied with de Hay's orders. He knew that he should get up and leave but he quite simply didn't have the strength. He knew that he could expect no help from the neighbours as they cowed in their own huts, for they were little better off than he, being one step away from eviction themselves and they would not want to bring that moment forward by incurring de Hay's displeasure through aiding him in any way. They couldn't even give him any food for they had none themselves. In the times of An Gorta Mor it was every man for himself.

Himself he thought, and what of himself? He stared down at himself, at his grimy bare feet with their blackened jagged toenails and his dirty ragged clothing that was in tatters. He stared at his filthy, spindly arms and at his calloused hands. He was a peasant, he was a wretch and his life was worth nothing, he knew that. There were lots of peasants all over the world, he knew that too. Somebody had to be a peasant but just the same as everything else in this tragic world and this pathetic useless life there was a composed order, a table, a league, even for peasants and he was down at the bottom of it. He was the poorest, most wretched and vilest of peasants. He was mired in poverty. He was broken and humiliated. He was the lowest of the low in the order of the most miserable and most undeserving peasants in the whole world. He was – an *Irish* peasant.

The Breathnachs hadn't always been Irish peasants, the Breathnachs hadn't always been peasants, the Breathnachs hadn't even always been Irish. Finbarr's great ancestor, Owen Welshman, had originally come from Wales. He was that rarity, a Welsh puritan. He'd landed in Ireland with Oliver Cromwell's army on one of the first thirty-five ships on August 15, 1649. He'd fought with valour at the battle of Drogheda and had been at all the subsequent big battles and sieges as Cromwell pursued his conquest of Ireland.

At the end of it all in 1653, Owen had been given land in lieu of pay. He was important enough to Cromwell's army to be given land with rich fertile soil just outside Enniscorthy, County Wexford and he'd settled there. That was almost two hundred years ago. Over the first hundred years Owen and his descendants would become gradually more and more prosperous. Over the second hundred years, there was a complete reversal of fortune as the Breathnachs and their descendants would turn to drunkenness, gambling and profligacy. The lands would gradually be mortgaged and sold and the returns squandered away. The Breathnachs would become poorer and poorer. All this was bad enough and then came the *Great Hunger*.

By 1845 all that was left of Owen Welshman's descendants in Ireland was Finbarr's father, his family and Finbarr's uncle by marriage and his family. They eked out a living grubbing around their separate one acre plots that Owen had once owned with many hundreds more but which his own descendants now rented from the middleman and judged the year as a success or failure by whether they and their families were still alive at the end of it. The reality was that stark and all that was left in the way of a future for Owen's descendants in Ireland was destitution, penury and premature death.

Now, after two hundred years, all the lands had gone and all that was left of the people was a fourteen-year-old peasant boy, evicted from the land by the middleman. Some would say a just and deserved end for Cromwell's conduct and for one of his brutal soldiers' progeny, for there was no doubt that the *Lord Protector of the Commonwealth of England, Scotland and Ireland's* presence in Ireland had been a disastrous one for the Irish people.

Finbarr sat there on the ground amongst the rubble of his home. He knew that soon he was going to die. He didn't think that he wanted to die but he didn't think that he wanted to live either, he just did not care and he knew that he could do nothing about any of it, one way or another. Finbarr Breathnach heard the sound of anticipated horses hooves, only this time they were accompanied by the clatter of another sound and they stopped in front of him. This time Finbarr did look up. Gazing down upon him from a rickety, open-backed wooden cart was the old priest, Father Malachi Drumgoole.

'Finbarr,' said Father Malachi looking down kindly on the young, ragged peasant boy, 'hop up.'

The young peasant boy turned his head to the old priest and gave him a look that indicated that he did not have the physical strength to rise from the ground and get onto the cart.

The old priest responded, 'Finbarr, rise, rise up or die here and now.'

The peasant boy, with his last particle of strength, dragged himself slowly to his feet and stood erect beneath the three trees. He staggered over to the cart. He collapsed, exhausted, into the open back and fell onto its floor. Father Malachi Drumgoole gently prodded the horse into movement and the old horse, the old cart, the old priest and the young peasant boy rode off slowly together into the bright, September, Irish morning.

Chapter 4

Danny Senetti

The hard, mid-morning rain lashed down onto the roof and the half-open skylight. Some of it cascaded through the window and came to a halt on the outlined duvet wherein the prostrate figure lay asleep.

The rain woke Senetti up. He lay there for a moment and allowed some of the cooling drops to find his face for a few seconds. Initially they felt refreshing to him but very soon they were coming down too hard as he pulled back the bedclothes, jumped up, stood on the bed and heaved the window upwards so that it shut into its sash. He'd probably opened it last night for ventilation and in his over refreshed state had overlooked the possibility of morning rain.

Save for one sock on his left foot he was naked. He reasoned that this wasn't bad for him as there had been occasions in the past after a drinking stretch that he had woken up almost fully clothed, except for his shoes of course, he somehow always managed to get his shoes off although sometimes he could never find one of them the next day. How is it that after you've been drinking heavily you often lose one shoe, he thought to himself, never the complete pair, just one of them? He sat down one-socked on the edge of the bed and as he did he accidentally back heeled an empty wine bottle across the polished wooden floor. It spun around as a whipped top would and was then arrested when it collided with the skirting board at the opposite side of the room. He looked at the empty bottle and concluded that with what he'd had in the pub, together with the tell-tale bottle which he didn't remember drinking, he'd had his share of the bank holiday frivolities. In fact, he'd not done the reading that he came home to do, he'd just tagged another day's drinking on for himself on the Tuesday.

Rummaging around in the bedclothes he found last night's underpants and put them on, one handed. He arose, grabbed his old black and white dressing gown from the hook on the back of the door and put it on. This, he promised to himself, would be his attire for the rest of the day. He had to attend a meeting at 6:00pm but until then, as he was now, this would be as splendid as he would be. If visitors came to call, not that he was expecting any and not that any ever did come to call, this would be how he would receive them. He looked in the wardrobe mirror and took an exaggerated bow to his own shabby reflection.

Tea, toast and marmite, that would set him up. It was his favourite food and drink in the morning, although this was more a testimony to a combination of convenience and his paucity of culinary skills than to his preference. He moved out of the bedroom, entered the bathroom for some brief ablutions after which he descended the stairs, walked down the polished lobby floor and collected today's newspaper from where it lay on the mat well. Then he went into the kitchen, 'Tea, toast and marmite,' he repeated silently to himself. He looked in the cupboard and extracted the jar of marmite. His happy anticipation was short lived as he discovered that he had no bread and furthermore no breakfast tea, although he did have some Earl Grey tea. He was reminded of that silly old adage that his mother used to recite in these situations, what was it now? Oh yes!

'If we had eggs, we could have eggs and bacon, if only we had bacon.'

He thought of her fondly and he smiled ruefully, he would visit her next week.

He decided he'd have the Earl Grey. He made it in his old brown pot and poured himself a mug full. The half bottle of milk that he'd had since last week had turned sour so he'd have to drink it black, no matter he thought! He still had the marmite so he undid the jar lid and stuck a teaspoon into its neck bringing the spoon out heaped with the brown compound. He placed it into his mouth and then withdrew the spoon almost clean and proceeded to lick it so. Marmite and black Earl Grey tea for breakfast. He thought to himself that it sounded either completely sophisticated or obviously disgusting, he couldn't quite make his mind up which.

He looked at his wristwatch: 9.59am. He turned the radio on and sat down at the kitchen table with the mug of un-milked tea. The announcer's voice leapt out of the radio speaker, 'This is BBC radio and this is the ten o'clock news for Wednesday...' He sat back in his chair to listen to the news, debating in his head whether he should have another spoon of marmite. The male newsreader continued, 'A painting of the Queen hanging in Westminster Abbey has been disfigured.' This was followed by something about Syria cutting off their internet connection with the rest of the world. Then something about the World Trade Organisation appointing a new Director in turn followed by some well-worn and used stuff about the Eurozone, which he didn't listen to.

For no reason he mentally retraced his steps over the holiday weekend: left Winton Kiss on Thursday for Beaumaris, yeah, Thursday, Friday, Saturday and Sunday, drinking and sleeping, sleeping and drinking, home on Monday, then Monday afternoon and evening, The Black Swan, Wheatsheaf and that poncy bar in River Street that he could never remember the name of, back to the Swan, then exactly the same again Tuesday. He had done that crawl dozens of times before, no hundreds of times if you excluded the poncy bar. Then taxi home, one in the house and off to bed. Wake up about 9:45am. Exactly right, that's what he had done. Just then his phone rang, he made his mind up not to answer it but when he looked at the displayed name and number it was Christine Harris, his personal assistant at the council. She was a good woman, she knew his weaknesses and his strengths and she looked after him. He both admired and respected her, he pressed the accept button.

'Hello Christine, how are you, did you have a good holiday?'

'Morning Councillor, to tell you the truth I'm glad to be back, the kids have been playing up from start to finish and as for him, well, how are you and did you have a good holiday?'

'Oh, you know, quiet, uneventful.'

'Oh dear, that worries me, I know all about your *uneventfuls*. Where've you been, those pubs in Anglesey again? Anyway, you can tell me another time.'

'No truly it was, and quiet too, in fact it goes so quickly I don't know where some of it went. I keep thinking that it is still Monday and it's actually Wednesday.'

'I know that you've been away but I wondered if you'd heard about Mrs Day?'

'Mrs Day, which Mrs Day is that?'

'She's on the Safeguarding Panel with you.'

'Oh! Helen Day, sorry Chris it didn't register, what of her?'

'She was found dead yesterday.'

'Oh no! She was such a vital, energetic woman, how?'

'We know very little at this stage, we have no details whatsoever but I think that it is being treated as suspicious. The Leader was informed over the telephone by the police, all in line with procedure, and she informed me. She told me to let you and a couple of the others know.'

'The police? Why are they involved?'

'As I've just said, there is talk that her death is being treated as suspicious, but you know what they are like here in the town hall. If there is no intrigue there is no interest, so just to create some they'll make it up themselves. As I say, we don't have any details, I'm not big on death protocols, maybe the police have to be involved, maybe that's just what happens. Anyway, your panel that was scheduled for this evening has been cancelled, probably as a mark of respect to Mrs Day. I thought that I'd let you know that too. Did Mrs Day have any family, did you know her well?'

'I didn't really know her at all although she is both a constituent and a neighbour of mine. Every two months at the panel and a cup of coffee waiting for the same train, that more or less sums up my contact with her. Anyway, thanks for letting me know and if you discover anybody to pass my condolences to, then please do.'

'I will do.'

'See you later, bye.'

He took a slurp of his Earl Grey. He overlooked the fact that it was hot without milk in and he scalded the underside of his top lip. He glanced at the front page of today's newspaper. Just then his doorbell rang, he decided that he wasn't home to visitors. He waited in silence, it rang again, he still waited, it rang again. They were persistent whoever they were, he heard the letter box flap open and a man's voice shouted through, 'This is the police, is anybody in there?'

He decided that he would answer it this time. When he opened the door it was Dominic Dimbleby and Lisa Dobbs both of whom he knew. Dimbleby was to the fore and Dobbs was a pace and a half behind him, they stood there in the doorway. Dominic Dimbleby was a chief inspector now, he'd heard that, and Lisa he thought was a sergeant. Three years ago he'd signed a thirty-second birthday card for her when she was stationed at the town hall, she'd been temporarily seconded to the child protection team working on a gang sexploitation case. They always had a police officer attached and more often than not it was a woman. At the time he'd been the executive member with responsibility for that portfolio. He remembered that he'd had some involvement with her over a written report. He remembered more now, they'd co-authored it, him and her and he had to present it to the All Party Scrutiny Committee and he couldn't help thinking that he found her a little bit dim and a bit lazy. Dimbleby and Dobbs were both police detectives. They showed him their warrant cards and introduced themselves. Dimbleby he had no first-hand experience of, but he knew that because of his forename and surname he was known by his police colleagues as Dom Dim. Senetti thought that perhaps that was indicative of something else entirely, though exactly what he wasn't absolutely sure, but he felt that he could guess.

'I know who you are,' Danny said.

'I know you do,' said Dimbleby, who was the older of the two police officers by about ten years, 'but we're here on official business so we thought we'd start the way we intend to go on.'

'Why don't you come in,' said Danny.

'Thank you,' Dimbleby responded and the two detectives entered the narrow lobby, one behind the other. It seemed to fill up immediately with the largeness of their physiques. Senetti looked at them briefly, their eyes darting everywhere, it occurred to him that they both presented the same, not exactly physically, for the older man was hawkish in feature and thin and tall, whereas the woman had a cheery round face and obviously one was a man and the other was a woman, but they were both large in their own ways and they both gave off the same aura, they both wore the same expressions on their faces and they both dressed in the same way with chain-shop suits, in a kind of his and hers presentation. It was their eyes as well, they both had exactly the same stare, which was a combination of harshness and scepticism.

He thought about the idea of plainclothes police or undercover detectives and he chuckled inwardly to himself, for you could place these two in any imaginable setting of your own choice and anybody and everybody would have been able to guess their occupation, just the same as if it had been stamped in blue on their foreheads.

'Come through to the kitchen,' said Danny. They followed him through and he beckoned them to sit down at the table. 'I would offer you a cup of tea but I don't seem to have the makings. How can I help you?' He tried not to sound mocking but it was a fact that he held certain views about the police. As with every occupation there were some good officers and some bad ones and some in between, but he'd spent two years on the police authority after which he'd concluded that many police officers looked down on the public and were disrespectful, even contemptuous, of them and he didn't like that.

'I heard that you had been away for a few days,' said Dimbleby.

'How did you know that?' said Danny.

'Detective,' replied the detective.

'Yeah, I've got a little place over in Wales, I thought I'd go over there for a few days with it being bank holiday.'

'Whereabouts in Wales?'

'It's in Beaumaris on the isle of Anglesey.'

'Have you got an address for it, a postcode?'

'Yeah, it's number one Gaol Street, I don't actually know the postcode.'

Danny observed that Lisa Dobbs had produced a notebook from somewhere and she began writing, 'Did you say Gaol Street as in eh, prison?'

'Yes, exactly the same.'

'When did you leave for Beaumaris?' she asked.

'Thursday evening.'

'When did you get back?'

'When was it now? Monday, late afternoon, about three o'clock I think.'

'You don't sound too sure,' challenged Dimbleby.

'I'm absolutely certain, it's just that sometimes you get a bit confused with the days over these bank holidays.'

'What did you do between 3:00pm on Monday and now?'

'On Monday I went down to Winton Kiss, I went into some of the pubs down there, the Black Swan and the Wheatsheaf.'

'Any witnesses?'

'Witnesses, do you need witnesses now to go into your local pub, why would I need witnesses?'

'We ask the questions sir, you answer them, it's always been that way, it's the protocol,' Dimbleby said sarcastically.

Danny fell silent for a moment.

'Well were there?' urged the sergeant.

'Probably half of Winton Kiss,' Danny countered. 'There were a lot of people out that day, it was a bank holiday.'

'Would any of them recognise you?'

'Well, I've not really had a reason Chief Inspector to ask anybody that question, but I suppose that I am fairly well known around here and I suppose most of them would, so yes.'

Danny Senetti thought that this was beginning to sound as if he needed some sort of alibi. He was a fan of silence when it was necessary and he thought that this was an appropriate time to use that response. He waited for the next question.

'After the Black Swan where did you go?'

'To the Wheatsheaf.'

'After the Wheatsheaf where did you go?'

'Back in the Swan, after that I came home.'

'How did you get home?'

'Probably in a taxi.'

'Probably?'

'Chief Inspector, I don't really keep a record of these things either mentally or otherwise. The important thing to me is that I got home.'

'What did you do on Tuesday?'

'Tuesday?'

'Yeah, it's the day between Monday and Wednesday, it always seems to fall that way, virtually every week.'

Danny thought that Dimbleby's sarcasm was becoming tiresome, but he kept his temper for the moment, 'Exactly the same as I did on Monday, only I started off from here instead of Beaumaris. I should have had a meeting, today actually, but it's been cancelled which I was completely unaware of until fifteen minutes ago, and I had a lot of catch-up reading to do for it, you know how the council is, it's all writing and when it's not writing it's all reading.'

'It's the same in the police,' Dimbleby said with apparent empathy. He was silent for a few moments before saying, 'you look as if you had a rough night reading.' As he said this he eyed Danny's dishevelled state.

'Well it won't be necessary now.'

'Why is that?'

'Because, as I've just said Chief Inspector, the meeting has been cancelled so no meeting, no reading. Anyway, if I'd known you and the sergeant were coming I'd have shaved my face, combed my hair and put my suit on.' Danny thought that it was his turn for a little sarcasm whereas Dimbleby thought he'd try a different approach.

'How well do you know Helen Day?'

'Is that what this is about, I've just heard she's died?'

'Please answer the question Councillor.'

'Well she's..., she was a colleague, she's on a panel that I sit on, it convenes bi-monthly and I see her then.'

'Anything more than that Councillor?' this time it was Dobbs' turn.

'Can you be more specific?'

'Well, did you socialize with her in any way?'

'I went for a drink with her a few times after the panel. Usually one of the bars near Piccadilly and once we used the bar in the station, sometimes we used to get the same train home you see.'

'Has Helen ever been in here?'

'What, in this house?' As soon as the words left his lips he thought it was a silly response and he wished that he hadn't raised it. He could see from the look on Lisa Dobbs' face that she thought the same.

'Yes, in *this* house.'

'Not as far as I know.'

'It is your house Councillor, so it is reasonable to expect that you would know who comes in it - innit?' Dobbs uttered the last word as some kind of chav joke that wasn't really funny, nobody laughed, not even her.

Danny thought that he was perhaps beginning to look and sound a little foolish, even worse he was perhaps beginning to look and sound as if he had something to hide, which he did not. He determined to be more forthright.

'Have you ever been inside her house?'

He mentally recalled he had on about five occasions, 'Yes, a few times over the years.'

'Why only a few times, why not more, did you have some kind of disagreement?' Dobbs said, as the Chief Inspector looked on in silence. The Sergeant continued to take notes.

Danny thought for a moment, he remembered how Helen Day's mood could change when she'd been drinking, she often became quarrelsome or tearful or sometimes both, 'Helen was alright for the first few drinks. She was good company, intelligent and interesting, in the bars in Manchester. When she got home though she would have house measures and more of them. After that she would become difficult, you know, belligerent and weepy, it's not a big thing, I fully understand it, there's a few people

43

around that are the same but I didn't need it and I didn't want it, I was just appearing for a fun thing, not for anything else and after three or four occasions it became rather tedious so I just stopped going altogether.'

'Did you quarrel about that?' Dobbs asked.

Danny could see where that question was leading, 'No, we didn't quarrel, it wasn't that, I just declined the next two or three invites, graciously I think, but we'll never really know now will we. Anyway, she stopped asking.'

'Did you still meet up in the bars in Manchester?'

'No Sergeant, we did not meet up in the bars in Manchester, please don't write that down because it is wholly inaccurate.'

'What in your view would you say *was* accurate?'

'What *is* accurate is that we occasionally went for a drink together in Manchester after the panel while we were waiting for the train, it was all very ad hoc. We discussed the happenings at the panel and we had a few mutual interests in history, politics and literature and that was it.'

'Were you in some kind of relationship with Helen?' Dimbleby chipped in.

Danny was beginning to tire of their challenges and their questions which, though seemingly direct, had veiled insinuations and innuendos, 'Yes, inasmuch as any connection between two people is a relationship then we were in the one that I've told you about, which was that of an occasional colleague and a now and again drinking partner.'

'Nothing more?' Dimbleby responded.

'No, nothing more,' repeated Danny, 'absolutely nothing more. Now if you two good people have got to be somewhere else then I won't keep you and even if you haven't, I can assure you that I have.'

'I thought that you said your meeting had been cancelled?'

'If only my whole life revolved around one solitary meeting, it would be far less complicated than it seems to be.'

'Do you know if Helen Day had any enemies or anybody that might wish her harm?' Dobbs enquired.

'I don't know of any, no.' He decided now that he would exert some kind of his own control over the situation so he said, 'You won't mind if I don't show you to the door, I'm a little underdressed at the minute and I need to change that. If you need me you know where I am.'

With that he rose from the chair to his feet. For some reason he didn't know why, and furthermore he didn't know why it mattered, but he thought, for the moment anyway, that he had finally got the better of his unfriendly visitors.

Dimbleby and Dobbs both got up from their chairs, as if in one choreographed move. Dimbleby spoke, 'Councillor, details are still coming out every minute and the picture is not yet complete, but it will be soon, probably in the next few days. If you think of anything, anything at all no matter how trivial, anything that might have a bearing on the case, then please feel most welcome to give me a call.'

He placed a business card on the kitchen table. It occurred to Danny that it was placed there more as a warning or a threat, not as a gesture of support, 'Exactly what are you referring to Chief Inspector? Is there something suspicious about Helen Day's death?'

'At the moment we're waiting on various reports, the pathologists and others, so nothing is official yet. Tell me, how did you know that she'd died?'

'I had a phone call from the council just before you arrived.'

Danny mused over Dom Dim's previous words, '...please feel most *welcome*...', there wasn't anything that they'd said or done that made him feel that with either of them. The two detectives walked out of the kitchen and down the passage, the Sergeant again a pace and a half behind the Chief Inspector. They left by the front door, Danny heard the latch click in the keeper as they closed it behind themselves.

After they'd gone he sat there alone and he began to think of Helen Day. How had she died? Why were the police involved at all? And why had they come to visit *him*? The last question was probably the easiest to figure out. They would probably visit anybody who was in her acquaintance and with Helen that wouldn't be too many. There certainly wouldn't be many that had been in her house, Helen had actually confirmed that to him the very first time he'd been in it. She'd been quite friendly with Theresa Rafferty, the foster mum on Hippings Lane, so perhaps Theresa had been in Helen's House. Helen had acted as the Guardian ad Litem for Theresa's two foster daughters some years ago and she'd got quite close to her, well, inasmuch as Helen Day got close to anyone.

Danny and Helen didn't talk much about personal things, their conversation was usually about politics and history and sometimes a little poetry. They were both big fans of Philip Larkin and W.B. Yeats and when they got onto the subject of the work of these two poets they often debated their verse late into the early morning hours. Helen had told Danny a few things when she was in her cups. The only thing was, he was usually in them with her so he'd forgotten much of what she had said. There were though two things in particular concerning Helen that stuck in his mind and he'd not forgotten either of them.

The first was this: Danny's paternal ancestors had been Italian, the name was a dead giveaway, *Senetti*, so he couldn't hide it and he didn't want to. His maternal ancestry though was Irish, his mother was Margaret Higgins from Ballina, County Mayo and although Higgins didn't sound as if it was a particularly Irish name she had assured Danny from early childhood that it was one of the commonest names in County Mayo. Although Danny's mother didn't say *commonest* she used the term *original*. As a child and an adolescent Danny and his sister had spent most of the school summer holidays in County Mayo with their grandparents, Molly and Barney Higgins, on their farm. Danny also had a good ear for accents, he'd made an amateur study of them years back and he knew as a fact that nobody could ever completely disguise the accent they gained in their formative years, no matter how hard you tried it just wasn't possible. There would always be a trace, some little nuance in your annunciation, the way you pronounced a particular word, it might be very slight but it would always be there and it would always give you away to the keen listener, especially if you were a little off-guard as you were when you had been drinking.

Furthermore, Danny recognised a County Mayo accent when he heard one. Helen Day most certainly wasn't an Irish name but there were lots of people with Irish names that weren't Irish and there were lots of people with non-Irish names that were. What Helen Day did have to Danny's ear was an ever so slight trace, much more so when she'd been drinking, of a County Mayo accent. It was, he had to admit, really none of his business where she came from and he didn't even really care about it, but one night, or in accuracy one early morning, during a drinking bout in Helen's house he'd allowed his curiosity to overtake him and he'd asked her about it. To his amazement she almost flew into a rage, she'd pierced him with her eyes, she'd grabbed his shirt saying that not only had she never been in County Mayo but that she'd never set foot on the island of Ireland in her whole life.

Danny thought that she did protest too much, but he didn't know why it should be such an issue. He sensed that it was a bit more complicated than that, she seemed frightened that somebody would find out that she was lying and as well as her vigorous denials she made him swear that he would not repeat what she called his *stupid assertion*. He couldn't work out why she was so upset and he certainly couldn't see what was wrong with being in Mayo, or for that matter any other part of Ireland, for he thought that it was a grand country and he'd had many a good craic there, but she obviously didn't share his view. One thing he did know for sure and that was, for some obscure reason, she was telling lies and he didn't believe her. At some stage in her life, maybe in her early life, he knew that she'd been in County Mayo, and for a sustained period.

The second thing that he remembered was a response that she gave to what he thought was a fairly harmless question. He asked her quite casually why she had decided to move to, of all places, Winton Kiss. She looked wistfully beyond him as he finished the question and appeared almost trance-like and he saw the glistening of tears in her eyes as she said, 'All my life I've had to keep my distance, away from the only person in the world that I've come to realise I ever really cared about, the only person alive that ever meant anything to me.' She went on, 'Many years ago I did the wrong thing, made the wrong decision, I was much younger and as a result I've missed so much. No person should be made to do that, whatever the reason, it's not human and it breaks your heart and it saddens your life through and through. It's the same as walking around with a rock in your stomach and that feeling never goes away, it lives with you all the time. Before I moved over here I decided that I wasn't going to live a life of constant sadness anymore. I wasn't going to intrude upon people's lives, no I wouldn't do that. It's much too late for that and it might cause them unhappiness and that's the last thing I'd want, but if I can just see them now and again and know that their life has not been unhappy the way mine has, then that would mean everything to me.'

Then she'd snapped out it, as if coming out of a trance. Danny had been dumbfounded by the intense emotion, he didn't think that he'd ever witnessed a more dramatic statement from anybody. She'd shown so much feeling that he'd not said any more, he just accepted the statement for the obvious integrity that it had. He'd never mentioned it again, to anybody, and he felt he never should, or he would feel as if he was betraying somebody's special, vulnerable, humane moment – but he had not forgotten it either.

He came out of his thoughts about Helen Day. He was concerned about the visit from the two detectives. There was obviously something about her death otherwise why would two senior detectives be investigating it? Did they think that he had anything to do with it? How exactly had she died? He didn't yet know the answers to either of those questions. He couldn't afford to be accused, even suspected, of something like this although he didn't know exactly what *this* could be. He was up for election next year and his majority was far from unassailable. He had good name recognition in the ward and although his reputation as a person was not what you could call lily-white, as a councillor he cared about his constituents and over the years he had proved it and some of them even cared about him, he knew that. He also knew that just one move in the wrong direction and all that can evaporate in half an hour. He'd seen it before with other councillors, if the electorate gets a fixed idea into its head, rightly or wrongly, then there is nothing you can do to move it and you might as well just shut up shop and go home. He wouldn't exclude any action from Dim and Dobbs, in his view they had demonstrated to him that they weren't the brightest and he still had political ambitions, and he had just about got over the last mess.

Two years ago he'd been cruising on the council and he'd also been one of two official candidates for the next parliamentary seat. It was rumoured that the sitting MP, Alan Mulvane, was standing down at the next election and Danny had definitely been on the shortlist, probably even the front-runner in the event that it happened. He was definitely on the up. That was until he hooked up with young Katrina Buckley. That word *young* turned out to be the problem. At first he just didn't know how young she actually was. He'd been blinded by the fact that a beauty such as Katrina could be interested in an old hack such as him. Oh he had nearly all his own teeth still and his own hair and he only needed his glasses for really small print and as well as that could still run a short distance for the train without being too breathless, but he wasn't under any illusions.

She had looked older, and she certainly acted as if she was, and if he'd have asked her, he knew now, that she would have lied about her age. He didn't think he was doing any wrong, after all he was new found single again. By the time it came out it was too late, it turned out he was actually ten years older than her own MOTHER! She wasn't actually legally underage, just about, thank god for that, for that would have been the end of him altogether. There were only two things on the council that were worse than underage sex and that was racism and homophobia, and even that was debatable. There were of course plenty of racists and homophobes at the town hall, in fact the place was riddled with them, just the same as lots of other places were. It was just that in that politically correct environment if you held those views you made damn sure that you kept them to yourself. Any indiscreet disclosures in that area would very quickly see you joining the ranks of the unemployed, probably the unemployable, or in his case the unelectable. If you held any of *those* views, which incidentally he didn't, you learnt quickly to suppress them.

Katrina had turned out to be eighteen and she was studying for her A-Levels but she was still a schoolgirl. He could just see the headlines now, 'The Councillor and the Schoolgirl.' To make it the worst that it could be, at the time he had been the executive member for education.

The Leader had told him, in no uncertain terms as she had raged at him in her typical forthright way and her falsetto voice, 'On behalf of the council you are holding the Executive Portfolio for Education. It's always ultra-sensitive this one, you are supposed to be facilitating young students to achieve their educational aspirations and ambitions and helping them get the best out of themselves, not taking it for yourself.'

He knew that she was right and he had to just stand there and take it. Even now, two years later, he squirmed visibly as he thought about it. His own political party didn't want a fuss for obvious reasons and Katrina's mother didn't because she thought it would undermine her daughter's forthcoming exam performance so the matter was kept as quiet as it could be kept. He'd had to make political concessions and any career aspirations he had harboured about Westminster were now well and truly shot to smithereens. He'd had to get over that and he had done. He'd also had to keep his head down in the council chamber.

'None of that rodomontading that you're famous for,' the council leader had ordered after she'd calmed down.

At the time he didn't even know what the word rodomontading meant, but he'd conformed and had done everything that was asked of him for nearly two years, it had not been easy but he'd done it. He'd stood down from the Council Executive and he'd resigned from all prominent committee positions. He'd sat in the most obscure seat, that nobody could see, in fact it was actually behind a pillar, on the back benches. Now though, he'd paid his dues and he was ready to bounce back. He was still a backbencher but he was just about back on track. The time was right and albeit slowly he was moving and he was on the up again.

The news about Helen Day and the visit from the two detectives had left him feeling very concerned and very unsettled indeed. As for young Katrina she wasn't that far away either, Sheffield University to be precise, thirty odd miles and fifty-eight minutes down the railway line. She was probably sharing some scruffy hovel of a house with half a dozen other students, living off pasta, cheap cider and twenty-five thousand pounds in debt, going around with some rather seedy PhD who'd sell his own children for the price of a course fee. If he was implicated in this situation by those two, Dim and Dobb, and Katrina heard about it and some journo offered her a few thousand for her side of the story then it would all come back to haunt him. He could see it all, his mind was racing now.

Just at that moment Danny glanced out of the kitchen and down the lobby. He saw, sitting squarely on the little table, the letter he had placed there on Monday, he'd completely forgotten about it. He went over to the table and collected it. He looked at the envelope again. This time he realised that he actually did recognize the handwriting, he also realised that he should do, for he had sat next to the writer for the last six years whilst she'd made copious handwritten notes at the Safeguarding Panel. It was the hand of Helen Day. He gently tore open the envelope and felt inside. There was a small, neat piece of white paper folded in two. He took it out gingerly and gently unfolded it. There was just one solitary word written on the whole piece of paper.

'Speranza.'

Danny realised that at first glance he didn't understand it. He read it out aloud to himself twice and he still didn't understand it. Why would Helen Day, for he now knew without any doubt that it was her, send him an unsigned letter with one word on it? What was it, some kind of puzzle, some kind of statement? If it was either, he couldn't solve one and he didn't recognise the other.

He knew enough Italian to translate *Speranza*, which was the Italian word for *hope*, although that didn't really get him anywhere and there didn't seem much hope for Helen Day now.

Momentarily he had a vision of her lying naked on some cold mortuary slab waiting in deadly silence for one of her last visitors, the pathologist, and he shuddered at the thought of it. Back to the note, why was she writing to him in Italian? She obviously knew of his Italian connection, but as far as he knew, she herself had no connection whatsoever to the place. She'd never mentioned anything or anyone or any place Italian to him.

Danny reflected upon his whole current situation, his life had seemed back on track and uncomplicated when he'd arrived at Gaol Street at the beginning of the holiday but since he had returned home to Winton Kiss at the end of it, he'd come back to a lot of potential problems and a lot of, as yet, unanswered questions.

Chapter 5

Finbarr's Oath

Finbarr had been at the Old Priest's house for almost two weeks now. The Priest lived there with his housekeeper, Mrs O'Flynn. She'd been kind to Finbarr, for the first three days she had spoon fed him like a baby on gruel mixed with nettles, she had cut his hair, his toe nails and his fingernails and slowly his strength had come back and after the gruel he was able to eat soup and bread.

He had luxuriated in the old tin bath out in the yard which Mrs O'Flynn had filled with warm water for him. He couldn't remember when he'd last had a real bath or even if he'd ever had one at all. Father Malachi had brought him a set of clothes that even included a pair of boots. He had never owned a pair of boots in his life. He knew that he was safe for the time being, for even Padraig de Hay would not violate a priest's house, but he also knew that he couldn't stay for too long. For one thing the Priest had told him so and for another de Hay the middleman wouldn't allow him anything such as long term sanctuary, de Hay would ignore the situation for a while but after that Finbarr would have to move away from Enniscorthy. What was here for him anyway? What was there here for anybody, only misery of one kind or another? He was all alone now, his family were all dead and gone and he had no friends. There was nothing to keep him here and any future that he had he would have to make for himself, and he would have to make it elsewhere.

He had no money, he owned nothing, no land, no house, all he had was his mother's tiny wooden crucifix and the clothes he stood in and they had been given to him. He was destitute of land, of home and of possession. He was though, and he knew this, not destitute of talent. Different to many Irish peasants of his age he could read and he could write and he could do it in two languages Irish and English, his mother had seen to that. He thought that if he could only get himself somewhere civilized then he could trade his talents for employment. Someone, somewhere would want him, he was convinced of it. The only decisions he had to make were where to go, when to go and how to get there?

His first chosen place would be America, he'd heard that if you could speak, write and read English you were valued there and even if you couldn't, nobody in America actually starved, not even the slaves. They were beaten but they were always fed. He reasoned that he would take a beating over starvation any day. One was over and done with whereas the other lingered on and never was.

He had an uncle, an aunt and two cousins who had sailed to America on the *coffin ships*. As far as he knew they were the last of his relatives alive, although he didn't really know if they were alive, for he had heard no word from or about them and it was well known that as many people died on the coffin ships during the journey as did on the land that they were trying to escape from. He'd heard that sharks followed the coffin ships as they threw so many dead bodies overboard. The only difference being that on the ships if you died and you were lucky you might just get a sea burial whereupon you would be despatched to a watery grave, but with religious rites, whereas if you died on the land you were just left where you fell for the wild dogs and carrion and perhaps no religious ceremony at all. In the end though, in one you were eaten by fishes and in another you were eaten by animals. Either way, in both you were dead, gone and forgotten.

Finbarr knew that despite his physical recovery in the hands of Mrs O'Flynn he probably wasn't strong enough to survive the journey across the Atlantic, it would be too long and arduous. Perhaps he could attempt it when he was stronger and he was now determined that he would be stronger. In addition to this a sailing ticket had to be purchased. There was nobody he could turn to for the price of a ticket to America. Those who had that sort of money had used it for that very purpose and had gone already.

There were only two types of people left in Ireland now. Firstly, there were the ones who were stuck there and couldn't get out of the place and then there were the others who were profiting from the first types' misery. So America, as a destination, had many attractions but at this moment in time the journey to get there had just too much against it. After this analysis he discounted it but in the same thought he knew that he had to get out of Enniscorthy, and then out of Wexford and after that he had to get out of Ireland. The first two would be relatively easy but the third one – not so.

There and then he made his mind up he would go to England. It was a relatively short journey and he had heard that in Dublin the coal ships that sailed back and forth across the Irish Sea would take you to Liverpool for free if you agreed to act as human ballast. That would be his route then, he decided that there was no time to dwell, tonight he would say his goodbyes to the Old Priest and Mrs O'Flynn. They had been kind to him but tomorrow at first light he would chase the road to Dublin and from there on to England.

The autumn sun was peeping out of the Wexford sky as Finbarr left the Old Priest's house for the last time. His spirits were good and he bounded along the boreen clutching the newly gifted shilling that Mrs O'Flynn had pressed into his hand the night before. He had never held money before and he wasn't sure what he was going to do with it. It was around seventy miles plus to Dublin, he knew that. Initially he headed north towards Gorey then continued towards Wicklow. He walked for two days from dawn until dusk, stopping just outside Wicklow Town on the first night where he ate some of the bread and some of the cabbage that Mrs O'Flynn had given him for fortification throughout the journey then slept under a hedge. The weather was good for October, it didn't rain at all and the route was clear and even, though strenuous at times.

On the second night he was lucky again with the weather, he slept in the Dublin Hills. He'd never been to Dublin before, he had never been anywhere before that wasn't near Enniscorthy and he didn't want to arrive in the city after dark. He knew the countryside, it held no unknowns for him but he didn't know the city and that did. He awoke early and bathed in a nearby stream. Again, just as the day before, the sun was starting to come out. On that third morning just after daybreak he walked into Dublin Port. Nobody in Dublin knew him and if they had done then they would not have recognised him: he wasn't ragged, he wasn't filthy, he wasn't a wretched peasant anymore or even if he was, he didn't look like one and most importantly he wasn't starving with the hunger. Now he could think, his mind was clear and he knew exactly what day of the week it was.

As he walked along the dockside he carried with him a sense of achievement, of hope, of optimism. He remembered that he still had Mrs O' Flynn's shilling and he remembered he also had his mother's crucifix. He was amazed that the very first coal ship he asked agreed to take him and the captain, a kindly Englishman, said that he could work his passage on deck and he didn't have to go below. He saw this as a sign that his life offered prospect and change and he was uplifted, he wanted to forget about the past but he also knew that there was a score to settle.

Later that day, as the ship pulled out of Dublin bay, Finbarr Joseph Breathnach looked back across the sea to Ireland. His eyes glistened with tears but they were not tears of sadness. He hated the place. In reality he had known nothing but unhappiness in all his life there. He hated everything about it. He hated the hunger and he hated the despair, the poverty, the plagues, the diseases and the deaths. He hated the constant humiliation of being a peasant. He hated its land and he hated its sky. He hated the fetid stench from the failed crops that permeated the fields and putrefied the air. He hated what Ireland had done to his father and to his sisters and most of all to his beloved mother. More than anything his deepest hatred was not for the place but for the person who was in it and had made it the way it was. That person was the middleman, the Gombeen, Padraig de Hay.

The middleman was responsible for the desecration and destruction of his family. He had snuffed their lives out with his avarice just the same as if he had killed them with his bare hands, just so he could charge a few more pennies on the rent. He had no more regard for them than the regard he gave to the flame as he snuffed his bedside candle out at night. The Gombeen still had his family as he lorded it in the big house behind the demesne wall with his fat wife, his ugly daughter and his spoiled brat son.

Finbarr burned with hatred and rage. He wept for the loss of his dead mother and his sisters, he was torn inside with his grief. He swore that come the time, and it would come even if it took years, he would wreak havoc on the middleman and on his family. The middleman was free and so were his womenfolk. It was the womenfolk who bore the children, it was they who would see to it that his vile name of de Hay and its despicable nature would be perpetrated through the years.

Finbarr took an oath to himself which he swore to his great ancestor, Owen Welshman. He would live long and he would keep track of the de Hay womenfolk, those now and those to come. Wherever they went he would find them. He would connive and plot, he would be ruthless and he would penetrate their place of safety by any means that he could. Then he would kill them just as de Hay had killed his sisters and his mother. It wouldn't be murder, no, it would be legal execution! Well it might not be legal but it would be lawful and it would be just and proper retribution. It would be retribution for all the crimes against his own family and against the families of the Irish people that de Hay and all his ilk had committed. You bear responsibility for your family and your family bears responsibility for you, his mother had taught him that. Your family never lets you down and you must never let them down, his mother had taught him that too.

He cursed the de Hay women through the years gone and the years to come. He would hand that curse down onto the de Hay female line and their daughters and their daughters' daughters and their sons' daughters. He would never forget and in turn he would ensure that his own children and his own children's children never forgot. The curse would be passed on through the decades and centuries until there were no de Hay women left and that name would be obliterated. He would seek these women out and wherever he found a de Hay woman then ritual execution would follow. He decided that he would not inflict the curse on children or the male line, the men would be exempt from death but left in their own grief, but the adult womenfolk would be damned and there would be no escape, as there had not been for Finbarr's sisters and his mother and all the sisters and mothers of Ireland.

He swore an oath to himself, the promise was made, the vow attested to, there was no going back. This was for the honour of his Great Ancestor and for the memory of his mother and for the death of his sisters and for all the mothers and sisters of Ireland. As if in a type of two-faced hypocrisy for his terrible and murderous intentions he slowly and deliberately blessed himself with the sign of the cross and then he spat venomously over the boat side into the Irish Sea.

Chapter 6

The Doctor's Interview

The sleek, silver Mercedes convertible paused momentarily at the traffic light filter then turned off the main A6 road and cruised smoothly and slowly down Reginald Street past the side of Norford Town Hall. It came to a stop outside the new brick building that is Norford Police Station.

Dr Maxine Wells got out of the vehicle. She crossed the courtyard and made her way towards the door underneath the overhead sign that read 'POLICE.' She paused at the desk marked 'Reception' and was greeted by the civilian officer. The officer had a badge pinned to her police-issue shirt. Written on the badge in yellow letters against a blue background it read 'Marianne Banks, Civilian Support Officer.'

After Maxine had discovered Helen's murder that fateful evening she'd phoned the emergency services and had spoken to the police. After the phone call she had left Helen's house and had stood outside. The sky was still drizzling, she didn't really mind the rain, it seemed to have some kind of cleansing effect on her face as she had waited in the front garden for their arrival. She didn't have long to wait, two uniformed police constables, a man and a woman, arrived.

For some reason Maxine noted both officers appeared in their early thirties. The female officer introduced them both as PC Nigel Jamison and PC Michelle Delaney. PC Delaney took a brief notebook statement from Maxine whilst PC Jamison proceeded to stick red and white tape everywhere in an attempt to cordon off the house. After she took the statement the officer had then dismissed the doctor by saying, 'Thank you Dr Wells, that will be all for the moment. Somebody from CID will probably want to talk to you in the next few days, I'm sure that they will be in touch. You're not planning any holidays are you, you will be around won't you?'

Maxine assured PC Delaney that she would be.

By Friday, Helen Day's murder had been all over the local papers and in one or two nationals too. Even though Helen's house had been cordoned off as a crime scene with what seemed to be a permanent police guard outside, some journalist had somehow managed to find a way to take a photograph through the window of the murder room. It wasn't a very clear photograph but it indicated some of the degradation and wreckage. They ran the photograph on the front page of the *Norford Messenger* under the headline, 'Ritual Wrecker Killing in Winton Kiss.'

On Thursday, the day before the newspaper headline, Detective Sergeant Lisa Dobbs telephoned Maxine at her morning surgery.

'Dr Wells, I'm DS Lisa Dobbs and I'm conducting an investigation into the death of Helen Day.'

'Oh yes, tragic business, I've been expecting your call.'

'Can I talk to you about your involvement?'

'I did give a statement to your officer. I do realise that it was very brief but I answered everything that she asked me. I don't think that I've got much more to offer.'

'We do appreciate that Doctor, it's all been very helpful, it's just that we need a bit more, we will try not to take up any more of your time than is needed. That's all it is Doctor, you know how it works.'

'When and where were you thinking of?' said Maxine resignedly.

'Well, I could come to your surgery after you've finished today, at a convenient time to yourself naturally.'

Immediately Maxine thought, *no chance!* She'd seen nosey coppers in action before, poking around in Ireland, but English or Irish they were all police and the police suspected everybody of everything and didn't believe anybody about anything. They would be upsetting both staff and patients not to mention her own equilibrium. She'd do what she could to help them, naturally, but they could stay away from her surgery.

'Perhaps it would be better if I came to you,' she suggested helpfully.

'As you wish,' responded the detective.

'Monday about midday?'

'Yeah, that'll be fine.'

'Where exactly are you?' asked the doctor.

'I'm at Norford Police Station, it's at the back of the town hall behind the juvenile courts, it's all clearly marked.'

'How long will you need me for?'

'Shall we say two hours at the most?'

'Ok, I'll see you Monday then, about midday. Have an enjoyable weekend.'

'Yes, you too, bye,' said the detective.

The weekend had come and gone, as they all do. Maxine had spent much of it at home with her father, he was in good spirits. On Saturday they went out for lunch together and he went off to play golf with Ben Goldstein on Sunday. Sunday evening she'd watched television alone until ten o'clock, some hammy detective crime show with all the usual clichés, but it had served a purpose for her, then she went to bed. As she dropped off to sleep she heard her father come in, slightly drunk she'd guessed. He was whistling softly and tunelessly to himself, he often whistled if he was in good spirits, and she was comforted by his tuneless effort.

'Hello,' she said to Marianne Banks the Civilian Support Officer, 'I'm Doctor Maxine Wells and I have an appointment with your Detective Sergeant Dobbs.'

'Just one moment please,' Marianne said, 'what did you say your name was again?'

Maxine repeated her previous introduction trying not to let the irritation in her voice show for having to do so. The young woman disappeared into a smaller office and Maxine could hear the muffled sounds of a telephone conversation being carried out. The next moment a rather stout lady, in her mid-thirties, wearing what appeared to be a man's suit, appeared from the side door.

She smiled and to Doctor Well's pleasant surprise showed a perfect row of even, white teeth.

'Dr Wells,' she said more in exclamation than question. She stretched out her hand, 'I'm Detective Sergeant Lisa Dobbs.'

'Pleased to meet you Sergeant, I'm Doctor Maxine Wells.'

The detective then opened a door in the corridor and peered in, Maxine could see it had four chairs and a table inside, little else.

'We'll be alright in here for an hour or so Doctor.'

The two women entered the room and the detective shut the door behind them. They sat down at either side of the table. They eyed each other across it. One considered that the other eyed her with suspicion whilst the other considered that that she was being viewed through the eyes of class superiority. More by natural instinct than deliberation both of them were right to a certain degree.

The detective began, 'I can tell you now that we are treating the death of Helen Day as a murder enquiry.'

The detective looked at Maxine's face, the doctor's features were relaxed and remained implacable.

'You don't seem the least bit surprised.'

'Sorry, the least bit surprised about what?'

'That we are treating this as a murder enquiry.'

'Oh I see, well that's because I'm not in the least bit surprised.'

'Why is that then?'

'Well, I don't see any reason to be. For one thing it's been in the newspapers all week.' Maxine paused thoughtfully.

'And for another,' Dobbs interrupted her thoughts.

'Well for another, I'm a doctor,' said Maxine, 'and I discovered the body. I also have some experience with murdered bodies and I know one when I see one, so no Sergeant, I'm not in the least bit surprised.'

'Yes, the discovery, I was coming to that.'

Both women became quiet.

'Doctor, what exactly was your relationship with Helen Day, how well did you know her?'

'I didn't really know her at all, she has been my patient for the last seven years, it was a stereotypical doctor patient relationship.'

'So you were fairly close to her?'

'No Sergeant, I don't think so, I thought that I'd just confirmed the opposite.'

'We've checked and we've discovered that over the last seven years Helen Day had seventy-nine doctor's appointments and they've all been with you, that's about one every month, is that number of appointments over that period normal?'

Maxine pondered on how the detective had been able to obtain this information, she concluded that it could have only come from her own surgery. She was puzzled as to why the detective had not asked her the question in an objective way but instead had presented her with the answer in a challenging way. She thought that this was disrespectful, she had come here in good faith to help but now she was being treated with suspicion, she felt a little irritated by this treatment but she decided not to show it nor to say anything.

'That number of appointments, is it normal, it seems a lot to me? I think that in the last seven years I've only seen my doctor four or five times.'

'Well, you are very fortunate Sergeant to be blessed with such good health. As for being normal, I'm a doctor, I suppose it's a bit similar to police work, there is very little that could be classed as normal.'

'What exactly did she come to see you about seventy-nine times, did she have some kind of condition?'

'Oh a variety of things.'

'What sort of variety, give me an example?'

'Oh the vast majority of it was trivial, when some ladies get to a certain time in their lives, anxiety sometimes sets in.'

'Exactly what sort of anxieties, please explain?'

'Sergeant, you know that I can't do that, what goes on between a doctor and a patient is wholly confidential.'

'Doctor, this is a murder enquiry, this lady is dead, I'm trying to bring the killer to justice.'

'Why do the police think that such assertions supersede everything? If I can assist then I will but I won't compromise my professional integrity.'

'I could ask for the records,' Dobbs said.

Maxine edged her chair in and moved a little closer to the detective. She sensed that there was a bit of cat and mouse developing and she didn't really want to play at police interviewing techniques. Nevertheless, if she had to then she had some of her own.

'Sergeant,' she said, 'I don't really know what is at the bottom of this but let us be candid, Helen Day was one of my patients and she came to see me with a variety of illnesses, some serious, some not so, some possibly even imaginary and perhaps non-existent, it's not for me to judge and its even less for you. She wasn't unique in this, she wasn't even uncommon and when you've been practising medicine for a few years then perhaps you can have a valid opinion on it, in the meantime, accept mine, which is that I'm fairly sure that none of these illnesses, real or otherwise, actually killed her, which is something that you are supposed to be finding out about. As for the rest of it, it will only serve to side-track you and is it really any of your concern?'

The sergeant thought that she had been *told off*, nevertheless, she carried on unfazed and changing tack slightly she asked, 'Doctor, what would your reaction be if I was to say to you that our investigating officers found many sets of your fingerprints at the scene of the crime?'

'My reaction, would be a combination of acknowledgement, agreement and astonishment.'

'That's a curious answer, would you care to explain?'

'Well, as I found the body in the first place and as I wasn't really expecting to find a body, I expect that I accidentally and deliberately touched quite a lot of things in the house. Therefore, as a consequence of this touching, my fingerprints would be in abundance. So that is where my acknowledgement would come in. These fingerprints would prove my presence in the house, which is a fact, as I was most definitely there, as I found the body, something that I seem to have to keep repeating and I could not have found it without entering the house. So these fingerprints would prove that I was there, which I agree I was, so that is where my agreement comes in.'

'And your astonishment?'

'Well as far as I am aware, I have never had my fingerprints taken in my life. There has never been any reason for anybody to take them you see. As far as I know, an individual's fingerprints can only be taken if he or she agrees to have them taken, or if he or she is arrested on suspicion of a criminal offence and neither of these are true in my case. So, unless somebody has taken them without my knowledge, say perhaps when I was asleep, then my astonishment would be that as there is no record of them, exactly how you'd managed to match something up to something that doesn't exist in the first place. I also have to say Sergeant that I think that for reasons best known to yourself that you are telling me lies and I didn't come here for that.'

The detective was not used to being so outwitted and although she felt a little frustrated and beaten on the inside, she was determined not to show it on the outside. Her facial expression therefore remained unmoved.

'Doctor, why were you at Helen Day's house that evening, the evening that you made the discovery?'

'She'd missed an important appointment at my surgery, I was concerned for her as a patient and I wanted to make sure that she received a proper diagnosis and the correct treatment and there was also some urgency about the situation.'

'Is it normal conduct for a doctor to go chasing around after patients who fail to keep their appointments? You must get lots of people that miss their appointments. Don't you have receptionists that are supposed to do that?'

'There you are with that word again Sergeant, no it isn't something that I would do as a rule, although this was not the first time I've done it, but not with Helen Day. However, on this occasion I considered it appropriate because of the urgency of the situation. I must remind you again Sergeant that I am a doctor and as such I am empowered to make decisions that I believe are in my patient's best interest and this decision was one of those.'

'Did you ever meet Helen in any other capacity than the doctor patient relationship, have you ever been to her house before for any reason?'

'No, I've never met her outside my surgery. She very much kept herself to herself and by all accounts she was a little reclusive and she didn't go out much. I've never been to her house before.'

'Winton Kiss is a very small village doctor, you both live there and you work there, did you never see her out socially, in the shops, the pubs or the cafes?'

'Sergeant, I don't go into pubs or cafes or shops much myself and I don't really know whether Helen did. All I know about her came from medical consultation, so if you need to know anything else other than that then I suggest that you ask someone else.'

'Surely you go into the shops Doctor, you have to eat?'

'Sergeant, my father does all the shopping, he's retired you see and he insists on doing it. It's his contribution to the household chores, but are my shopping arrangements relevant to anything?'

Maxine wondered what the police investigation had actually discovered about Helen Day. She thought to herself that you wouldn't really have had to ask too many questions before you discovered what sort of a person Helen Day was and this detective didn't even seem to know the basics about somebody that had been found murdered and the investigation was almost a week old. She now concluded that this detective was not the best at being one, but even accepting this she was surprised at the next question.

'Do you own or have access to a gun Doctor?'

'No Sergeant, I don't own a gun nor would I know where to find one. Why do you ask, do you think that I shot Helen Day?'

'How did you know that she'd been shot, did I say that she'd been shot?'

This conversation was now beginning to remind Maxine of the television programme she'd been watching the night before. 'As I said before Sergeant, it has been in the newspapers, I found the body and I'm a doctor. There really is no point in answering these questions if what I say is not registering with you. Anyway, shouldn't you be writing this down?'

Lisa Dobbs rocked back on the chair's hind legs and rested her head against the grey wall, she ignored the doctor's last comment. 'Doctor,' she said, 'forgive me but everybody that has some kind of connection to a murder victim is a suspect until they are ruled out. As far as I am aware you were the very first to see Helen Day dead. Indeed it was you who raised the alarm.'

'Yes?' said Maxine puzzled by the hypothesis.

'If you were the first to see her dead then it follows that you may, and I only say may, also have been the last person to see her alive.'

Maxine thought this deduction had no apparent, sensible logic to it. As well as this she was beginning to have her initial opinion of the detective sergeant's lack of natural application for her chosen calling confirmed. Lisa Dobbs she thought was, as Doctor Tom would say, a bit of a Toc H Lamp.

'Not quite,' said Maxine.

'I don't follow?'

'The murderer, perhaps?'

The two women rose from their chairs as if in concert and as if some inaudible signal had told them the meeting was over.

'Just a couple more questions Doctor.'

'Really?'

'As far as you know did Helen Day have any enemies, anybody that wished her harm, anybody that wanted her dead, did she ever mention anyone to you?'

'No, I don't know of anybody.'

'Did she have any friends?'

'I didn't really know of any of those either, as I have already said, she tended to be alone and a bit aloof.'

'What about Danny Senetti, wasn't he friendly with her?'

'Do you mean Councillor Danny Senetti?'

'You know him then?'

'Just so there is no doubt Sergeant, I don't know Councillor Senetti at all. I have never met him in any capacity whatsoever and I know absolutely nothing about his connection to Helen Day that is not plain and simple gossip, which I won't repeat, because I don't deal in such stuff except that sometimes it is forced upon me and I have no alternative but to listen to some of it. Can I suggest that if you need an answer to that question then I think that you should ask it of the councillor himself *Detective* Sergeant.'

As Maxine said this she stressed the word detective as if to question that the detective was one.

'Councillor Senetti is also one of your patients.'

'Yes Sergeant, that is quite correct.'

'That's interesting Doctor, how many times has he been to see you?'

'I'm surprised that you don't know the answer to that one, particularly as you knew all those facts and figures about Helen's appointment schedule, and actually I don't find it interesting in any way whatsoever, not even in the slightest. In fact it is completely uninteresting and very obvious to me. Most people around the Winton Kiss area are my patients, the reason for this you see is that the place is so small and my partner and I are the only doctors in town. As for Councillor Senetti, he has never been to my surgery, not even once and as I have just said it is a fact that I have never met him and I have never even spoken to him, not even on the telephone. Before you ask Sergeant, I've never seen him in the pubs, cafes or shops, although I did once see him at the train station,' she teased.

Doctor Maxine Wells gave Detective Sergeant Lisa Dobbs a withering look which made the detective feel rather ridiculous, which was exactly what Maxine thought she was and which was exactly the effect she wanted the look to have.

A few minutes later the two women were sat down, deep in thought. One sat in a police station interview room her chair rocked back on its hind legs and her head resting against the wall, the other sat in a sleek, silver car. Both were thinking about the content and implications of an interview that had just taken place between themselves.

Chapter 7

Llandudno, c1883

As is often the case in life it happened completely by accident and coincidence.

He was stood in the queue in Llandudno post office telegraph section. He'd been taking a short holiday after his demob from the army, just an idea of his to adjust back into civilian life. Thirty-two years in the army was a long time for anyone. He'd booked into a small hotel in the seaside town and was content to stroll about the place aimlessly for a week or two and so far, as if by an added bonus, the weather had been good.

The whole situation was totally unexpected as he waited patiently in the post office queue immediately behind a fierce old lady dressed in black. In front of the old lady was a young trades boy and in front of the boy was a young woman, in front of her was a nondescript gentleman. He focussed on the young woman. He could only see her from the back, she was quite tall and very slender, reasonably well dressed and he supposed that she was around thirty years of age. He guessed that she was perhaps a schoolteacher or similar although he did not quite know what similar could be.

Although he'd done nothing about it for some time he'd never given up on his oath and not one day of his life passed by without it being in his mind and when he did think about it, even for a second and after all these years, the anger and rage welled up in him as strong as ever. He was though content to wait for the right moment to strike, even if it took him years or to the last day of his life. He believed that someday the opportunity would present itself and retribution would be his.

In the autumn of 1875 he'd taken some leave and visited Enniscorthy. He was a captain by then and acting as Adjutant to General Havering so his leave had been easy to arrange. He went there ostensibly to update himself on the de Hay clan but he knew that if the opportunity arose he would not shirk it, he would work out a plan of action and he would strike. He would strike fatally and with grave consequences to others but without any trace of himself.

Being in Enniscorthy had brought back bad memories about the lives and circumstances of his dead family and he wanted to get out of the place almost as soon as he'd set foot upon its soil. However, he had a task to perform and needed to stay until it was complete. He'd stayed at the local inn under an assumed name. Nobody recognised him, why indeed would they? He'd left the place twenty-seven years earlier and he was now totally beyond any kind of recognition as the person that he had once been. People now called him sir, he enjoyed such an address, and since his elevation to officer fifteen years ago he'd cultivated an unassuming, gentlemanly persona.

He knew that he would never get past the rank of captain. Soldiers that came up through the ranks, especially in peacetime, never did. Nevertheless, captain was alright, in fact it was better than alright, it was certainly a complete change for him from when he'd last been in this little workaday Irish town. He'd changed his name when he'd enlisted in 1850, his old one was just too Irish to offer him optimum advancement in the British army.

Now he was Captain Barry Walsh, although he didn't use that name when he'd stayed at the Enniscorthy local pub. He'd also grown a beard for his visit to further disguise his appearance. Any connection no matter how removed or indirect was exactly that, a connection, and when he was on the business of the oath he was careful to make as few of those as possible.

He knew coldly in his heart that the time would eventually come when he would strike, so at every episode concerning the oath, even one of inaction, he arrived and disappeared without trace. It had been comparatively easy to find the information he needed, he didn't even have to ask any questions. He discovered a long time ago that the subject that most people wanted to talk about was themselves and what was going on around their own lives, they weren't really interested in what you had to say or in what was happening in yours. He also discovered that you could steer a conversation one way or another with just a few well-chosen words.

On that Saturday night in Enniscorthy he'd taken a walk around the town and he'd purposely visited a few of the bars. That was where all the chatter and gossip was, in the bars, that was always the case whatever part of the world you were in, it was always the bars and where there was talk there was information. That night he'd casually engaged people in conversation. He'd bought his new, temporary companions a few drinks, taking care not to drink too much himself, and just listened to everything that came back to him, analysing what he needed to keep in his head and discarding the rest. He had trained his mind in this way.

Captain Walsh knew from his own personal reading that the reign of the middleman was coming to an end in Ireland, and the middleman himself, Padraig de Hay knew that also. The captain listened in the bars that night and through his listening he'd learnt that Padraig de Hay, the middleman, was not a middleman anymore. He now owned the local bank and was extremely wealthy and was now a *gentleman*, the town's mayor and a respected family man. He still lived in the mansion house that had once been owned by the absentee English landlord, his crimes and atrocities long since forgotten by most and only vaguely remembered by a diminishing few. Padraig de Hay's son, Fergal, had died in India, in military service in 1858, the boy was barely twenty-one years old. This fact evoked no sympathy at all in the captain and anyway he wasn't interested in the male line, that was not part of the oath's business. As he listened attentively to various speakers he knew that sooner or later some of them would say something of interest and sure enough some of them did.

After he'd pieced it all altogether, the information that he had was that the middleman had three daughters and that his second wife, his first had died, was pregnant with a fourth child. He even had names for the womenfolk: Sybil, Clodagh and Siobhan.

Sybil lived in England somewhere and Clodagh and Siobhan lived in Enniscorthy still. Sybil however was the middleman's stepdaughter and the captain was not interested in step-lines, only bloodlines but he was intensely interested in Clodagh and Siobhan. Padraig also had a young son but the captain was not interested in the male line. He'd learnt all that without barely uttering a word and certainly without saying anything about himself and when he had been asked anything about himself, no matter how trivial it was, if he thought that a connection could be made back to him, past, present or future, he'd simply lied with his answer. He was on his own high alert all the time.

After much deliberation it was plain to him that Enniscorthy at that time was not the place for a strike without a properly thought out plan, it was too remote, too sparsely populated and too difficult to get out of quickly. It was also a place where few strangers came and if you did visit and you stayed around for more than a couple of days then you would draw attention to yourself, for no other reason than you were a stranger. He toyed with a few ideas but decided that they were hare-brained and convoluted. No, he would return home and be patient, he was convinced that patience was the answer. So he did return home, he left Enniscorthy without a trace of him ever having been there and returned to England and almost immediately he was posted to India.

The nondescript gentleman completed his business at the post office counter and the tall, slender young lady moved to the front of the queue and approached the counter grille.

'May I send this telegram?' she said. He nonchalantly detected that she had a refined Irish accent. The young woman handed a piece of paper to the bespectacled, balding, young clerk behind the grille.

'Who and where would you wish to send it to Miss?'

'I've written the complete address on the other side of the note.'

The clerk turned the piece of paper over and read out aloud, 'Mr Padraig de Hay, The Mansion House, Enniscorthy, County Wexford, Ireland. Is that correct?' he said.

'That's quite correct,' said the young woman, her voice seemingly and slightly agitated.

If anybody had observed Captain Barry Walsh at the precise moment the telegraph clerk read out the information on the paper as the captain stood waiting patiently in the same queue then they would have noticed his handsome, suntanned features drain into a deathly pallor, his hands visibly shake and very small beads of sweat appear on his forehead, but of course nobody did observe him.

'What do you want to say?' asked the clerk.

'I've written it on this piece of paper.' She produced another piece of paper and again handed it to the clerk.

Once again he read out loud, 'Arrived yesterday, safe and sound, everything fine, Siobhan.'

'Is there no privacy in my conversation, must you read out all my private business in public?'

'It's the rules ma'am,' said the clerk 'we have to make sure that we send exactly as you request, not one word more, not one word less.'

'Well they are very intrusive rules,' she retorted. 'Would you *please* send the same message to this address in Dublin. I suppose you're going to read that message out to the post office queue as well,' she said haughtily and perhaps a little tearfully.

The clerk leaned forward and read the Dublin address out but in a much lower voice than before.

'Thank you so much.' She paid the receipt, turned abruptly and left the building.

Captain Walsh immediately abandoned his place in the queue and left the building also. He knew that whatever happened he must not lose her, he must keep her in sight. He had no plan yet in his head but he said to himself again that come what may, he must not lose her. As soon as he came out of the post office he saw her immediately walking along the seafront, this time she was under her parasol. He still couldn't make out her features as she moved along the path in the July sunshine of 1883. He followed her at a distance taking care that he was not noticed by her. This was relatively easy to achieve as she was obviously preoccupied with other business and totally unaware of his existence. After she'd been walking for ten minutes she stopped at a bench on the seafront and sat down. Furling the parasol she wedged it between the bench slats and opened her purse. She produced what appeared to be a letter and began to read. Then she put the letter to one side on the bench and delving once again into her purse, produced a small ladies handkerchief from inside it. He could see and hear her clearly in the bright sunshine, even from a distance, her eyes were moist and she began to cry softly. Captain Walsh saw his chance, it's now or never he thought to himself, he walked slowly over to the bench.

'Good morning Miss,' he said.

She looked up at him with slightly tearful eyes.

'Forgive my intrusion but are you alright Miss?' he asked gently, looking down at her as she nervously sat on the bench.

'Oh, oh, er, yes I am really.'

'You're Irish aren't you Miss?'

'Is it that obvious?'

'No, no, it isn't obvious at all, well I wouldn't have thought it was to everyone, well not to most people. It is to me, you see it's just that I'm Irish too and well, I recognise a kindred accent and it's actually very nice to hear, for me anyway.'

'I wouldn't have thought that you were Irish,' she said.

'Well, I must be honest and say that there are times in my life when I'd wished that I wasn't but the fact is, yes I most definitely am. I left Ireland at a young age and I've done a lot of travelling since then, so I suppose the accent has become a little influenced over the years.'

His use of the word *influence* amused her and she laughed slightly. He could see her face clearly in the sunlight now. She had blond hair peeking from her cream coloured bonnet, a broad forehead, small saucer-like blue eyes, a small tight mouth and a small straight nose. Individually he considered these features may have been attractive but all together they presented her not as ugly, no she certainly wasn't ugly, but he thought of her as being on the unattractive side of plain.

He began to think that this might be easier than he first thought and a plan now started to formulate in his head.

'Yes, I can just detect it now but it is very feint.' As she said the words she smiled, she didn't actually feel that she wanted to smile but she found that she couldn't do anything to stop it.

'Oh that's much better,' he consoled, 'homesickness can be a serious ailment if you allow it to take hold.' As he said the words he smiled, his smile was different than hers, although she didn't know it, it was a most deliberate and *contrived* act.

She thought how his smile lit up his face and made his eyes twinkle. He had perfect teeth, she thought he had a nice smile, actually it was much more than that, he had a tremendous smile, a wonderful smile.

'How did you know I was homesick?'

'Oh, I'm more than delighted to be wrong Miss.'

'No, you're quite right.'

'Homesickness is no stranger to me, I've suffered from it myself in most parts of the world, I think everybody has and I've never even had a proper home to be homesick for.'

She laughed once again. She was impressed by this straight-backed, sensitive man, he made her laugh and just then she realised that he was very handsome with his tall athletic physique, fair hair, blue eyes and perfectly balanced symmetrical features. In fact she thought that never had she seen a man so handsome in all her life.

'If it's not too forward a question, what part of Ireland are you from Miss?'

'I'm from a little place in County Wexford, I doubt that you'd know it. My name is Siobhan, Siobhan de Hay. What part of Ireland are you from sir?'

'I beg your pardon Miss, my name is Patrick Smith, Captain Patrick Smith,' he lied. 'Originally I'm from a little place called Dublin,' he lied again, 'I expect that you will have heard of it.'

She laughed yet again, 'And now it's my turn to be a little bit forward, what brings you to Llandudno?'

'Oh, I'm recently out of the army and I thought that I'd treat myself to a little holiday by the seaside and you never know your good fortune, I thought that perhaps I might find a wife, start a family before it's too late,' he smiled again, then he laughed again.

She felt absolutely enthralled, 'Oh, you're not married already then?'

'Oh no, never have been, it's not fair to inflict army life on a lady and I've never really found anybody that would tolerate me for any more than a short interlude.'

She considered that there would be many women who would be more than prepared to tolerate the handsome captain for *much* longer than a *short interlude*. She hoped that this would not be the end of her conversation with him, just the beginning of it, but she didn't quite know how to bring this about. She felt sheepish and tongue-tied.

The captain recognised that Siobhan wished to progress their short conversation, he wished this too and he knew exactly how to bring this about. He sat down beside her on the bench and looked into her eyes, 'It's a glorious day Siobhan de Hay, I appreciate that this is very forward but would you give me the pleasure of taking a stroll along the seafront with me. I'm all alone and if you are too we could keep each other company. We could finish up at Granelli's ice cream parlour, you can just see it about a mile away, it's that bright pink and white building shining in the sunlight straight ahead.'

Siobhan was caught by both relief and surprise, she tried very hard not to let the delivery of her response betray her absolute pleasure at his invitation but as the words left her lips she knew that they did exactly that but she didn't care. She giggled, 'Oh I'd love to Captain.'

'Please call me Patrick.'

They got up from the bench together, he looked into her eyes again and smiled at her again. The smile she knew to be a tremendous smile, a wonderful smile. They strolled along arm in arm together, the plain, young, tall, slender lady and her newly-found handsome captain.

As Siobhan de Hay walked slowly along the Llandudno seafront in the midday summer sunshine, arm in arm with Captain Patrick Smith, they chatted and although she had only known him for half an hour she thought him to be the kindest, funniest, exciting, most handsome man that she had ever met.

She knew there and then that he was exactly what she had ever wanted and she just could not believe her own good fortune.

As Captain Patrick Smith walked slowly along the Llandudno seafront in the midday summer sunshine, arm in arm with Siobhan de Hay, they chatted and although he had only known her for half an hour he thought her to be the most naive, dullest and plainest-looking woman that he had ever met. He also believed her to be already totally enamoured of him, he knew there and then that this was exactly what he wanted and he just could not believe his own good fortune.

Chapter 8

The Council Meeting

Just as the Reverend Bel was finishing off the delivery of the lesson that opened the council meeting, and right about the time that she arrived at the Amen itself, Councillor Archibald Douglas Forsyth Hamilton, OBE, unbowed his head and looked up and around at the civic ensemble. Hamilton's eyes scanned the hundred-and-twenty-year-old council chamber searching methodically along the long, oak-benched, leather-covered seating, his perusal came to rest upon one particular bench wherein a seat was vacant. By the expression on Councillor Archie Hamilton's face this empty place was causing this veteran local politician some degree of anxiety.

Just then the mayor, Councillor Neville Penderyn, high up in his seat of office at the head of the chamber asked for apologies, absences and declarations of interest. Councillor Karen Spencer, the leader of the council, rose to her feet and as if by signal all the other councillors sat down as she began to speak, 'Councillor Paul Dixon is currently recovering in hospital from his brief illness and will be in absentia from the meeting this evening. I'm sure that everybody in this chamber will join with me in wishing him a more than speedy and complete recovery.'

This statement caused some incoherent mumblings around the chamber.

'If nothing else,' she continued, 'we will miss his sense of humour, in fact we would terminally miss anybody and everybody's sense of humour in this chamber, if only there was somebody who had one.' As explained to the new member in the chamber this was a typical council leader type joke, unfunny.

'During the course of proceedings this evening there will be a get-well card circulating for Councillor Dixon, I'd be most grateful if members would sign it when it gets to you,' she exhaled. 'Also, Councillor Danny Senetti sends his apologies, he has received a very late and urgent demand upon his time and is unavoidably running late, but he will be in attendance when he arrives.'

'How could he not be, it would be impossible to be in one without doing the other?' said Mayor Penderyn. There was some, but it has to be said not much, laughter around the benches. As explained once again to the new member in the chamber this was a typical, council mayor type joke, again – unfunny.

The announcement about Senetti seemed to ease the anxiety shown in Hamilton's face and his composure took on a more relaxed state from then on. The meeting real then commenced. It progressed laboriously through the listed agenda items and approximately two thirds of the way through Executive Question Time, which was item four of a fifteen item agenda, Councillor Danny Senetti entered through the doorway of the council chamber. He waited patiently at that doorway for several minutes and until the last executive member answered the final question on the item. Senetti then crossed the floor purposely but quietly and took up his usual seat in the third row of the council backbenches next to Councillor Victoria Quilley.

Following the mayor's direction the ensemble of elected members progressed through each item on the agenda, arriving finally at the last one which was a proposed and seconded motion whereupon the member who had seconded reserved the *usual rights*. This motion seemed to manage quite easily to be all of specific, vague and pointless at the same time. It was also a motion that was not without precedent and it stretched the bounds of repetitive tedium beyond previously unsurpassed lengths.

Finally, the vote was taken and recorded after which elected members rose, the metaphorical guillotine came down and the mayor announced the colours and numbers of the winning raffle tickets and declared the meeting closed. The inevitable outcome of this full council meeting was exactly the same as all the other full council meetings that had preceded it for the last one hundred and twenty years and it was declared triumphantly, that there would be – another full council meeting.

As the members both filed and fled out of the chamber in a disorderly fashion, Councillor Archibald Douglas Forsyth Hamilton, OBE, followed Councillor Danny Senetti out of the council chamber and the Reverend Bel followed them both and several councillors in turn followed her. At the same time Councillor Hamilton looked at his wristwatch, two minutes past ten. 'Danny, a moment.'

Senetti stopped and turned around. 'Archie, how are you?'

'I'm never better Danny, how are you?'

'Never better too, as they say.'

'How are Charlotte and the children?'

'Archie, how would I know the answer to that? Charlotte is my ex-wife remember, we're not together anymore, we live separately. I've not spoken to her for three months or rather she hasn't spoken to me and as her father you probably see more of her than I do. As for the children, well they are not children anymore and as you well know they're both away at university, at opposite ends of the country, Newcastle and Norwich, which if nothing else should at least prevent them from killing each other. In addition to this, both those places are about two hundred miles plus from here only in opposite directions. So, unless they're after money I don't hear much of them and even when they are and I do, it is usually in the form of what they call a text, and just in case you don't know what a text is Archie, well it's a kind of babble that they use these days, you know where a letter takes the place of a word and a number takes the place of a syllable. I don't understand why we encourage them to learn English as children when they refuse to speak it as adults. Anyway, I can't fathom the babble out, in fact, I can do the crossword in the Guardian in half the time it takes me to unravel a text message. So, I usually don't even bother trying to read it let alone respond. So what I am trying to tell you Archie is that as far as my ex-wife and my kids are concerned, I know sod all about sod all.'

'Danny boy, you're a cynical bastard, it's a good job that I love you.'

'Archie, I want to believe you, I really do, it's just that over the last twenty-odd years any evidence for this love of yours has been scarce on the ground. Anyway, I may be wrong but I don't think that you have followed me out here to ask after Charlotte and the boys, you must want something else. What short lived cause of yours do you want me to sponsor this time?'

'Well, I don't really want to talk here, too many listening. How about we meet in twenty minutes in the Town Hall Tavern across the road.'

'Archie, there are at least three reasons why I'm not going in the Town Hall Tavern with you.'

'Go on, I suppose that I'm going to have to listen to them all. Couldn't you just tell me one instead of the whole three, or two maybe, I'll meet you halfway.'

'One is that there will be as many councillors in there as there are in here, too many listening as you say, but for me after almost four full hours in a council meeting I need to get away from the company of councillors, not get deeper in with them. Two, I'm driving and I can't drink, and three, and this is the most important reason, the one that supersedes everything else, the last time I was in a pub with you alone, which was some years ago, you sat there all night drinking apple and mango or was it pineapple and melon something or other. If a man's going to have a drinking partner then there is a prerequisite qualification that goes with that relationship and that qualification Archie, is that the drinking partner actually has to drink and as we both know you don't. So, after the last marathon apple and mango tango with you I filed for divorce on the grounds of an irrevocable breakdown brought on by our drinking incompatibility. That application was granted and the decree is now absolute.'

Archie laughed first then Danny did.

'Decree absolute, the same as your daughter did to me really only the other way around, as they say, like father like daughter.'

Both men laughed again.

'Ok Danny, well can we go into the corridor then, at least that'll give us some degree of privacy,' said the older man.

Danny nodded and both men walked together through the hall. They passed the marble statues and the glass encased civic memorabilia and the photographs on the wall of the many mayors past and the one present. They walked out of the chamber foyer and into the corridor where they both stopped at the marble staircase, they leaned against the shiny brass handrail and momentarily looked down into the marbled stairwell and then turned to face each other.

Archie's glance darted around nervously but there was only the clergywoman in earshot. Danny noticed her also but for a very different reason, he thought how beautiful she was for a priest. He'd seen female priests before but never one so attractive as her. He could see that she had her earphones in and she was looking at her mobile phone, obviously she was catching up on her messages whilst she'd sat through the council meeting. Danny reflected that it seemed that the mobile phone epidemic had even encroached upon ecclesiastical matters. It was obvious that she wouldn't be able to overhear and in any case she wouldn't be interested in what they had to say for it was a known fact that the only people who could bare to listen to what councillors had to say immediately after a full council meeting were other councillors.

Archie began to speak, 'Danny, it's about this murder in Winton Kiss, what was her name now, Helen Day?'

'Why do you want to know about that?'

'It's just something that I've taken a passing interest in.'

'Archie when have you ever taken a passing interest in murder?'

Archie appeared exasperated. 'Danny, it doesn't really matter one bit does it? It isn't important in any way is it? That's the issue with you, you always want to know the ins and outs of everything and you always answer somebody else's question with one of your own, that's bad enough but it's usually embedded in a five minute speech. I'm after short answers, not questions and long speeches, and you're the local councillor over in Winton Kiss so why can't you just tell me what you know.'

'Well that's easy, I know absolutely next to nothing.'

'You must know something, at least more than I do.'

'What makes you actually think that I know any more than you do? Between you and the police...'

'Why, what have the police got to do with this?'

'They came to see me about it the other day.'

'Well that's a start, what did they tell you?'

'They didn't tell me anything Archie, the police don't come to tell you things, if they came to tell you things, we'd see even less of them on the streets than we do now, they came to ask me things.'

'Why would they do that?'

'Because they're the police Archie, and that's what they do, they ask you questions.'

'Yes, but why would they ask them of you Danny, what have you got to do with this crime?'

'I knew the victim.'

'So you do know something, how did you know her?'

'I had a relationship of sorts with her.'

'Surely you're not being serious Danny, she was old enough to be your mother. You know, you take some getting over you do, first you're baby-snatching with that schoolgirl, what was her name now? It doesn't matter, but what does is that her own mother was young enough to be your daughter. Then you're going grab-a-granny with somebody that's your own mother's age and as if that's not enough she actually gets herself murdered. Haven't you learnt anything from last time? If I wrote this down and sent it off to the BBC they wouldn't believe me.'

'I'm not even going to respond to any of that exaggeration that you've just uttered, it wasn't that sort of relationship.'

'What sort of relationship was it?'

'It was a kind of semi-professional relationship.'

The older man laughed out loud, 'A kind of semi-professional relationship, listen to yourself, what's a kind of semi-professional relationship? Where do you go to find one of those? You can't have a semi-professional relationship, it's either professional or it's not. Semi-professional, it's the same as being nearly pregnant or half drunk, you are either one or the other.'

'How would you know Archie, you've never been either? I don't know where you drew that analogy from but it's not big and it's not clever. My relationship with Helen Day was totally appropriate. We sat on a council panel together, she lived near me and now and again we had one or two little drinks together.'

'Danny, you've never had one or two little drinks in your life. Are you sure that you're not getting your numbers and measures a little mixed up?' Archie said.

'One or two drinks together whilst we were waiting for the train and that's the extent of it,' Danny repeated. 'I suppose the police were just following up a routine connection along with dozens of others. If anybody knew her then they went along and spoke to them and that's why they came to see me. Now speaking of drinking partners, she was a good drinker Helen Day, none of your apple and mango tango for her, I'd have gone to The Town Hall Tavern with Helen.'

'What was her story, where was she from originally, what was she doing in Winton Kiss?'

'I don't know the answers to any of those questions, I didn't know that much about her, not many did, she was the keep-yourself-to-yourself type.'

'Where was she from originally?'

'I've just told you Archie, I don't know.'

'You were on a panel together, you had a drink together, you must have heard her speak, what kind of accent did she have?'

'Well it was very slight, but as you ask, I thought that she had an Irish accent.'

'Irish!' Archie almost shouted the word.

Danny also thought that there was more to Archie's response than a raised voice. Archie exclaimed the word more than questioned it, it was as if it supported or even confirmed something to the older man. He also detected a tremor in Archie's voice when he himself repeated the word *Irish* and if he was mistaken about that then he certainly wasn't mistaken about the older man going positively white in the face at its mention. He observed all of this but he made no reference to any of it.

'She was shot wasn't she?' asked Archie. 'How many times and where?'

'I don't know how many times, but it was in her house. This has all been in the newspapers Archie, why don't you go home and read them?'

'No, I don't mean where in the neighbourhood she was shot, I mean where exactly did the bullet or bullets go and what type of gun was it? There's something else, what was the condition of the room that they found her in?'

'Bullets, type of gun, condition of the room, you're asking some really odd questions Archie and I keep telling you I don't really have any answers for you. Why don't you go and ask the police if you're that interested?'

Undeterred the older man persisted, 'I was reading the newspaper reports before I came out tonight. The local GP found the body, the report said so.'

'As I said before Archie, why don't you go home and read them again? You might have missed something, you'll get much more out of them than you will out of me. What really is your interest in all this, come on tell me?'

'Danny, don't press me on it please, it goes back a long time, almost a hundred and fifty years. If there's anything worth knowing then you'll know in due course.'

Archie looked at Danny sideways, 'The village doctor found the body didn't she?'

'I think that I read that, yes.'

'The local GP Danny, that's *your* GP, I've heard Charlotte talk about her, Doctor Maxine Wells, that's who she is, she knows more about this than anybody.'

'Alright Archie, if that is what you think, why don't you go along and interview her?'

'No Danny, not *me,* I want *you* to go along and interview her.'

'Me, I don't even know her, I've never even met her or spoken to her, I'd forgotten her name until you just said it now. I've only seen her maybe twice, three times in my whole life and then I didn't know it was her and I'll tell you what, I know her type and...'

The older man interrupted, 'Danny, how old are you now, do you mean to tell me that you never even been to see your own doctor?'

'What do I need to go to see the doctor for?'

'What does anybody go for, it's obvious?'

'Archie, didn't anybody tell you that doctors don't know anything about anything these days? They are not in the ways of the old time physicians who carried out a diagnosis and found cures for things and gave you prescriptions and examinations. It's all lifestyle now, whatever you've got, to them it's all your fault. They just ask you if you smoke or drink and how much you do it and what your diet is and how much exercise you take. Then they look at you in disgust and tell you that you're an overweight slob and you're unfit. If you don't have any of these habits, and who doesn't these days, and who isn't these days, apart from you of course Archie, then they blame your parents. I don't need to go and see Doctor Maxine Wells just to be told to cut down on my drinking and lose some weight. Any of the drunks in the Black Swan can tell me that and none of them have been to medical school and I don't need an appointment to talk to them. Once those doctors get their clutches into you your life isn't your own. Intimidation and threat, that's how they operate, telling you what will happen to you if you don't stop doing this or what will happen if you don't start doing that. They're the medical equivalent of a bullying teacher, but at least you can get away from teachers when you leave school. You never get away from doctors, one of them signs you into life and one signs you out of it and another one of them keeps watch on you in the meantime.'

'Danny, you're changing the subject and what do you mean she's a type, what type are you talking about?'

'The type that has no truck with my type, that's what type.'

'Danny, she's a material witness, she's your local doctor, that's her type and you, Danny Senetti. are her local councillor. What could be more natural than the local councillor having a chat with the local doctor?'

'That's not much of connection is it, not much of a let-in.'

'It's enough for what we need to know, anyway, it's the best one that we've got, it's the only one we've got.'

'What exactly do you need to know Archie, you've not said, and what do you mean *we*?' repeated Danny. 'Exactly when in this conversation did this fantasy of yours elevate itself to *we*?'

The older man cogitated for a while and concluded that the conversation was not moving in quite the direction that he wanted it to. He decided to change his approach, 'Danny, I'm not asking you to do much, it's just a short conversation that I'm asking you to have and you owe me.'

'You know what Archie, you never disappoint me, but you must be losing your touch a little, you usually get that into the conversation in the first ten seconds, this time it has taken you all of ten minutes.'

The older man lowered his voice, 'Danny, you'll be interested in this, I'm standing down from the council.'

'Archie, it's common knowledge, everybody in the borough knows it, you announced it yourself three council meetings ago, it took you ten minutes to tell everybody something that should have taken you two and when you sat down after your speech we knew no more at the end of it about your reasons for going than we did when you stood up at the beginning, only that you're retiring next May.'

'No Danny, I'm not, nobody knows this, you'll be the first.' He lowered his voice even more to an audible whisper, 'I'll get to the point, I'm bringing it forward, it's going to be on my seventy-ninth birthday in September. I'm eighty next year and I don't want to celebrate my eightieth birthday sat in on some pointless scrutiny committee discussing the significance of the fact that there has been a nought point nought per cent increase in the take up of free school meals during the last half-quarter. What exactly is a half-quarter anyway? I've done my civic duty and beyond, it's time to let someone else in, a younger someone else, a cleverer someone else maybe, a more energetic someone else, I don't really care as long as it is a different someone else.'

'Well Archie, you know best, it's your life, good luck with it, just promise me that you're not going to inflict another one of those BAFTA award winning speeches on us. Maybe you could let everybody know by email or even better by text.'

'You said that you don't read texts.'

'Exactly.'

'What my retirement does mean is that I'll be off the council, and in preparation for this I'll be standing down from all committees next month except the Airport Committee, I'm going to stay on that one as an ordinary member until I officially retire but I'll be resigning as chair of it next month with immediate effect.'

Danny was silent, there weren't many elected members that didn't covet the influential position that was Chair of the Airport Committee. It was one of the most important positions in the region let alone the borough. That was without mentioning the very generous special responsibility allowance that went with it and his finances as usual could do with any support that they could get. In fact he'd been thinking about it whilst he'd been in Beaumaris and if things didn't improve he might even have to consider looking for a regular job of some kind, or cutting down on his drinking. He wasn't sure which perceived remedy was the worst.

Just then Archie's words broke back into his thoughts, 'Everybody knows how the succession works, unofficially of course, the outgoing chair recommends the incoming chair, it's tradition and you'll never beat tradition. Danny, I'll be direct, I'll come to the point, I'll recommend you if you're interested.'

Again, the younger man was silent.

'Come on Danny, everybody in the council knows where you should be and where you want to be, I mean Karen Spencer, she's nice enough and straightforward enough and she's more attractive to most men than you could ever be, probably to most women as well, but you're not completely devoid of talent and your pig-headed cynicism and your plug ugliness should not be allowed to hold you back.'

The old man's voice trailed off and he looked at the younger man intently, then he started speaking again, 'Danny, Chair of the Airport Committee is your route back, it's your second chance, everybody deserves one, even you, and this is yours, it's what you've been waiting for and all you've got to do in return is go and see your doctor. Some people do that every week, it's their idea of having a good time.'

'Well it isn't mine and what will I say to her, I can't just march in to her surgery and start asking questions about a murder. She's a doctor, that probably means that she's an intelligent woman, what if she throws me out or calls the police? They're already suspicious, I told you they came to see me.'

'Danny, obviously you need to be a little more subtle in your approach than that. Give it some thought anyway, that's your problem to solve and if I know you, you'll think of something.'

'I haven't said I'll do it yet.'

'So you are thinking about it then?'

'When are you going to make the recommendation to the Airport Committee?'

'I'll do it as soon as I've had your report on your meeting with the doctor.'

'You're really serious about this murder thing aren't you, is there something about all this that you are not telling me Archie?'

'Danny, there will probably turn out to be nothing worth telling.'

Then the older man said, 'There is just one more thing concerning Helen Day, if you were on this panel with her, you must have seen her quite regularly and you must have got close to her physically, in a semi-professional way of course,' he added in mock sarcasm.

'Archie, less than five minutes ago you were being direct, you were coming to the point. Now you are doing the opposite so what are you talking about?'

'Well you must have noticed things about her, physical things.'

'Archie, I keep telling you this, I didn't really look at Helen Day that way. I'm becoming a bit apprehensive about your answer here but what sort of physical things are you referring to, can you be more specific, have you got an example?'

'What colour were her eyes?'

Danny began to laugh, 'Her eyes, I've got absolutely no idea, why would I know the answer to that? Anyway, she always wore glasses every time I saw her, what reason could you possibly have for wanting to know that?'

'Alright forget it Danny, it isn't that important anyway. I just thought in all those years you might have noticed.'

'Archie, I've known you much longer than I've known Helen Day and I don't know the colour of your eyes, actually what colour are they?'

The older man looked a little exasperated, 'Danny, I said forget her eyes, just go and see the doctor will you.'

Danny kept it up, 'And why would you want to know the colour of someone's eyes?'

'Danny, you are being disrespectful now, the lady has only just died in tragic circumstances.'

'Fair enough Archie, but it's an odd request.'

'Trust me Danny, I'm a councillor.'

Both men laughed and then with silent mutual acceptance realised that their conversation for the moment had finished. Councillor Danny Senetti and Councillor Archie Hamilton separated as they came out of the side exit at the town hall. It was raining heavily, Danny turned left and made his way across the forecourt to the underground car park to retrieve his car. The older man, declining Danny's offer of a lift, turned right, slipped down a side street, unfurled his black umbrella and began his usual short walk to his usual taxi rank.

For entirely different reasons both men were completely oblivious to the dark saloon car that came screaming out of the night at speed. Nobody heard the Spanish guitar music emitted from within its door speakers and nobody saw it stopping momentarily, as it ploughed into the older man, hoisting him up in the air and over the car bonnet onto the car roof, dropping him on his head and leaving him in a bloodied, broken-boned heap and for dead, seven metres from where he'd been originally walking. The wheels then spun and screeched as if in panic as the vehicle sped off into the dark, wet night.

Chapter 9

Dublin Tryst

Siobhan de Hay was on her way to a tryst. She was meeting a man and she had a secret that made her heart jitter and her brain go light-headed. It was as if she was a young schoolgirl all over again. Even if she was behaving in a schoolgirl way none of it mattered to her, all that did was that she was in love with him and he with her.

It was all so incredible and hard to believe for her because all of ten weeks ago she had been resigned to her life in Dublin with her elder sister Clodagh. A life of teaching, sowing, reading, gossiping, drinking endless cups of tea and occasionally visiting her father and her younger brother in Enniscorthy, County Wexford. Although she didn't see much of young Dermot as he was away at boarding school in England.

She'd long since accepted that at the age of thirty-three she was never going to be anything other than the younger de Hay spinster girl to those that spoke of her and *Miss Siobhan* to those that spoke to her. Then completely out of nowhere on a beautiful summer's day on the Llandudno seafront she'd just been sat on a bench thinking of home and who'd come along out of the sunshine but Captain Patrick Smith. He'd been a soldier in the British army. Siobhan's older brother Fergal had also been an officer in the British army but he'd been killed in India, barely twenty-one years old in 1858.

They were going to get married, Siobhan and Patrick, and live in London, it was all so exciting. Patrick didn't have any family, he'd been an orphan, he'd never married and he'd never had a family to look after. He'd saved most of his money throughout his army career, he'd had some good advice and he'd invested wisely and by any standards he was quite well off.

Siobhan wanted children, lots of them, sons or daughters it didn't matter that much to her, as long as they were with Patrick. She and Patrick had stayed up all night talking about it. She'd never talked about anything of that nature before, not with a man anyway. It was all a wonderful dream come true.

Even though she was a thirty-three-year-old woman and long past the age of needing consent on any mortal issue and Patrick was respectable she knew that there might be some opposition from her father. However, she also knew that once he saw Patrick he would take to him, but her case would be strengthened, and virtually certain, if she could get her sister Clodagh on her side. Clodagh was Old Padraig's favourite and she could always bend the old man to her will.

Now Siobhan was back in Dublin and Patrick was here too. As she approached the little teashop she saw him standing outside its entrance. He was a tall, straight man with a definite military poise. Even on this chilly autumn evening with his coat pulled up and his hat pulled down it was unmistakably Patrick. She thought that he looked more handsome still, in the early evening darkness, in his smart blue-grey overcoat, his hat to match and his shiny black shoes that glistened in the dark. She looked in his direction and jumped in the air and waved in a vigorous schoolgirl way that belied her thirty-three years. He came over to her and took hold of her outstretched hands and kissed her on the cheek. She wanted him to kiss her passionately on the lips and hold her in his arms but she knew, as he did, that such open air displays of affection, even in modern Dublin, would not be tolerated, particularly on a Friday evening.

'Siobhan,' he said tenderly and with a warm smile.

'Patrick,' she said in reciprocal tenderness, 'I've missed you, I thought today would never come.'

'Me too, but it has my love,' he said.

They strolled hand in hand over to Logan's Teashop. He opened the door for her as they both stepped inside. A smart liveried waitress dressed in black and white came over to them and ushered them to a table by the window.

'How have you been?' he asked.

'I've been fine really although sometimes I get nervous with all this,' she replied.

'You're not having a change of heart are you?'

'Never, it will happen, I know it will, we'll be together, I know we will.'

'I know we will too.'

They fell silent for a moment.

'Have you kept our secret?' he said.

'I have, although I must admit I've found it very difficult to do. Clodagh never stops asking questions, trying to prise things from me. I've kept a few secrets over the years and they were easy to keep compared to this one, probably because I didn't really care that much about them but with this one, I've been bursting to tell everybody.'

'It won't be long, just another twenty-four hours, and we'll know if she's on our side then we'll make a plan to see your father. Then after that there will be no need for any more secrecy and we can tell anybody that we wish to tell.'

'Oh it all seems so complicated!' she said in anguish, 'Why can't we just be together, why do these other people have to be involved, why can't we just tell them that we want to be together and why can't they be happy for us?'

'They will be, please be patient. It has to be done the right way, there are other people involved, there always will be, members of your family, their happiness is important too and I know that you wouldn't be happy if they weren't happy.'

'Oh Patrick, you're so kind and so understanding of others, sometimes I think that I just don't deserve you.'

'Siobhan, if there is anybody undeserving here it's me. This is much easier for me to do, I have no family to consider.'

'You've got the army.'

'Yes, the army has been good to me but it's not the same as a real family, one that you've grown up with and anyway, I'm out of it now.'

'Have you ever had any kind of family Patrick?'

'No never, just the army.'

'Not just one single relative, somebody to grow up with?'

'I did have two cousins once but I heard that they had both died sailing to Boston on the coffin ships. Apart from that, there are no relatives, not any that I know of. Tell me about your family again, I find it interesting.'

'Well you know it all already.'

'No, tell me again, you know you love to talk about them all and I love to listen to you talking about them.'

'Well, I'm originally one of seven but two of them didn't survive infancy. I'm the second youngest, Fergal my brother died in India, he was an army officer as you were Patrick, only he was a lieutenant I think, oh I don't really understand army ranks, and he was killed in some sort of skirmish in India. I remember him, but I didn't really know him that well, he was twelve years older than me, it all happened when I was a little girl. Nobody in the family talks about it anymore, I think it's all too sad for them even to think about, he was barely twenty-one.'

'The army is the place for cutting young men down in their prime, that's for sure,' he reflected.

'Have you been in that situation Patrick?'

'More times than I want to remember,' he answered.

'You're so brave.'

'What about your sisters?' he asked.

'Well, there are three of us still, Sybil, Clodagh and myself. Clodagh and I live here in Dublin, we have done for the last three years. Sybil is actually my half-sister on mother's side, she married an Englishman, Albert. Albert has got some sort of important job on the railways and they are always moving from place to place, every time she writes it seems that she's got another address. The last time I heard from her she was in Edinburgh and the time before that she was in some place in Wales with a completely unpronounceable name. Father was telling me the last time I saw him that he thinks they are going to stay in Edinburgh for a while.'

'A lovely city.'

'Have you been there?'

'Oh yes.'

'Is there anywhere that you haven't been Patrick Smith?' She squeezed his knee under the table.

'When you've been in the army as long as I have you've been to a lot of places.'

'Don't sound so resigned to it all, I envy you, I've been nowhere. I had a battle with Father before he would agree to me coming to Dublin and that's only seventy miles from home and when I told him I was going to help Mrs Lloyd with her school in Llandudno, you'd have thought I was going to the other side of the world, when in fact it is the best place in the whole world because it's where I met you.'

'Has Sybil got any children?'

'She's got two, a boy and a girl.'

'What are they called?'

'Alexander and Lillian.'

'Good names, what's the family name?'

'Hamilton.'

'You've got a brother.'

'Well, he's actually my half-brother, Mother died a few years back and Dad married again, but his second wife died also, giving birth to young Dermot, he's only twelve, he's back in Wexford with Dad although he's away at school a lot.'

'Well that sounds like a lovely family, I expect that you love them all and you are very fortunate to be able to do it.'

'Soon *you'll* be able to love them all and they'll all be able to love *you*.'

They both sat quietly gazing into each other's eyes.

'Tomorrow night,' he asked, 'is it all organised?'

'Yes,' she said.

'What exactly have you told Clodagh,' he asked in earnest.

'I've told her that I want her to meet somebody who is very important to me, somebody who I want to spend the rest of my life with.'

'No names, no background information?'

'No, nothing, just as we agreed, exactly as we agreed.'

'Didn't she ask?'

'Oh she asked, more than once actually, but I was firm with her and in the end she had no choice but to respect my point of view. I feel sure that she knows that tomorrow night she will be meeting my future husband, but she has no idea about what or who you are or even where you are.'

'Well, not long now, it will be all over tomorrow night. Oh, just one more thing, the servants, they've still got the night off? We don't want them listening in to what we've got to say.'

She reassured him, 'they won't be there, just you me and Clodagh.'

'What time, still six thirty?'

'Yes, are you alright with that?'

'I suppose if anything I'm a little nervous.'

'It's natural, you've got the address haven't you?'

He nodded his head and patted his breast pocket gently.

Chapter 10

Dom Dim and Dobbs

The doorbell rang in the distance and Senetti looked at his bedside clock, it was 7:47am. He always had a bit of a lie in after the late finish of the Full Council Meeting, particularly as he'd spent two hours at the pub lock-in after it, so he decided to ignore the bell. It rang again and then again and then constantly. He realised that the intruder into his sleep was now leaning on it so that it would just ring out permanently. Albeit reluctantly, he got up and put on his black and white dressing gown, he couldn't find anything to put on his feet so he padded barefoot down the stairs, up the hall and opened the door.

'You again!' he exclaimed as he saw Dimbleby and Dobbs stood there.

'What do you want this time, at this time? I suppose you'd better come in.' They all went through to the kitchen and resumed the seating arrangements they'd had a week ago.

Dimbleby spoke first, 'Good Morning Councillor, we are truly sorry to disturb you at this early hour when only ninety-seven point two per cent of the working population are awake.'

Danny made a mental note of the chief inspector's sarcasm, it was something that he was becoming rapidly accustomed to. He determined that this interview would go along different lines than the previous one.

'How well do you know Councillor Archie Hamilton?'

'He's my father-in-law, sorry ex-father-in-law, why do you ask, has something happened to him?'

'I'm afraid he's been involved in a car accident.'

'Are you sure it's him? He doesn't drive anymore, the doctor stopped him some years ago, he was having blackouts, had a couple behind the wheel. He was very lucky so I suspect...'

'In this particular instance he was a pedestrian.'

'Oh God, he's not...'

'No, he's still alive but he's badly injured and he's not regained consciousness yet. He's in Norford General Hospital.'

Danny felt saddened by the news, 'Have his family been informed? What actually happened?'

'Yes his family have been informed, as for what happened we don't really know for sure, nobody has come forward so we've no witnesses. We suspect a hit and run but we don't know. Were you on good terms with Mr Hamilton?'

'I'd say so, yes.'

'You had a long conversation with him after the council meeting, were you talking about anything in particular?'

'Of course we were talking about something in particular, have you ever had a conversation where you don't talk about something in particular, what kind of conversation would that be?'

'What were you talking about?'

'Council business, the usual committees, meetings, motions, all the political intrigue that people think goes with politics. When councillors converse with each other they only ever talk about two things, the council and the councillors.'

'By all accounts, over the years you've often clashed with Archie Hamilton in the debating chamber.'

'By all accounts of whom?'

'The other councillors.'

'There's sixty-four other councillors in the borough, you've interviewed them all in the last few hours have you? What you actually mean is one or two councillors who you've managed to contact or they've probably contacted you. Now I wonder who that can be?'

Dimbleby felt a little foolish at Danny's deduction, Danny could see it in his face.

'Of course I've clashed with Archie over the years, he's an opposition councillor, that's what we do in the council, we

98

contradict and argue with each other, sometimes sensibly, sometimes not, it's called political debate. That's what the council chamber is for.'

This time it was the sergeant's turn to speak. 'Do you own a car councillor?'

'I do Sergeant.'

'What make and colour is it?'

'It's a Mercedes.'

'A Mercedes eh, things must be improving with councillor's allowances.'

'In difference to police overtime Sergeant, councillor's individual allowances are a matter of public record and, not that it's any of your business, but my car is eight years old going on nine. In fact it was Archie Hamilton's old car, he gave it to me when he had to stop driving, I was married to his daughter then. It's a kind of dark red, maroon I think, I'm not very good on colours.'

'I notice that it isn't parked outside on the road, where is it at this precise moment?'

'It's in the car park at the Black Swan, where I left it last night.'

'I should remind you Councillor that drinking and driving is a serious criminal offence.'

'Sergeant, driving away from the pub after you've been drinking is a criminal offence. Driving to the pub before you've had a drink and then leaving the car behind after you've had one is the opposite of a criminal offence, it's what I call responsible citizenship.'

'What's the registration of the vehicle Councillor?'

'Now you're asking me something, I think that I've got absolutely no idea.'

'What, and you've had the car eight years?' said Dobbs.

'No, you haven't been listening Sergeant, that's not what I said, I didn't say that I'd had the car for eight years, I said that the car was eight years old, they are two entirely different facts. You seem to be a little careless with facts Sergeant and I find that a little disconcerting in a detective. Anyway, it doesn't matter, even if I'd had it fifty years I still wouldn't know the registration, I don't look at registrations, I'm just not interested in them.'

'Has your car been in any accidents recently?'

'No, not recently, not at all. Why are you asking these questions, do you think that maybe I ran my own father-in-law down with his own car because of a difference of opinion that we had at a council meeting?'

Now it was Dimbleby's turn again, 'All we know Councillor is that Mr Hamilton has injuries that are conducive with being the victim of a hit and run car crime. Nobody has come forward to explain and Mr Hamilton is not saying anything at the moment. He was found just after ten forty-five last night by a shift worker who was on his way home. If the shift worker hadn't have been around we are reliably informed by the medical experts that Mr Hamilton would probably have died from his injuries and then we may have been looking at a murder enquiry. At this stage we don't know whether it was accidental or deliberate, we hope that he pulls through then maybe he can tell us. What we do know is that you were probably the last person to see him before the incident.'

Danny parodied the officer, 'All I know Detective Chief Inspector is this: in the last two weeks there has been two serious crimes in this town, a town in which the police are supposed to protect us. One a murder and the other possibly a hit and run and maybe, potentially as you say, another murder. On both these occasions because I have connections to both victims you have visited me and asked me questions and I can understand that. What I can't understand is the manner that you ask them in, which I can only describe as being extremely disrespectful and accusatory.'

The two officers looked at each other in an uncomfortable silence.

Danny continued, 'Now I am not perfect, but I can say to you in all honesty that I have never murdered anybody, by any method, and that includes running them over. If you don't wish to accept my assurances then feel absolutely free to do so, even arrest me if you wish but before you do, let me tell *you* something, if you are thinking about doing this, even if it's only for half an hour, then I shall put everything I can into instructing my lawyers to cause you both as much professional embarrassment as they can possibly think up. In addition to this, as a local councillor, an ex-member of the police authority, a council taxpayer and all the rest of it, I'm beginning to wonder, apart from harassing me, what else you are actually doing to solve these crimes, what other leads you are following up and what else you are doing to find the person or people responsible for all of this.'

He could see that his bluster first tactic was having an effect, so in an attempt to hammer home his point he carried on with it, 'Now it's true, I did know Helen Day and obviously I know my own ex-father-in-law and I've had many a disagreement with him over the years, that's both inside the council and out of it. In fact, isn't that what fathers-in-law are supposed to be for, disagreeing with? I do recall that some years ago when he was a younger man he punched me in the head. It's also true that I was drinking last night and just to compound the felony I don't know the registration of my own car. I'll tell you what, forget the other leads. I'll ask your chief superintendent the question tonight at the local committee, I understand that he's giving another one of his presentations there. In the meantime, perhaps you can tell me why any of this warrants two visits from two senior detectives, one of these visits at 7.45 in the morning. I had a working day yesterday that started at 7:00*am* and finished at 10.45*pm* and no, I don't get paid overtime. Does any of that register as far as you are concerned? Do police officers not consider the public anymore or are you just focussed on your own pursuits to the exclusion of everybody else's? Let me ask you a question, why were you, whichever one of you it was, leaning on my doorbell, acting as if you were an eight-year-old, what gives you the right to behave in such a impertinent, unprofessional way?'

Senetti wasn't expecting an answer to any of his questions but he paused just for a few moments in the event that one should arrive. Dimbleby looked anxious, he knew that much of what the councillor had said had the ring of truth about it and he also knew that even though Danny Senetti had a bit of a wayward reputation he was respected in some quarters. He also knew that Senetti would carry out his threat to raise the question at the Local Committee and he didn't want Chief Superintendent Matt Showman on his case.

'Mr Senetti, we're just trying to get on with our job.'

'Mr Dimbleby, I'm sure that's true, and I'm just trying to get on with mine, so perhaps we should leave each other to do that.'

'I'll say good morning then.'

The two detectives got up from their seats and as they had done on the previous visit, walked out of the kitchen, down the hall and out the front door. Danny stared after them as they left and shook his head twice. He began to doubt that any crimes that took place in the borough would ever be solved if Dom Dim and Dobbs were on the case. He also resolved mentally that, as far as those two police officers were concerned, he wasn't just going to leave the situation where it seemed to be at that particular moment.

Chapter 11

The Local Committee

Dr Tom Wells looked a little agitated and his daughter Maxine noticed his discomfort, 'Dad, we are going to be late, what have you lost?'

'It's my black and yellow tie.'

'You've got drawers full of ties, put another one on.'

'I always wear my black and yellow tie with this shirt and I always wear this shirt with this jacket and this jacket with these trousers and these trousers with these shoes.'

'Why do you need a tie at all, we're only going to the LC, nobody wears a tie to that?'

'I'll change my shirt, but then I'll have to change my jacket and if I do that then I'll have to change my trousers and then my shoes,' he muttered.

Maxine went into his room, she loved her father, she quite simply owed everything to him and her late mother, but living alone with Dr Tom could be difficult at times. She came out of the room a few seconds later with a black and yellow tie draped over her right hand, 'Is this the tie?'

'Ah, that's the one, where was it?'

'It doesn't matter now, what matters is that we've found it so just put it on.'

'Who's driving, you or me?' asked Maxine.

'You drive, you enjoy driving, it bores me, you don't mind do you?'

'Not at all.'

Doctor Tom came out of the front door first followed by Maxine. She locked the door, placed the keys in her bag then she walked over to the silver Mercedes and took them out of it again to open the car before getting in. Doctor Tom climbed into the passenger seat beside her. Maxine turned the key in the ignition, the engine fired quietly and powerfully into life and the car moved smoothly and silently off the gravel drive.

Any police officer who knew Chief Superintendent Matthew John Showman even slightly knew exactly what he was, a career copper from the toe tips of his shiny shoes to the glistening peak of his polished cap. He had joined the county force twelve years ago, straight from Manchester University on the graduate-accelerated promotion scheme and as far as accelerated promotion was concerned both he and it had certainly lived up to the promise that such a name gave. Now, as he approached his thirty-fifth birthday, he was already a chief superintendent, a rank and pay scale that most officers aspire to but a position that few ever attain.

He was the youngest chief superintendent in the whole county and one of the youngest in the country. His recognition and reward at such an early age had not been attributed to him because of either his policing skills or his ability to catch criminals. In fact he wasn't that good at, nor was he that interested in, either of these two lines of duty and he was more than content to leave both these tasks to his un-accelerated and un-promoted colleagues, as long as he could have the reflected glory, and, as he scampered at lightening pace up the police promotion pole, those same colleagues ultimately became his subordinates. Oh, he had done his early, compulsory stint on the beat. In fact he had done it in one of the toughest parts of Manchester, that nobody could deny, but this was now a long gone and distant memory to him and all others.

His rapid promotion had been due in large part to his own still current pursuit, which was, still is and probably always would be, his propensity to attend and make presentations at various committees, gatherings and conventions. He was what is known to other police officers as *a politician's policeman* and he would attend any meeting that contained both an audience and politicians of any kind. He saw this practice, if achieved regularly, as his own personal route to chief constableship. This evening he was due to attend yet another committee and deliver a paper of his own authorship: *Local Policing and the Dynamic*. As opposed to most of the intended recipients of this paper, he was actually looking forward to it.

In similarity to most cities and towns throughout the UK, the public services in the borough of Norford are managed by an elected chamber. In Norford's case this comprises of sixty-five locally elected members, or councillors as they have come to be known. For ease of administration in Norford this whole is divided up into eleven separate parts, each part is governed by six councillors except for one, where there are five.

Most things that effect a particular local area, from refuse collection to planning applications to street sweeping, from car parking to graffiti, from health and wellbeing to cutting the grass in the park, from serious crime to stray dogs and cats, all these and more besides find themselves on the agenda of a particular and regular convention, this convention is known as the Local Committee. The councillors who preside over the Malton Local Committee are, in alphabetical order: councillors Christopher Conley, Ben Goldstein (chairperson), Daphne Hunter-Hobbs, Sylvia Starr, Monica Schultz and Danny Senetti.

The LC, in its abbreviated form as it has come to be known, convenes on the first Wednesday of every month at the local library at 6:00pm sharp.

Entrance is completely free and it is a public meeting open to all constituents and anybody else who feels that they have a vested interest, or anybody who is agile enough to sneak past the council's democratic officer as she mans the door. This is a comparatively easy task to complete as the unofficial entrance policy seems to be if you want to come in and you can get in then you are in, although it has to be said that many people having gained entrance just the once, try to sneak out almost immediately, never to attempt re-entry ever again.

The vast majority of Malton residents have never attended the LC in their lives and fully intend, with firm resolution, to go kicking and screaming to their respective graves or funeral pyres without ever having done so. There are however some civic-minded individuals who attend each convention as if it were a moral duty and there are others of course who just come in to listen to the bother, or indeed to be the cause of it. There are also those who just turn up in the winter months for a warm and a cup of builder's tea.

The LC was exactly the place that Superintendent Matthew Alan Showman was attending to give his crime briefing. It was planned that the LC would be particularly well attended tonight. A few who were attending were: the local vicar, the Reverend Bel, the local senior school head teacher, Mrs Petra Kowalski, Dr Tom Wells, who was accompanied by his daughter, Dr Maxine Wells, Estelle Boassara, esteemed chair of the Malton Civic Society, an abundant selection of the civic minded and, most importantly, or at least as far as Chief Superintendent Matt Showman was concerned, the six local politicians that made up the LC.

The two cars arrived simultaneously in the library car park and both came to a stop side by side. Dr Tom Wells and Dr Maxine Wells got out of one and Councillor Danny Senetti got out of the other. Senetti had seen Dr Tom on many occasions but couldn't really claim to know him, he nodded and smiled at father and daughter. Senetti looked at Maxine and thought how elegant and cool she looked, almost beautiful in her obviously-expensive, fitted, black-linen dress. Maxine thought that Councillor Senetti looked as ragged and crumpled as he did the last time she saw him. She wasn't sure but apart from the overcoat she thought that he seemed to have exactly the same clothes on now as he did then, and that was six months ago. She remembered the dark suit and the scuffed shoes, although the beer gut seemed to have disappeared, in fact he did look decidedly slimmer, perhaps he'd been on a diet. The symbolism of the two motor vehicles parked side by side in the library car park struck her, her own sleek, silver, shiny convertible next to his dusty, dirty whatever-colour-it-was-underneath saloon. She noticed that the back number plate was covered in mud, or something or other, and was completely unreadable.

The three of them walked towards the library where the LC was being held. Senetti allowed the two doctors to ease in front of him. As Maxine approached the library entrance she noticed the tall, upright, immaculate figure of Chief Superintendent Matt Showman in his neatly pressed uniform suit and his immaculate white shirt, his whole appearance seemed to shine. She mused how two men, Senetti and Showman, could both be representing the community yet be turned out in entirely opposite ways. She told herself that appearance was all cosmetic anyway but she didn't really believe that. She recalled that her late mother used to have a saying, *handsome is as handsome does*. If that was correct she thought, with what she knew about Senetti against what she knew about Showman, then the high-ranking police officer was winning easily and without effort.

Then she had another thought, which was a type of juxtaposition, she considered that Showman wouldn't appear quite as handsome if it wasn't for his uniform yet Senetti would be much more so if it wasn't for his. She dwelled on the philosophical point of what was really the reality and what was really the mirage. Was it Senetti or was it Showman and which was which or who was who?

As Maxine and Dr Tom entered the library hall she noticed that tonight's LC was unusually well supported, she expected that this was because of the supermarket issue, she estimated that at least two hundred people had turned out which was probably a record for the LC. There was hardly a seat to be found but eventually she found two together and she and her father sat down amongst the audience and to the back of the hall.

The LC commenced in the usual way, Ben Goldstein as Chair asking for approval of the previous committee's minutes, declaration of interests then questions and petitions from the public. There was a lot of nodding and sayings of *agreed* from the other five councillors. Maxine noticed that Senetti was silent throughout. Dr Tom asked a question about the proposed new supermarket and Ben Goldstein announced that they would be discussing the issue specifically, further down the agenda, and if the good doctor could be so kind as to be a little patient then he would probably find his question answered in that discussion. The good doctor seemed satisfied with chair Goldstein's answer.

Superintendent Showman took his seat by one of the four guest microphones ready to deliver his paper. Before speaking he took his wristwatch off and placed it in view on the table. He seemed quite pleased with and proud of himself as he gave forth with his fifteen minute, twenty second presentation. He stated at every opportunity that presented itself that the police were winning the war against crime. He added that crime in the borough was the lowest in the county and in turn crime in Malton was the lowest in the borough and that it therefore followed that Malton was the most crime free area in the whole county. He showed statistics to prove this on a large white screen and in general he sang the praises of the local police force in a direct way and in particular in an indirect way he sang the praises of himself. After he had concluded he looked at his wristwatch evidently pleased that his presentation was on schedule to the second. He said that he was more than happy to answer any questions.

A civic-minded audience member asked the shiny, high-ranking police officer about unruly youths in the park on Sunday morning. She seemed content with the answer.

Maxine Wells paid attention as Councillor Danny Senetti raised his pen slightly above his head signalling that he had a question. Chair Goldstein nodded towards the councillor and said, 'Councillor Senetti.'

Senetti stood up from his seat and began to speak. Maxine observed that although he was ostensibly speaking to the chief superintendent he was really speaking to the gathered audience. Senetti wanted to know exactly what the police were doing about the recent murder in Winton Kiss and also the more recent hit and run in Norford town centre. He said that crime may be down in numbers and detection rates may be up on last quarter's figures, but in severity crime seemed on the increase, for where else have you had two crimes of such severity in as many weeks? Furthermore, Senetti wanted to know what progress was being made in investigating these crimes and when could the community expect news of arrests? In additional furtherance he also wanted to know from the policeman if the rumours that he'd heard about local people being interviewed by his officers in an accusatory way were true and finally, did the police believe that the perpetrators of these crimes were living amongst us in the community?

Senetti resumed his seat. Maxine could sense the discomfort in the audience yet she also sensed that they were behind Senetti. Matthew Showman was definitely uncomfortable and she supposed that such a high-ranking officer was not accustomed to being challenged in such a way. She also thought that the points the councillor had made needed saying and were absolutely right on. She recalled her own recent, accusatory experience with Detective Sergeant Lisa Dobbs and wondered how Senetti could portray her own experience so accurately. She thought back to his own alleged relationship with Helen Day and half guessed that because of it he may have had a similar police experience to the one that she had had. In that instance she warmed a little towards Senetti, if only for having the courage to say what she thought but couldn't or wouldn't say herself in a large open forum.

The shiny chief superintendent didn't give a clear answer, he mentioned the usual stuff about *prejudicing investigations* and *can't divulge at this stage*. It was just the type of typical stonewall, dishonest answer that Maxine did not expect but as she observed Senetti she could see that he did expect it. She also thought that Senetti could easily have challenged the superintendent's response but that he was quite content just to have raised it in the first place and that he was also quite content to leave it at that, though he concluded and retained the initiative by saying, 'Well thank you for that Superintendent, we all appreciate that you have your duty to perform but I do also, so you won't mind if we ask you to keep us informed of the police situation regarding these two serious incidents as it develops. Perhaps you could give us an update at the Local Committee next month?'

Maxine noticed the irritation in Showman's voice as he almost forced the words out of his mouth, 'Yes Councillor, I'd be happy to.'

Whilst Superintendent Showman was very accustomed to keeping tabs on everybody else he was very unaccustomed to them being kept on him and he made a mental note to speak to the officers on both cases and ensure that councillors in general, and Councillor Senetti in particular, were satisfied with the investigations.

He certainly didn't want to have to turn up at the Malton LC every month to give a progress report only to face criticism and be portrayed in anything less than a glowing reflection.

Maxine thought to herself that Senetti's point was well made and she thought that he did too. As the chief superintendent shuffled off back to his seat in the audience she considered that even in those few short steps his gait seemed a little less assured than when he had come in. She didn't know why that should please her but it did. Dr Maxine Wells also made another observation to herself which was that in that brief interchange between policeman and councillor, the shiny superintendent had dropped a point or two in her estimation, whilst the crumpled councillor had definitely gained a couple.

The meeting then moved on to the big issue of the night and the reason Dr Tom was here and thus the reason Maxine was. It was not that she had any interest whatsoever in the planning application for the supermarket but Dr Tom did and if her dad was interested then she was interested too. The supermarket debate opened up with the planning application being presented by council officers, representatives from the supermarket had their say, Councillor Daphne Hobbs spoke out in support of the project and then it was Danny Senetti's turn. This time Senetti remained in his seat and, as an anticipated dead silence filtered through the library hall, he spoke out, 'As others here tonight have, I've also seen the documentation in relation to this scheme. In fact, it's been forced upon me more than once, as if familiarity with it will have an effect on my decision.'

Maxine observed that he spoke in a clear and unfaltering way.

'I am not opposed to supermarkets, I use them myself on occasions but as a rule I prefer to shop in local shops. There are several problematic planning issues with this scheme, but the biggest by far is the fact that it is not in the town centre and as such it is detrimental to the town centre and in my view it would harm it badly, if not kill it off altogether. In Malton we want our town centre enhanced not harmed. I am not a planning expert, nor a traffic management expert, nor a retail expert. I have read with respect what the independent experts say about this supermarket scheme and it appears to me that they are all united in their opposition to it. Council officers in particular have put a great deal of endeavour, expertise and resources into this, looking at the scheme from all angles and they say reject! Their recommendation is being made in the best interest of the community of Malton, they could have no other reason for making it. I am a local councillor, it is my responsibility to represent the people of Malton to the council and to represent the council to the people of Malton. I've lived with the proposal of this scheme for almost two years now. During those two years I have come across very little support for it. What I have found is wholesale opposition to it. I have had a constant mailbag opposing it. I have had an orchestra of telephone calls about it. People of Malton have stopped me in the park, in the street, in the pubs and cafes, in the shops, at the train station, at the bus stop, even when I was waiting at traffic lights and on several occasions when I've been on my bike, the list is truly endless, people that I know, people in the community that I represent, and they've all had one thing in common to say to me: we don't want that supermarket in that location in Malton.'

Senetti paused for a moment and looked around the hall. Maxine observed the pin-dropping silence in the room and she realised that he had their complete attention.

'I've had letters from Malton businesses opposing it. I've had a three thousand signatory petition opposing it. I have received communication from every society that has Malton as part of its name, all opposing it. Our local MP opposes it, my ex-wife opposes it, my mother opposes it, my children oppose it and I haven't actually asked the dog but I'm sure if I did he'd oppose it too.'

Maxine doubted that Senetti even had a dog, she also doubted an earlier reference that he'd made to being on his bike and she doubted that he even owned a bike, or that he could even ride one. She supposed that both the bike and the dog were creatures of myth but there was no doubting the effect upon the audience.

Senetti carried on, 'The community doesn't want it and I as a local councillor would be wholly unrepresentative of the community if I didn't oppose it too. So, you won't be surprised to know that I do oppose it. There is one final point that I wish to make and it is to the people connected to this scheme, we are only a small community in Malton, you knew that before you came here, but we are a strong community and we are united on this issue and we don't want you here.'

Senetti left his chair, rising to his feet, his voice now a little impassioned, he continued, 'You came here uninvited by our community and your stay here has become that of an unwelcome suitor. So, can I politely advise you, on behalf of the community, to do what all unwelcome suitors have to do in the end, and what you will eventually have to do, and that is to transfer your affections – somewhere else!'

With that he sat down looking a little exhausted after his emotional delivery. As he did the audience rose to their feet and applauded uproariously. Maxine thought how happy and triumphant they all looked and, though his words were simple, that it was a very effective speech. As she looked around the faces of the people of the community she could see the support and affection for this enigmatic and contradictory figure and the point of realisation dashed upon her, as a tidal wave breaks upon a rock, that perhaps there was more to Danny Senetti than his drunken, ragged, crumpled appearance belied.

After the vote had been cast, five against, one in favour, the application was lost. The head of the supermarket faction glared at Senetti who smiled back at him, which in turn only made his glare even fiercer. The crowd began to disperse and Dr Tom walked across to the councillors' table. Maxine followed and her father proceeded to speak to Ben Goldstein.

'Doctor Wells,' said a man's voice behind her, she turned around to find Councillor Danny Senetti.

'Councillor Senetti, hello, nice to meet you, you spoke well tonight, it must have been difficult to remember and deliver all that. I think that you put into words what a lot of people were actually thinking.'

'Well,' he smiled, 'you're very gracious. I'd written it all down in advance and rehearsed it in front of the mirror a few times and the delivery is always easier when it's from the heart.' He paused and looked at her seriously.

She felt a little disarmed and surprised by his candour yet she found herself saying, 'You mean that it's not always from the heart Councillor?'

He chose to ignore her question as he reasoned it to be one of those questions that was looking for trouble and he didn't want any, not with her anyway, and not tonight. 'Doctor,' he paused again, 'I'm pleased that you are here tonight as I need to have a conversation with you.'

'Well here I am!'

'No, no this is absolutely not the right time nor place.'

'Alright then, your surgery or mine?'

'I wasn't really thinking of either, why do you say that?'

'Well this conversation of yours, it's either medical business, as I'm your doctor, or council business, as you are my councillor, so your surgery or mine?' she repeated.

'Well no its neither, well no that's not right, it's probably a bit of both, so let's make it neutral ground eh?'

'Did you have anywhere in mind?'

'I'd not thought of it until just now, perhaps the local pub?'

'I don't really drink Councillor.'

He felt a little irritated by her reticence and he said, 'Well, it's not compulsory, you don't really have to drink Doctor, just because you attend the circus that doesn't mean that you are expected to hold a chair up to the lions or ride the bareback ponies. It's not a condition of the conversation, you can have a coffee or one of those apple and mango or pineapple stuff things that people who don't drink are so fond of. I'm not asking you on a date Doctor, you won't be there all day, you can drive home after an hour, and this is serious community business.'

Straight away he regretted his own typical, cynical outburst and as he could see he was not getting off to a good start with the beautiful doctor. To make things worse he could clearly see that she had irritatingly risen above this and that she was keeping her good grace and humour as she said, 'Serious business, no date, I'm not sure that I want to go now Councillor,' she teased. 'What about my house then?'

'It's very kind of you to invite me there, and I'm very honoured, but your house is not really neutral ground, you can throw me out of there if you don't agree with what I say, whereas in the pub you'll at least have to listen.'

'I can walk out of the pub just as easily if I don't agree with what you say.'

This was getting worse he thought. 'Doctor, I'm actually doing this for somebody else, a valued member of the community. I knew that it wasn't going to be easy and now you just seem to be going out of your way to make it harder and I can't really see why. I'm not asking much, just an hour of your time when it suits you.'

'Somebody else, why can't they do it for themselves?'

'Just trust me.'

'What, trust a councillor, trust me I'm a doctor?'

They both laughed, that's better he thought, 'Alright, don't trust me then, but at least hear me, as I say for an hour, that's all I'm asking, at your convenience, you can manage that surely?' He waited in silence for a few moments, then he said, 'It might be important to the community. The community of which you Doctor, are an important and much valued member.'

She noted his councillor speak and supposed that he had played the community card many times before. 'Alright,' she responded, 'I'll take a chance.'

'Thank you,' he said almost in completion. Danny Senetti took a business card out of his shirt pocket and pushed it into Maxine's hand, 'Give me a call on that number when you get an opportune moment, please make it sooner rather than later.' Then he picked up a bundle of papers from the table and he was gone.

Maxine was intrigued, she really couldn't imagine what he needed to speak to her about that was neither medical nor council business. She promised herself that she'd ring him in the next twenty-four hours. She looked around for her father and noticed he was still in conversation with Ben Goldstein. She thought again, for the third time tonight, that Councillor Danny Senetti was perhaps not quite the useless, drunken blackguard that she had been all too ready to accept him as.

Chapter 12

The Peasant's Decree

John Gresham was a foundling child in London but as a young man he made his way to Ireland. It would prove to be a journey against the futuristic trend as thirty years hence people would be clamouring to get out of that country in their millions. In the year of 1817, Gresham was still a young man when he became the butler to a prosperous family household in Dublin. In a Georgian house, with its complicated domestic and social structure, being a butler at that time was the most important servant's position to be held. Even so, a servant, no matter how well regarded, is still a servant and nobody in the world has ever been able to establish exactly how, or even venture a believable guess as to where, a person of such comparative low status and income as the young Gresham came upon the not inconsiderable capital sum required for the challenging task that he undertook. For in that year he purchased the buildings of 21-23 Sackville Street in Dublin's city centre. In the ensuing years he turned those buildings into the highest class lodging house in the whole of Ireland. Its clientele included the aristocrats, gentry and honourables of the day and anybody who was anybody that happened to be in Dublin at that time.

As is the case with some honourables through time and the world over, the *honourables of the day* that came to reside at the Gresham did not always have intentions that were compatible with their perceived status of honour and nobility.

Room 304, on the third floor of the Gresham Hotel was occupied that particular afternoon. The sole gentleman occupant had arrived in Dublin in order to honour two previously arranged and very important appointments that he would fulfil over two days. Upon arrival the previous day the occupant of room 304 had checked into the Gresham and, after he had instructed the hotel porter to take his bags to his room, he had then departed immediately for one of these appointments. The outcome of this first appointment could have been declared a resounding success, that is to say if there was any intent to make such a declaration, which decidedly there was not.

Today he would fulfil the second appointment, which though dependent upon the success of the first one was by far the more important of the two and had been the reason for the first. After a late breakfast he had taken a leisurely stroll around Dublin.

Four hours later the occupant of room 304 had shaved, bathed and dressed. Now he sat on a chair facing the side of the bed. On the bed was a small, narrow leather case. He placed both hands on the two brass clasps at either side of this case and slid them both to one side, the lid unlocked with a click and he lifted it open. Inside the case resting snugly in two, specially made for the job, velvet apertures were two unusually small handguns.

These weapons were not just any ordinary small handguns, they were special guns. Apart from the objective of killing people, which they could do with chilling ease, these guns were made specifically with one other objective in mind, this objective was – concealment. They were Remington, Model 95, over-under, double-barrelled derringer pistols. Each gun had a bluish gunmetal stock and was finished off with an exquisite ivory, handle-grip. The most apparent aspect of these weapons was their smallness and each gun, from handle edge to barrel tip, was no more than about five inches long and was easily hidden in a hat, pocket, bag, up a sleeve or even in the palm of a man's hand. Each gun held two shots, four of them in total, the first shot with the correct aim being as deadly as the second, third or fourth. The occupant of room 304, or Captain Patrick Smith as he referred to himself these days, took both derringers out of the case and laid them down upon the bed. Picking them up individually he inspected first one and then the other. Satisfied with his own scrutiny, he then placed them on the mahogany writing desk that sat beneath the window of his room.

After all these years, today had finally arrived, it was to be a monumental occasion both for himself and for others, he knew this. His actions this day would have grave repercussions both for him and for the Middleman, and for future generations to come. These future generations included both Captain Patrick Smith's descendants and the middleman, Padraig de Hay's.

The captain knew that his was a terrible deed in contemplation but there could be no going back. The deed was his destiny and he had waited many years and was bound to it, bound by an irrevocable oath made by a fourteen-year-old peasant boy, who stood on a boat as he left Ireland in ignominy and forever. Bound thirty-five years ago, by a duty recognised then, but stretching back two hundred years earlier to his Great Ancestor. Circumstances were completely beyond the captain's control and he was nothing more than a servant in their bidding.

His eyes sought out a black leather valise that yesterday the porter had carried to his room. Out of this valise he produced a very small wooden box. This was a small writing case that contained implements for that very task. From this case he extracted a piece of plain white writing paper, a pen, a bottle of black ink and a blotter. He placed them all on the writing desk next to the two derringers. The captain, in pensive mood, paced back and forth by the window for two or three minutes. Then he sat down at the desk by the same window and in the Dublin autumn afternoon he began to write. He wrote slowly and deliberately but easily and without preoccupation, only pausing momentarily to dip the pen nib into the ink bottle. It was as if he knew exactly what he was going to write before he put pen to paper, as if what he was going to write was well rehearsed and thought through for many a year, as indeed it had been.

Finally after he had completed his written piece he laid his document down and pressed the blotter to the damp ink. He got up from his seat and walked around the room for a minute, then looking out through the window at the hustle and bustle of

Sackville Street below, he picked up his document, read it and once again paced the room in deep thought.

After several minutes he then took out another identical piece of white paper from his writing case, picked up his pen again and made an exact handwritten copy of the first document. Having completed this second document to his own satisfaction he blotted it, put the top back on the ink bottle, swilled the pen clean and packed up the writing case. He then placed both documents side by side on the desk, they read identically:

The Peasant's Decree   *October 6th, 1883*

Padraig de Hay,

I knew you many years ago in An Gorta Mor when you were a younger person and I was a younger one still. You were an evil, despicable man then and save that you are now deemed 'respectable' I doubt that little has changed with you since.

I have waited many years to place what will now come to be the de Hay Curse. After this, the lives of you and those people belonging to you will change forever. You are a much older man by now and cannot yourself be too far from death. When it inevitably does come to you then neither that state you find yourself in nor the cold grave you lie in will give you any grain of comfort nor peace from this curse.

For now you sit content in your gated mansion house with your established but swindled wealth and your complete family. With almost immediate effect this contentment will be short lived, it will not reign for you and it will not reign for those that follow on from you even after you have long departed.

For the crimes that you have committed against the Irish people, for you and for those de Hays that come after, you have been tried, convicted and sentenced. I and those that come after me have been appointed as your judges and executioners. In difference to you and your avaricious ilk we will not be responsible for the deaths of broken-spirited men and starving children. So the men and the children that bear your name are pardoned. However, throughout the decades and centuries to come there will be no pardon for the adult female line that bears your name. For small mercies sake, and unlike your own countless victims, the end will not linger, it will come quickly to them. The adult women will suffer the deed and their end will be ruthless and shocking yet swift and conclusive. The men and children will suffer the consequences of these deeds which will be endless, leaving havoc, tragedy and misery for those left behind in heartbreak, suffering and tears, as was my own fate, as I was left behind through the deeds dealt to me by your own merciless hand.

Signed: A Man of Insignificance.

Captain Patrick Smith then folded both his documents into two and placed each of them in separate envelopes that he had pre-addressed and stamped. He then sealed the envelopes.

For a full ten minutes he sat motionless in contemplation, the legs of his long lean frame stretched out before him and his own back erect against the back of the chair. Then, as if some insurmountable, mental blockade had finally been breached he rose to his feet and as he did so he scooped the two derringers up, one in either hand, and placed them in their purpose-made holsters that were fastened around his waist. Then he put on his topcoat, scarf, hat and gloves in that order. Picking up the letters he scanned the room one final time to detect any tell-tale sign of his presence then, satisfied with his surveillance, he put his writing case away, completed his packing and picked up his valise.

The autumn air was chill as he stood on the bottom step outside the Gresham and looked out at the statue of Nelson's Column. He'd read somewhere that it was one hundred and twenty one feet tall. It seemed to him, as an Irishman, that such a statue of a very English hero should be erected in a very Irish square was nothing less than an act of imperial subjugation.

It was 5:15pm and the light was hurrying along the day on its way out. He turned left onto Sackville Street and commenced the short walk to the Georgian square where the two sisters Clodagh and Siobhan de Hay lived. He noticed the new electric street lighting that he'd heard had recently been installed and along the way he posted both his letters. The exact time of the posting was a matter of precision and not a matter of frivolity for at least one of these letters. The captain knew that today, being Saturday, and the last weekend postal collection being at 5:00pm, that it would be Tuesday before this letter found its recipient and this suited his purpose. It would give him all of Sunday and all of Monday to make his escape out of Dublin, should he need extra time, although he planned to be on tonight's midnight boat for Liverpool, but it was wise to have a contingency. The second letter had no such time sensitivity as it had been posted to himself back in England.

He walked slowly but with purpose for he knew exactly where he was going and exactly why he was going there. In less than twenty minutes he had completed the walk and stood on the edge of the Georgian square that overlooked the small, tiny private park in the Trinity ward of Dublin. He was a little early and punctuality played a part in his task so he decided to take a turn around the square and he walked clockwise around its railings for fifteen minutes until he came back to the place where he had started from.

He found the house that he was seeking at the end of an elegant Georgian terrace. As he gazed up at it from a short distance he saw the impressive four-storey, brick-built building with its stone portico at the front entrance. There were eleven windows on the front facade, two on the ground floor and three rows of three aligned above. Each window row reduced in area as it ascended the height of the building so that the size of the three windows on the fourth floor were almost half the size of the two windows on the ground floor. The three windows on the second floor had iron balconies. At street level there were black and gold painted iron railings around the entrance to each house, as if to mark out the boundary of one from its neighbours. All these features together gave forth an image of prosperity, strength and elegance. He noticed that there were lights on throughout the terrace including the house that he was visiting. He rapped the big brass knocker on the door as softly yet audibly as he could and almost instantaneously he heard the hurried, light tread of a woman coming down the stairs. It was Siobhan, she pulled the door open, pulled him inside and kissed him passionately on the lips.

'Oh it's so good to see you again Patrick, I never tire of it and I never will,' she said as she ushered him down the hallway and shut the front door behind him.

In stark contrast from the street outside he noticed how deathly quiet the house seemed be. He took off his hat and placed it upturned on the coat stand shelf then he took off his topcoat and hung it on the coat hook and his scarf and gloves he placed in the hat. 'It's wonderful to see you,' he replied, 'I've had enough of that hotel room for a few hours.'

'Yes, they can get to be a bit stuffy can't they, especially if you spend any length of time in them.'

'You're right, although I did go out for a walk this afternoon.'

'Oh really, where did you go?'

'Oh nowhere special, just a couple of turns around old Dublin Town, quite interesting really, looking at the buildings. Yes, and I notice that you've got electric street lighting, fairly advanced eh?'

'We've had it for a couple of years now, it's only in the centre of Dublin.'

Just at that moment Siobhan noticed the small valise he was carrying. She seemed a little troubled by it as they had planned to travel to Enniscorthy on Monday and she didn't understand why he would bring any luggage now. 'Patrick, you've got some luggage?' she queried.

'No, it isn't really luggage, it's just a few belongings, sentimental stuff, a writing case, some other bits. I prefer to have them with me.'

'Are you going to write me another love letter?'

'If that is what you want then that is what you shall have. I shall compose one tomorrow.'

She kissed him again passionately on the lips, 'I love you,' she said.

'How is Clodagh?' he asked, 'I'm really looking forward to meeting her.'

'She is in extremely good humour and she is looking forward to meeting you. In fact she's spoken of nothing else for the past two days, to hear her carry on you would think it was Clodagh who was marrying you.'

He smiled at her and laughed softly.

'Shall we go up then?' she asked.

'Lead the way, I'll follow,' he smiled at her.

She turned away from him, lifted her skirts a little and began to climb the staircase. She continued this climb for two flights until she arrived at a wide landing. Around this landing were five doors, each with a room leading off. He followed her as she stopped outside one of these rooms, the door was slightly ajar and there was light coming from inside.

She knocked softly on the door as if in announcement, 'We're here at last,' she whispered. She opened the door fully and entered the room, he followed her in. Inside the room there was a tall slender lady sitting in a chair. As the captain entered the room she rose from this chair. The captain thought that she looked the image of her younger sister in almost every way.

Siobhan spoke first, 'Clodagh, please allow me to introduce you to Captain Patrick Smith, the man I love and the man I intend to marry. Patrick, please allow me to introduce you to my sister Clodagh who I also love but have no intention of marrying.' She giggled, surprised at her own inventive wit.

Clodagh stepped forward smiling and with an outstretched hand which the captain took in his. He also smiled, Clodagh noticed that he had perfectly shaped, even white teeth and that his smile lit up his features. Clodagh thought that rarely, if ever, had she seen a more handsome man.

The captain looked around the elegant Victorian drawing room. He noticed it was long in shape and high ceilinged. It was also large, probably about twenty-two feet by sixteen he thought, and from floor to ceiling about ten feet high. The ceiling was painted plain ivory cream and from its centre hung a four lamped gasolier, the walls had been expertly painted a pastel lime green.

Adjoining the walls and the ceiling was a complex Italian plaster cornice, also finished in ivory cream, and some two feet below that a highly polished brass picture rail ran around the perimeter of the room. The floor was covered with a lightly patterned carpet which was a similar green colour to the walls. A discoverer looking into the room from the doorway would see the focal point as being the white marble fireplace with its caste iron insert. Inside a fire burned brightly and a scuttle full of coal rested on the hearth. The fireplace's mantle was home to an array of china and porcelain ornaments. Fixed to the wall beneath the mantle and the picture rail was a huge mirror, which gave the room an even more elongated perspective when you looked into it. The promontory of the chimney breast had two large recesses at either side of it, each recess containing two framed pictures which hung from the rail in perfect symmetry. In the right hand recess stood a walnut davenport writing desk, which was neatly closed and apart from five books arranged along its lid was unashamedly naked. In the left hand recess stood a walnut piano with an open music sheet on its easel stand and the lid up, its ebony and ivory keys gaping at all who entered the room. On top of the piano and at either end were two ornate candlesticks and exactly equidistant from both candelabra was a brass pendulum clock. On the left hand side of the drawing room was a large bay window which was curtained and laced and just up from the window and out of its gaze rested a circular table that was covered in a pristine white linen tablecloth and surrounded by three red velvet and walnut chairs. On top of the table was a lighted gas lamp and a tray that contained a white bone china tea service and all the ingredients to take early evening tea.

The captain could see that the de Hay women lived in luxury and he briefly and mentally drew a juxtaposition to the small, cold, empty and bare cottiers hut with its dirt floor that used to house him, his mother, his father and his four sisters many years ago where they all had to sleep in stradogue in a feeble attempt to preserve everybody's modesty. An iced rage welled up inside him.

The captain also noticed that the room was deadly silent and that no noise whatsoever from outside penetrated its sanctuary. It was as if he found himself in a contained soundproof box, this would further suit his purpose.

Clodagh's voice broke tersely into his thoughts, 'Do sit down Captain Smith. A captain, Siobhan didn't say anything about you being a captain, a military man or is it the navy? In fact Siobhan didn't say anything about anything really, she's been keeping me guessing about you for weeks.'

The captain smiled again, he ignored the last part of her statement, 'You were right the first time, it is actually military, or it was, I am retired now.' He eased himself effortlessly into one of the velvet and walnut chairs.

'Really Captain, you look far too young to be retired from anything.'

'Thank you ma'am, I'll take that as a kind and generous thing to say.'

'It may indeed be kind and generous but it is also a true thing to say.'

'How long have you been retired Captain?'

'Not long, earlier this year.'

'And what do you plan to do with your retirement, is it going to be a big change from all that activity in the army?'

'Well I did have many plans, they were very drawn and detailed, I was going to travel extensively. I've become fond of painting and I thought that I might travel in Europe and do some, but then I met Siobhan and I've become fonder of her than I have of either of those, so now my plans have all changed. I've found that life can surprise you that way sometimes.'

'You're Irish Captain aren't you? I've only just noticed.'

'I am ma'am, years of travelling around to different places have changed the accent, to exactly what I'm not quite sure, but it did start out as Irish, I'm fairly sure of that.'

This amused the elder sister and she laughed slightly. She found him charming. 'I teach elocution and pronunciation and you have a good accent Captain, it's what they would call here in Dublin a refined Irish accent.'

The captain did not know the reason why as the conversation was completely and totally irrelevant, whatever was said in the next five minutes by this woman, her sister or indeed himself would have absolutely no bearing whatsoever on anything that he could think of, but despite this he wished to change the subject of it so that it all pointed as firmly away from himself as he could get it. In an attempt to do so he said, 'Siobhan tells me you and your family are all from Wexford.'

'We're from County Wexford yes, a place called Enniscorthy.'

'I can't say that I know it, I'm fairly sure that I've never been there.'

'I wouldn't expect that you have Captain, there isn't really any reason for anybody to go there. It's just farmland and very little else, there's not much to do there in the way of interest, leisure or occupation and there's certainly not much fun to be had there. That's why Siobhan and I are here in Dublin, if we had spent any more time back there I think that we would both have been taken by terminal boredom.'

'But your father, he is still there?'

'Yes he is, we'll never get father away from Enniscorthy and we wouldn't want to try. He was born there and he'll die there, although we hope not for a while yet.'

'Would you take some tea Captain?'

'That would be very nice, thank you.'

They all sat around the white linen tablecloth facing each other, the handsome captain with the refined Irish accent and the two plain looking de Hay sisters from Enniscorthy, County Wexford, each one a reflection of the other.

'Is your father well?'

'Oh yes, hale and hearty, he's got young Dermot with him, I think having to look after a twelve-year-old boy keeps him young.'

'I think that Siobhan said that you had a sister in Edinburgh?'

'Yes, Sybil, she's married.'

Siobhan who had been silent up to now decided it was time to engage in the conversation, 'Come on Patrick you must know all my family details and history by heart now, let's tell Clodagh about you and me and why we're here tonight.'

'Yes you're right darling, I'll get to the point. You see Clodagh, I hope that I can call you Clodagh?'

She smiled and gave a perfunctory nod.

The captain now realised that the moment was upon him. He continued, 'You see, the truth of the matter is the sole reason that I've come here tonight...' He looked across at Siobhan and smiled, as he did his words trailed off in mid-sentence, his eyes hardened, he rose to his feet and placed both his hands inside his jacket. In one movement, in the space of less than two seconds the derringers were drawn, one in each hand. In the space of another second he fired one shot from each gun. The first bullet hit Clodagh de Hay in the middle of her forehead and the second hit Siobhan de Hay in exactly the same place. Both sisters were jolted back in their chairs almost simultaneously and blood began to ooze from their head wounds. As they sat in their separate chairs, the captain looked down upon them and he could see that both sisters were indisputably and instantly – dead.

The captain then walked around to Siobhan's chair and pressing the gun to her flesh fired a second bullet from point blank range into the left hand side of her temple. Then he did exactly the same with his final bullet to Clodagh. After this he stood in complete silence and waited for five minutes then he replaced the guns in their holsters.

He stood silent for five more minutes to see if his exertions had attracted any attention. Standing back from the window he looked down on the square but all was as normal with people seemingly and obliviously going about their business in the Dublin evening. He waited again, still in silence, his breathing was heavy but he knew that the walls to the houses in the square were fortress thick and that they would not betray any audible secrets.

Then he set about the room, he pulled a switchblade knife from his jacket pocket. He became in a frenzy and crushed, broke, smashed and cut everything that he could lay his hands on, just as the Wreckers had done to his hut many years before. No object escaped his manic hand and he had to fight back an impulse to hurl one of the velvet and walnut chairs through the window. He decided against this as he thought that any such action would draw attention from outside in the street.

In a kind of symbolic gesture he took the sole surviving ornament from the fireplace. He looked at it with a look that was a mixture of disgust and satisfaction and he said out aloud in the now silent room, 'Even a man of insignificance should have something to remember himself by.' Then, with disdainful contempt, he tossed the ornament onto his dead lover's lap where it lay as motionless as she was, trapped in her skirt folds.

Checking once again that his guns were secure he picked up his valise, left the room and descended the stairs. Collecting his belongings from the coat stand he put them on and left the house being careful to shut the door quietly behind him. Nobody had noted his arrival and nobody noted him leave, he was confident of that.

As he walked back across Dublin carrying the small valise and the now discharged derringers, he called into a bar and ordered himself a large glass of Irish whiskey. As he stood at the bar with his whiskey in hand he considered his mind, he thought himself to be solemn yet triumphant. He thought of his mother and her face leapt into his mind's eye, he felt somehow vindicated and decided that he had atoned in part for her death with his actions tonight. He raised his whiskey glass slightly and toasted himself silently in the bar-room mirror. His memory raced back to Padraig de Hay's words to him many years ago as he grovelled in the night in his peasant's rags at the feet of the middleman's mighty stallion and as he sat in the dirt amongst the rubble of what had once been his home. On that night he had been too full of fear and hunger to even look up from the ground. The middleman's words came back to him with crystal clarity:

'You have shown yourself to be a man of insignificance to me.'

He considered that the opposite was now true and his actions this evening had now proved it, for Captain Patrick Smith, Captain Barry Walsh and Finbarr Joseph Breathnach were all men of great and equal significance to Padraig de Hay. Great significance because of the deed that they had just done and the deeds that

127

would come to be done and equal because the three identities all belonged to one and the same person.

Tonight he had no fear, he had no hunger. He felt important, as if his destiny had arrived. He felt an excitement. As the last surviving member of the Breathnach family, he had life and death power over the de Hay's and he intended to use it. He also knew that this power was not yet extinguished and his actions tonight against the de Hay women must continue through the years, through the decades, through the centuries.

As he stood at the bar that night looking up and out at his own reflection in the mirror, he thought to himself that after all these years the Oath and the Peasants Decree had finally begun, it was unstoppable, and at that moment, he crossed over the line to calm insanity.

Four hours later he was sleeping soundly in his berth on board the midnight boat to Liverpool.

Chapter 13

An Unlikely Alliance

If you head out from Winton Kiss and go out along River Street, towards the county border of Derbyshire, about halfway between the end of River Street and the actual sign that reads *Derbyshire,* and just before you come into open country, where the already narrow road narrows even more, you will come upon a pub. This pub is not remarkable for the area or for that matter any area, it is mainly a straight up and down, stone-built structure. The name of the pub itself comes from the name of the village, the Winton Kiss, known as the *Kiss* to locals. On the A-board that stands outside on its frontage it boasts to serve fine ales and home cooked food.

The Kiss was where Doctor Maxine Wells had arranged to meet Councillor Danny Senetti or, more accurately, she had arranged to meet him *outside* the Kiss in the beer garden. She'd objected to his suggestion of meeting inside the pub and insisted that she just would not do it, and despite his own logical argument he was beaten into submission by both her own determination to preserve this stance and his own need for the live conversation he wished to have with her, so he'd ended their telephone conversation in compliance and by saying, 'Well I only hope that it isn't raining on the day then.'

Now, as he headed for the destination sat in the back seat of a private taxi-cab he was watching the windshield wipers slosh left and right across the screen, it was raining, and very heavily too.

Senetti pondered: he failed to comprehend the attitude of some women on this issue of waiting alone in a pub. A man would wait for you alone, he would meet you at the bar but a woman, he knew many of them that just would not do it. It seemed to him the more successful and confident the woman was then the stronger the likelihood that she would not agree to it. She would meet you in a railway station, miles away from anywhere, she would meet you in the middle of a park, she would meet you in the light or dark, inside a theatre, up a mountain or by a riverbank, there were in fact countless places that women would meet you in or at, the list was truly endless. Then, when you asked them to meet you in a pub in the middle of the day, a place that was full of people, often people that they knew and probably one of the safest places in the world that you could meet somebody in, you could use all the explanation and argument that was in your head and they just would not agree to the liaison, they just would not wait for a man in a pub on their own. Take Maxine Wells, she was beautiful, intelligent, successful, full of confidence, she was a doctor. She took life-saving decisions as a matter of routine and she'd probably travelled all over the world yet she wouldn't wait inside her own village pub for a man on her own. It was a complete mystery to him and the only reason he could think of was that it was a hereditary stance and that regarding this particular issue these women were still in the mind set of their own grandmothers.

As his taxi pulled up he looked out at the appointed spot in the beer garden, it was empty. Well of course it was, it was raining heavily and everybody was *inside* the pub. Everybody that is except him and the beautiful doctor, for she was not to be seen. He mused upon the weather and considered that perhaps because of it she had actually found the attitude to go inside, if only for the sake of shelter. He thought about it for a while then decided that she wouldn't do that, so he would just have to wait outside in the rain until she arrived. Which is exactly what he did.

To the observer he cut a forlorn figure as he sat there hunched and all alone on the bench seating in the empty beer garden under the summer sun umbrella, his raincoat collar pulled up on his neck with water dripping off the edges of the umbrella, as the rain tippled down all around him.

Ten minutes later he saw the silver Mercedes glide past him and stop at the Kiss car park. Two minutes later Maxine Wells appeared at the beer garden entrance under a huge golf umbrella, she gave Senetti a smile, a dazzling one. He had to admit once again that she was a very beautiful lady, so he did admit it, but only silently to himself.

'So here you are Councillor, hiding under the umbrella.'

She noticed that he'd cleaned himself up a little for the occasion, he'd shaved and he was wearing a crisp, clean tan raincoat that looked new. In addition to this he, or someone else, had polished his shoes. However, she also noticed that he had combed his hair with his hands again and underneath the raincoat he was wearing a black shirt with a button down collar and one of the buttons was missing, so one collar was buttoned down and one was stuck out. It gave a sort of comical effect but Senetti himself was completely oblivious to it all. Oh well, she reasoned he'd made a sartorial effort of sorts, a Danny Senetti type sartorial effort.

She knew that she was late and expected some kind of admonishment or at least some grumbling reference to her unpunctuality from him. She knew many others that would have made it, her father dished out a lecture if you were just one minute late for anything, the more you were late the longer the lecture, which itself usually lasted longer than your period of lateness, but the councillor himself made no such comment about it whatsoever. She sensed that this failure was more out of deliberation than accident, she further thought that Councillor Danny Senetti did not want to be known as a person who states or does the obvious.

'Under the circumstances,' he said, raising his eyes to the teeming sky, the rainwater beginning to drip off his black hair, 'shall we go inside?'

'Yes, I think that is much more than a good idea.'

He hurriedly walked the five paces required and joined her under her umbrella. They both half ran in step to the pub entrance and went inside. It was Saturday afternoon and the pub was fairly busy. Whilst Maxine shook her umbrella outside from the safety of the pub doorway, Senetti engaged in an activity that he was well versed in, he approached the bar.

'Pint of bitter for me and I don't know about my friend.'

'I do,' said the young barman, 'it'll be one of those apple and mango drinks.'

Senetti smiled in his own reassurance. He also recognised the barman, it was young Joshua Ellis, he knew the Ellis family, they were solid voters of his and Mrs Ellis always helped out with his election campaigns. Joshua was at university, Sheffield Danny thought, English literature, he remembered Mrs Ellis telling him.

Senetti took both drinks and sat at an empty table in the corner. The front bar was small yet cosy, it didn't seem very private to him but on the other hand customers were preoccupied with their own business, they weren't really interested in his. Maxine joined him and they sat around the table facing each other.

'This is cosy,' she said. She raised her glass slightly in his direction and flashed that dazzling smile once again, 'so eventually we're here.'

'We are indeed Doctor.'

She leaned slightly forward. 'Tell you what,' she whispered, 'just for today, and today only, I'll call you Danny if you'll call me Maxine. It's not that I'm trying to be friendly or anything, it's just that normally the people in here won't be interested in what we've got to say but if I keep calling you councillor and you keep calling me doctor then we're going to attract attention and our onlookers might start to wonder, is it the councillor that's being doctored or is it the doctor that's being councillored, if you see what I mean?'

They both laughed.

'I do absolutely Maxine, but just for here and now you understand.'

'Agreed.'

They shook hands.

'Is this your local pub then?' he asked. He said it more as a conversation ice-breaker than something that he actually wanted to know the answer to as he really couldn't have cared less about anything in the world than where Maxine's local pub was.

Recognizing the ice-breaker, Maxine courteously responded with one of her own, 'Sometimes on a Sunday, and if it's a nice day, I come here with Dad but we usually sit outside, this is the first time I've actually been inside.'

'Me too,' he said, 'it's quite pleasant, and then again I tend to feel at home in most pubs.'

She deliberately refrained from passing comment but she'd heard that this was the case.

'Do you know a man named Archie Hamilton?' he enquired.

'No, I don't think so.'

'You think, don't you know Doctor, sorry I mean Maxine?'

'Danny,' she said slowly, 'I've got seven thousand people on the register, I can't remember all their names. Do you know the names of all your constituents?'

'He's definitely not one of your customers.'

'Then I don't know him, who is he, is he relevant to our conversation?'

'He's my ex-father-in-law and he's very relevant to our conversation, we would not be sat here now if it wasn't for him.' He paused momentarily before continuing, 'As we speak he's in the hospital.'

'Well I'm sorry to hear that and I hope that he makes a quick and complete recovery but please tell me that you've not brought me here to discuss one of your sick relatives. Talk about a busman's holiday.'

'No, of course not Maxine, please be patient.' He smiled slightly at the unintended pun. 'As well as being my ex-wife's father he's also a fellow councillor and on Tuesday we had a full council meeting.'

She interrupted again, 'This is going from bad to worse, first its sick relatives now its council meetings, this is just the kind of stimulating conversation I was looking forward to on a wet Saturday afternoon.'

'Maxine are you going to let me get to the full stop, or are you going to interrupt at every comma?'

'Sorry,' she said and she put her finger across both lips as if to demonstrate her future silence.

'After the council meeting Archie deliberately sought me out and asked me questions about the murder of Helen Day. When I asked about his interest in it he said he was involved with some project or something but I didn't actually believe what he was saying. I couldn't help thinking that there was some connection between him and Helen Day.'

'What do you mean by a connection, do you think that he might be involved in the murder?'

'No not that, he's an old man, he's eighty years of age.'

'I'm sure he wouldn't be the first eighty-year-old murderer.'

'That's surely true, but no, he's not involved in the murder, I'm sure of that.'

'What then?'

'I don't know but there is some connection, I'm sure of it.'

'This might seem a little radical,' she teased, 'but have you thought of asking him more directly?'

'I intend to but at the moment he's lying in a coma in the hospital and it's just not possible.'

'Oh, how did that happen?'

'Well that's another thing you see, after we separated on the night of the council meeting, we both went our own ways and he was the victim of a hit and run accident and that was the outcome. There is another possible connection, it might not have been an accident at all. I mean, and I have to admit that this is pure speculation on my part, but what if Helen's murderer and the hit and run driver are also connected, what if they are the same person?'

'Danny, you're right about one thing, that is pure speculation, you've just jumped straight from A to Z without stopping.'

'Maxine, a friend of mine has been murdered. Helen was a kind of friend and when Archie shows an interest in it, he's nearly killed by a car, something could be a little bit connected here don't you think?'

'Danny, you're talking like one of those characters from a TV detective show, have you mentioned any of this to the police?' she asked.

'No, I have seen the police on two occasions, once after Helen's death they came to see me and they also came to see me after Archie's hit and run. To be perfectly honest I've not been too impressed with the way that they have conducted themselves, in fact they treated me more as a suspect than anything else.'

'Was it Detective Sergeant Dobbs?'

'And her boss, Detective Chief Inspector Dimbleby. It seems to me that they are both as bad as one another. They didn't seem to have any ideas about Helen and they didn't seem to have any about Archie and it's obvious that neither of them has ever been in the council chamber. They seemed to think that me crossing swords with Archie in the debating chamber is a motive for running him down. If that was the case there'd be no councillors left, we'd all be running each other over every month.'

He thought that he heard her silently mouth something, he thought that she'd said the word *bliss* but he let it pass without response.

'I've got a question for you Danny, I have been as patient as you've asked me to be, but my question is, what does all this have to do with me?'

'When I had my conversation with Archie he knew that you had found Helen's body at the murder scene, he probably got that from the newspapers and he wanted me to find out what you knew, in fact that's more or less what our whole conversation that night was about.'

'I see, and here's me all along thinking that you found me irresistibly attractive.'

'There is that as well but that's a bonus just for me,' he ventured.

She doubted the sincerity of his last remark and they both fell into silence for a few minutes as Senetti picked up his by now empty glass. He walked over to the bar and came back with two fresh drinks, which he placed down on the table.

'How many of those do you have a day?' enquired Maxine.

'If you are going to start that, I'm going to have to start calling you Doctor again, as many as I require,' he quipped. 'Tell me, what were the circumstances that led you to find Helen's body, what exactly was your relationship with her?'

'I'm not sure that I can tell you that, you know, doctor and patient confidentiality.'

'Maxine, we're not here in any kind of official capacity, we're just two people in the pub having a conversation about a murder that took place in our local village. I expect half the village population is talking about it, we're just a bit more informed than most because I knew her better than most, you were her doctor and discovered her body. Anyway, she's dead so exactly whose confidence would you be breaking?'

She fixed her eyes upon his as if she was searching for an answer to a question that she had not asked.

'Maxine, I'll tell you what I know, if you tell me what you know.'

'My relationship with her was exactly that, one of doctor and patient although she did attend the surgery more than most.'

'What, you mean she was some sort of hypochondriac?'

'I don't really use that word Danny, but there's a lot of people, probably more than you think, who believe they have all these illnesses or, and this is just as real, that they are going to get them. In my line of work I get to meet many of them, but it wasn't really that with Helen Day, most of it I think was that she just wanted someone to talk to and I'm your local GP and as such I am a sitting target. If a patient makes an appointment then I have to see them, it's really as simple as that.'

'Wasting people's time, that's what that is. I've never been to see a doctor since I was a child and then it was only because my mother took me. Trying to get her money's worth out of the NHS.'

'Well good for you Danny, doctor dodgers we call you and you're either very fortunate or very silly, some people get ill and that's why we're here. I see people all the time who have never been to see me and I have to tell them that they are dying, yet if they had come to see me earlier they might not be. When you die we can all say did you hear about Danny Senetti? He died and nobody even knew he was ill because he never went to see a doctor, he just went straight from midwife to mortician without stopping in between.'

He laughed at her sarcasm, 'That seems to me a reasonable, uncomplicated and painless road to travel.'

She continued with her story, 'No matter how imagined or trivial Helen's complaint she always, without exception, kept her appointments. That day, the day I found her, she'd made one at 4:15pm and she didn't keep it, no phone call or anything. This time there was actually something wrong with her and I was concerned so I stopped off at her house on the way home from work, that's when I made the discovery.'

'Tell me exactly what you did and try and remember every detail.'

'Well, I'd left a couple of telephone messages which she didn't respond to. I went to her house and rang the doorbell, I got no answer so I went around the back. The back door was unlocked so I went into the house, she was in the lounge in the chair, obviously dead. She'd been shot, I could see that.'

'How many times had she been shot and where? What sort of gun would you say she'd been shot with?'

'That's a lot of questions even for a pseudo TV detective. As far as I could see she'd been shot twice, once in the forehead and once in the temple but you understand that I didn't exactly examine the body, I just found her and telephoned the police.'

'What sort of gun would you say was used?' he repeated.

'Danny, I'm not a ballistics expert.'

'No Maxine, but you're not just an ordinary GP either and you do know a bit about the subject.'

'How do you know that?'

'Maxine, I'm a councillor, people tell me things, sometimes they tell me things that I don't want to know, I say to them *I don't want to know* but they just tell me anyway and I heard that you'd spent some time working with the murder squad in Dublin so you must have picked up something.'

'I am not an expert of any kind,' she emphasized, 'but if I were to guess then I would say at point blank range with a low calibre hand gun.'

'One last thing Maxine, was their anything significant about the room that you found Helen in?'

'Danny why do you ask that, do you know a bit more about this than you are letting on?'

'Maxine, all these questions, they're Archie's questions they are not mine.'

'Well then, perhaps Archie knows a bit more than he's letting on.'

'I am beginning to think that too but currently he is not in a position to be of any help one way or the other, I just hope that he pulls through and if and when he does, I'll be one of the first at his bedside, but until then...'

'You care about Archie don't you?'

'He's been good to me in the past, helped me out a time or two and when I was having all my problems with Charlotte he didn't take sides, even though Charlotte is his flesh and blood daughter. As well as that he's my children's grandfather and he's the only one that they've got.'

Maxine began, 'In one way the room shocked me more than the actual murder.'

'What makes you say that?'

'Well, it was absolutely devastated. Everything had been smashed, broken, cut. There wasn't anything that was left untouched, even the skirting board and the architrave had been ripped off and even the light fitting had been dragged from the ceiling. It was as if some ritualistic symbolic gesture had been executed. There was one thing, I'd forgotten about it, there was a small statue that had been left untouched, either deliberately or because the murderer missed it, we'll never know.'

'That's the thing Maxine, we need to know, we need to find out.'

'You're serious about this aren't you?'

'You were at the LC the other night weren't you when I asked the shiny superintendent about the murder and Archie's hit and run and what him and his people were doing about it?'

'I was, I thought that the points you were making were well made and needed saying.'

'I made them because Dimbleby and Dobbs on two occasions, as I said before, came to see me and I really thought at one stage they were going to arrest me for basically no other reason than I knew Helen better than most and also because I was talking to Archie just before he was run over. Now that may sound ridiculous to you but take my word for it Maxine, it isn't and I just can't afford to even be suspected of any of this. I can't trust the investigators so I thought that I would do a little investigating on my own behalf.'

'Actually it doesn't sound ridiculous, I was treated in the same way, that's why I understood exactly what you were saying at the LC. I didn't think that I was going to be arrested but my position in all this was challenged. I haven't met the other detective, but if he's as you say then I understand what you're saying, but how exactly are you going to go about this investigation, where are you going to start?'

'I thought that we'd start by just re-examining exactly what we know. We both have our own contacts, so perhaps we could make a few phone calls and maybe ask a few questions, nothing too intrusive, keep it low key for the moment. You also have access to Helen's medical records perhaps they may tell us something.'

'I'll look at them again, it's amazing how this has suddenly become *us*!'

'I thought that we could work together on it, you could think of it being an unlikely alliance.'

Maxine was intrigued by the situation and, let's face it she thought to herself, her life at the moment wasn't exactly brimming over with excitement. She needed a distraction from her surgery. She also thought that whatever Senetti was, and that was probably a lot of things but boring wasn't one of them, she might as well go along for the ride, for the time being anyway.

She wasn't surprised when she heard herself say, 'What's the harm, I'll try it for a while but this is an equal partnership, there is no management structure here.'

'Great news,' he said.

Maxine considered they would not be able to gain any access to forensic or medical evidence and as most serious crimes these days were solved by these it would make their task very difficult indeed. She mentioned this to her new found ally.

Danny doubted that all crimes were solved by forensic evidence and he thought that she'd just made the whole thing up just to suit her argument, she was after all a doctor, something that he should never forget. He said that there were crimes before there was ever modern forensic evidence, detection rates in the Victorian era were better than they are now and forensic evidence was very limited then.

Maxine doubted this and she thought that he'd just made the whole thing up to suit his own argument, he was after all a politician, something that she should never forget, but she didn't respond to his assertion.

'Alright,' she said, 'where do we start?'

'Well, the first thing is to ask the basic question. Then let's go away, concentrate on what we know and on what we can find out and meet up again, compare notes. How does Wednesday evening sound?'

'The basic question being why, Danny, would anybody want to murder a seventy-year-old harmless reclusive spinster?'

'That would be my idea of it yeah!'

'And have you got an answer?' she asked.

'No, not a glimmer of one.'

'Danny, the way that I read Helen was that she was on the run in Winton Kiss, she was hiding from something or someone that's in her past, so the answer is somewhere in there. There is something else too, there was a large amount of money in Helen's bag that night, hundreds maybe thousands, I didn't count it but it was completely ignored by the murderer.'

'Maybe he didn't see it.'

'No, you couldn't really miss it. I don't know why but I think that it was deliberately not taken.'

'Hmm, interesting, I agree with you about her past, it's just that we don't know what or where her past is.'

'Well, we'll just have to discover it Councillor, won't we.' With that she rose to her feet.

'I thought that you weren't calling me Councillor any more Doctor?'

'See you Wednesday, bye.'

Chapter 14

Joseph's Father

As far as the dead are concerned, and they are the people who actually occupy these places full time, we will never know if their perception is the same as ours, but for those of us who are still alive and are only in these places as occasional, reluctant visitors the cemeteries of London are not particularly warm and welcoming places at any time of the year, though they do seem to be especially cold and lonely in the month of November.

There had been three significant deaths for Joseph that year, all three had affected him. The first was the death of his dog Bruno, a companion of almost eleven years, who had died in the month of March. The second was of a man that he had never met, nor did he know of anybody in his own acquaintance that had. That man was King Edward VII who had died in the early summer. Both these deaths had had an effect upon Joseph but neither of them had affected him as much as the third death in November that year, which was the death of his own father.

Joseph had duly paid his respects on all three occasions. He had dug the grave himself and buried Bruno in the back garden. He had lined up with the thronged thousands on the streets of London and stood there in solemnity as the late King's royal funeral cortege had passed by. The late King's funeral would bring together one of the largest gatherings of royalty the world had ever seen. For many of these privileged aristocrats it would be their last international convention as in the space of a few short years there would be an epidemic of these royal families being deposed and assassinated across Europe during World War One and during the repercussions that immediately followed that epic event.

Now, in great contrast to the London crowds and his own back garden, Joseph stood alone in the November morning as the sole mourner by his father's open grave. He genuflected and cast a handful of soil onto the closed coffin lid, his only other companions graveside being a mumbling Catholic priest, inaudibly saying the burial rites, and two identically dressed gravediggers, who stood leaning on their shovels several paces to one side in silent respect, waiting patiently to back-fill the grave with the excavated earth that lay piled on one side. As the priest mumbled on and the gravediggers bowed their heads Joseph's father was finally laid to rest.

Now Joseph was all alone. This year he had lost his dog, his king, and his father.

The few that had a view on Joseph's father, and it would indeed have only been a few for he was a solitary man and somewhat of a loner with no friends or relations, would have said that he was a handsome man, in fact they may have said that rarely had they seen such a man more handsome. They would also have said that he was a man of simple pleasures who, for most of the time, was content either in his own company or in the company of his only son who he clearly loved and who, seemingly, was his sole purpose in life. They would have said that Joseph's father preached no harm to anybody and his apparent total preoccupation was to see his son grow into a man of respectable, decent industry and adulthood who would in turn raise his own family and have respect for others. It could not be denied that this was a noble ambition for any normal father to hold for any son, let alone an only one.

All this was true, Joseph knew it as such, for save a succession of live-out male servants and eleven years of Bruno, he had lived alone with his father all his life, all his life now approaching twenty-two years, and he knew all of what others knew about his father and much of what others did not.

What others would have known was that Joseph's father was no different to anybody else inasmuch as he had a private side to him. What they wouldn't have known was that unlike almost everybody else it was a dark side, a more sinister side, a side that had its secrets and these secrets were terrible secrets. As with most secrets they had their roots in the past, in his formative years. Joseph's father's dark side spread out its tentacles wherever Joseph and his father went and this side often put Joseph's father in that dark place. From this place there would be brief moments of sanctuary and long moments of continuous pretence towards those who could never gain admission to this place, but there would never be any real escape for Joseph's father. For although Joseph's father, to all outward appearances, was handsome, balanced, calm and measured, beyond that veneer he was actually quite insane and he dwelt almost permanently in his own house of insanity.

He was not insane in a way that could be easily detected for this was a controlled insanity, it did not manifest itself into open violence nor antisocial behaviour, nor did it show in erratic conduct nor incoherent or spiteful speech. It did not show at all in any way through outward appearance. His insanity was a direct connection to a murderous obsession that he had first thought up in his own mind, an obsession that had taken total possession of his life many years ago as he sailed out of Dublin Bay for the first time, as an exile and a boy refugee from his own country, an obsession that had started out as his servant, but one that had rapidly become his master. In the cause of this obsession he had seduced, lied and murdered and he had done all this knowingly and with deliberation. Worse than all of this, he had indoctrinated another person into the same school and invested him with the same dark mind and insane murderous obsession. This other person was his own and only son, Joseph.

Joseph's father had not been a young man when Joseph was born, fifty-five years of age to be precise. Joseph's mother had disappeared without trace when Joseph was a very young child and he had no recall of her. She had left the house one day as she often did, but this time she had never returned. If there ever had been any trace of her in the house Joseph had never seen it.

Joseph's father did not speak about her, nor make any reference to her in any way whatsoever, so neither did Joseph. In later years on the occasions that Joseph witnessed his father being asked about his mother, his father would reply with four words, always the same four words, 'I am a widower', to which the enquirer would always reply with three words, always the same three words, 'I'm so sorry.' Then that would be the end of that and there would be no more questions on the matter and the subject would be closed.

In every other way to the onlooker Joseph grew up quite naturally, just the same as any of the other children in his neighbourhood, only he was without a mother's love and without a mother's teaching and influence of any kind, and as far as any aspect of a mother was concerned, he was completely and infinitely motherless. It didn't seem to concern anybody else, so he didn't let it concern him. He had no interest or curiosity, nor had he any feeling for a mother that had never been there for him, only for a father that always had.

His father had financial means, Joseph knew that, and from a very early age he sent Joseph to good schools. Initially his school attendances were interspersed with educational bouts from various professional tutors whom his father had selected and engaged and who taught Joseph at home. These tutors were different from each other in many ways but in one way they were all the same for they were always men. Sooner or later Joseph's father would always find disagreement with these tutors or the tutors themselves would find disagreement with his father. Sometimes their disagreements were audible and Joseph would overhear some of their argument. In the end the result would always be the same, the tutor would leave the household and soon after a different one would appear who eventually would also find disagreement. Whether his father actually exhausted the pool of tutors in London, Joseph never found out, but in the end they stopped coming altogether.

Joseph still attended his London school but his father's announced intention to install him as a boarder never materialised and instead he became a permanent day pupil. Neither the curriculum nor school life was any different than if he had been a boarder, except every night he went home to his father. Sometimes if Joseph felt that he wasn't doing as well as he should with some of his lessons he confided in his father and his father would take on some of the lessons as a tutor. His father was a good teacher and Joseph was an attentive student and it worked very well. As Joseph grew to adulthood and his father grew older there seemed to be very little need for other people in their lives. Throughout these twenty-two years Joseph had been everything to his father and his father had been everything to him.

It was on the morning of his tenth birthday, it was a Sunday and Sunday was a no school day. The previous evening his father had summoned Joseph to come into the study at 11:00am. Three days prior to this Joseph had asked his father about having a dog and his father had said that he would consider it. Joseph considered that he was about to be given his father's decision. At the appointed time Joseph had rushed off excitedly to the study and taken his seat, his father had been waiting in his own seat. Joseph remembered the conversation as if it had taken place five minutes ago.

'Joseph, although my health and strength is good, I am no longer a young man.'

'You are strong Father.'

'For the moment, yes it is true, but we need to prepare. This lesson today is the most important lesson of your life, you must remember it for the rest of your life, it must govern your life and you must teach this lesson to your own children as soon as they are old enough to understand and you must ensure that they realise the importance of it also. Without this realisation, and without our actions upon this realisation, we as a family have no honour, no pride and no significance. Do you understand what I am saying Joseph?'

'Yes Father.'

'Joseph, do you know what the most important thing in a man's life is?'

'Is it his health or his wealth Father?'

'The most important thing in a man's life is not his health and strength, nor his physical countenance, it is not his financial position nor his influence, nor his intelligence nor anything else that you can think of, for all these aspects are completely out of our own control and their importance to us reaches a peak at some stage in our lives and then begins to diminish. After you are dead the importance of these aspects disappears altogether, as they do themselves, and they become just a memory for others to dwell upon. No, the most important thing in a man's life is his significance. A man's significance can be found in many different ways, but it is vital that by the time you finish your life you are not a man of insignificance.'

'I don't understand Father.'

'I know Joseph but you will, you will.'

'Do you know what the second most important thing in a man's life is Joseph? It is almost equal to significance.'

'No Father.'

Joseph's father caught his breath before he continued, 'The next most important thing in a man's life is his family Joseph.'

'Yes Father.'

'Joseph who is your family, who are the members?'

'You are Father.'

'Do you have any other family?'

'No Father.'

'That is correct Joseph, all families are different in size and composition, some are big, some are small. The size itself makes no difference to the completeness of one's family. A family does not have to have lots of members to be a family, two is enough. Our family is small in size, it consists of just you and I and nobody else, but despite our size we are a complete family. Do you understand and agree with this Joseph?'

'Completely Father.'

'A person has responsibility for the actions of his family and a family has responsibility for the actions of an individual family member. So, whatever you do reflects upon me and if I do something, it in turn reflects upon you. Remember all the time Joseph that actions have consequences. You must never let your family down and they must never let you down. This responsibility does not disappear when a family member dies, it is there for always. In example of this I will say if your father has done wrong then it falls to you to put right that wrong and if your father has had wrong done to him, then it falls to you to put that right also. Do you understand Joseph?'

'Yes Father.'

Then Joseph's father told him a story about events that happened in Ireland before Joseph was born. He started his story in 1649 with Oliver Cromwell and Owen Welshman. He said that Owen Welshman was Joseph's great ancestor and he must be honoured and that Owen had arrived in Ireland on the thirty-five ships. He said this was a great honour and he told him of all the battles that Owen had fought in and how he'd been rewarded with land for his valour and chivalry. He said that Owen was a man of *great significance*. Then he described events that took place in Ireland just over fifty years ago. He told of a whole country full of people, thousands upon thousands of them, a million of them who died of hunger, disease and despair and of how others looked on and did nothing to help. Then he told of another kind of people who exploited these poor people when they were at their most vulnerable and who cheated and swindled them out of their homes and of their lands and caused their deaths. He told of how many of those that lived had to leave their homeland forever and go to all different parts of the world just to survive and how many thousands of them died during those journeys and didn't even arrive at the destinations that they didn't want to go to in the first place.

Then he told of the year of 1848 and in particular of two families, the Breathnachs and the de Hays, who both lived in a place called Enniscorthy in County Wexford. He told of how one family was good and the other evil. He told him of the heroic, ragged, orphan peasant boy called Finbarr who, having seen his father, his sisters and his beloved mother murdered by cruelty at the hands of the middleman, was forced to grovel at the hooves of the Gombeen's horse. He told how de Hay had sent the wreckers to Finbarr and how they had left the young boy to die in humiliation and suffering. During the telling of the story Joseph could see the suffering and humiliation in his father's eyes and the young boy burned inside with rage. Finally his father told Joseph about the Oath and about the Peasants Decree and of the just and deserved execution in Dublin of the two sisters. He said that these were rightful executions and that they must continue throughout time. When his father had finished his story he turned to Joseph and asked, 'Do you understand Joseph that you are the last one and that you are the only one? The honour of our family must not die when I do and it must not die when you do. Do you understand what you will have to do? Everything must be done in a certain way, as this is justice and retribution not reckless murder and there is a code of conduct in line with the Oath and in line with the Decree. In the years ahead you will learn this code of conduct. You must learn certain things Joseph, are you prepared for this, do you have the courage to obey your father and our Great Ancestor?'

Joseph said that he was and he did, and indeed it was true for the pact was made that morning between the boy and the man and the pact would not be broken, for Joseph was everything to his father and his father was everything to him.

The lesson ended and as Joseph rose from his seat his father looked at him with kindness and control as he said, 'Joseph, you may have your dog, I thought that we should call him Bruno, what do you think?'

Chapter 15

Mademoiselle Antoinette Dubois

The battle of Vimy Ridge took place in the Nord-Pas-de-Calais region of France. It commenced at daybreak on Easter Monday, 1917 and ended at 6:00pm, Thursday, April 12, 1917. The two main nation belligerents were Canada and Germany, represented respectively by four divisions of the Canadian Corps and three divisions of the German Sixth Army.

A high point of this battle, if there could be said to be such a thing in any battle, were the acts of bravery carried out that would later see individual Victoria Crosses awarded to four Canadian soldiers. The Victoria Cross is the highest military decoration awarded to British and Commonwealth soldiers for bravery and valour. A low point of this battle, if there could be said to be such a thing, and this is often a significant outcome of many battles, was that there was much human injury and loss of life. The Canadians suffered a total of 10,602 casualties of which 3,598 were fatalities. The Germans would go on to say that their own casualty number was unknown.

By nature of the nationality of the main combatants, the vast majority of casualties were unquestionably either Canadian or German. Most casualties that is, but not all of them. The Canadian contingent would claim a victory, a victory disputed by the Germans and some historians. Amongst the reasons cited for the Canadians declared victory were a compound of newly found tactics, both physical and technical, absolute meticulous planning, unprecedented weaponry support and comprehensive training. All this, some claim, was aided and abetted by the Germans apparent puzzling failure to stand by their own plan of action. Some of those who have declared a vested interest in the Canadian, or indeed the German nation, together with some of those who claim no vested interest in either, hold the opinion that the Battle of Vimy Ridge has come to be the first and original defining moment for the Canadian nation as a whole on the world stage.

A defining moment was decidedly *not* how the beautiful blonde-haired French-born Mademoiselle Antoinette Dubois saw this battle six months on from its end. The amber-eyed, eighteen-year-old alighted the midday train from Dublin to Wexford at its destination station. Apart from a small well wrapped bundle which she cradled in both arms she had no other apparent luggage. Vimy Ridge had cheated Antoinette out of a life of comparative privilege and luxury. It had prevented her becoming an important, legitimate member of a wealthy family on the island of Ireland and robbed her of her intended husband, First Lieutenant Francis Eamonn de Hay.

Lieutenant de Hay had been seconded to the Canadian forces and had been cut down during the German counter attack to regain the northern half of Hill 145, he was barely twenty-seven years of age and his body was never found. The only legacies that the battle of Vimy Ridge had bequeathed to Antoinette Dubois were the memory of her dead twenty-seven-year-old lover and the three-month-old illegitimate bundle of a daughter, Marguerite, that she now carried in her own two arms. She hoped and prayed that she was taking her only child in a time of worldwide insecurity and depravation towards a life of security and privilege that she had fatalistically been made to walk away from by the happenings of Vimy Ridge. This conflict on the battlefield of France may have unified one whole nation and given another a rare military comeuppance, but to Antoinette's own personal knowledge and experience it had rendered at least one family permanently asunder.

It could and would have all been so different with Frank by her side and as Mrs Frank de Hay, albeit in a foreign country, she would have had the wealth and status befitting her name. This she realised was now impossible. At the young age of eighteen she recognised that she had neither the experience nor the inclination for motherhood and that if she pursued this course on her own, a course for which she had no ambition whatsoever, then her life, as she wanted it to be, was almost ended before it had begun.

The de Hay family had indicated to Antoinette that a place could be found for her with them in Ireland, but there were conditions attached to this place. These conditions had been devised and insisted upon by Mr Dermot de Hay, a man that she had never met. They had been communicated to her in letter by his daughter Roisin de Hay, a woman that she had never met. Antoinette had considered their proposals but in the end she had decided that she was not going to live her life through a set of terms and certainly not those imposed upon her by a man and a stranger.

There was also the matter of the theatre in Ireland, there did not seem to be much of it, at least not compared to France. She had made some enquiries as best she could. She had discovered that there was the new playhouse in Dublin, but very little else. Ireland had some wonderful playwrights but they had all been forced to go to either America or England to establish themselves and Antoinette had a desperate desire and an aching ambition for a career on the stage. Finally she had decided that the twin setbacks of having to live in Ireland and look after a small, needy, dependent baby could not be found a place in her plan.

Her motivation was not entirely selfish for she loved the little girl in the way that only a mother can love a child, but she knew that her daughter's best chance for security and advancement was with the de Hays in Ireland. She also knew that the best that she could offer little Marguerite back home in France was survival. No, all in all, and under the circumstances, what was about to happen was for the best. She herself was young and Marguerite was as young as anyone could be. They both had their lives in front of them and with time things can change, she knew this, but the important position to take now was to establish a relationship with Dermot and Roisin and to secure little Marguerite's welfare and prospects.

Much can happen in the future and whatever happened she, Antoinette Dubois, would always be Marguerite's mother, there was absolutely nothing that anybody, however rich and powerful they were, could do about that. So on this day, with her mind made up, she stepped out of Wexford train station with its single-storey, low-level roof and its triple chimney stacks. She climbed into the waiting chauffer driven car just before it sped off in a due northerly direction towards the County Wexford town of Enniscorthy. She was going to meet her late intended husband's father and sister for the first and possibly the last time and she had an important and very special delivery to make.

Upon first hearing of Frank's death, already heavily pregnant, she had written to Roisin de Hay, Frank's sister. Frank had told Antoinette all about his father and sister, they were the only family that he had and she reasoned she would receive a more sympathetic stance from a young woman barely much older than herself. She also hoped that Roisin would present her case to her father far more intuitively than she ever could. Hindsight had since proven that she was correct on both counts.

Everything though was not yet ultimately settled, for Roisin had informed Antoinette in letter that her father would only accept baby Marguerite if he was sure that the baby was his own granddaughter. This had driven Antoinette into panic and turmoil and she had written back to say that the new born baby was indeed Frank's child, but that she did not know a way that she could conclusively prove beyond doubt that this was the case. She had though been further reassured when Roisin had written back and told her, having discussed the matter with Dermot, that he had said that if the child was indeed his granddaughter then he would know. At the time she had accepted the integrity of this statement but now, as she sat in the back of a chauffeur driven car in a foreign land speeding towards a town, the name of which she had neither heard of nor could barely pronounce, she was beginning to have her doubts and fears.

What if the old man didn't know, what if he didn't recognise Marguerite at all? What if he thought that Antoinette was trying to trick or cheat him in some way? What would he say, what would he do, what would happen then? What would become of her and little Marguerite, trapped in a strange land with no family, no friends, no money and all alone? She had no answers to these questions as she looked down at the baby sleeping peacefully and hoped that little Marguerite would stay that way for a little longer.

As Antoinette's thoughts raced away from her brain and occupied the inner depths of her body and soul the chauffer driven car slowed down and passed through the huge, green, iron gates that silently announced the magnificent entrance to the mansion house. The car then coasted evenly along the gravel drive and came to a smooth, quiet, faultless halt outside an impressive stone portico entrance. Antoinette's amber-coloured eyes looked around, then they settled on the elegantly dressed, very slim young woman who stood on the steps to the hall entrance in the August sunshine. It was Roisin de Hay, for although they had never met before, Antoinette Dubois knew instinctively that it was she who stood there in elegance and serenity in front of the open door.

As the chauffer came out of the driver's side he walked to the back of the car and opened the rear passenger door. Antoinette stepped out of the car into the afternoon warmth as Roisin came down the front steps to meet her. The young Irishwoman held out her hand in reflex to the young French woman, then realising that Antoinette was holding the baby, she stepped back and said, 'Hello, I'm Roisin de Hay, I'm so pleased to meet you at last, may I hold the child?'

Antoinette replied in almost perfect, but heavily French-accented English, 'I'm Antoinette Dubois and I'm pleased to meet you,' then she dutifully handed over the baby. A thought came into her mind, she tried to dispel it, but it lingered there, she thought that this might be the last time she would hold her own baby. As Roisin took the child she parted the covers and gazed down upon little Marguerite's face. Almost immediately she caught her breath in excitement and silent tears rolled down her cheeks and onto the baby's swaddling clothes.

'Please follow me Mademoiselle,' she said to Antoinette as she walked back towards the house with the little bundle. Waiting in the hallway were two female servants. Roisin gave the still-sleeping child to the eldest of the two saying, 'Bernadette, please look after this child, her name is Marguerite,' and to the younger one she quietly commanded, 'Hilda, please show Mademoiselle Dubois to her room.'

Turning to the young French woman Roisin said, 'Please go with Hilda, she will look after you, everything is prepared just as we discussed in our letters but we have no time to lose, the photographer will be here in just over an hour and my father will receive you an hour after that. He will only have an hour himself before he has to leave for Wexford.'

Antoinette Dubois dutifully followed the young servant girl up the huge central stairway and Roisin disappeared down the long hallway.

One hour and fifteen minutes later the two women stood on the front lawn of the big house in the summer sunshine. Now Antoinette was also bathed, her hair done and was elegantly dressed. They were joined there by Mr Leopold Isaacs from Wexford town. Mr Isaacs could be briefly described as a little, portly man around sixty years of age, with a black moustache and black hair to match which was parted down the middle. He was dressed in a light-blue three-piece serge suit, a white shirt and a blue bow tie. Mr Isaacs was a professional photographer, he was in point of fact the best photographer in Wexford, he was in point of fact, the only photographer in Wexford. Mr Isaacs went about his business with aplomb but also in a professional and expedient way. He completely ignored Roisin as she stood aside on the lawn and gave total attention, interest and dedication to his subject, Mademoiselle Dubois. After an uninterrupted forty minutes he had directed and photographed the young French woman in seven different stances and poses and with several props that he himself had provided. As he took his photographs and after each one he produced a small black notebook and a pencil from his jacket pocket and looking the young French woman up and down made some annotations in this book. After he had taken what was seemingly his last picture, he once again produced his little book and pencil, made more scribblings and then put them back in his pocket. After this he announced his work as completed. After which he said his very brief but very flamboyant goodbyes to both ladies, gathered up his equipment and placed all of it and himself in his little black van. As the vehicle coughed and spluttered, Mr Isaacs left the grounds of the mansion house as noisily as he had arrived.

The two young ladies then returned to the house. They entered the drawing room where they sat in silence for ten minutes before being joined by the master of the house, Dermot de Hay. Antoinette Dubois regarded Dermot, she thought him much younger than she had expected and she placed him to be between forty-five and fifty years of age. He was a tall man with the thin build that was the de Hay trademark and Antoinette saw her dead lover Frank in him. All the de Hays, whether male or female, had the same type of lean build. Antoinette concluded that it looked good on a man but not so good on a woman. On a man it seemed spare and athletic, whilst on a woman it presented as thin, skinny and shapeless. Dermot's hair was flecked with silver but was still predominantly dark and even if slightly greying it was still thick and vital. He was dressed smartly in a dark jacket and grey striped trousers. He was not handsome in the traditional sense, but there was a certain assured strength that exuded from him and that was attractive. The young French woman thought that it was very attractive indeed. He was a successful banker and Miss Dubois thought that he looked the very epitome of one. When he spoke his voice was not too soft, nor too loud and his words were measured and calming.

'Let us first remove any anxiety out of the way,' he said. 'Please don't be nervous Miss Dubois, we all know exactly why we are here. We are to do our best for each other, particularly for little Marguerite. I can tell you that I have seen the child and all is well, she is truly the daughter of my son and she is a de Hay, of that there is no doubt.'

Antoinette sighed, many of her earlier concerns now dispelled, 'You are satisfied that the child is the child of your son Monsieur, as indeed I assured you that she was.' She uttered this more as a statement than a question.

'I am perfectly satisfied Miss Dubois, as soon as I laid eyes upon this beautiful little girl I knew it was the case. I should say further that, from the onset, I have never really had any doubts on the matter, but I am sure that you appreciate that I had to be absolutely sure.'

'So everything is settled Monsieur, it is as we agreed.'

'If nothing has changed from your point of view, then nothing has changed from mine. It is though important Mademoiselle, that once again we familiarize ourselves with the terms and conditions of our agreement, it is what my lawyer, Mr Scanlon, would call *contractual matters*. It is important that we do this so that there is no confusion either now or in the future. It is also important that we are all clear about our responsibilities to each other and above all, our responsibilities to little Marguerite, and whilst little Marguerite finds herself here in Wexford as a consequence of tragic circumstances, these must all be put behind her and a plan for my granddaughter's happiness must be the outcome of this meeting, here and now.'

Antoinette thought that the man's words seemed somewhat inconsistent, he spoke just as a grandfather would about his emotions upon seeing his baby granddaughter and of little Marguerite's happiness then, just as quickly, he spoke in the language of a banker, making reference to *terms and conditions*, and *contractual matters*. She glanced over at Roisin who sat there in silence. Antoinette sensed that Roisin was having similar thoughts. Nevertheless, the young French woman nodded in agreement. Antoinette could tell that Mr de Hay was accustomed to being listened to and to having his words obeyed.

Dermot de Hay continued, 'Miss Dubois, there are several contractual matters to our relationship, perhaps we could address the practical ones first. One of these practical issues is that it is my understanding from my conversations with Roisin that you wish to return to France, by yourself and at the earliest opportunity, is this still the case Mademoiselle? Before you answer I wish to make it absolutely clear to you that as the mother of my granddaughter we are more than happy to provide a home here for you, but there would be some rules and regulations that you would have to agree to honour if you were to choose this. It is also important to remember that whatever route we choose today there will be no changing, no going back. It will all be done, it will all be legalized and tied down by Mr Scanlon's documents and from my experience of Mr Scanlon, this tying down will be ironclad.'

'Thank you Monsieur but my mind is made up and I do intend to return to France at the earliest opportunity, alone.'

'Very well Mademoiselle, your wishes are respected.'

He produced a blue envelope from his inside jacket pocket, 'There is sufficient money in here to defray any travelling expenses for both the journey here and the journey back to France, the money is both in Irish and French currency. As today is Saturday, tomorrow is Sunday. I am afraid, for reasons which I have never been able to understand, the whole of Ireland seems to close down on Sunday. You will therefore not be able to commence your journey home until Monday. Needless to say you are most welcome to stay with us until then or even further.'

'Once again, thank you Monsieur.'

'If you have any important issues during that time Roisin will manage them, I believe that you have an appointed servant for your practical needs.'

'Yes, a lovely, cheerful girl called Hilda, I am fortunate to have her.'

'You are very gracious Mademoiselle.'

Dermot de Hay continued, 'Now perhaps we can discuss little Marguerite.' He paused for a minute and all were silent. 'In these circumstances plain speech is best. Marguerite will remain here in Wexford, she will be raised as an Irish girl, as a de Hay and I, as her paternal grandfather, will have all parental rights over her. Is this clear to you, understood by you and agreed by you Mademoiselle?'

'It is clear, understood and agreed Monsieur.'

'She will be aware of your identity and she will know that you are her mother and that she is your daughter. We will not try to hide it from her and we will show her the photographs as you have requested. We will make no attempt to hide anything from her, such an attempt would be both dishonest for us and unhealthy for the child as she grows up. When we speak of you in answer to her inevitable questions we will portray you in a good and positive light without exaggeration.'

He paused again, as if what he had just said troubled him, then he walked over to the other side of the room where a sideboard stood and poured himself a small glass of poteen from a decanter that rested in a silver tray on top of the sideboard. He raised the glass to his lips and emptied the contents in one.

'Merci beaucoup Monsieur, vous êtes le plus aimable et courtois,' she reverted momentarily to her native tongue.

Dermot spoke again, 'If in the future you, I and Roisin think it is in the child's best interest for her to meet with you then we will bring this about, but there must be no contact for the first eleven years of little Marguerite's life. She must be given the opportunity to establish herself here in Wexford without the distraction and young heartache of a coming and going mother. People will gossip and theorise about your absence, after all this is Ireland, but such gossip will be no concern of ours. Do you agree to what I have just outlined, Mademoiselle is it as you anticipated it to be?'

'C'est Monsieur.'

'I have arranged the next aspect with Mr Scanlon who in turn has arranged it with his own colleague in Paris, a Monsieur Guillaume Chevalier. Once you return to France if you have any issues of any kind, now or in the future, then Monsieur Guillaume Chevalier must be your first point of contact. Every month there will be a monetary allowance paid to you, it is on the generous side of modest and it will provide for all your needs, it will allow you to lead a respectable life in France. Please be aware Mademoiselle that it will most certainly provide for all your needs, but it may not provide for all your wants, it will be up to you to make the distinction between the two and you must learn very quickly how to manage within your income.'

He paused yet again for a moment and looked straight into her eyes and as he did this he buried both hands deep into his trouser pockets.

'There is just one more point, it is not for me to tell you how to run your life, but I understand again from my conversations with Roisin that you have ambitions to pursue a career on the stage. Is this the case Mademoiselle?'

'Yes, this is true Monsieur.'

'I wish you good luck. Being an actress can be an artistically and financially rewarding profession, but it can also be a precarious one. I have known some actors in my time and they can sometimes have a different morality than the rest of us. I don't say all of them, just some of them, and I cast no particular aspersions. However it is important to me as Marguerite's grandfather, and indeed will be to Marguerite herself, to know that her mother is leading an honest, moral and productive life whether it be on the stage or anywhere else.'

'It is my intention anyway, but you have my word that this will be so Monsieur.'

'Having met you I am convinced that this will be the case but I felt bound to say it anyway. Then as far as I am concerned that is all Mademoiselle, unless there is any more you wish of me?'

'Non Monsieur.'

'I have some papers that Mr Scanlon, my lawyer has prepared, I will expect you to sign them before you leave, Roisin will guide you through them. If they still present any difficulty in understanding then Mr Scanlon can be contacted if necessary, but whosoever is involved these papers are of the utmost importance and they must be understood and signed by you before you leave Ireland for France on Monday, even if you have to delay that departure. I hope that this is clear Mademoiselle?'

'I will give them my attention Monsieur.'

Dermot de Hay was impressed, he was compelled to think that, despite her very young years, Antoinette Dubois had conducted herself with the utmost graciousness and maturity in what after all was a most sensitive and delicate situation. He had noticed all of this as well as her astounding physical beauty. He made no reference to any of it.

Satisfied with the interchange, Dermot de Hay concluded, 'Then I will say good day and good luck Mademoiselle. Please accept my apologies for not joining you for dinner this evening. I have a long-standing business arrangement in Wexford that I have been unable to get out of and I will be travelling over there immediately. Roisin will be here to keep you company.' He held out his right hand and once again looked into her eyes as he said, 'Then au revoir and bon voyage Mademoiselle.'

She took his hand and fixed her amber-coloured eyes on his. In a fleeting moment she sensed a physical attraction between herself and the older man, then it was gone. She sensed that he was not a sentimental man, but what was more important was that she knew that Dermot de Hay was a man of his word and she repeated the words that he had just said to her, 'Au revoir and bon voyage Monsieur.'

Chapter 16

Two Young Women

The two young women were at last alone with each other and seemed to be in adversarial pose. They were separate yet totally encompassed within the large, elegant, Edwardian-style dining room of the mansion house. This illusion of adversary was further added to by the fact that they were sat at opposite ends of the large twenty-two-seater mahogany dining table.

The impression of challenge was further emphasised by their own physical differences. These differences were in fact at great variance to each other, for in this aspect they were total opposites. The slightly older young lady Roisin was very slender and tall to the exact point of thinness. She had no figure of any shape and her physique had once been described some years ago, by an insensitive and ungracious school friend, as not going in and out in any of the right places.

The young Irishwoman had achieved what many women would have readily entered into a pact with Lucifer himself for, inasmuch as she had so far managed to retain her schoolgirl figure through to adulthood. Only for Roisin herself this retention was not considered as an enhancement but was thought of as a detriment. From top to toe she had: no bust, no waist, no hips and no bottom. She was the same shape all the way up and the same shape all the way down. This shape was really no shape at all, save one that resembled a straight vertical line. Her eyes were crystal clear and a piercing blue colour, but they were small and saucer shaped and had been put together with a broad forehead and a small mouth and in a cruel finality her teeth were crooked. Her sole redeeming feature to any kind of beauty was her hair, it was thick, lustrous and naturally blond. However, on its own it was nowhere near enough to redress any kind of balance and this small redemption was easily outweighed by everything else that has been mentioned. The complete physical picture was one of a tall, skeletal, fierce looking lady.

She knew this of course and had come to accept it. She was also headstrong, politically minded, intelligent, knowledgeable and opinionated. Men in particular did not enjoy her company and tended to avoid it. If in their view by some misfortune they found themselves embroiled in it then they usually looked for a way to extricate themselves as quickly as possible.

On the other hand the mademoiselle that currently sat at the opposite end of the table to Roisin was a veritable beauty. She was approximately the same height as Roisin, possibly an inch shorter and she had similar glistening blond hair but however hard you looked for another identical factor with her Irish contemporary the resemblance terminated there. Her figure was both trim and voluptuous and went in and out exquisitely in all the right places. Her features were a sensation and were in perfect symmetry. In particular her eyes were crystal clear, perfectly shaped and were an unusual amber colour. Her lips were perfect, her teeth were even and glistening white and her smile was dazzling, the overall image was one of a sleek, beautiful, graceful feline. There were very few men that were not captivated by her and they almost challenged each other to be in her company. Despite her tender age, Mademoiselle Antoinette had known of her allure for several years, and was acutely aware of her charms.

Despite their obvious differences the two young women were decidedly not adversaries. Nothing could be more to the contrary and as Roisin and Antoinette were acutely aware of the other's different ways, they were very pleasantly disposed to each other and neither one of them had any intention of being anything other than a friend to one and each. Since Frank's untimely death Roisin and Antoinette had exchanged thirteen letters in all, six from Roisin and seven from Antoinette and during that discursive interchange both felt that they had come to know each other and about each other reasonably well.

They had commenced a light dinner together half an hour after Dermot de Hay had left in the chauffer driven car to make his way to Wexford. Now they were concluded and were conversing over their cups of tea.

'Is there any news of your father Antoinette?' enquired Roisin.

'We actually received a letter from him last week and at the time of writing he was in good spirits, he was free from injury and alive and we were happy to hear that.'

'Yes, it's strange how this war has seemed to make us expect death for someone near to us. It's made us so insensitive to death, it's as if we expect it to happen and that it will be to somebody we know.'

'Yes I know, it was exactly the same with Frank...'

'If you don't mind Antoinette,' Roisin interrupted, 'I know that I have just raised this, I now wish that I hadn't. I would really appreciate it, and accept it as a kindness, if we could agree not to mention Frank. I'm not suggesting in any way that my loss is greater than yours, it's just that it's all still a bit raw for me. He gave his life for nothing, all for some political ideal, it is all so futile. I am against this war, I have been from the start. Both sides are completely in the wrong. This war is a complete disaster for everyone involved. Men, it's all about men. Men, some of them as old as my father, behaving as if they were children. It makes me so angry and I don't want to spend my life in anger. It is a waste of my good energy and these days with all that has happened I only have so much.' In an attempt to change the subject she asked the young French woman, 'How is your aunt, how is her language school doing?'

'Oh she's fine and as she says, she makes a living.'

'And what about you, didn't you say in your last letter that you had an audition for some big show?'

'Yes, it's a big show in Paris, it's not such a big part in the show itself but if I get it, it will be big for me. The audition is two days after I return to France, so I am saying a little prayer.'

'I am saying one for you too, Antoinette.'

'What about you Roisin, what plans do you have?'

'I still have ambitions to be a lawyer but there are people in Wexford who need me to be here at the moment. My father has not been the same since this war started, so I will have to be unselfish and my ambitions will have to go somewhere else for a year or two yet, but not for too long I hope.'

'Yes, as far as ambitions go it is always the women who have to be unselfish. It is always the women who have to make the sacrifices. If a man has ambition he feels that he has the right to just go out and fulfil it. Nobody objects, and even if they do, he does it anyway even if it gets him killed.'

Roisin knew that this was another reminder of Frank but she chose to ignore it in the hope that Antoinette would take it no further. In turn Antoinette recognised that she had unwittingly made another reference to the dead lover and brother and she didn't pursue it.

'In France,' Antoinette continued, 'we have a society that is supposed to be based on liberty, egalite and fraternity, but who is free, who is equal and who is in the brotherhood? Not the women, if you wish to stay at home and manage your house and have as many children as you wish, then you are free and equal to do this, if you wish to have an ambition to be admitted to the higher professions then you are not free and equal, if you are a woman you can be the nurse but you can't be the doctor, you can be the nun but you can't be the priest, you can be the clerk but you can't be the lawyer, you can be the politician's wife or the politician's mistress but you can't actually be the politician, any one that is important, any role that is significant, women are not allowed to be part of it.'

'It's the same in Ireland, Antoinette, it's the same in England, it's the same in many parts of the old world, we are not even allowed to vote. If you take our government, all the members of parliament, every one of them with no exceptions are men, yet the women make up half the population. So where is the representation for women there in our system?'

'It has been this way since men and women have been around Roisin and it will never change. If what we are saying is right and I believe that it is, then how are you going to realise your ambition to be a lawyer?'

'In the new world Antoinette, things are different, in America there have been women doctors and women lawyers for fifty years.

In New Zealand women have been able to vote since 1893. So it is simple Antoinette.'

'Sorry, but I do not understand. How is it simple Roisin, surely it is the opposite of simple it is très difficile.'

'What will have to happen is that the situation will have to change.'

'Yes, but the situation has not changed much for women in the last five hundred years, why should it change in the next five hundred?'

'It will change for women, slowly at first but it will change, I am convinced. It is changing now and it would have already changed once and for all if it had not been for this war. God knows this war has taken over the whole human race, but the real oppressed people in this war have not been a tribe, nor a nation, nor a race, they have been a gender, they are the women whether they have been Irish, English, French or German. They may not have been oppressed deliberately or even knowingly but as a direct consequence of men's preoccupation with this conflict, men have been able to abdicate their responsibilities to women. All these battles and ideals and this rescuing of freedom have given men a place to hide. Soon though, as with all episodes in history, it will come to an end and there will be no more hiding places. At the end of this war after the heat has cooled there will be no victors nor vanquished, all there will be is a lot of dead men who have been killed by their own fraternity and there will be women to take their places. The most important thing is that women must have the vote. Once that happens we can no longer be ignored by the men that run the country. They will have to listen to us after that and they will have to represent us. If they do not then we will not vote for them and they know this, they are not stupid, only when it comes to war.'

'Do you have a particular time when you think this will come about?'

'Yes, I think that the next five years will be absolutely crucial. Let's get this awful war out of the way, this is a man's war, it was never a woman's war. It's coming to an end now and you will see some big changes in England, Ireland and across the whole continent of Europe. In our lifetimes you will see many women take on the higher roles as you call them, doctors, lawyers, politicians, priests, believe me.'

Antoinette seemed pensive, 'I think that it will be a long time before women get the vote in France. It certainly won't be in the next five years. It may even take another war before that happens. France will be behind everybody else in this respect. I agree about the important positions but I personally don't think that the majority of women in France want the vote, it would give them responsibility that they don't wish to have.'

'Isn't that what all women want Antoinette, to be equal to men, isn't that what you want?'

'No Roisin, I don't want to be equal to men, je veux infiniment superieur a et que je veux les faire tomber à mes pieds.'

'Sorry Antoinette, I missed that.'

Antoinette translated, 'I do not want to be equal to them, which is what I would be if I had the vote, I want to be superior to them, as I am now, I want them to fall at my feet.'

'Surely before women can be superior then first they must be equal when right now we are inferior.'

'The whole situation Roisin, in relation to men and women is indeed one big conundrum. By my own reasoning, and this is purely personal, what men worship in women is drama, drama and passion. So you may have your vote, you may have mine too if you wish, for I probably would not use it anyway. I can get what I want from men without it and I have to say that I rather enjoy it when men hold open the door for me. If women do win the vote we will lose all this as men will see equality as a challenging thing.'

'I much prefer to open my own door Antoinette.'

'Yes, I fully understand this Roisin, but when you have no choice because no man will attempt to do it, will this be a forward or a backward step for women?'

The two women giggled spontaneously at their own philosophy. They both accepted fully that they were friends and they both accepted fully that they were women and finally they accepted fully that they were different.

Chapter 17

Speranza

Apart from the young barman, Joshua, and the elderly man dressed in head to foot beige: beige hat, beige golfing jumper, beige shirt, beige trousers, beige socks and beige shoes, who was absorbed in his evening newspaper crossword, there was nobody else in the Kiss when Maxine and Senetti came in together on the Wednesday evening. Maxine went straight to the table she'd sat at last time and Danny bought and brought two drinks over to that same table.

Danny was the first to speak, 'When I came back from Beaumaris after the last bank holiday this letter was in my post box.' He handed an envelope to Maxine.

She took the envelope and read out softly but aloud, 'Councillor Danny Senetti.'

Then she extracted the letter and opened it, 'Speranza,' she read out aloud.

She turned the piece of paper over and examined the other side, 'Is that it? No name, address, date, signature, anything, just one word?'

'That's all, that's it.'

'Who is it from, what does it mean and is it connected to any of this?'

'Well, I can answer some of that but I'm not sure that it doesn't just muddy the waters even more. It's from Helen Day, and Speranza I believe is the Italian word for hope.'

'How can you be so sure it's from her, its only four words? Can you be absolutely sure from just four words?'

'Yes, I can be sure, it is a very distinctive hand and also Helen and I were both members of this Social Services Panel for about six years and I sat next to her for all that time. She was one of those people that made copious notes about everything, I spent a lot of time looking at those notes and I recognise the writing, it's definitely hers, I've also got something in the house from her and I've compared it and it matches perfectly so there's no doubt whatsoever. The questions are why she would send an unidentified letter to somebody with one foreign word written on it and what was she trying to say? If you want to write a letter why not just write a letter?'

Maxine became pensive for a minute, 'Suppose you were reaching out to someone and you didn't really want them to know that it was you.'

'Reaching out for what, you're not going to go all mystic and caring on me are you?'

'Are we here to take this seriously or not?'

'Sorry,' Danny apologised.

Maxine continued, 'suppose you knew that you were going to be murdered,' she looked at him sternly stifling his intended interruption. 'Alright, perhaps not exactly that but you were concerned for your personal safety and something had made you suspicious and you thought that you might be in danger of being harmed.'

'Go on,' he said.

'You wanted to tell someone just in case you were right and you wanted their help, but just in case you were wrong you didn't want to draw attention to yourself by letting them know that it was you. Then an anonymous note would do that job, wouldn't it?'

'This isn't even an anonymous note is it, it is just one word, but go on Maxine, carry on with your thought process, I might be able to tune in eventually but I'm not quite there yet.'

'Yes,' she continued, 'you think that you are in danger and just in case you are, you want somebody to know so you send them a cryptic message.'

'I still don't think that I know what you are talking about, but just for a minute if I pretend that I do then there is just one problem with what you've just said, you'd be dead wouldn't you, which she is, so what would be the point in the letter?'

'Well, if you were wrong about the danger and nothing happened to you then that's fine, it's just one word on an unsigned letter. The recipient would probably just ignore it anyway. The only reason we're paying attention to it is because we know that Helen's written it and we know that she's been murdered. If what I'm suggesting is right and you do end up dead, then you've hopefully put someone on the trail.'

'The trail of what, Maxine?'

'Danny are you being deliberately obtuse in this? The trail of the murderer! What else are we talking about here? Helen was murdered, have you forgotten?'

'No, I haven't and I think that I'm beginning to pick up on what you're saying now. There's something else that's just come into my mind about that letter, what if you were trying to protect someone else as well?'

'You mean that you were trying to prevent someone else from being murdered, why do you say that?'

'I didn't actually mean another murder I meant it more in the sense of a protective instinct that say, an older brother has for a younger one. It's just something that Helen said to me once when I asked her why she'd moved to Winton Kiss. Something about being close to someone.'

'Danny, let's just deal with one thing at a time shall we. Let's just stay with the letter for a while, *Speranza,* what exactly is she trying to tell us with that word? Is she trying to point us towards something Italian?' They both looked at each other as if neither of them had an answer.

Maxine had downloaded the photographs that she'd taken at the crime scene with her mobile phone onto her laptop and she'd had some prints made. She took these prints out of her bag and set them down on the pub table. There were four of them: one showed the crime scene in all its devastation, another showed the writing on the mirror and the other two showed the little statuette and the faded inscriptions.

Danny and Maxine focussed on the crime scene first. Danny spoke, 'that room, it's absolutely trashed, why would you do that? Obviously it's been done after the murder. You'd think if you had just shot someone then you'd want to get out of it as quickly as possible, not stay around to wreck the place. Is it the actions of somebody that's crazy?'

Maxine responded, 'I'd say yes and no, obviously you are not exactly of sound mind if you would kill somebody in the first place, but the cleanliness and precision of the killing doesn't fit in with the devastation of the scene. I stood amongst that carnage and it was eerie. I think that it was ritualistic and it was just as much a part of the murder as the murder itself. It was important to the murderer that the room was attacked in that way. To support my ritual theory there are also the bullet wounds which to me have been made in a meticulous way. I don't know for an absolute fact but as a doctor I'm fairly sure that either of those wounds would have been instantly fatal and that there was no need for both of those shots so one of them was fired into the victim after she was dead. It is as if those bullets had to be fired into Helen, dead or alive, as if they were something that had to be done in a particular way, just the same as the ritual of the room. There was also a large amount of cash on view in Helen's bag which was completely, and I think deliberately, ignored.'

'Why would you do something in a ritualistic way? Rituals are connected to sacrifice, to tradition. Was Helen a victim of some sacrificial, ritual tradition?'

'Yeah, but perhaps not so much a sacrifice more an act of something else.'

'Another thing Maxine that's been bothering me, the murderer must have created a bit of noise, the gunshots would be loud and breaking up everything the way he did must have taken quite some time to do, all increasing your chance of being seen, being heard, getting caught.'

'You would think so,' she said, 'providing that there is somebody around to hear you. However, I've learnt something that's interesting on that subject. I've been asking around, well more listening around really, there isn't much that goes on around here that doesn't pass through my waiting room and that one of my receptionists doesn't get to know about. It seems that every May bank holiday the people that live in the two houses, next door and next door but one to Helen take a week's holiday together. They have been doing it every year for the last ten years. So the neighbours were away when the murder took place and within those two-hundred-year-old walls you could have made as much noise as you wanted to make without fear of disturbance as there was nobody around to hear it.'

'That is interesting, but you would have to know that information about the neighbours to feel free to do that.'

'Well of course you would and the murderer almost certainly did.'

'Then you would have to be connected to the community in some way.'

'Again of course you would and he probably is, although there are many ways that you could have that connection.'

'I don't think that Helen really knew who anybody was in the community.'

'She wouldn't have to, as long as they knew who she was and that her neighbours were away on holiday.'

'So you think Maxine, that the murderer is in the community?'

'I think that the balance of probability says yes and even if it didn't then we shouldn't rule it out. Do you agree?'

Danny said, 'I do agree and that would also account for the murderer being in the house in the first instance.'

'How do you mean?'

'Well, Helen was reclusive and on her guard at the best of times. If she was afraid and suspicious, as we're saying she was, then she would be on her guard even more than usual. Not many people saw the inside of her house under normal circumstances. She wouldn't just let anybody in. She certainly wouldn't have let a complete stranger in. To gain entrance it would have to be somebody that she was expecting or who she knew, or at least recognized, or if not any of those at least someone she accepted.'

'Good point Danny, another aspect is that I'm fairly sure that she was shot as she was sitting in that chair.'

171

'What does that tell us?'

'It tells us that as she was sat down she was probably relaxed in the situation and that she was probably engaged in some way, probably in conversation with someone that she wasn't expecting to shoot her. Again this points to her knowing or accepting her killer.'

'Do you think that you would engage in conversation with somebody that was threatening to kill you Maxine, don't you think that you'd notice if somebody was trying to shoot you?'

'No you wouldn't, that's exactly it Danny, you wouldn't notice at all, why would you? We're used to reading about these situations or seeing these television programmes where the murderer points a gun at the victim and makes a threat or a huge speech. It is all done for dramatic effect, but in reality if you do neither of those things, murder can be carried out very quickly, especially gun murder, it can be done in two or three seconds, even less, especially if it has been practised. Draw, aim and fire, it's as simple as I've just said and it takes no longer. One second you're engaged with your victim, then the next second you've shot them dead and they didn't even see it coming. The key is your planned deliberation and the victim's complete ignorance. It sounds as if it's a cliché but you can be shot dead before you even know it.'

The colour in Danny's face drained at her chill account and as he realised the authenticity of her description he nodded in solemn assent.

The couple turned their attention to the photograph of the writing on the mirror as Danny picked up the image and studied it, 'I can't make the word out very well, it could be several things, the letters could be a date or they could be a code or something else altogether. The question I have is why are they there in the first place, especially as they don't seem to mean anything to anybody? Why write a message that nobody understands? Why give a clue at all, that's if it is intended as a clue, or is it a statement? Who are you actually writing this for? If the numbers represent a date then what is significant, what happened in 1848?'

'I had a little trawl through the Internet and I couldn't find anything that seemed to connect,' Maxine added. 'If anything it seemed an unimportant year. No major disasters or discoveries but of course it doesn't have to be major to anybody else, other than the person that thinks that it is.'

The beige man drained the remnants of his drink, picked up his newspaper and left the pub. As he did he muttered and gave a hostile stare in the direction of Danny and Maxine's table as if to say, you have ruined my evening with your presence and your ruminations. Now there was only Maxine, Danny and Joshua, the young barman, left in the Kiss.

Danny stopped studying the photograph of the writing on the mirror and picked up one of the photographs of the statuette. It was the one of the statuette plinth and the inscription underneath with the missing words. He read them out aloud, *'de in no,'* it didn't make any sense. He'd seen lots of similar statues. Latterly they had gone out of fashion, but at one time he recalled that virtually every Roman Catholic household had seemed to have a statue similar to this either on the mantle-piece or in the window. In fact his grandmother had one and when he was a young boy she'd once taken him on a pilgrimage to Knock in County Mayo. In Knock there were thousands of them. Every shop in Knock seemed to have their windows crammed with them.

Just then his train of thought stopped and he breathed out slowly and gave Maxine a knowing look, *'de in no,'* he said.

Maxine looked back at him quizzically.

'It's not Latin at all,' he explained, 'it's much closer to home than Latin, it's English. 'Made in Knock,' that's the inscription on the base of the statue.'

'Knock, where is Knock?' asked Maxine.

'Knock is a place in the west of Ireland, in County Mayo. I've been there as a boy. It is quite famous, about a hundred and fifty years ago, I'm not quite sure of the exact date, but a group of people saw an apparition on a wall. The images were of the Blessed Virgin, Saint Joseph, John the Evangelist and I think that Jesus Christ appeared too, they were all there. Ever since then, it's become the Irish equivalent of Lourdes. I think that I've read somewhere the biggest church in Ireland is in the place. Some say that recently Knock has lost a bit of its spiritualism and has been given over to religious memorabilia and commercialism, but people still flock there by the thousands. There are dozens of shops selling rosary beads, holy water and statues just like this one, the one in the photograph. They are all probably made in China now and some of the letters have worn away over the years but that inscription when it was new read, *Made in Knock*, I'm sure of it.'

'The question is why, when everything else in the house was torn to shreds, why was that left alone?' said Maxine. 'What about the other inscription on the scroll at the front?'

Danny looked at it for the first time:

To a l n e en fr th S ers Oct   196

'I don't know, a name, another date, I can't make it out. The fourth and fifth word could be *from the*, obviously if that is a date and it makes sense that it is, then its October, nineteen-sixty something. If we had the actual statue maybe, but not from these photos. What if we put them under a microscope?'

'That wouldn't help us in any way. Again, if we had the real statue but that will be locked away in the vaults of police evidence.'

'Let's look at what we think we've got,' said Danny.

'Let's then,' said Maxine.

'A murder, maybe a ritualistic one. I agree about the wreckage and if you're right about the bullets that also supports your theory. The murderer may be close to the community, the knowledge about the neighbours' holiday supports that, but what's the motive, what's the reason, something in Helen's past? Where is her past, what is the Italian connection and what is Speranza?' His voice rose as he said the final word.

'Jane Francesca Elgee,' said a young voice that seemed to be detached from human form. Maxine looked at Danny and he looked at Maxine, then they both realised that the owner of the voice was the young barman, Joshua, who had looked up from his bottling behind the bar.

'Who is Jane Francesca Elgee, is she Italian?' Maxine said, looking in Joshua's direction.

'Jane Francesca Elgee, later to become Jane Francesca Wilde, she was Oscar Wilde's mother,' said Joshua authoritatively. 'You do know who Oscar Wilde is? I think her antecedence actually was Italian, but that was in her past, possibly her great-grandfather. Her father I think was Irish and if he wasn't she definitely was. She was an established poet, wrote for a radical magazine called the Nation. She wrote a lot about the famine. The point is she was a poor, but famous, Irish nationalist poet and she wrote under the pen name of Speranza.'

Danny got up from his seat and walked over to the bar. 'When exactly was this?' he asked.

'Eighteen-forties mainly.'

'Thank you,' said Danny. 'Maxine, where is that photograph of the writing on the mirror?' He picked up the photograph and scrutinized it, '*An Gorta Mor.*'

'What language is that,' asked Maxine, 'Italian or Irish?'

'It's Irish, it translates loosely as the *Great Hunger*.'

'I didn't know that you had the Gaelic.'

'I don't but I know a little, I don't know what that word is on the mirror but if the numbers allude to a date then its *eighteen forty-eight*. That date is right in the middle of the Irish potato blight, one of the biggest tragedies of modern times, arguably the biggest in Ireland's history. Helen wasn't trying to point us in the direction of *Italy*, she was trying to point us in the direction of *Ireland*. The statue is made in Knock in Ireland. The look on Archie's face when I told him that I thought that Helen might be from Ireland. Ireland has worked its way into this puzzle too many times, featured in this too much. The answer to this is in Helen's past and I am sure that is to be found somewhere in Ireland. Maxine, we need to go to Ireland!'

'Danny, your enthusiasm is infectious and suppose you're right, and I think that you could be, we need a bit more than that, we can't just ship up in Ireland, it's a big place to look for something that is no more than half an idea. If we go there, which is easy enough, what exactly would we be looking for and where exactly would we be looking for it? Exactly what part did you have in mind: Dublin, Belfast, Cork, Limerick?'

'County Mayo!'

'Why County Mayo, because the statue was made in Knock and that's in County Mayo?'

'No, it's a bit more than that. Anyway, we start by asking after Helen Day.'

'Danny, we can't just hop over to Ireland looking for somebody called Helen Day, chances are it isn't her real name anyway. If you were leading your life the way she seemed to be, your name is the first thing you'd change and then there is that date, if it is a date, eighteen forty-eight, which as you say, is in the time of the Irish potato blight, well so what? Why has somebody written a date on a mirror after they've murdered somebody? That date must have more relevance to the murder than it just being in the middle of the Great Hunger.'

'Maybe somebody from that year is responsible for all of this,' Danny said.

'What, you mean that somebody from eighteen forty-eight murdered Helen Day, that would make them at least one hundred and sixty-six years old.'

'No, I don't mean that at all, I'm not sure what I mean.'

'Danny, before we go haring off to another country looking for a woman called Helen that has a connection to the Irish potato blight in 1848, I think that there is somewhere a little bit closer to home where we might find some answers.'

'Where's that?'

'Archie's.'

'I thought that might be your answer.'

'Well exactly Danny, it's much easier to look around a few square feet of a flat in Norford and in silence than to tramp around a whole county in Ireland asking everyone we meet do they know a woman who's been murdered in England called Helen? The Irish are renowned for their sense of quirk, but I think that we might even be stretching their patience a bit too far. How is Archie anyway?'

'Somebody would have been in touch if there had been a change in any way, so I'm assuming that he's just the same.'

'Danny, the last time we met in here you told me that you were asking his questions, but then they became a bit blurred with yours so exactly what were his questions?'

'Well, he wanted to know the detail about the bullet wounds, whereabouts on the body they were and he also asked about the condition of the room that Helen was found in. He also said something about the colour of her eyes, but he didn't really pursue that.'

'Apart from the one about the eyes they are very astute questions, they are about the ritualistic aspect of Helen's murder. They sound to me as if they are questions where the questioner is trying to confirm something that he has some prior knowledge of.'

'That's exactly what I thought but what could it be?'

'I think Danny, that we've had this conversation before, it could be that he's directly or indirectly involved in this or it could be that he's seen or heard about this type of thing before. He's lived a long time, maybe he's just an inquisitive amateur.'

'What, you mean just like us? No, I think with Archie that it's a bit more than that Maxine?'

'Alright then, maybe he actually knows something as you've said. Maybe there is a connection, possibly something that's happened in the past that he knows about, what exactly do you know about his own background?'

'Not a lot really, his generation always seem to have something to hide, you know an illegitimate child or somebody in a mental home all their life, a cousin who was an army deserter and was shot at dawn. Things that mattered then but don't seem to matter much now. Illegitimacy and army desertion I mean, not being shot for it. So they don't seem to say much about their own past. I think that they just find it less complicated than if they make statements that raise questions in the first place, so they stay quiet. I know somebody Archie's age who has recently been tracing their ancestors and they've just found out that the person who they thought was their sister was their mother and the person who they thought was their mother was their grandmother and their father wasn't their father at all. Their actual father was some kind of itinerant trumpet player with an exotic name, he was Irish so it's topical. That generation seemed to get themselves involved in all kinds of fixes. My mother had a friend, it was also in Ireland, again topical. This friend of hers, her own uncle had to smuggle her over to England rolled up in a carpet in the back of his van, all the way from Port Laois to Blackpool. Her crime was that she was pregnant and she was sixteen and she was unmarried. This was in the early 1960's, it wasn't the dark ages.'

'Danny, I love it when you take me along on these philosophical trails of yours, but what about Archie?'

'Most of what I know about Archie, at least as far as his background is concerned, I got from Charlotte so it's second hand really. As far as I know he is originally from Edinburgh. Some old Scots family, old money. He came down from Scotland to Manchester University in nineteen fifty-seven. He met his wife who was local, he had kids and he settled here. His wife died, his kids are here, his grandkids are here and now he's been here too long to go anywhere else, he's been on the council forty years, it's a story as old as the hills.'

'Well the way I see it, he is our biggest lead and as soon as he comes round we need to speak to him, but in the meantime it might help if we can get to look around his place.'

Quite suddenly a memory of a word came into Danny's head. A strange word that his grandparents used to use, an old Irish word. He remembered that his grandmother used to recite a poem to him. He tried to visualise it in his head in stanza form as he recited the verse softly to himself:

> '*Behind a web of bottles, bales,*
> *Tobacco, sugar, coffin nails.*
> *The Gombeen like a spider sits ...*
> *Surfeited; and for all his wits,*
> *As meagre as the tally-board*
> *On which his...*'

'I forget the last bit but that's it Maxine, *Gombeen,* that's the word that was written on Helen's mirror.'

178

'Gombeen, I've never heard of it, is it in the Oxford English Dictionary?'

'Probably not, it's an old Irish word, loosely defined it means swindler, crook, usurer, that sort of person.'

'Do you think that the murderer was referring to Helen when he wrote it?'

'My knowledge of her doesn't point to that and she doesn't seem to fit the typical description of one but, as we keep saying, the answers are in her past and who knows what's in there waiting to leap out at us.'

'Alright,' said Maxine, 'we've got the Gombeen, we've got Speranza, we've got the statue in Knock, we've got 1848 and we've got all roads lead to Ireland. Back here in Winton Kiss we've got a ritualistic killing, possibly committed by an unidentified somebody connected to the community, but as of yet with no apparent motive. There are a lot of bits but they don't actually add up to much, do they? None of them actually give us anything about Helen Day. We're not any further forward with her. Who are her parents, what is her background, where is she from, why has a non-Catholic got a statue of the Virgin Mary and the big question, what has she done that would make would make somebody want to kill her?'

Danny looked thoughtful, 'I'm just thinking about what you said about Archie's place. If I approach the situation the right way I can probably get the keys from Charlotte. His place is in Woodhall, close to Norford town centre. We could probably meet there one afternoon. I'll just have to be careful with Charlotte, sometimes she just chooses to remember all the wrong things about me. That's when she turns on me and gets difficult.'

'Danny, I've not known you for very long, but I can think of a few reasons why someone might turn on you and get difficult.'

'Maxine, let's not go off the subject eh, I'll speak to Charlotte, I'll telephone her tomorrow evening when she's finished work and she's at home relaxed.'

Chapter 18

The Professor and
the Female Solicitor

Another Monday morning had inevitably arrived in Manchester and the newly polished, gleaming brass plate that was fixed to the large, shiny black door of the nondescript, brick-built office building that was situated half a mile from the city centre was clear, concise and unequivocal in its announcement: *Roisin de Hay, Solicitor.*

The Professor stayed outside on the path of the busy Manchester street studying the plate for at least three minutes. To the observer it would seem to be an unusual occupation, as there was very little to peruse upon for that length of time, for in those few words there was nothing at all that was not absolutely instant and totally self-explanatory. Having completed his research he then produced a street map from inside his jacket pocket and began to study that document with the same concentration. Eventually, carrying the map, he made his way methodically to the other side of the road and appeared to study the happenings around him from that perspective for a further ten minutes.

He looked back down the street, across the street and up at the roofline of the building and he noticed the stone tablet high up in the front elevation, it read: *Royal Market Buildings 1870.* He stared down at the kerb line on the ground and he surveyed all around him in every direction, again referring to the map. Then he crossed the road once more, checked his pocket watch and loitered for another ten minutes in more surveillance. Only then, seemingly satisfied he walked through the shiny, black door and into the office and as he did he took off his hat. Once inside he announced himself to the bespectacled young secretary who was sitting, writing behind the desk, 'Good morning, I am Professor Jeremy Weedon and I have an appointment with Miss Roisin de Hay.' As he said this he produced a small white card and handed it to the young lady.

The secretary glanced down at the card and mentally read its content, *'Professor Jeremy Weedon, International Financier, 52 Kendal Road, Chorlton-cum-Hardy, Manchester.'*

'Good morning Professor Weedon,' said the secretary, 'Miss de Hay is expecting you and will see you shortly. Meanwhile, would you please take a seat sir.' As she said this, with a flourish of her hand she indicated at the four chairs that she herself had cleaned, dusted and placed in a neat row along the adjacent wall less than half an hour earlier.

'Thank you,' the Professor responded as he sat down in silence and reached for the newspaper that lay on the small table in front of him. The headline that leapt out of the newspaper that day was a monumental one concerning an adventure in prospect. It announced that Charles Augustus Lindbergh was going to attempt a non-stop, solo, transatlantic flight from New York to Paris over a weekend and as such if his mission was successful he would become the first person ever in history to be in New York on the Friday and Paris on the Saturday.

After reading briefly about Lindbergh's biography, the Professor put his newspaper down and turned his attention to the young auburn-haired secretary. He smiled and asked, 'have you worked here long?'

'Since Miss de Hay opened the office sir,' she said.

'How long ago was that?'

'Almost two years now.'

'Do you work here every day?'

'Monday to Friday, nine until five, four thirty on a Friday.'

'You don't work Saturday then?'

'I never do sir, the building is closed on a Saturday at one o'clock prompt until 7am on Monday, but Miss de Hay sometimes works on casework on Saturday morning.'

'But you don't work with her when she does?'

'No never sir.'

'Does anybody?'

'As far as I know she works alone sir.'

The Professor gave an indication of being content with this information, he smiled again and returned to his newspaper.

The Professor was visiting a rare official in Manchester and an even rarer one in the rest of England, a female solicitor. The passing of the Sex Disqualification (Removal) Act 1919, some eight years ago, meant that women were no longer barred from what was, or what had been known as, the higher professions. Two prime examples of these professions were medicine and the law. It was as a consequence of this act that women were now enabled to qualify as doctors, solicitors and barristers, perhaps in future years, even as judges. Such a legal qualification had been the long-time ambition of Roisin de Hay from Enniscorthy, County Wexford. She had studied for and passed her Law Society exams at Oxford. Newly and fully qualified she planned ultimately to move back to Ireland and practice there, but she had decided to give herself a few years' experience in a large city. Initially her choice had been London and she had been practicing there a year, but if the truth was recognised she had become a little bored in the capital with its long standing legal conventions, old established ways and ancient, unwritten codes of conduct.

An opportunity had presented itself in Manchester two years ago and she had taken it. She found Manchester a tough and grimy town, sometimes the air there was dark and damp and in the winter it was black with the myriad of mill and house chimneys emanating their thick black smoke all day and night. The place itself though was dynamic and unconventional, the people straightforward, plain-speaking individuals who defied convention. If there was a rule to be broken then Mancunians would break it. As an added incentive her father was involved in some of the finance for the Cottonopolis aspect of the city and visited it at least three or four times a year so it was also an opportunity to see him. All these things considered she decided to gain her city experience in Manchester, at least for the time being.

The Professor shook Roisin's hand as she came out to meet him and he noticed of her that she had a regal bearing and that she was a tall, very thin, plain yet alert looking woman around thirty years of age. She noticed of him that he was tall, well dressed, athletically built and that he was a very handsome man probably in his early to mid-thirties. She thought that he seemed a little young to be a professor. He thought of her that it seemed odd that a woman should be a solicitor.

'Do come through Professor Weedon,' she said and she indicated to a door, which opened up on a medium sized office with all the usual office equipment of the time. Adjacent to the window was a large, green, leather-topped desk with one chair on one side of it and two on the other. The female solicitor shut the door behind the Professor. This action was mainly to preserve an air of solicitor, client confidentiality. She then occupied the solitary chair whilst the Professor took one of the two that were paired.

She spoke first, 'to start with I will need a few but brief particulars.'

'What would you need to know?'

'Oh nothing intrusive I can assure you, we can start with your name.'

'Jeremy Weedon, Professor Jeremy Weedon.'

'Do you have a middle name or any other name?'

'No.'

'Do you have an address Professor Weedon?'

'When I am in England I stay at this address.' He handed her a business card which was an exact copy of the one he had given to the secretary ten minutes earlier.

Roisin observed that on the card was a Manchester address, which she recognised as being fashionable, 'Do you sometimes live outside Manchester?'

'Yes, more time out than in these days, my business takes me all over the world, sometimes for months at a time, Canada, America, Europe and as you can see Manchester and also other British cities including the dreaded London. I do always think of Manchester as home and wherever we are in the world, we always keep a house in Manchester, this house actually.'

'What exactly is your business?'

As she asked her questions and received her answers she wrote them down.

'It's all to do with international banking and finance.'

'Do you plan to stay in England for a long period this time?'

'No, unfortunately I'm planning another trip abroad. How long I will be there, I don't know exactly. It all depends on several things.'

They studied each other momentarily and in silence.

'Tell me Miss de Hay, yours is an unusual name, are you any relation to Dermot de Hay from County Wexford?'

'Yes, he is my father, do you know him?'

'I've met him a couple of times in the line of business, but I'd hardly say that I know him, they were just professional encounters.'

'Oh, when exactly was that?'

'You know, I'm not absolutely sure, one meets so many people these days.'

'Oh, can you remember where it was then?'

'You know I'm not sure of that either, possibly London, yes I'm almost sure it was London, 1925 in London. Yes, at the International Bankers Convention.'

Roisin knew of this convention and she knew that it had been in London in 1925 exactly as the Professor had stated. She also knew of a few other things. She had heard her father mention the International Bankers Convention. He loathed it and he called it the *Pompous Pigs Ensemble*. She also knew that he hated London intensely and avoided the place whenever possible and that if anything was in London he always sent a representative but that he personally didn't go to it. She also knew that people are often forgetful or mistaken about where and when they've actually met someone, particularly if they did a lot of travelling, whereupon time and place would probably blend into each other. With all this in mind, and even though she had only just met this man, she thought to herself that there was something that was possibly distrustful about him.

'One more thing Professor Weedon, for the record I need your date of birth.'

'This is actually turning out to be a lot of brief particulars Miss de Hay.'

Roisin thought that this wasn't actually turning out to be a lot of brief particulars. In fact she thought that it was exactly the opposite of what a lot of brief particulars really were. In addition to this she was a little bemused as to why anybody would be seemingly reluctant to offer these fundamental facts about themselves. Unless of course they really didn't wish for anybody to know who they were, where they lived, what their age was and if they didn't want anybody to know those particulars then they didn't really want anybody to know anything about themselves, because until you divulged these three points of information then you have remained anonymous. Surely an anonymous profile in international finance was no profile at all. Indeed, if the Professor wanted to be anonymous then why be in international finance and why consult a solicitor?

'That will be all Professor Weedon, name, address and date of birth, it's just protocol and it's all completely confidential, I assure you.'

'In that case, it's the fifteenth of March.'

'What year?'

'1887.'

Roisin didn't know why but she didn't believe him. She thought that it really was very unsettling when you couldn't trust your own client to tell you the truth about something as black and white as his own date of birth. At that precise moment she was tempted to listen to what he had to say and then politely dismiss him and say that she really couldn't help him. The truth was though that she sensed that there was something intriguing about the Professor's real motivations, possibly even something sinister, and because of the person that she was, she was curious to know more. She was nevertheless determined to be in control of the situation whatever it turned out to be. She would think about this later but for the moment she would continue as normal.

'So you are exactly forty years of age?'

'Yes, I suppose I am.'

She thought that the Professor looked young for his age. 'Now that we have those brief formalities over how exactly can I help you?'

'I have some affairs that need settling in case of my death.'

'You mean you wish to establish a will?'

'Yes, but there is a little bit more than that, I need somebody to act as an executor for my estate, somebody to ensure that everything is carried out in accordance with my wishes in the event of my death.'

'Do you have all the details?'

'I do, I have all the details worked out to the finest, but I do not have anything written down yet, it is still in my head, and that of course is where you come in Miss de Hay.'

'This seems straightforward Professor Weedon.'

'That part of it is Miss de Hay. It is my diary that isn't. You see I only have so much time in England and even less in Manchester. I have business in Edinburgh, Birmingham and London. I have already filled up my normal office hour's capacity. I'm off travelling again in a few weeks, this time to the United States for what will probably be a lengthy stay, probably at least six months, and I want to have the peace of mind of knowing that everything is in good order before I go and whilst I am there.'

'May I ask you a question Professor Weedon? This time it is a little intrusive.'

'We will try Miss de Hay.'

'How is your health, may I say that you look very well, but are you aware of any illness that you may be suffering from?'

'No, there is none at all, no my health is good and I have no illnesses that I am aware of. This is not to do with my health, which as I've said is fine, although anything can happen, particularly in America where in some parts they all seem to wear guns as much as they wear those jeans that they are so fond of. No, this is more a case of good management than anything else.'

'It is a wise move to have such a plan and as a Solicitor I would recommend that every person should have one. Do you have any dependents Professor Weedon?'

'Can you name a person that doesn't Miss de Hay?' he said hesitantly.

She watched his face and thought that perhaps he said this with an ever so slight trace of a sneer and she found this odd. As well as this, even though she had clearly heard him say the word *person* she knew instinctively that he meant to use the word *man* but had avoided it. Perhaps it was because he considered it inappropriate to use the word in front of a female solicitor. Despite his word choice she knew that his nature was different than the way he spoke and that for all his comparative youth and even more youthful looks, he was a solid member of the old guard with its traditional establishment attitude. She also thought him to be a very calculating man.

'Do you have a wife or any children?' she asked.

'I have a lovely wife and three young children. They are the most important things in the world to me.'

Roisin contemplated on this response too. She found it strange that somebody would describe his own wife and children as *things* and not as *people* or *persons*. She herself had neither children nor a husband but she had a father and a niece and she would never describe either one of them as *things*.

Then the Professor said, 'as I mentioned earlier, my diary is in an awful mess and I need to address this situation most urgently and also I need without fail to keep the appointments that I already have, they are most important to the development of my business.'

'I sense that perhaps you have thought about this and that you have a suggestion to make,' Roisin responded.

'Well the only time that I appear to have free is next Saturday morning, would that offer any convenience to you, perhaps you don't work Saturday?'

'No, I don't really regulate my hours in such a way. I do always take Sunday off but apart from that I try to accommodate my client's requirements and normally Saturday morning would not be out of bounds.'

'I sense that this particular Saturday will be out of bounds Miss de Hay?'

'My father will be visiting me that weekend, he's travelling over from Ireland. I've not seen him for some months now and our reunion has been planned for quite some time. He's the only parent that I have and I have planned to spend some time with him that weekend.'

'By all means, I understand fully, we each of us have only one father. I lost mine some years ago. I completely understand your wish to spend time with him and I suppose if I tried really hard then I could rearrange my diary for the following Saturday.'

Roisin had already observed the Professor's good looks, now she became aware of how charming he could be, a dangerous combination she reflected. 'You're very gracious Professor Weedon, would it be at all possible to rearrange the Saturday morning to a weekday?'

'I am afraid that would be completely out of the question, as I said, I quite simply have too many commitments throughout the week.'

'Then shall we say a week on Saturday? That would make it Saturday the twenty-first.'

'Yes, let's settle on that then, shall we say 10:30am?' As the Professor concluded his sentence he rose from his chair as if to leave.

'10:30am will be fine. There is just one more thing Professor Weedon.'

'Yes, what's that?'

'The witness.'

'Witness?' The Professor sat down again.

'Yes, if we are going to conclude the business on the day, which shouldn't be a problem, then there will be papers to sign. In these situations the law insists that any signatures are witnessed.'

'Oh! I don't require a witness Miss de Hay, your very own word and signature would be good enough for me.'

'Thank you Professor Weedon, your very gracious sentiments and comments are appreciated. However, although my very own words and signature may be good enough for you, unfortunately they would not be deemed to be good enough for any probate situation that might arise and any will without such a witness signature could be viewed as weak and in an extreme case even invalid. It would certainly not be strong in the event of any subject challenge. As well as this such a witness is a legal requirement, it is the law we are dealing with.'

Roisin thought that this last revelation seemed to make the Professor a little edgy, it certainly took him by surprise and she detected a miniscule lack of composure on his part.

'In short, it would be poor advice on my part to suggest such a document with so obvious an omission, so there is no doubt really that we do need a witness. There is a further point to this, the witness should be independent and not a family member nor a close friend nor an employee. If you do not know of such a person then I can provide for somebody to attend on the day. There are professional people that carry out this duty. They are very discreet and confidential. It is after all a witness to the signature and not to the actual content of the document.'

'And there is no way of avoiding this?'

'Absolutely not, I'm afraid it is as inflexible as your own Saturday morning seems to be.'

'Very well, if that is the law then that is the law.'

'So shall I make arrangements for the professional witness to attend on the day?'

'No, that will not be necessary Miss de Hay, I do know of such a person and I can arrange for her to be in attendance on the day.'

'Can I enquire as to her particulars?'

'I would sooner withhold them at this stage.'

'Why do you wish to do that?'

The Professor appeared hesitant but only for a moment, 'Out of respect for her really. I feel that the right course to take is to discuss the matter with the lady first, just in case she does not consent, although I can think of no reason why she wouldn't readily agree.'

'This is a little irregular Professor Weedon, I must insist on knowing something of her.'

'She is neither a family member nor a close friend nor an employee. She is a professional contact of mine who lives in Manchester. Will that be in order Miss de Hay?'

'Does this lady have a name?'

'Yes, she is called Olwyn Jones,' he said hesitantly.

'All right, that will do for the time being.'

'Then until the appointed time a week on Saturday.'

The Professor for the second time during their interview rose from his chair. He shook Roisin's hand and left by the same way that he had arrived, pausing at the doorway to put on his hat.

The female solicitor sat in her chair quietly for a few moments looking at the brief particulars that she'd taken down about the Professor. Then she thought about his strange reluctance to be forthcoming during the interview. She stood up and went over to the doorway, as she did she beckoned the auburn-haired secretary to her.

'Ivy, can you shut the front door and come in here for a moment?' Ivy duly obeyed and entered her employer's office. 'Has Professor Weedon left the building altogether?'

'Yes, I saw him go myself five minutes ago.'

'Are you sure?'

'I am.'

'Ivy, whilst he was here did he say anything to you?'

'Not really, not much, only chat.'

'What was the content of this chat?'

'He asked me how long I'd worked here and he also asked me if I ever worked on a Saturday.'

'What did you say to him?'

'I told him that I'd been here two years and I said that I have never worked on a Saturday.'

'Anything else?'

'What him to me or me to him?'

'Either.'

'I told him that you sometimes worked on Saturdays, have I said something that I shouldn't have said?'

'No Ivy you haven't, not at all.'

Roisin was pensive for a moment and Ivy looked on patiently. After working for the female solicitor for two years she instantly recognised her employer's look and she awaited her instruction.

'What was the name of that enquiry agent, the one we used in the Oxford Road case? He was a big bear of a man with a ruddy complexion, I think that he is an ex-police officer, he has a large, walrus moustache and wears a bowler hat.'

'His name is Stanley Oldknow ma'am.'

'Stanley Oldknow, that's the man! Do you know how to contact him?'

'Of course, he has an office in Shudehill, I sometimes walk past it on my way home when I go that way. I can see him through the window, he's always sat there drawing his pictures. He often waves when he sees me.'

'His pictures Ivy, what pictures?'

'Oh sorry ma'am, apparently he's a police artist and when the police are looking for somebody he draws a picture of them from information given to him by a witness. Oh I think that's what it is, I'm not sure. Anyway, apparently he's very good.'

Ivy became a little flustered and Roisin smiled, 'I know exactly what you mean Ivy and that's excellent, would you mind going home that way tonight?'

'Of course not.'

'Would you give Mr Oldknow a message from me? Tell him that I need to see him tomorrow if that's possible. Tell him that I appreciate that this is very short notice but that I have another enquiry for him. Tell him that I need his talents.'

'I will ma'am.'

Chapter 19

Dermot and his Daughter

At around 11:00am on the Thursday morning Mr Dermot de Hay left the mansion house in Enniscorthy. He travelled by road in his chauffer driven car in a northerly direction towards Dublin. Upon arrival in Ireland's capital city he attended a routine business appointment, which took around forty minutes. After concluding this appointment he walked around the city for a while. Eventually on that day he took the evening boat across the Irish Sea to Liverpool.

In due or undue course, depending upon the observer's singular perception, and after an uneventful crossing, the boat docked at Liverpool on the Friday morning whereupon Mr de Hay attended another routine business appointment, this time in Liverpool. Having in turn concluded this appointment he paused for a while and took some refreshment in the city. After this he boarded the train from Liverpool Lime Street station to London Road station in the city of Manchester. Travelling first class he finally arrived in Manchester at around 2:00pm. Shortly after this he kept his last and favourite business appointment of his schedule with an old Manchester based business colleague, Mr Arthur Finney. Mr Finney had an interest in several mills around the area of Ancoats in the city of Manchester.

After his appointment with Arthur, Dermot accepted his old friend's invitation to walk with him the approximate one-mile distance from Ancoats, down Oldham Street across Manchester's Piccadilly and down Moseley Street to the Midland Hotel. The Midland Hotel was certainly the most lavish hotel in Manchester and some would even argue in the country. The two wealthy businessmen, one Irish, one English, enjoyed each other's company, strolling along, talking away, through the late Friday afternoon carry on, all the way to the front entrance of the Midland hotel. Outside this hotel entrance Arthur and Dermot shook hands warmly and parted company easily. Arthur went off for Friday early-evening drinks, to his gentleman's club in nearby St Anne's Square.

As Dermot stood outside the Midland he looked up at the majestic building with its red brick and brown terracotta exterior. He then entered the building where the receptionist greeted him, 'Good afternoon Mr de Hay.'

'Good afternoon Ernest,' replied Dermot.

'I've reserved room 216 for you. Miss de Hay has not yet arrived, when she does I've allocated her room 217, is that to your liking?'

'It's very much to my liking Ernest, how are your family by the way, its four now isn't it?'

'Shortly to be five sir.'

'Five! Well congratulations Ernest, both to you and Mrs Robbins.'

'Thank you sir.'

'I'll see myself up, no need for any fuss, I'm still able bodied and I'm travelling light as usual.'

Ernest Robbins thought that Mr Dermot de Hay was a gentleman of the highest order and Dermot thought that of all the hotels he stayed in the Midland in Manchester was probably his favourite. He also made a mental note to tip Ernest generously upon leaving tomorrow, after all, the hotel receptionist would soon have another mouth to feed and he would need all the money he could earn.

Although Dermot wasn't comfortable to leave Wexford for too long he enjoyed these brief business excursions between Ireland and England for a variety of reasons. They gave him the opportunity, as he often explained it, to get out and about and meet people and he tried to undertake such trips as often as possible, at least three times a year. Yes, he enjoyed his gallivanting as Roisin often described it.

The best part though was always his visit to Manchester. Not that he actually had any fondness for Manchester itself. In fact the opposite was probably true for he found it a harsh industrial place with an utterly deplorable weather climate of reputedly permanent dampness. It always seemed to him that whether the sun shone, the rain came down, the wind blew, the snow fell or the Manchester smog descended, and he had witnessed all of these first hand on several occasions, he was even sure that he had seen and felt permutations of each and every one of them in one single day, that whatever the climatic symptom in Manchester there would almost always be that dampness in the air.

Save for a few weeks in the middle of summer Dermot was informed that the damp never left the city. This was something that he could readily believe as it didn't seem to have either an arrival time or a departure point, it just always seemed to be there, bone-chilling damp, it seemed permanent and there seemed no respite from it, whether it be January or June. He also recalled the Manchester smog, he had witnessed Irish mist, Scottish mist and even London fog and New York fog, but he had never seen anything that remotely resembled Manchester smog with its thick, yellow, green gruel swirl that clamoured all around you. As for the natives, the people, known as Mancunians, each and every one of them seemed to be always busy. Running around at a pace trying desperately to either sell something to somebody or to buy something from somebody else. Yes, the whole population of this city, a city that was at the centre of the industrial revolution, was divided equally it seemed into buyers or sellers.

No, the reason that Dermot took pleasure from his visits to Manchester, apart from the Midland of course, was that at the end of these business excursions this was the place where he would meet up with one of the two most important people in his life, his only daughter Roisin. He loved his only daughter in the way that only a father of an only daughter can. It was though, much more than natural paternal affection with Roisin, for he truly admired the difference in her against other people. From an early age this difference was apparent and she had never shown what was deemed to be any interest in following the traditional path of her contemporaries.

Unusually for a father towards a child he also admired and respected her more than any other person that he had ever known. As an individual she had not been endowed with the natural beauty and grace that the majority of women have placed upon them by nature. Even as her own father he recognised that the kindest way to describe her physical appearance was to say that she was plain. Though, beyond the physicality and the cosmetic aspect, Dermot knew that Roisin wasn't plain, in fact she was the exact opposite of it. She was a highly intelligent, single-minded and original woman, a determined woman of the utmost integrity and of the utmost kindness and over the years Dermot had witnessed many acts of her kindness towards her fellow man. He had watched her grow up without a mothers guiding hand, for her own had died when Roisin was a girl. He had watched and supported as she had done what very few women today can ever do. She had overachieved in a man's world. Moreover, and this was what was truly remarkable, she had achieved this without having to resort to impersonating a man herself, nor had she resorted to any kind of traditional so-called feminine ways. In short, Dermot de Hay was proud of his only daughter.

Father and daughter kept in touch regularly through writing, but in recent years it was their meetings in Manchester that gave them their real father and daughter togetherness. Dermot knew that Roisin had to lead her own life but he truly missed her being away from home and apart from little Marguerite, who was now almost ten years old and was the other important person in his life, they were all the family that each other had. Dermot had longed for more grandchildren but he had long since given up on his only daughter ever marrying. Her interests were in politics and the law and any slight hope that he entertained of being a grandfather was completely stifled the day that she graduated from law school. All this said, he loved her more than anything and was fiercely protective of her. After graduation she had flirted very briefly with professional life in London and then had decided to set up a practice in Manchester. A practice that he had been more than pleased to support her in, for although he had some dislike of Manchester and its smog he positively loathed London with all its sycophancy and hypocrisy and whenever an invitation to visit the world's capital city fell upon his desk he always did everything he could to ensure that he was well and truly represented, as long as it was not by himself.

This evening he was having dinner with his daughter. He was looking forward to seeing her and it would be the highlight of his trip. There was another reason that he was seeing his daughter and it was all to do with his granddaughter Marguerite, or more to the point to do with Marguerite's own birth mother, the renowned French actress Miss Antoinette Dubois.

Roisin's journey to meet her father that Friday evening had been much less convoluted and shorter than her father's, both in operation and distance, she had simply locked up her office after work, picked up her overnight valise and had taken a cab across Manchester, instructing the surly driver that *The Midland Hotel* was her destination. As her cab negotiated the Friday night traffic rush, neither its solitary passenger nor the surly driver took any notice of the other cab that also contained one driver and a solitary passenger and appeared to be following the same route a short distance behind. As if to stretch the bounds of credibility even more there was yet again a third cab with one driver and one passenger, this cab appeared to be taking the same route as both of them. In short, the second cab was following the first and the third was following the second.

During this short journey Roisin pondered on some aspects of her own life and on the lives of others that were connected to hers. Little Marguerite would be ten years old now, Roisin hadn't seen her little niece since last Easter. The time was fast approaching when her education needed to be considered. She thought that the child's educational needs would probably be best met if she moved out of Wexford, possibly even Ireland altogether but she knew that her father disagreed. Her father she knew would have a plan for his granddaughter, Roisin was sure of that. Then there was Marguerite's estranged mother, Antoinette Dubois. Antoinette had kept her side of the bargain and stayed out of the child's life for the agreed time. Roisin assumed that her father had kept his side of the bargain and paid her the money as promised. The only change was that the agreed time was now coming to an end and, by all accounts, Antoinette was doing alright for herself and didn't really need Dermot's money anymore. Roisin had an overwhelming feeling that somehow she herself was going to be dragged into all this and whilst she wanted the best for little Marguerite she really hoped that Dermot and Antoinette could sort the issue out between themselves. She loved her father, she loved Marguerite and she felt friendly towards Antoinette. After all, Antoinette was Marguerite's birth mother and Dermot was the child's birth grandfather so they both had legitimate concerns to ensure that little Marguerite had the best start in life and this they had done in their own individual ways thus far. Roisin didn't want to become involved in any *family at war* scenes. She had kept up the correspondence with Antoinette even after all these years and she was confident that Marguerites' mother loved the little girl. She also knew that Dermot did too. She hoped that both her father's and Antoinette's aspirations for Marguerite could somehow be brought together.

There was something else too, this was about her own aspirations. She was at a crossroads in her life. She wanted to go back to Wexford to be where her family was, where her heritage was, where she belonged. Yet on the other hand she now wanted to stay in Manchester. That hadn't been the original plan but plans change and so it now was. Manchester was a modern place, a radical place. She thought that things were done differently here. She was fascinated by the political scene in Manchester and she had become involved with it. There were female councillors in England now and they weren't all part of the suffragette movement. She had been offered a candidacy in Manchester at the local elections next year and she wanted with all her heart to stand.

There was also another issue that she didn't have a clear view on. It was not connected to the issues surrounding her family, but it puzzled her. It was one of her professional cases, it was the case of Professor Jeremy Weedon.

Ivy, Roisin's personal assistant, had called in to see Stanley Oldknow the enquiry agent on the way home from work as promised. Oldknow, reliable as always, had called on Miss de Hay promptly on Tuesday morning. After a brief interchange between them he had accepted the case and promised to present a report by this coming Tuesday. At the moment she awaited this. So why was her patience being tried? She didn't know, all she knew was that there was something that did not ring true about the Professor. She wondered if he had been sent for some political mischief by her political enemies. Then she reasoned that as her potential candidacy was just that, potential, and it was also a close kept secret, that she didn't at this stage have any political enemies as nobody knew of her connection to politics.

Then she told herself that she was being irrational. Jeremy Weedon was probably just a little eccentric, as were several of her other clients, after all, he was a professor and weren't all professors supposed to be eccentric in some way. What exactly had he done wrong? Nothing, he just wanted to conclude his business on a Saturday and no other day would do, his explanation for doing so was perfectly plausible, it was her that was making a mountain out of a molehill.

Finally her taxi arrived at its destination and stopped immediately outside the Midland Hotel. A little dapper man in a blue frock coat and a top hat came out to meet her, 'Good evening Miss de Hay.'

'Good Evening Ambrose, do you know if my father has arrived?'

'I believe that he has Miss.'

'Thank you Ambrose.'

Some two hours later Roisin and Dermot were enjoying a fine meal of Dover Sole and fresh winter vegetables, as described on the menu, together with a bottle of the Midland's finest French wine. They were seated in a private dining room, which Roisin had reserved for them. This room was away from the main restaurant but just allowed the slight refrains of the five-piece band to filter through to where they were seated. Her father was comfortable in that room.

Roisin thought how well, distinguished and handsome her father looked. He was still a relatively young man and she wondered to herself why he had remained a widower all these years.

Dermot thought that his daughter looked tired and drawn and he guessed correctly that she was probably working all her waking hours and doing little else. During the dinner they chatted about Wexford in general and about some mutual friends and acquaintances. They spoke at length about Marguerite but with very little reference to her future and with none whatsoever to her mother. In relation to the latter it was as if they were both avoiding the subject temporarily but with the knowledge that discussion about her was imminent to the night and could not be avoided permanently.

They had spoken about politics but in general terms with little specific reference to the political situation in either Ireland, England or Manchester and none whatsoever to Roisin's potential future political candidacy, as the father was totally ignorant of it and the daughter was waiting for what she considered to be the right moment to introduce the topic. In fact, they had spoken about many issues but both conversationalists, as if in some kind of telepathic agreement, had deliberately avoided the relevant points concerning any of them.

It was Dermot who made the first attempt to alter this, 'Roisin would you facilitate something for me?'

'You only have to ask father.'

'It is rather delicate.'

'Do you mean for me or for you, or for whoever I am facilitating with on your behalf?'

'Ah, my daughter, you know me far too well.'

'The most direct way is just to ask directly father.'

'Yes you're right, it is the best way. It is about Marguerite, you will recall that the initial agreement that we had with Miss Dubois almost ten years ago now has only a very short term to run, in fact all that is left of it is a few short months.'

'Then perhaps you should let it expire naturally. I didn't really think that it was a good idea anyway.'

'Roisin how can you say this, you were there throughout? You were consulted at every stage.'

'I was an attendant companion to Antoinette and a silent compliant to you.'

'You sat there and raised not one objection.'

'Father, that is what a silent compliant does, raises no objections.'

'Why Roisin, why?'

'Father, I was your daughter.'

'You are still my daughter.'

'I was ten years younger, I was little more than a girl. I had hardly been out of Wexford, I had never been out of Ireland. From a selfish point of view I took an easy, naive moral stance and from a selfless point of view I supported my father. I now realise that neither of these views was for Marguerite and they certainly weren't for Antoinette.'

'We were all only doing what we thought was the best thing for Marguerite.'

'No father, we were all only doing what we thought was the best thing for ourselves.'

'Well, it's all old history now, it's all worked out fine.'

'Old history can work out fine but that doesn't mean that we should feel that we have to repeat it.'

'I've been thinking about the situation a lot recently and I need you to help me negotiate a new agreement.'

'Are you absolutely sure that this is the right way to go about this? Do you think that this is a good idea father?'

'Why not Roisin? You're a lawyer, you have a relationship with Miss Dubois and you are the child's blood aunt, in fact after me you are the only blood relative that she has.'

'Well, as you mention this father, aren't you overlooking the fact that Marguerite has a birth mother, albeit one that she hasn't seen for ten years but nevertheless a mother, and you can't find a closer blood relative than a mother. It's also precisely for those reasons that you have just mentioned that technically it would be a bad idea for me to have any involvement. If we were ever to find ourselves in a courtroom then I don't think that a judge would be too impressed when it was revealed that one of the acting lawyers was a blood relative of the subject litigant. That is not exactly what I meant though.'

'Roisin, I'm your father, please don't speak to me in that lawyers language, blood relative of the subject litigant indeed. For a moment I thought that I was having dinner with Scanlon. If that is not exactly what you mean, then what do you mean?'

'Well, whilst a formal written and legally binding agreement may have been the right thing to do ten years ago it is not necessarily the most beneficial case now.'

'You're still doing it Roisin, it is not necessarily the most beneficial case now.'

'What does Marguerite say about this?'

'Roisin, she is a child.'

'She may be a child but it is her life that you and Antoinette are discussing or that is to say you would be if you were really discussing it instead of having legal agreements drawn up. As well as this Marguerite will not always be a child and I for one don't want her to grow up thinking that I was responsible any more than I have been for keeping her apart from her mother.'

'Please speak English Roisin.'

'Sooner than translate, permit me to make what I think is a constructive suggestion and the only real way forward for all involved.'

'Go on, suggest away.'

'What is important is what is best for Marguerite and even though she is a child, her wishes have to be taken very much into consideration here. The situation was entirely different in 1917. Surely her life is going to be better with both her mother and her grandfather on the same side. Without the enforcement of legally binding contracts that only serve to keep adults and child away from each other.'

Dermot looked directly at his daughter as she continued.

'This is my suggestion Father...' She waited for an interruption from him but none came. 'I will write to Antoinette in France. I will tell her that we all want what is best for Marguerite. I'll suggest that you and her meet up, not in Wexford, no definitely not in Wexford and not in France either, it should be on neutral ground, I'll think of somewhere. The place doesn't matter for the moment. I will not be at that meeting in any capacity, daughter, aunt, lawyer, companion, anything. It is not my place to be at that meeting. There should be no third parties, just you and Antoinette. It will be Marguerite's future that you will be discussing, the rest will be up to you and her, her grandfather and her mother. I will also say to Antoinette that I have spoken with you about this and that you are receptive to this meeting.' She paused and fixed her father's eyes with hers, 'Can I say that Father?'

He didn't respond directly to her question. They both sat with their own thoughts. Then he said, 'What if it is she who is not receptive and does not agree? What if she wants to reclaim Marguerite for her own and take her back to France?'

'I'm fairly sure that she doesn't want that. She knows such a course of action is not in the best interests of her own daughter. She is not interested in authority or custody, she simply wants to have more involvement in her daughter's life. She knows what you have done for Marguerite is good but she cannot stay out of her own daughter's life for another eleven years.'

'Roisin, how do you know this?'

'I have been writing to Antoinette over the last ten years mainly to give her news on Marguerite. We don't write frequently, but we do write regularly perhaps twice a year. She is not perfect Father but she is a good woman and she loves little Marguerite. I'm sure that she only wants what is best for her.' Then, undeterred, the young lawyer pressed her father again, 'Can I tell Antoinette that you have the same interest also and that you are receptive to the meeting?'

'When will you arrange this meeting?'

Roisin placed her hand over her father's, 'I will not arrange it at all unless you give me your assurance that you are receptive to it taking place in the first instance and also a further assurance that you will treat Antoinette as your granddaughter's mother and not as if she is some hired governess who you are just about to dismiss with a week's money.'

'Very well, you have my assurances in both areas.'

'Then I will write to Antoinette next week. There is one more thing Father that I feel that you should consider, if you wish you can look upon this as free advice from a lawyer, something that we do not dispense readily. I think that when you meet Antoinette that you should bear this in mind.'

'What is this consideration?'

'Although I have said that Antoinette's wishes are to the contrary, if she did wish, as you say, to claim Marguerite for herself and take her back to France, then her case would not be as it was ten years ago when we were in the middle of the chaos of a world war, women were seen as very much subservient to men and Antoinette was an unmarried young girl with no means of support. Her case would be as strong now as it was weak then.'

'Roisin, why do you tell me this if not to depress me?'

'I tell you this father because I know you and I know Antoinette and you are both of a type. I tell you this so that you at least will try and ensure that the discussion remains about Marguerite the child and does not become about the adults.' She stood up, 'Please excuse me father.'

As Roisin stood up and excused herself Dermot stood up also. She left the table and Dermot called the waiter over and ordered another bottle of the same wine.

After ten minutes or so Roisin returned and again took up her seat. Almost immediately she said, 'Father, I've decided to stay on in Manchester a little longer.'

'How little longer?'

'I've become involved in the political scene here. What's going on in Manchester is so exciting, particularly for women, and I've been offered a candidacy to stand at the next election. I am to become a councillor.'

'Don't councillors have to serve a fixed term of office?'

'Yes, four years.'

'Then we won't be expecting you back in Wexford in the near future.'

'At the moment father, my life is established here in Manchester. There is too much going on for me here at the moment.'

Dermot paused for a moment, he thought that perhaps Roisin had met somebody in Manchester, a man perhaps, a future husband perhaps. It was not good that he was losing his daughter in the first place, and to Manchester of all places, but if there was a husband on the scene then perhaps that was a little bit different, 'Is there somebody special in your life at the moment Roisin?' As he said this he smiled in optimism.

'No father, there is nobody special and I haven't found anybody yet that remotely resembles a husband.'

'Roisin, a woman of your age should have a husband and some children, you are still a young woman.'

'Father, how old are you?'

'You know the answer to your own question, I am fifty-seven.'

'Why have you remained a widower so long? You are still a young man father, by any standards, perhaps you should consider taking a wife yourself and starting another family?'

'Roisin, you and little Marguerite are all the family that I need. Anyway, I understand your response so let's change the subject completely shall we? Let's talk about something that has absolutely nothing to do with our family or your politics.'

He smiled rather foolishly she thought, perhaps it was more of a grin. She could see that the wine was having its effect upon him and she welcomed this change. 'Certainly father, and as you ask do you know a man named Jeremy Weedon, Professor Jeremy Weedon?'

'Weedon, no I don't recall but I meet so many people and I forget the names of at least half of them. That's what I love about Wexford, I know everybody there by name, I know them and they know me.'

Roisin thought that that was exactly what she didn't love about Wexford, but she went on to say, 'He says he met you in 1925 in London.'

'Well he's wrong there, at least about the place anyway, I have not been to London since the end of the war. Apart from a couple of specific appointments that I just couldn't find a way of getting out of and they weren't in London itself, I was just picking up a train connection. June 1919 was the last time I was in London, I remember it clearly because it was the same week that they signed the Treaty of Versailles. I just can't face London anymore, all that rushing around at twice the normal speed and all that boasting, it isn't to my liking at all. Whenever there is anything going on there I always make sure that the bank is well represented as long as it is by somebody else. I usually manage to send young Conlon, he is very able and he loves the place. He tells everybody about it for about three months before he's due to go and then for three months after he comes back. He drives everybody mad, all you hear is London, London, London. Even having to listen to Conlon for ever is still much better than having to go myself.'

'I just thought that I'd ask about him.'

'Who is this Jeremy Weedon anyway? How old is he, what does he do, what does he look like?'

'Oh he's just a client, he's nobody special.'

'Now that you are away from the sanctuary of Wexford and the protection of your family you need to be on your guard, alert at all times.'

'Oh I knew that I shouldn't have mentioned him at all. This is your peasant's decree curse again isn't it?'

'You shouldn't be so dismissive of it, it killed your grandfather, he just became a different person overnight. One day he was full of life the next day he was all hollowed out inside and that's the way he stayed, in less than twelve months he was dead.'

'Yes, but he died from the after effects of the killings, most of which was in his own mind and surely you don't believe in some silly old Irish curse that was made hundreds of years ago. No wonder the English sometimes laugh at the Irish when we still believe in such things.'

'Roisin, it wasn't hundreds of years ago. It was less than fifty, forty-four to be precise. I was there at the time, I was little more than Marguerite's age myself but I remember it, the misery and the anguish, as if it was yesterday.'

'Father, as you say it was fifty years ago and it was some madman, it was nothing to do with any curse, that was just some kind of coincidence. Anybody that was around fifty years ago and was capable of the things that you have suggested will by now either be extremely old or dead themselves. Just to put your mind at rest Weedon is barely a few years older than myself and wasn't even born then. As well as this I am a solicitor in a major city in England. I have dozens of clients at any one time and every other one of them is odd in some way. These are the times that we live in. This is not Wexford where nothing ever changes for centuries, this is Manchester where everything changes every year. The people here are unusual.'

'Roisin, I am sure that some of what you say is true but I am equally sure that some of it isn't. The person that murdered Siobhan and Clodagh is probably long dead by now, I agree with that. All that I say is that you are my only daughter. I will not be having another one now and if there is any substance to the Peasants Decree then we must be vigilant, we must be aware that our weakness in this is when we drop our guard and become complacent, that is when we are at our most vulnerable. If this Man of Insignificance is out there then we must be aware. To dismiss the whole business as silly undermines our vigilance, increases our vulnerability and strengthens his purpose, so be aware Roisin, *please* be aware of all this and take the necessary precautions, promise me this Roisin.'

'I am Father and I already have.'

Chapter 20

The Missing Letters

'Dom dom dom dom dom
Dom be dooby
Dom dom dom dom dom
Dom be dooby dom
Whoa whoa whoa whoa...'

This music, senseless to some, yet a melodic and harmonious tune to others, eased itself out of the car speaker system that was contained within the doors of the old burgundy-coloured Mercedes that stood parked in bay number twenty-four in the private residents car park of the very elegant and obviously expensive apartment block in Woodhall, Norford. Just like any juvenescent, 1950's boy racer listening to his rebellious tunes, the driver turned the volume up two notches. At that exact moment the high tenor lead came in with the first verse of a simplistic yet understandable, magnificent, sonorously-delivered lyric:

'Love, love me darlin'
Come and go with me
Please don't send me
Way beyond the sea
Love, love me darlin'
Come and go with me...'

Senetti pondered: he had always loved Doo Wop music. Not the contrived, master-mix stuff that sadly it had evolved into these days, but the real wizz from the 1950's and 60's. He wasn't sure why he was such a fan, it certainly wasn't the music that was contemporaneous to him, it had been born, breathed, lived, died, buried and been resurrected before he had even been born. He couldn't quite remember when he had first heard it, he wasn't sure so he settled on the self-suggestion that it was probably from the old 45 rpm record collection that his mother used to have when he was growing up. He wondered whether or not she still had the collection and decided that she probably did.

She had often played her record collection at the weekend when he was a schoolboy growing up in the late 70's and early 80's. She had a cream and red leatherette Dansette record player that used to stack twelve 45's at a time and it always seemed to be on when he was trying to do his homework, on either a Saturday morning or a Sunday evening, when his dad was at work or in the pub. The music would filter through from his mother's tiny living room, up the narrow staircase and fill his even tinier bedroom with all these Doo Wop tunes. He wasn't quite sure why it was called *Doo Wop*. He'd heard and read about two or three suggestions as to the origin of the name but he didn't really believe any of them and in the vernacular he thought that it was all *jive*. He didn't really care as he thought that Doo Wop was a great name anyway. He knew all the bands, all the members of the bands and all of their songs. He even knew some of the writers and even some of the musical arrangers.

He thought that if he ever found himself on one of those television quiz shows where you had to answer questions on a *specialist subject* then Doo Wop music would be the one that he would choose. The bands all had fantastic names: *The Marcels, The Flamingoes, The Cadillacs, Frankie Lymon and the Teenagers, Dion and the Belmonts* and his own particular favourites, *The Dell Vikings* and *Johnny Maestro and The Brooklyn Bridge.* There were many of them and he loved the whole genre, he had every Doo Wop track that was anything and when he was in his car and he wasn't listening to the news on Radio Four then he was listening to Doo Wop music.

He sat back in his seat, put his head on the headrest, closed his eyes and mouthed the singer's words in unison and in silence.

He stayed in this position for a full thirty seconds then his thoughts were penetrated by a sharp rapping on his window. He opened his eyes and turned sideways, as he did he looked through the glass and into the eyes of Dr Maxine Wells, her face only inches away from his on the other side. She was laughing freely. He pressed the switch in his car door armrest and the window fell into the door gracefully, to Maxine the music now seemed to play even louder, she swayed from side to side in both rhythm and gentle mockery. She gestured to Danny and in what seemed a reluctant move he switched the music off, the private car park immediately became silent.

'What was that you were listening to?'

'That Maxine, is called Doo Wop music, and that was the Dell Vikings.'

'I've never heard of it or them,' she said.

'Well you will have soon, because I'm taking this disc into Archie's.'

'Did you get the keys?'

He raised the window and got out of the car, pressed the key fob and turned to face her, 'Yes, they were in my outside mailbox when I got up this morning, Charlotte must have dropped them off early on her way to work.'

'You mean that you haven't spoken to her?'

'I spoke to her over the telephone when I originally asked her for them. She asked me what I wanted them for. I said that it was connected with something that Archie asked me to do for him when we spoke at the council meeting the night of the accident.'

'Did she believe you?'

'Course she believed me, there's nothing to disbelieve, it's completely true. Neither you nor I would be here now if it wasn't for Archie stopping me at the council meeting and asking me about Helen Day.'

'It's bending the truth a little though isn't it?'

'Maxine, I don't understand you sometimes, we are investigating a murder here, we are not trying to make our first holy communion. Perhaps you've forgotten but originally this was your idea, you have remembered that haven't you? The more I think about it, it is a good idea. We are not doing anything wrong, we've got complete permission and authority. We're just going to go in and have a good look around. We'll leave the place exactly as we found it and we won't deliberately break anything. Charlotte gave them to me without any question or argument. I must admit I was a little surprised myself, but there it is. So, are we going into Archie's or are we going home?'

'How is Archie, has anything changed?'

'No, nothing really, no change at all. Charlotte said that all the doctors keep saying is that we will just have to be patient. Oh I don't know really, it's a difficult time.'

Maxine thought that Danny looked strained at the mention of Archie, she sensed that he felt for his ex-wife and his ex-father-in-law.

Danny then brandished a small bunch of keys in his left hand. As if in silent agreement they both walked around to the front of the building. Danny selected what he guessed was the front door key, which it actually turned out to be, and he opened the door. Maxine and Danny stepped through the door and found themselves inside the lobby, they looked at the information board on the wall which displayed rows of numbers from one to thirty-two.

Danny said, 'Archie's flat is number twenty-four, it is on the second floor. Lift or stairs?'

'Stairs,' said Maxine, 'better for the heart.'

'Archie would have used the lift, let's stay in the persona,' said Danny.

'I don't know Danny, why do you ask me about my preferences and then overrule them? Why didn't you just say we'll take the lift?'

Maxine pressed the button that called the lift. As the doors opened they stepped in and a few moments later they stepped out on the second floor. They walked in single file down a short, narrow corridor and stopped outside the door, twenty-four.

'You do the door, I'll do the alarm.'

As Maxine opened the door the electronic alarm leapt into beep mode, Danny stepped forward and deactivated it. Maxine shut the door behind them and they both stepped into the silent apartment. It was a modestly sized apartment, modestly furnished, in fact, everything about it seemed modest, which seemed a little contradictory for the neighbourhood. Danny had been here once before just before Archie had moved in but he'd since forgotten about his visit.

'I'll do the bedroom,' said Maxine, 'you do the lounge. You'll have to look through all those pages in those books. Remember to put them back in the same order that you found them in.'

They both set about their separate tasks conscientiously. As Maxine looked around the bedroom she heard another one of Danny's Doo Wop tunes filter through to the study. Obviously he'd found Archie's music system and was playing his disc as promised although he had the volume turned down. As one track ended Senetti announced aloud the name of the band that was about to commence the next track, he announced them all, *Vito and the Salutations*, *The Flamingos* and *The Skylines* were just three of them. Maxine thought that this was a bit school-boyish and she didn't know any of them, nor did she remember their names after his announcements. Nevertheless, she half listened to about seven or eight different three-minute songs with a good heart as she looked through Archie's bedroom. Then, after about thirty minutes she popped her head around the door that separated the living room from the study, the CD carried on playing softly.

'*Frankie Lymon and the Teenagers*,' said Senetti.

Ignoring his musical identification she said, 'Well, I've searched in every place that I can think of in here. I'll try the other bedroom.'

Danny continued removing books from the bookcase that ran completely along one wall. By the look on his face he was experiencing the same outcome as Maxine.

There were two bedrooms in the apartment. It was obvious that one of them was being used as a bedroom whilst the smaller one was being used as a study. Inside the smaller room there was a single bed and the rest of the furniture was made up of a desk, a chair and a large safe that sat on the floor in the corner. Maxine could see that the safe had a large silver dial with numbers around it. On the desk a computer sat idly, Maxine pressed a button and it came to life, the screen glared at her in computer-style defiance, demanding a password that she didn't know. She called through to Danny who came into the room.

'I don't suppose that you know the password to the computer or the number to the safe?' she asked.

'No I don't, I can think of things that it might be, but then again it might not, you know, grandkid's names, dates of birth and that but we could be here all day and as well as that, I'm not sure that I want to look at his computer nor inside his safe, I think that they are probably a little too private and I might see things that I don't really want to see.'

'No, I think that you're right, there is probably nothing in either of them anyway.'

Maxine watched as Danny looked around the room. It seemed to her as if he was searching for something in particular, 'Did you think of something?' she asked.

'It's just that when I had the conversation with Archie at the town hall, on the night he was involved in his accident, he said that he'd been reading about Helen's murder in the newspapers. I distinctly got the impression from what he said that he had been doing that reading immediately prior to the council meeting a few hours earlier. Obviously he didn't come home, he went straight to the hospital after he was run over so where are the newspapers he was talking about?'

'All the bins and baskets are empty and everything in here has been cleaned very recently. So Denise has probably been coming in whilst he's been in hospital and she's probably thrown them away. Do you think that they are important?'

'They are not important in themselves and you're right he does have a cleaner, she's probably has thrown them out. Who keeps old newspapers, how did you know that she was called Denise?'

'I don't know,' she said.

Just then Maxine remembered that she'd seen a small stack of newspapers in the first bedroom with a hand written post-it note on top of the stack, it read, 'Denise, don't throw these away.' She returned to the kitchen and retrieved the newspapers, placed them on the dining room table and began to go through them.

Danny asked, 'have you found something?'

'It's the newspapers that you were talking about, I've seen the articles before. It's just the same report in all of them, about the murder. They are all saying more or less the same thing, it's just syndicated journalism.'

Maxine flipped through them. As she came to one edition, a local one and one that she'd read several times before, she noticed that somebody had written something in purple ink in the white space at the top of the page above the headline – *Ritualistic Murder*. It was obviously scribble, a doodle and the type of note that you make when you are thinking of the subject but it could be read quite clearly. It said:

'Helen Day – Kathleen Helen??? MO.'

'Danny, is this Archie's writing, do you recognise it?'

'I've never had to recognise anybody's writing in my whole life, now all at once, I am being asked to recognise everybody's.'

'Is it Archie's?' she repeated.

'Yes, I'd say so.'

Maxine opened her bag and produced the four photographs that she'd taken at the original crime scene. She carried them around with her all the time now and studied them periodically but she was still no nearer to understanding the mystery of the scroll's missing letters. She placed the photograph of the Virgin Mary on the table, it illustrated the partially erased scroll on the base, then she placed Archie's scribbled newspaper next to it. She studied them, first the photograph, then Archie's scribble on the newspaper. After this she produced a scrap of paper and a pen from her bag. Danny looked over her shoulder and watched her in silence, not quite sure what she was trying to do.

On the scrap of paper she reproduced by hand the inscription from the photograph exactly as it was written on the scroll. When she had done this she sat back and studied it for a while, it read:

To a l n e en fr th S ers Oct 196

Maxine beckoned Danny to sit down beside her which he did. She said, 'You know when you're doing one of those crossword questions, where you have half the letters but you can't find the rest of them because you don't fully understand the clue?'

'I know what you mean, the question is, can we solve it?'

'I think we can.'

'How?'

'If we consider the letters to be an inscription on a memento that was given to somebody, we already know that the first word is *to* so we ask ourselves, who exactly is this being given to?'

She looked across at Danny and his silence seemed to acknowledge his understanding.

'Take the word after *to* and for the sake of the argument assume it is the name of a person. We have a blank and then the letter *a,* so let's assume the letter before it is a capital letter and it isn't a vowel. So, running through the word we have capital letter, then letter *a*, then blank, blank, letter, followed by blank, blank then letter *n*.'

Danny remained quiet whilst she carried on with her hypothesis.

'That is a lot of letters and it would normally be enough letters for one name.'

Then Maxine placed the scrap of paper she'd written on earlier on top of the newspaper immediately under Archie's scribble.

'Kathleen Helen,' said Danny triumphantly.

'Of course,' said Maxine, 'the scroll when it was originally written said, *To Kathleen Helen.*'

'When was it originally written?'

'I'm coming to that, just be patient. Let's be progressively conclusive here and not jump to the conclusions, if there are any.'

'Alright Doctor, carry on.'

'Archie was trying to see if there was a connection between Kathleen Helen, whoever she is, and Helen Day, that's why I think he scrawled this on the newspaper.'

'It sounds sensible to me, even progressively conclusive.'

'I think that we can even go on a little further than that, I think that he was asking himself whether Kathleen Helen, whosoever she was or is, and Helen Day were one and the same person.'

'I think you could be right again Maxine, in fact I think that you are, what about the rest of the inscription, any ideas?'

'Yes I have, the letters *Oct* are obviously representing the month of October and the numbers, I think that they refer to a year in the nineteen-sixties, nineteen sixty-two to be precise.'

'Why do you say that, why not sixty-five or sixty-six, we've got ten to choose from?'

'Alright, Danny let's think about this. Why would you receive a statue with a date on?'

'As a gift.'

'Yeah, what sort of gift?'

'Possibly a leaving gift.'

'That's what I thought, you're given these sort of things when you leave somewhere. It's a going away present and you don't usually get a going away present unless you've been somewhere long enough to qualify for one.'

She lapsed back into concentration for a moment and Danny picked up the photograph from the table.

Danny spoke, 'If all of us are right, and that includes Archie's guessing games, about Kathleen Helen and Helen Day being one and the same, and if you're correct about it being nineteen sixty-two, we already know Helen's age was seventy when she died, that would make this young woman eighteen in nineteen sixty-two.'

'That's precisely why I think it was that year because she was eighteen, and eighteen was one of three land mark ages in those days, the other two were twenty-one and sixty-five.'

'*Sisters!*' Danny exclaimed, 'that's what the last word on the scroll says, *Sisters!*'

'You're right again,' said Maxine. 'So filling in all the blanks the complete scroll reads, *To Kathleen Helen from The Sisters, October 1962.*'

'Where would you find sisters, in a hospital, in your family? No, *they* wouldn't give you a going away present. So, where else would you find sisters? A convent! A convent, that's where, that's where the statuette comes from, it's so obvious now, she left the convent at eighteen and the sisters gave her this statuette as a souvenir.'

'I think souvenir is the wrong word here Danny, but yes you're right.'

'Now that we've worked this out it opens up a new set of questions.'

'You mean such as how long was she in the convent, which convent was it and the big question, why was she in there in the first place?'

'I know that you'll say that this is nothing more than pure speculation on my part Maxine, but I am fairly sure that we will find that convent in Ireland. I can even be more specific than that, I think that we'll find the convent in County Mayo. I always thought that Helen had a slight trace of a Mayo accent and where Archie has written *MO* on the newspaper, that's a well-known abbreviation for Mayo, they even have it on the car registration plates over there.'

'As we're speculating then Danny, why was she in the convent in the first place?'

'I don't know, but let's say that she wasn't a nun and that she'd been in there for quite some time, and as she was only eighteen when she left, then let's say she was there because of something that somebody else had done.'

'I'm not quite sure I follow you on that one.'

'What I mean Maxine, is that she was too young to put herself in the convent – so somebody else did it for her.'

'Maybe she was an orphan and she had no family.'

'Maybe you're right but there must be other reasons why people go into convents other than they are orphans or they want to be nuns.'

'I suppose there's lots of reasons why people do things, particularly to other people and particularly to children who often have no say in the matter and can't offer any resistance or any argument simply because they are children. Children just don't have a voice, even now and they would have had even less of one in nineteen sixty-two and that's the year that Kathleen Helen *came out*. We don't know yet when she went in. In fact, I have a friend that was brought up in a convent and she wasn't an orphan, she had both a mother and a father. It's just that neither of them were able to look after her and of course there was the other reason.'

'What became of your friend and what exactly was the other reason, did she ever tell you?'

'She became a doctor and yes in fact she did tell me, it was all rather sad.'

'Well come on Maxine, what was it? tell me.'

'She said that they put her in a convent because it was the only place that they could safely hide her away.'

'Who were they hiding her away from?'

'I don't think that she knows the answer to that even now after all these years, probably themselves.'

'Perhaps that's what happened to Kathleen Helen in her early years, she was hidden away. It certainly happened to the Helen Day that I knew as that's all she seemed to do, hide from everybody. So Kathleen Helen started her life in hiding and then she turned into Helen Day who ended hers the same way. The question here is, what exactly was all that hiding for, all those years apart?'

'There are a thousand reasons why you hide Danny and nine hundred and ninety-nine of them are because you're afraid.'

'That's probably a very good point you make Maxine.'

'Right, that's enough philosophy for now, what is our next move then?'

'I think that we've put it off long enough. There's no doubt about it, at least one of us will have to go to County Mayo. Find the convent and you find the real Kathleen Helen, find Kathleen Helen and you find Helen Day, find Helen Day and then, and only then, do you have a chance of finding the murderer.'

Maxine said, 'there are now two things that I think we've more or less established today.'

'What are they?'

'That one way or another, Archie Hamilton knows a lot more about this than any of us.'

'That's one thing.'

'The second is that this hit and run of his, now that we know all that we do know, is a bit too much of a coincidence to be an accident.'

'What, you think that somebody has tried to kill him by deliberately running him down?'

'I think it's a very strong possibility Danny.'

'Do you think it's the same person that murdered Helen?'

'I think that's a strong possibility too.'

'Why would somebody want to kill Helen and Archie?'

'Maybe there is some kind of connection between the two of them.'

'If there is, then that connection is to be found in Mayo, I'm convinced of it.'

Chapter 21

The Enquiry Agent

When you are six foot five, when you touch the weighing scales at around nineteen stones and when you take size 13 shoes then it is never going to be an easy task to do anything with discretion and to remain unnoticed.

Nevertheless, growing up in Manchester, as the son of a Manchester policeman, then spending fourteen years as a Manchester policeman himself, ten of those fourteen years as a detective, and then after that a further five years as a private enquiry agent, had taught Stanley Oldknow a *few tricks*. With these credentials, and his native Mancunian background and connections, there was very little that he didn't know about that city and its inhabitants and very little that he couldn't find out about its visitors.

This was now his fourth day on the Professor Weedon case. He had been retained by the female Manchester solicitor who had summoned him to her office by sending Ivy Beck around to his. In covert opposition to many in Manchester's legal circles, and also against many of the city's senior police officers, Stanley actually supported and even respected the female solicitor. He would go further than that, for if she was a typical example of female solicitors then he wished, secretly of course, that there were more of them. Indeed, he knew that given time there would be. He had worked for her before and found her to be a respectful and intelligent client. Furthermore, she paid him without quibble, in full and on time, which was more than could be said for many of her male counterparts.

When he attended her office that Tuesday morning she had told him that she was just taking some precautions, but that she had become suspicious of a man calling himself Professor Jeremy Weedon. She had raised several points with Stanley, mainly about the Professor's conduct during her recent interview with him. Stanley had written them down in his notebook. He wrote everything down in his notebook. Stanley had listened quietly to what she had to say. He had asked Roisin a few questions but as he left the building he spoke to Ivy Beck at length. Amongst other things, he asked Ivy for a physical description of the Professor. He did a lot of work for solicitors and he had learnt from experience that they could be very perceptive people who could often tell you most things about people they'd interviewed. They could tell you about their client's wealth, education, culture, intelligence, honesty and much more but they couldn't always tell you the colour of their clients' hair or their eyes, even when they had been sat four feet across from them and in the same room for two hours. So, if you needed a reliable, detailed physical description of a person then never ask the solicitor, always ask the secretary. Ivy didn't disappoint him, even down to the Professors fancy, tan Oxford brogue shoes. Stanley also asked for a lot of detail about the Professor's facial features and he wrote down every miniscule item.

After his interview with Roisin, Stanley had spent the next two days trying to find out about the Professor. During his enquiries Stanley had discovered that virtually everything that the Professor had imparted to Stanley's client was bogus. The address the Professor had given was valid but he didn't live there, somebody else did. His name was bogus too, nobody had ever heard of a Professor Jeremy Weedon or his *fictitious family*, Stanley had checked everywhere. By the time Friday morning came around Stanley Oldknow was satisfied that Professor Jeremy Weedon was an alias and that this man, whosoever he was and for whatever his reasons, was an imposter of some kind.

Roisin had told Stanley about the Professor's insistence that they meet on a Saturday. She had also told him about her forthcoming appointment with the Professor a week next Saturday. On the Friday morning of the week before the Saturday appointment, Stanley had an idea of his own. As he sat having breakfast he reasoned that as the Professor was meeting Roisin in just over a week that he may have already stayed in Manchester, in fact he might be still here. He decided to call around some of the city centre hotels and enquire about anybody answering the description he'd taken from Ivy.

Before he set off on his round of the hotels, Stanley had a little task to perform, which he often used to great advantage when identifying or tracking down suspects and he decided to employ it. Opening his notebook he read back on his notes from his discussion with Ivy. He studied them intently then, placing the notebook on the table, he closed his eyes and sat perfectly still for a full five minutes in concentration. From a wooden box resting on his breakfast table he withdrew a piece of white card, a set of pencils and an India rubber. Using these implements he worked away sketching, pausing, erasing and studying for a further fifteen minutes. The end result of his artistry was, he hoped, a very accomplished sketch of his quarry, which he had drawn completely from Ivy Beck's descriptive powers.

From the descriptions that Stanley had received about the Professor, Stanley didn't think that he would be staying in a doss house or a hostel. So, armed with the sketch he set off to visit the better hotels around Manchester city centre. Even without the doss houses and hostels, there were eighteen such hotels, he knew this from his own knowledge, from the regal Midland Hotel to the no nonsense Piccadilly Lodge. His visits to the first five hotels produced nothing. None of Stanley's contacts had seen anybody that resembled the drawing that Stanley showed them but just about a third of the way through his mental list and on entering his sixth hotel of the day at about 2:00pm the enquiry agent struck lucky.

Stanley knew the porter of the Queen's Hotel from his days with the police. He was a wiry little Liverpudlian named Jackie Black and he'd been the porter there for many years. In his younger day Jackie had been a Marquess of Queensbury rules flyweight boxing champion. He was an example of what was often described in police circles as an *honest rascal*. If there was anything going on in the hotel trade in Manchester then Jackie

Black knew about it. In fact, Stanley thought that Jackie must be near retirement age by now and he said so, 'Jackie, I thought that you would have dug up all those hefty tips that you've been stashin' away for years and retired by now.'

'Mr Oldknow, are you still hacking about? Bleedin 'ell, somebody said to me the other day that the police seem to be getting younger these days. If that's the case then why are all the coppers I know all bleedin codgers.'

'Jackie, I've not yet reached my fortieth birthday.'

'Perhaps I'm getting you mixed up with your old feller, god bless him.'

They shook hands and laughed together. Stanley produced the sketch from his inside pocket, 'I am on a case Jackie, have you seen this man recently?'

'Did you draw that Mr Oldknow? It's the image of him.'

'You know him then, has he been here?'

'He's been here all week.'

'What, you mean he's here now?'

'Room 117.'

'You sure it's him?'

'Either it's him or his identical twin.'

'Who is he, what's his name?'

Jackie lowered his voice and moved closer to Stanley, 'He goes under the name of Jonas Watt, Major Jonas Watt, but it's an alias.'

'How do you know that?'

'When you've been doing this job as long as I have you get to know and understand things about people. You could listen to someone for half a minute and you can tell things about them just by doing that.'

'What, and you've got to know and understand that his name isn't Jonas Watt?'

'No, not that, that's not what I mean Mr Oldknow. I don't know what his name is, it could be bleedin' Gene Tunney for all I know but what I do know is that he's never been a major, in fact he's never done a day in the bleedin' army in his life.'

'I'll take your word for it.'

'You can, believe me, and if he's assumed the bleedin' rank, he's assumed the bleedin' name.'

'You should have been a copper Jackie.'

'I was considering it at one time but they wouldn't consider me, especially at five feet bleedin three.'

'What else do you know about him?'

'I know that he's never been married and he's got no family. Probably brought up by his dad. There's been no women around his life. Loner, he's got it stamped all over him. They're a breed on their own. It's a combination of things, it takes years to learn, but once you have they're easy to spot.'

'Do you know anything else about him?'

'Such as what Mr Oldknow?'

'Such as where he's from and what he is doing here?'

'Well, he's got a posh voice but his accent, only slightly traceable mind you, to the discerning ear of course, says that originally he's from London. As for what his business is I don't know. You could talk to men like him all day and he wouldn't tell you. He's trained his mind and his conversation so he could say a lot and at the same time tell you nothing. I could get one of the girls to poke around in his room when he's out, he goes out a lot. Whatever he's up to, it's a serious business.'

'Why do you say that, because he's carrying a false name?'

'No Mr Oldknow, the name in itself is neither here nor there. There's lots of people come here under false names, usually for reasons to do with other people wives or husbands. The week before the war ended we were full every night and I swear every bleedin' one of 'em was called Smith. It was all the soldiers' wives and their spiv boyfriends having a last fling before their husbands got demob. We didn't make a fuss, discretion is our middle name. No, we don't concern ourselves with names at the Queen's.'

'Then what is it Jackie about the Major?'

'He's a troubled man, as if he's being eaten up inside by something he's done or by something he's got to do. As I said, its serious business he's on. He reminds me of one of those Italian agents whose about to carry out some kind of vendetta crime.'

'Jackie, what do you know about Italian agents and vendetta crimes?'

'You'd be surprised what Jackie knows Mr Oldknow.'

'Alright Jackie, get one of your girls to poke about in his room but do it discreetly. I don't want him to have an inkling that he's suspected of anything. You know where to find me if you discover anything. Remember, anything, any scrap of any kind. Nothing is irrelevant, nothing is trivial.'

'Alright Mr Oldknow. One more thing, a couple of hours ago he asked me to get him a cab, said he was going on a short journey across town then he had second thoughts, said that he'd changed his mind about the taxi and that he'd walk.'

'What time did he originally ask for the cab?'

'Five o'clock precise.'

'Stanley took a wad of paper money out of his pocket, he peeled three bills off and gave them to Jackie who quickly put them into his own trouser pocket.'

Stanley said, 'Jackie, forget I'm here, forget that you've seen me. I'm going to sit down in your lobby and read the newspaper for an hour or two. Do you think that I could have some tea and a few of those fancy biscuits that you do here? Not too many mind.'

Jackie marched off and Stanley sat down by the revolving door, he picked up one of the newspapers that were arranged neatly on the table in front of him and quietly awaited the appearance of his afternoon tea.

Approximately two hours later Stanley Oldknow was still sat there as he saw the Professor, or indeed the Major, come down the sweeping staircase, go out through the revolving doors and head off purposely across the city. Stanley mentally congratulated himself on the accuracy of the sketch that he'd drawn. As he did so he quietly moved through the revolving doors himself and followed the Professor on foot and about ten paces behind, through the Friday evening crowds.

After about ten minutes Stanley realised that he knew exactly where the Professor was heading so he dropped back a little. The Professor walked for about half a mile then he entered the Blackbird café, which was adjacent to a cab rank and opposite the

Royal Swan Buildings where Roisin de Hay's office was located. He sat in a chair by the café window. Stanley remained outside on the other side of the road, he could clearly see the Professor as he looked into the brightly lit café from the dark street outside. Stanley loitered on the corner and then drew himself a couple of pinches of snuff. After a few minutes he saw the female solicitor herself come out of the front door of the building and step into a waiting cab. As she did this the Professor came out of the cafe and stepped into a second cab. Stanley hurriedly stepped into a third taxi and the three cabs moved off as if in cavalcade.

After a short journey across the centre of Manchester the leading taxi stopped outside the Midland Hotel as did cabs number two and three. Roisin got out of the first cab and as she did she was met by one of the hotel porters. Stanley recognised him as a man called Ambrose Hughes. As Roisin de Hay walked through the door of the Midland Hotel the Professor's cab moved off with the Professor still inside. Stanley paid his fare and stepped from the cab into the street, he had seen enough for the time being.

Stanley was now convinced of two things. Firstly, he was convinced that the Professor was not in the least bit interested in settling legal matters of any kind. His objective in seeking out the female solicitor was nothing to do with these. His objective was actually the female solicitor herself and Stanley instinctively knew that the Professor intended to place her in harm's way. Secondly, he was also convinced that the Professor would take no further action of any kind until the appointed time next Saturday.

Stanley walked through the city towards his own lodgings, he planned to have a few drinks in the Lord Abercrombie with some old police colleagues before he reached his destination. As he walked through the Friday evening Manchester swirl of people and traffic the enquiry agent felt confident that he blended into the crowd and remained unnoticed. In some other occupations this would have been a symbol of failure but to the enquiry agent it was the exact opposite of this. It was also a remarkable achievement for a man of six feet five, who touched the weighing scales at around nineteen stones and who took size thirteen shoes.

Chapter 22

Three Options

Stanley had kept himself informed in relation to the Professor. On the Tuesday morning following the Friday night's taxi cavalcade he had visited Roisin de Hay and reported the results of his enquiries to his client. He informed her of all the detail and was careful to leave nothing out. In summary, Stanley advised Roisin that the Professor was an imposter and although he didn't know why or in what way, his professional opinion was that the Professor intended harm to her. He added that the Professor's story about the will and settling his affairs was an old tactic, was made up and was really a diversion. The real purpose of that tale was to secure a situation whereby the potential perpetrator was alone with his potential victim with little chance of anybody else being around to witness whatever it was he was going to attempt to do or say, hence the Professor's insistence on the meeting being at her office and it being on a Saturday.

Roisin said, 'Well, I'm not sure that I'll get any enjoyment out of being called a *victim*. Putting that aside for the moment, suppose you are right Mr Oldknow and I have respect for your professional judgement, so I'll say that you are. What would your advice be, what shall I do about the situation?'

'The way I see it Miss de Hay, we probably have three options.'

'I would be interested to know what those options are.'

'Well the most obvious one is that you could call the police in.'

'I could do this quite easily. When I call them in though what will I say to them? Will I say that a new client of mine has an appointment this weekend, and although I have only met him once, and that being for less than an hour, and I have no evidence to support this, I believe him to be an imposter and I also believe that he means to do me harm, although I have not the slightest idea why, in what way or how he is going to achieve this?'

Stanley said, 'as far as the Professor is concerned it is the most immediate and safest option. If the police were to station an officer outside the building on Saturday then the Professor would probably not even keep the appointment and would indubitably and hastily leave town.'

Roisin became thoughtful, 'Can you tell me Mr Oldknow, is there any law against calling yourself a professor when you are probably not one, or against calling yourself a major when you are probably not one? Or for that matter calling yourself whatever you have the inclination to call yourself? What if we are wrong about Weedon or whatever his name is? What if he is just a harmless fantasist who does nothing more than go around pretending that he is somebody else? I have heard of such people, I expect that in your line of work you meet them regularly. You do accept Mr Oldknow that we could be wrong?'

Stanley took a pinch of snuff, 'I don't believe Miss de Hay, that there are any laws against the situations that you mention, at least not any that the police would be interested in enforcing. I once knew a man who used to seriously claim that he was the king of Mesopotamia. We all knew that his real name was Ebenezer Snodgrass but we still called him *Your Royal Highness*. He was, as you say, a harmless fantasist who never did anybody any harm. You are right, you can call yourself anything you wish. You are also right, we can always be wrong Ma'am, that possibility can never be discarded. A lot of my work is assumption and second guess so there will always be possibility of mistake. So yes, I have to say that we *could* be wrong.'

'You don't know how pleased I am that you've just said that Mr Oldknow.'

'I have to say though that I don't believe on this occasion that we are, *wrong* that is.'

'No, I can see that you don't.'

'I would also want you to know that I fully understand your position, your wider, professional position that is, if you'll forgive me for saying so, perhaps a little more than you realise Miss de Hay. I have given consideration to it and I understand that it is precarious.'

'Please explain your meaning Mr Oldknow.'

'If I can be forward ma'am this is how I read it.'

He paused and she could see that he felt a little awkward.

'Please be as forward as you wish Mr Oldknow, there could be much at risk here and we will achieve nothing by observing etiquette and excluding candour.'

The enquiry agent began, 'You are a solicitor and you are a woman, it is a new combination and many do not want such a mix. These critics are, of course, almost exclusively men, but they are there and they are in the established positions of power and authority. I work amongst them all the time and I have heard what some of them say. They say and they believe that you should not be here at all. If we are completely wrong about Weedon then they would relish the opportunity to paint you as the neurotic *female* solicitor who has no discernment and who treats the confidentiality of her client's business with disrespect. They would say reporting your own client to the police indeed! They would take this opportunity, there is no mistake to be made about that. They would say, they say it now but this time they would have reason to say it, that you have no credentials to be in Manchester let alone in the legal profession. Your professional reputation and any other reputation would be in tarnish if not in tatters overnight. All this for no other reason than you are a woman in what they see as being exclusively, a man's profession.'

Roisin could hardly believe her ears, never before had she witnessed such an intelligent sensitive rendition on an issue of gender from a man, any man let alone a man of such rugged appearance and seedy occupation as Stanley Oldknow.

'Mr Oldknow, I have to say that you amaze me, you astound me you really do.'

They both sat there in silence taking in the impact of what Stanley had just said. The woman was silent because she had never heard anything like it said before by a man and the man because he had never said anything like it before to a woman.

'You said that there were three options.'

'The second would be that you cancel the appointment completely and altogether, send a third person message to Weedon. If it helps then I will deliver it myself personally, so that it is without question and to ensure that he fully understands it. I would explain, quite politely but firmly, that you cannot help him and then you can completely remove him from your client list.'

'And what is your opinion of this course of action?'

'It would probably bring some resolution, but only if we are wrong and Weedon is, as you say, a harmless fantasist. If that is the case then he will just move on to his next fantasy, if he has one, and completely forget about you.'

'And if we are right Mr Oldknow and he isn't harmless and he doesn't move on.'

'Then any resolution would only be permanent in our own heads. It would be temporary in his and just a momentary pause as far as he was concerned and we would always be wondering when he, or possibly one of his agents, was going to appear again. We could be wondering this for a long time, perhaps even the rest of our lives. Is that a level of uncertainty that we want?'

'I have to say that you are a man of some psychology Mr Oldknow, you never fail to impress me.'

'Thank you ma'am, I am an easy agent.'

'The third option, what is the third option Mr Oldknow?'

'The third option at this stage is a little vague and is little more than half an option. It would involve us working very much together on this. We would have to trust each other as if our lives depended upon it, as indeed they may, and both the risk and the danger could be much greater than either the first or the second option.'

'Are there any benefits to have for selecting this option?'

'It is possible that it could result in a conclusion.'

'Sounds to me as if you have the semblance of a plan Mr Oldknow.'

'As I said ma'am, I am an easy man but even I know that to call this either a semblance or a plan would be to elevate the idea to a much higher station than it deserves.'

'Then that's the one, yes that's the option that we will go for Mr Oldknow.'

'Very well Ma'am.'

'Just one more thing Mr Oldknow.'

'Anything.'

'A few moments ago you referred to his agents.'

'Did I?'

'Yes, you said something along the lines of he or one of his agents, I don't recall your exact words. The point is, what did you mean, do you think that there is some sort of organisation involved here?'

'No, I think the opposite. Whatever the Professor is up to, he is most certainly acting solo. It was just something a contact of mine said last week and it came into my head. A slip of the tongue and trick of the mind as my old grandmother used to say.'

'That sounds as if it's an old Irish saying Mr Oldknow.'

'Well, after all she was from Donegal Ma'am.'

Later on that week, when Stanley was enjoying his regular Friday night refreshment in the Lord Abercrombie he received a pencil scrawled message on a piece of Queens Hotel letterhead notepaper. The author was Jackie Black and the message informed Stanley that Major Jonas Watts had settled his bill in cash half an hour ago and that he was leaving the Queens Hotel at 8:00am tomorrow.

This message from Jackie Black confirmed to the Enquiry Agent's mind that the female solicitor had chosen the most dangerous option.

Chapter 23

Saturday Morning

The Blackbird Cafe opened from 7:00am to 7:00pm six days a week. The outside activities and comings and goings of the street scene on Saturday morning could be seen clearly through its large plate-glass window. The Professor sat in a chair near the window. He read his newspaper, apparently avidly, but even the nonchalant observer, had there been one, would have seen that his attention was fixed on the building opposite. From this situation he could see everybody that passed, entered or left the building from that entrance.

He had been sitting there since around 8:15am and was now on his third cup of tea. At a few minutes past 9:00am the Professor had seen a small man in a grey suit and a cap arrive at the building. This man had unlocked the huge front doors of the building and pushing them inwards had secured them open. The man hadn't entered the building itself, his job done he had then walked off purposely, possibly to open another building as he was carrying a huge metal ring from which hung many keys. As the small man in grey disappeared so the postman appeared, entered the building briefly and then continued on his rounds down the street. It reminded the Professor that he also had an important letter to post.

For the next hour the Professor sat there with his successive cups of tea and his newspaper. During that time nobody else entered or left the building and this satisfied him. At around ten o'clock he observed a cab, it stopped outside the building and he momentarily saw a tall, thin, young and elegantly dressed lady alight from the vehicle. Initially the taxi obscured her from full view through the

Blackbird's window but as it pulled away she became visible from head to foot and he could see it was the female solicitor, Roisin de Hay. She stood outside and looked at the building for a few seconds then entered it. The Professor left his table, left the cafe, immediately followed her and entered the same building. As he did he was pleasantly surprised to find Roisin in the reception area where the secretary was normally to be found.

'Good morning Professor Weedon.'

'Oh good morning Miss de Hay, you caught me a little by surprise, I'm not used to seeing you in that context.'

She led the way through to her office, 'Do come through Professor.'

They both arranged themselves around the table assuming almost identical situations and positions to the situations and positions they had at their last visit.

'I am afraid that I can't offer you any refreshments, there is nobody in the building today apart from you and I and I wouldn't even know where to start looking for the tea.'

'That's perfectly alright Miss de Hay, I had some breakfast earlier in the cafe across the road.'

'Oh I keep meaning to go over there, was it to your liking?'

'It was very satisfying indeed.'

'Professor, I was expecting you to be accompanied.'

'Ah yes of course, my witness, she will be here shortly.'

'I made a slight mistake with the time, I asked Olwyn to meet us here in this office at eleven. I meant to say ten-thirty, I've just realised my mistake now. I do apologise, as it is not even ten-thirty yet. I sometimes get myself a little mixed up with all these appointments, locations and times that I have to keep in my head.'

'It's perfectly understandable, do you have any of the paperwork?'

'No I don't have it, Olwyn has it, she is bringing it with her.'

'Ah well, as we have at least half an hour to wait there is a little task that I have to perform. Would you excuse me Professor, I'll be gone for no more than five minutes.'

Roisin stood up and left the office. Closing the door behind her she travelled quickly through the building whereupon she arrived at the door of the rear entrance. A curtain hung from this door, which she drew open and then turned the key anticlockwise, the heavy mortice lock opened with a metallic clunk. She opened the door, left it ajar, and returned to her office and the Professor.

'If you recall, the last time I was here we spoke about your family from County Wexford Miss de Hay, which part of County Wexford?'

'It's a small town called Enniscorthy.'

'Oh yes, Enniscorthy.'

'Do you know it Professor?'

'No, strange as it may seem I've travelled to many parts of the world but I've never actually been to Ireland at all. Although I did actually know somebody from Enniscorthy itself.'

'Oh really, who was that, perhaps I know him too?'

'That's highly improbable Miss de Hay, he was around a long time ago and he didn't move in the circles that you would have done but for the record his name was Finbarr Joseph.'

'I don't recognise the name, did he have another name perhaps, what did he do?'

'Oh he didn't really have another name, not one of any consequence anyway, and he didn't do that much. He just sat there on the ground, on his own little piece of land.'

'Well, I don't suppose he was doing anybody any harm just sitting there.'

'That's just it you see Miss de Hay, I mean you wouldn't think that he was doing anybody any harm, but he was. He was being harmful just by sitting there. Or even if he wasn't, others thought that he was, and that's what counted in those days, what others thought, not what Finbarr thought.'

'Who exactly was Finbarr?'

'He was a peasant boy in the Great Hunger.'

'An Gorta Mor, that was a long time ago.'

'For most it was, but for some it is just as if it was happening today.'

'So what happened to Finbarr?'

'He had to leave Ireland.'

'Where did he go?'

'Oh he travelled everywhere.'

'Did he ever go back to Ireland?'

'He visited it yes, but he didn't stay there. He was very typical of his generation and over a period of time millions left Ireland and very few ever went back.'

Roisin knew enough about the history of her own country to know all this, but *Finbarr's* story interested her so she continued, 'What happened to his family and his little piece of land?'

'His family died before he left Ireland, that's one of the reasons why he had to leave, he had to grow up without them.'

'That's a very sad story Professor, a person's family is most important.'

'You are right Miss de Hay, your family is of the utmost importance, you must never let your family down and they must never let you down.'

'What happened to Finbarr's land?'

'Oh, somebody took it off him and he became a man of insignificance.'

'That's an unusual way to describe somebody, I don't think that I've ever heard of a human being described in such a cruel way before.'

'Well, it may seem a cruel description, and I suppose that it is, but if you have no land, no family, no money and no country and all that you actually do have is failure and humiliation then how would you describe such a person Miss de Hay?'

'Well, surely feelings are important and humiliation is after all a feeling.'

'Do you speak from personal experience? Forgive my candour but how would you know, when was the last time that you were actually humiliated? I don't mean when did you last make a little mistake or when did you last feel a bit of a fool. I mean when were you so humiliated that you felt that you couldn't face anything and you had to run away from everything?'

'I have to say that I've never really felt that way.'

The Professor knew that what Roisin had said about it being a cruel description was an honest answer. He also knew that what she said was not really of any consequence. He had at one time during their conversation considered telling her about the relationship between his father and her grandfather but he was under strict protocol in the way that everything had to be done and this protocol did not include divulgence. He considered that he had engaged long enough in conversation and in fact that he may have over engaged. The time had come to realise his task. He didn't feel agitated inside as he thought that he might have done. No, instead he felt unfeeling and numb as if everything before him was unfolding at a very slow speed. He rose from his chair with alarming grace and in the method that he had been taught and practiced he pushed back the folds of his topcoat in one and the same movement. His hand flew down to his sides and when it emerged he held a small but deadly gun.

A split second later two simultaneous events occurred, a gunshot rang out and as it did a large figure appeared in the room behind the gunman, it was the enquiry agent, Stanley Oldknow. In his hand he had a soft lead cosh, which he smote down twice in heavy but quick succession on the back of the gunman's hand. The derringer fell to the floor and with a bang instantly discharged the remaining bullet, which flew through the glass window. Stanley Oldknow then smote two further heavy blows to the head of the Professor, he slumped to the floor unconscious and as he fell the enquiry agent rained down another blow. The assailant was rendered helpless and motionless on the floor. Stanley Oldknow turned his attention to Roisin de Hay, she was still sat behind her desk slumped in her chair. The solitary shot which had been aimed at her head had been deflected down by Stanley's intervention but it had entered her upper body in the middle of her stomach, she was conscious but the wound was haemorrhaging blood.

In one easy move Stanley pushed the heavy desk aside then he leaned forward and, surprisingly gentle for such a large man, scooped the stricken woman from her chair.

She looked up weakly at her rescuer, 'I am shot Mr Oldknow, it feels strange, I have never felt this way before, am I going to die?'

'No Miss de Hay,' said Stanley, 'you are not going to die but you may just have to sleep for a while.'

'Sleep for a while, do you promise I will wake up?'

'I promise, Roisin, I promise!'

As Stanley carried her out of the building he could feel the life and breath and perspiration coursing through her body. He walked quickly for a large man with an injured woman in his arms. Once outside he laid her down on the pathway then he took off his coat and rested it under her head for a pillow. By now she had lapsed into unconsciousness.

Stanley didn't know what to do so he shouted at the top of his voice, 'This lady is injured, help!'

People came running out of the Blackbird Café, an off duty nurse appeared and then, after what seemed an age to Stanley but was actually only six minutes, an ambulance appeared and took Roisin off.

After the ambulance sped off a policeman who Stanley knew came upon the scene. Stanley ran back with the policeman to Roisin's office but it was empty, the Professor had gone. They looked around the immediate area but there was no sign, no trace. Finally they both returned to Roisin's office and as the policeman spoke to a detective who had arrived on the scene Stanley noticed a derringer and a small cartridge case next to it on the floor. He quickly knelt down, picked them up and surreptitiously placed them into his coat pocket.

Chapter 24

Noel O'Malley and the Holy Conception

From the front and the outside, the sturdy and apparently single-storey house that situated itself right in the middle of the terraced row in Castle Street, on the edge of Ballina town in County Mayo, would originally have looked no different than any of the other houses that had stood either side of it for a hundred years or so. The reason that it now appeared completely conspicuous from its neighbours was that Sean Christopher Higgins who was the co-owner of the house had decided on a whim four years ago to have the whole outside front of it painted bright pink. The neighbours didn't really object, in fact in the main most of them were quietly amused, in their own quirky Irish way, by his choice of tint and others thought that this colour splash brought a bit of light and spontaneous relief to what was otherwise a rather unpainted and sedate street frontage.

What they did find perplexing though was the reason why Sean Christopher Higgins would use his own time and money in pursuit of this dawn-tinted endeavour. This puzzle was made even more interesting to them as for the last forty-one years Sean Christopher Higgins had resided permanently in Tallahassee, Florida and in those forty-one years he had rarely set foot on the island of Ireland itself, let alone across the doorstep of the little pink house. It therefore seemed to some that perhaps his choice of colour was a symbolic gesture to the local authority who had decreed five years ago that Castle Street be designated a conservation area. This designation prohibited such acts of wanton colour as

Mr Higgins had perpetrated. The neighbours considered that Mr Higgins was perhaps thumbing his nose at the council from across the Atlantic ocean or metaphorically poking his fingers into their eyes or, possibly even worse and more disrespectful and irreverent than any of these, that he was showing these conservation clots, as they are sometimes known, his big, pink arse. Anyway, paint it pink he did and pink it now was and, as far as Sean Christopher Higgins was concerned, pink it was staying.

Sean Christopher Higgins was Danny Senetti's *Uncle John* on his mother's side and Danny's mother was the other co-owner of the pink house. Senetti himself was staying there alone and as family his stay was naturally rent-free. He planned to stay for five days whilst he continued his investigations into the background of Helen Day, also possibly known as Kathleen Helen until proven otherwise. This burden of proof was proving difficult to establish, but whilst he did try to establish it Danny Senetti's part of the agreement, in exchange for this rent-free accommodation in his mother and uncle's house, was to give the little place a *bit of an airing*.

Danny's investigations had not got off to a good start. One reason for this was that he didn't really know where to begin. He kept hearing Maxine Wells' words ringing in his ears, 'We can't just walk around Ireland asking people if they know a woman called Helen who has been murdered in England.' The problem was that he agreed with Maxine about the shortcomings of such a plan but he didn't know what else to do, and as of yet he hadn't even done that!

There was also another reason why his progress had been curtailed a little. His initial travel arrangements had been fine, taxi to Manchester airport, plane to Knock airport, collect hire car and drive over to Ballina, all easily accomplished, and he'd arrived without interruption at the pink house around 6:00pm, Monday evening.

After a little bit of airing, which for him involved opening the sitting room window, opening the kitchen window, lighting a fragrant candle in the kitchen and leaving a couple of lights on, he had decided to go for a walk around Ballina. It was a pleasant evening and he walked along by the river Moy. As he passed Saint Muredach's Cathedral he paused and looked up at its majestic spire, half hoping for some inspiration and half praying that some kind of plan would come into his head, but it didn't. During the rest of his walk he thought hard about what his first move tomorrow should be, but he couldn't come up with much that he could impress himself with so inevitably he resigned his thinking on the subject and looked for a pub. Fifteen minutes later he turned up at Harrison's bar. Even though his last visit had been almost five years ago he had been in Ballina many times and he knew that he could easily find his way back to the pink house from there.

When he woke up the next day he estimated that he had left the pub around 11:00pm. In the pink house Danny's bedroom was downstairs from street level and as he had made his way gingerly down these stairs after his evening drinking bout he had lost his footing. He wasn't injured at all but in order to steady himself he had grabbed at the wooden stair spindles on the ornate staircase. The end result, as he saw in the morning, was that two dislodged spindles lay on the stair treads exactly where he had left them the night before. One of them was broken into two pieces, which was bad enough but when he looked at the other it was broken into three which, he reasoned, was one and a half times as bad as the first one. A makeshift, bodge-up repair was completely out of the question as he knew that a neighbour would be inspecting the house after he'd left and he didn't want any tales, exaggerated or otherwise, getting back to his mother or his Uncle John, even though Uncle John was in Tallahassee. He therefore decided that the investigation would have to wait until he'd fixed the spindles properly.

With this in mind, for the best part of Tuesday he drove around Mayo in his little hired car looking for an exact match to the broken stair rail. Initially he headed south and stopped off at Castlebar then Claremorris and then Balinrobe but to no avail, as he could not find the parts. Finally he stopped off at the Mayo town of Westport. He was guided by a local to a small joiner's shop just outside the town centre. The man in the shop said that he could turn the two new spindles and 'you wouldn't know the difference,' but that they wouldn't be ready until tomorrow. Danny agreed, made the arrangements and left the shop.

He paused outside on the pavement wondering what to do next and as he did he listened to the conversation of two elderly women. One said to the other, 'Oh yes, I do remember that place, I used to take my daughter there when she was a child, it was up by the old convent.'

When Danny heard the word *convent* he interjected, he hoped that it was politely. 'Excuse me ladies but where exactly is the convent that you refer to?'

The lady who was speaking stopped talking to her companion and addressed Danny, 'It was the Convent of The Holy Conception. As far as I know it was the only real convent in the whole of County Mayo. There were convent schools and there was once a convent college but this was the only real thing with nuns and girls who lived there and all.'

Her companion joined in, 'The strangest thing about that place was that of all the girls in it, and there must have been a hundred of them, not a one of them came from County Mayo. That convent had girls from every one of the thirty-two counties of Ireland except one, this one, and there was plenty from this county who would have benefitted from being in there, what do you say Angela?' both women laughed.

'Where exactly is the convent?' said Danny.

'It's just this side of Liskarney,' said Angela. 'It's about three miles out of Westport, you won't miss it, as soon as you see the building you'll know exactly what it is, well what it was before the fire, it couldn't be anything else but a convent.'

'Won't do you any good going up there though,' said the other woman, 'there's nobody there now, it's empty. The nuns and the girls have all gone years ago. Been nobody in there now for twenty years.'

'What about all the records?'

'I don't know about the records, I don't know what they did with them. Perhaps you should try the library.'

'I'm looking for somebody who was in there in 1962,' said Danny.

'That's a long time ago,' said Angela.

'Old Noel O'Malley,' said her companion.

'Oh yes he'd know, he knows everything about that place, worked there all his life. He must be nearly ninety now.'

'No, he's not that old, eighty-five I'd say, but accordingly his mind is still clear and all there.'

'Where can I find Mr O'Malley?'

'He lives in Crossmolina, I don't know where exactly but Crossmolina is only a small place, and he's famous in that town so if you just ship up there and mention his name somebody will be sure to point you in the right direction.'

'Thank you ladies,' said Danny, 'thank you very much.'

'Good luck,' they both said in unison.

Danny wandered off to retrieve his car. He knew that Liskarney was a little to the south of where he was and Crossmolina was a fair distance to the north, he guessed at about thirty miles. The convent building itself didn't matter that much, especially since it was empty but the old man might give him another clue. If he went via a circuitous route then he could fool himself that the journey to Crossmolina was on his way back to the pink house, so he decided that he would head north in search of Noel O'Malley. There was nothing to say that it was the right convent and even if it was there was nothing to say that the old man knew anything. It was a long shot, he knew that, but so were a lot of things in life and he'd sooner talk to a person any day than look at a building, especially a burnt out one.

About one hour later Danny Senetti walked into the Dolphin Hotel in Crossmolina. It was early evening, the place was empty, the early-doors drinkers had all gone home and the night drinkers were yet to arrive. The attractive, dark-haired young barmaid was having a conversation into her mobile phone. She was explaining to the person on the other end who was called Alison that she had been trying to make contact with her for two days and that she had not been able to do so. Senetti pondered: he mused on why mobile-phone people did that. They contacted you and then when you took the call they spent longer telling you about the where's and why's of how they had been unable to contact you previously

241

than they did telling you what they actually wanted you for now that they'd actually managed to get hold of you. When the phoning barmaid actually saw Danny she made her apologies to her friend and hung up. Danny thought that this was a small mercy but he was glad of it.

'What can I get you?'

'Hmm, I'll have one of those mango-tango things.'

'Oh yes, I know what you mean, what flavour? Funny, you don't strike me as a mango-tango person.'

'No you're right, I'm not normally, it's just that I'm driving and I'm working.'

'Certainly, for sure,' she said.

Danny tried to think of the word that described what she had just said. When you use one word after another and they both mean the same thing. He tried to think of examples in his head and he came up with, *baby infant, continue on* and *two twins*. He wondered if the barmaid knew that she was doing this with, *certainly, for sure.*

He thought that he'd try his nice person approach so he gave her his best smile and he said, 'my name's Danny Senetti, I'm English and my father is Italian but my mother is Irish, and I'm looking for a man called Noel O'Malley, have you heard of him?'

'I certainly have,' she said, 'everybody has heard of Noel, they built this town around him.'

'Do you know where I can find him?'

'I certainly do.'

There was that word again Danny thought. He once had an acquaintance who used the word *flippin* in every sentence that he uttered. If he couldn't get the word in he would separate syllables to insert it. Danny recalled how he had once said fifty-flippin-per-flippin-cent and also how he'd once said cere-flippin-mony, for the word ceremony.

She looked at her wristwatch, 'He comes in here every weekday evening, Monday to Thursday and also on Saturday, although he's a bit later then. He's as regular as clockwork for his three and a half pints of Guinness. He'll be here in about twenty-one minutes,' she said.

Danny had an afterthought, 'Do you do rooms?'

'Certainly, for sure.'

'Have you any tonight?'

'Certainly we have.'

'Excellent!' exclaimed Danny, 'Book me in and cancel the mango tango, you can have it if you want, I'll have a pint of Guinness and a small Irish whiskey. When Mr O'Malley comes in please tell him it would please me immensely to buy him a drink or two in exchange for half an hour of his company and put his drink on my tab.'

'Certainly, I'll bring your Guinness over.'

Danny went over to the seat by the window and sat there gormlessly. In the meantime the barmaid, who he now noticed had a name badge on which read *Christina*, brought his drink over.

After what seemed to Danny to be precisely twenty-one minutes, the bar door opened and an elderly yet sprightly man came through it. He was small in height and build, he was tidily dressed with a casual jacket and trousers and was bareheaded. He had sparse white hair brushed back over his head and one of those cherubic faces that looked as if it had been scrubbed smooth pink. Danny noticed that all his clothing was predominantly green, he also noticed his eyes, they were a piercing hazel colour. It was obvious, as Angela and her friend had claimed a couple of hours earlier, his mind was still clear and he was all there. Danny knew without introduction that it was Noel O'Malley and, as if in confirmation, Christina said, 'Evening Noel.'

Noel and Christina went into a little semi huddle at the bar. Then, after a few minutes the old man walked over to Danny's seat. 'Hello Danny,' he said, 'I'm Noel O'Malley, thanks very much for the drink.'

Danny stood up, 'Pleased to meet you Noel and you are most welcome to the drink. I'm Danny Senetti, would you join me for a while?'

'Certainly,' said Noel and they both shook hands.

Danny thought, that flippin word again. He sat back down, as did Noel.

'You're English aren't you, and Senetti that's Italian isn't it?'

'Only on my father's side.'

'And on your mother's?'

'She is a Higgins from Ballina.'

'Higgins, oh that's a good old Mayo name.'

Then Noel became silent. Danny could sense and see that Noel was in his own backyard and was quite comfortable with the silence. He also didn't want to scare the older man off, so he sat in silence for a while too. Noel then made some comments about the weather and a football match that he was looking forward to this coming weekend. Danny listened and after ten minutes he went over to the bar and ordered two more pints of Guinness. The barmaid said that she'd bring them over. Danny returned to his seat.

'Can I call you Noel?'

'Yes.'

'A lady called Angela, who I met for the first time today in the street in Westport, said that you would be the man to help me.'

'You need to be careful picking women up in the street. Anyhow, I'll do my best. Can I call you Danny?'

'Yes.'

Another silence ensued.

Danny still wasn't quite sure how to manage this situation to get the best out of it. He mulled over various presentations in his mind. Then he decided that the most straightforward approach would probably be the simplest, 'I'm trying to establish the identity of somebody who died recently in England, though I think that she spent some time in County Mayo, her name was Helen Day.'

'I've only ever been to England once, it was over sixty years ago, a place called Blackpool. I remember it cost me three month's wages for a week's supply of fish and chips and some coloured water that was masquerading as stout and the company of a beautiful, dark-haired long-legged lady whose name I've long since forgotten. Is the place still there?'

'It is, very much so.'

'I've never known anybody by the name of Helen Day.'

'We think that she may have lived in a convent in Mayo for many years up until probably 1962.'

'The Convent of the Holy Conception?'

'Yes, would you be prepared to tell me about the convent?'

Christina brought the two drinks over.

'I'm eighty-six next birthday, I started work there when I was fourteen, third of September, 1943, straight from school, the war was on in Europe at the time. General Apprentice they called my job, which basically meant jack-of-all-trades, master of none. If the boiler packed up I fixed it, if the door came off its hinges, I put it back on, if somebody broke a window I repaired it, if one of the nuns locked herself in the lavatory then I got her out, anything and everything. In the end, after Old Cleary died, apart from a succession of visiting priests and occasional contractors, I was the only regular man in the place.'

'What about the girls Noel? How many were in there, why were they in there, how long were they in there?'

'You are taking me back now Danny. There were usually around one hundred girls in the convent at any given time. The answer as to why they were there was a different one for each girl. Some of them were in there years, from being a baby to being a woman. Some weren't in as long as that. Some you knew quite a lot about, others you knew nothing. You never really got to know why they were in there, not the true story anyway. The nuns never gave out any information, so the girls made stories up and after a while these stories became half-truths. It was said that some of the girls were orphaned, some of them were foundling, some of them were just abandoned and some of them had other stories told about them. In the end you didn't know where the fables stopped and the facts started or even if there was any fact at all. It didn't matter really. Whilst they were in the convent they were all in the same boat. You weren't allowed to get too near the girls, you couldn't befriend any of them. You had to call the nuns *Sister* and the girls *Miss*. You were constantly warned about getting too close to the girls, *conduct unbecoming* it was called. That could be anything: a wrong word, a look, a gesture. If you did it once too often you were warned and if you didn't heed the warnings you were fired. *Confidentiality*, that was another one, you were told not to discuss the business of the convent outside the convent, if you did then the you would suffer the same consequence, I saw it happen to a few over the years. There are no jobs around here now and there were even fewer then so I kept to the rules, I wouldn't have survived so long if I hadn't.'

'Did you know any of their names?'

'Any of their names? I knew all of their names, or at least the names that they went by. Some of them were around a long time, eighteen years for some. Every year a few would leave when they got to be eighteen years old and then a few more would come in to take their place, but there wasn't a big turnover. The most that ever left in any one year I think was twelve and in one year only two left. Occasionally a girl would leave before she was eighteen, probably to go back to her family, but I wouldn't get to know about that, nobody would tell me. You'd just think to yourself one day, I've not seen her for a while and then somebody would say that she'd gone home and that's all you got. Nobody had any surnames except me, I was called O'Malley, the nuns were called Sister Edith or Sister Colette and the girls were called Susan Anne or Elaine Margaret or Miss Elaine Margaret if I addressed them. It was a kind of class thing, the girls were on the top and people such as myself were on the bottom and the nuns just stood off it altogether.'

'Do you recall a girl called Kathleen Helen when you were there?'

Noel took a long swig of his Guinness, put down the glass and looked straight at Danny, 'You know,' he said 'you're the second Englishman in over fifty years to ask me about Kathleen Helen.'

'Oh yes, who was the first?'

'Some detective a long time ago. Is Kathleen Helen the one that died in England, the one that you mentioned before?'

'We think that she might be, yes. Will you tell me about her?'

'Kathleen Helen, that's going back a long time, she came in not long after I started, yes I remember her. The official version was that she was a foundling on the convent steps, there were many foundlings, too many to be true really. She arrived just around the end of the war, she was a little baby. They had to hire a wet nurse in from the village to feed her. She was there until she was eighteen.'

'Do you remember when she left?'

'She left in the early nineteen-sixties. I can't remember exact dates, I'm not very good at that, but names and faces, that's different. I remember though that year there were three leavers, they all went out on the same day, I remember them, there was Morag Fiona, Justine Joanne and your girl Kathleen Helen. The Beatles had just come out with that song, *Love Me Do*, it was being played everywhere.'

'What do you remember about her?'

'She was a tall girl with blond hair, wore glasses, very thin, no shape, plain looking, small features, serious, very intelligent, nice enough person and always polite.'

'Anything else?'

'As I said, there were stories but you never knew if they were true and you have to remember this was Mayo in the 50's and 60's, some of us still believed in fairies and pixies in those days. If there hadn't been any stories then we'd probably have made some up just for our own amusement.'

'What were the stories about Kathleen Helen?'

'The girls in that convent were from all over the United Kingdom. One story about Kathleen Helen was that she was a foundling, that she was Irish originally but from the other side of Ireland. Somewhere over by the south east and that she came from money.'

Danny signalled for more drinks and Christina duly obliged.

Noel O'Malley continued, 'there was another version about Kathleen Helen, it was said that she wasn't a foundling at all and that the real reason that she was in Concepta's was that her family were hiding her away. That they put her in Mayo because it was as far away from where she came from that you can get without leaving Ireland altogether.'

'Which story did you believe?'

'I didn't really give either of them much thought, they weren't really any different than the stories about any of the other girls inasmuch as you couldn't establish them one way or another. They were just stories and you just took them with a pinch of salt.'

'What were her family hiding her from, were there any stories about that?'

'Ah well Danny my boy, that's when it got a little bit silly, even for Ireland and even in those times.'

'Go on Noel, I've come a long way to hear this.'

'Alright but don't laugh, it's not my story, I didn't make it up and I didn't believe it any more than you will.'

'I understand that but tell me anyway.'

'Well, it was said that her family had a curse placed upon them from the last century, that this curse meant that all the female line in the family would be murdered. So in order to prevent this happening to Kathleen Helen, who was the last female of all this family, she was hidden away in the convent. I mean, I have to say that it was pretty far-fetched even by Concepta's standards.'

'Did she have any visitors while she was in the convent?'

'I don't recall seeing or hearing of any.'

'Was that unusual?'

'No, not really.'

'What about the records for the convent, where are they kept?'

'There aren't any, they've all gone.'

'Gone? Gone where?'

'In nineteen ninety-four, I'd only just retired one month previous, there was a fire. It was a fearsome blaze, you could see it across all of Mayo. It burned for a day and a half. How people weren't killed I'll never know but thankfully nobody was. They got everybody out before it got hold but all the records of course were destroyed in the blaze.'

'Is there anything in any of the local libraries?'

'I don't think so, Concepta's was a law unto itself. The nuns wouldn't have wanted outsiders poking around in their business. The convent was opened in 1890 and I expect in a period of one hundred and four years that they would have had a few secrets to keep. Any records would have been on the premises and would have gone up with the fire. What sort of record are you after?'

'Absolutely anything, a name, an address, another scrap of information, another piece of the puzzle. Where did Kathleen Helen go when she left the convent?'

'As I said before, we wouldn't get to know that. We knew that she was due to go out because of her age and everybody went at eighteen, but it was the same procedure as everybody else, one day she was there and the next day she was gone. All those years eh, and then you never saw them again.'

'Well thanks Noel, I appreciate what you've told me.'

'I wish that I could have told you more. Anyway I've got to go now, I've had more than my drinks quota for the night. You're staying here aren't you? Don't miss the breakfast it's a good one. Thanks for the drinks and the company.' With that the old man was gone.

Danny sat there with an empty glass feeling a little deflated. He had enjoyed the Guinness and the little Irishman's company but he hadn't really learnt much from the conversation. Certainly nothing that could be considered conclusive. The time was about right, the woman's age was about right and he could see an older Helen Day in Noel O'Malley's physical description of a much younger Kathleen Helen. Yet it was all conjecture and all that he could say with any conviction was that Helen Day was possibly, even probably, the same person as Noel's Kathleen Helen but that was only through his own instinct and a little bit of circumstantial evidence. It quite simply was not conclusive!

What to do next? He didn't know. Where to go? He didn't know that either. He got up and walked over to the bar, there were a few evening drinkers now corralled around and he wondered whether he should join them. Unusually for him, especially as he was staying overnight in a pub, he went to bed early that night.

Senetti was in the bar of the Dolphin the next morning. During the morning the bar room doubled up as the breakfast room for the previous night's accommodated guests, of whom Danny was one. In fact, as he looked around the fully set out but completely empty dining room he seemed to be the only one. He was half way through his full Irish breakfast when he looked up from the plate and saw Noel O'Malley standing in front of him.

The little Irishman's eyes were as impudent as ever and his face had been scrubbed even pinker than Danny remembered it. He had entirely different clothes on than he had been wearing last night and this time all his clothing was predominantly blue, his outfit was topped off with a dark blue felt cap.

'Noel,' said Danny, 'sit down and have a cup of tea.' Danny reached across to the unoccupied table next to him, which had been set out for two diners and took a clean cup and saucer from it. He poured Noel a cup. Noel took his cap off and sat down.

'I thought that I'd find you here,' said Noel, 'I was thinking about our conversation last night and early this morning I was up with the lark and I sprang into action. I know where there might be some more information.'

Danny chuckled at the little Irishman's prose but Noel's comments excited him and he pulled his chair closer to the table, 'What sort of information?'

'You said that you were trying to establish the identity of Kathleen Helen and your woman in England, what was her name, Helen Day?'

'Yes.'

'Would a photograph, albeit an old one, of Kathleen Helen help?'

'Well yes, absolutely, have you got one?'

'No I haven't, well not personally, but I think that I know where there is one, as I said it's an old one mind, taken when she was eighteen, but sometimes people are recognizable from old photographs.'

'That's very true, where is it?'

'Edinburgh!'

'Edinburgh?'

'Do you remember that I said that we never knew where the girls went when they left the convent?'

'Yes.'

'Well, I remembered there was one girl, just one, and we knew exactly where she was for at least two months after she had left the convent.'

'Don't tell me, when she came out she was arrested outside the convent gates where she'd been in hiding for the last eighteen years and whisked off to jail to complete the last two months of a previous sentence that she'd escaped from when she was six months old.'

The Irishman laughed, 'Did anyone ever mention to you Danny that sometimes there's just a trace of cynicism to you, it must be the Italian side of you for there is no cynicism whatsoever in the whole of Ireland.'

Danny smiled back at Noel, 'You'll have to hear me out on this one Danny, it's a bit convoluted but I promise you it's worth listening to and if you want to know more about Kathleen Helen then this is your only lead, or at least the only one that I can give you.'

'Ok Noel, you've got the floor.'

The little Irishman took a slurp from his teacup, 'At Concepta's, as well as the regular nuns and the girls, we had some outside teachers. Some of them were just now and again, but some of them were regulars. They were all women but they weren't all nuns, some of them were lay. They didn't live in the convent but they worked there. One of the regulars was a lady called Magdelene Fionella Deborah Chriscoli. The girls just called her Miss Maggie.'

'I'm not surprised.'

Noel carried on, 'Miss Maggie wasn't much older than the older girls herself and she had a fondness for modern music. One day she brought the Beatles LP into the convent, there was a bit of a scandal about that. The girls related to her and she was very popular amongst them. Now we'll just digress a little bit but it is a meaningful digression.'

'You're very articulate Noel for a retired general apprentice.'

'Danny, I've been around a long time and I've read a lot of books and I'm only telling you this because your mother is Mayo Higgins.' He paused and took another slurp from his teacup. 'When you're brought up in a convent, the other girls are your family. The ones that you have the closest relationship with are just the same as your closest sister. Like your closest sister you tell each other everything, no secrets from each other.'

'I can understand that.'

'There was actually a name for such relationships, they were called *convent sisters*. Kathleen Helen's convent sister was a girl called Morag Fiona, she left the convent on the same day as Kathleen Helen. Kathleen Helen and Morag Fiona went through the whole convent experience together. They both came into the convent the same year. I've thought back hard, it was the summer of 1944. There were actually three of them on that discharge in 1962 but the other girl is irrelevant apart from the fact that she's on the photo.'

'The one in Edinburgh.'

'The one we hope is in Edinburgh.'

'Noel, don't go back on it now.'

'Danny, don't drag me off my train of thought, right, the photo. A couple of days before the girls left the convent there was a little ceremony. Only a small private thing in the courtyard lawn between the nuns, the girls that were leaving and those girls closest to them. A few speeches and well wishes, a little religious gift, usually a set of rosary beads or a statue of the Virgin Mary from one of the shops in Knock and a photograph of the leaving girls together, just to remind them of their happy days in the convent. The photograph would be posted onto them at a later date, there was probably some photographic developing time involved in those days. Are you following so far?'

'Yes, I'm up with you.'

'Morag Fiona was originally Scottish and she was going back to Scotland to live with some relative. On the very same day that she was due to leave Concepta's the convent received word that this relative had been involved in a car accident, she was hospitalized, and Morag Fiona couldn't go. The convent said that they would extend Morag Fiona's placement until her relative recovered but Morag Fiona wouldn't have any of it. Apparently she said she waited eighteen years to get out of the place and she was not going to stay a minute longer and that was that. The nuns couldn't do anything about it as she was eighteen. They couldn't keep her in the convent against her will and they didn't want to send her back to Scotland until her relative had recovered.

They were in a bit of a panic so, as a compromise, Morag agreed to go and live with Miss Maggie until her sister got better. Ten weeks she was there and after she'd been there a few days the photograph arrived in the post.'

'Noel, I don't know where all this is going, but why didn't you tell me this last night?'

'Danny, I couldn't tell you last night because I didn't know it last night. I didn't know any of it until I got home.'

'So what you're saying is that Morag Fiona has kept this photograph all these years and it's now in Edinburgh. So, find Morag Fiona, find the photograph!'

'No Danny, I'm not saying that, you're saying that. If you want to know what I'm saying Danny, why don't you wait until I've said it? Then you'll know for sure, because you'll have heard it from my lips, not yours.'

Danny smiled at the old man's contrariness, he could tell that Noel was in tale-telling mood, he was relishing the raconteur's role, he was going to tell it his way and the listener would just have to be patient.

Noel resumed, 'We know exactly where Morag Fiona is.'

'Where, Edinburgh?'

'Yes, Old Calton cemetery.'

'She's dead!'

'Last year.'

'Noel, what good is that?'

'Miss Maggie and Morag Fiona kept in touch through all those years. Miss Maggie was godmother to one of Morag Fiona's kids and now and again through the years they'd meet up. She went to Morag's funeral in Edinburgh and after the funeral she went back to Morag Fiona's house. Morag Fiona's husband, who is a retired teacher, got all sentimental, as people often do at funerals, and he was showing around some old photographs of his late wife. Sure enough the leaving photograph of the three girls taken all those years ago was amongst them. Maggie said it made her feel all strange inside to see it after all this time.'

'Noel, how do you know all this?'

'Because Danny boy, Miss Maggie, who by now is a young woman of seventy-five, is alive and hearty and living in a little place called Ballintubber which is a few miles from here. I've known her for all those years and I remembered Morag Fiona staying with her and I knew that they'd kept close and that Morag Fiona was close to Kathleen Helen when she was in the convent. So, on your behalf I spoke to her last night, because Danny, that's the kind of guy I am.'

'What, you've been over to Ballintubber?'

'No, Miss Maggie was actually at my house last night, neither of us ever married you see and we've been well, what shall I say, er, close for over forty years now. When I got home we were talking about you and it came out.'

'You old rogue, at your age.'

'Well, what started as passion has now become compassion. Anyway, back to the photograph all you've got to do is to make contact with the late Morag Fiona's husband and go and look at the photograph. I've even half done that job for you, here's his contact details: name, address, telephone, email, inside leg, shirt neck, everything.' He pushed a folded piece of notepaper towards Danny, 'Now the next time you ship up in Mayo it will cost you a lot more than a few jars of Guinness.'

Danny leaned forward, he cupped the little Irishman's pink face in both hands and kissed him soundly on both cheeks, 'Noel, I love you as if you were my own father,' he said, 'have another cup of tea. Christina can we have some more tea please?'

'Certainly, for sure.'

Chapter 25

The Widower's Photograph

Just one day after she had received the phone call from Danny Senetti, Maxine Wells was travelling northwards to Edinburgh. As well as the story about the photograph Danny had told her some mixed up tale about two stair rails and driving around Mayo. He said that he was staying in Ireland for a couple more days to fix them. That was the thing with Senetti, Maxine realised this, in fact she hated to admit it to herself, but it was one of the things that she found interesting about him. He was different from many people she knew, they just made the mundane out of everything. Danny Senetti, no matter how mundane a situation was, he always tried to create a perspective of interest from it.

As the mid-afternoon train pulled into Waverley station in Edinburgh Maxine searched in her handbag for the scrap piece of card that she'd written the contact address of Morag Fiona's husband on. She read her own writing mentally, 'Hamish Lennox, 265, Mayfield Rd, Edinburgh.' Memorising the address she walked through the extensive concourse to street level. She stepped into the first of a line of taxicabs that waited there and as she did she spoke Hamish Lennox's address to the cab driver and off they went. The Edinburgh traffic was lighter than she had once remembered it and half an hour later she stood outside the honey-coloured, Cragleith-sandstone house with its long and narrow front garden. Hamish greeted her with a smile and a handshake as she went inside. She thought he presented as a little, round jolly man probably with a quick laugh and a thoughtful perspective. She put him to be about seventy years of age, he had a shock of white hair and a beard to match and he peered over his silver rimmed glasses when he looked at you. He was wearing a pristine open necked white shirt, a battered old green cardigan and a pair of brown corduroy trousers. He showed Maxine into a comfortable looking lounge and they sat down opposite each other.

Maxine said, 'it is very good of you to see me at such short notice.'

He smiled genuinely, 'I'm glad to see anybody these days, I don't get a lot of visitors. Morag received all the visitors but then she was always looking for a reason to stay in the house, whereas I was always looking for a reason to get out of it,' he chuckled at his own observation.

'You keep busy then?'

'Well, I try not to, I don't really do busy, I generally find the opposite more rewarding.'

'Were you and Morag married long?'

'Forty-three years.'

'That's a long time.'

'Yes, it's a lifetime.'

'You must miss her.'

'I do yes, but I think of her fondly and when I do it makes me happy. You know, when you get to a certain age and you've been together with someone for a long time you realise that it can't last forever. You know that something is going to happen to one of you, you don't really talk about it, apart from the practical issues. You don't know you are doing it but you make a plan in your head for when this happens, it just happened a little bit sooner than I thought it would. It always does, to everybody, but you've still got your plan and if you stick to it you'll be alright. Anyway, you've come to talk about the convent haven't you, not to listen to my sentimental rambles.'

'Did she mention the convent a lot when you were married?'

'Well that's a funny thing because at first she did. When we were both young she talked about the place all the time, it played such a big part in her life, it was as if she was trying to come to terms with it, you know, get it out of her system. Then, once she had the children she stopped. She didn't mention it for years. She never spoke about it to them. She never denied it, how could she? It was her childhood but she would never elaborate, it was as if she wanted to protect them from that world. When they asked her any questions about it she would say, oh that was then and this is now. When the children eventually left, the whole convent episode seemed to go full cycle and she started talking about it all over again. After she got her illness, and especially when she knew that she was going, she spoke about very little else.'

'Did you find that upsetting?'

'No, not at all, in fact the exact opposite, it seemed to give her comfort, which in turn comforted me.'

'How many children have you got?'

'Three, they are all doing well in their own way and I see them all, and the grandkids, so I'm lucky. I've no complaints about my life, I'm safe and secure, healthy and strong. I've got a good family, a wife, children and grandchildren, it's just that they are all in different places.'

'When Morag spoke to you about the convent did she mention a girl called Kathleen Helen?'

'Oh yes, all the time, they were convent sisters, they grew up together.'

'Did Morag and Kathleen Helen know much about each other's background?'

'They knew everything there was to know or at least they thought they did.'

'Why do you say that Hamish, did the truth turn out to be different?'

'Morag was told that she was an orphan but she didn't know the details. The nuns wouldn't give you any details. She later found out that her father was a marine biologist, he was killed in a boating accident. Her mother couldn't stand the pain of being without him and died of a broken heart. Morag and her parents were living on Achill Island at the time and there was only one other living family member, an aunt in Edinburgh who was little more than a girl herself and was too young to be given custody of a baby so that's how Morag came to be in a convent in Mayo. She was only a few months old when she was taken in, so in a sense she was an orphan, both parents were dead and there was nobody else, so it was true.'

'What about Kathleen Helen?'

'Kathleen Helen always thought that she was a foundling child. Nobody knew if she had any family or not and in the true sense of the tradition she was told that she'd been found on the convent steps, around the same time as Morag went into the convent, apparently they were only a few weeks apart.'

'So what was different?'

'Well, Morag used to say that because none of the girls really knew the facts about themselves and also because they had virtually no contact with the outside world they made up stories about each other and that there were always stories going around about many of them. The stories were repeated and embellished so many times that after a while nobody could recall the original version, they just became accepted. Nobody tried to establish if they were true or false. These tales became a kind of folklore. The one that used to go around about Kathleen Helen was that she was the subject of an old Irish curse and that somebody was out to kill her and that she had been hidden away in the convent by her family for her own protection. It wasn't the most outrageous story that went around but it was outrageous. Morag told me that one child was said to be the illegitimate daughter of film stars John Wayne and Maureen O'Hara, the result of an illicit affair that they had when they were filming in Mayo in the early 1950's. This girl later turned out to be the progeny of two fraudsters who were serving long stretches in jail for embezzlement and upon their release they reclaimed her. Another girl was said to be a member of one of the royal families of Europe. So all the girls just lived with these tales, it was just that in the end Kathleen Helen's turned out to have some truth in it.'

'How do you know that Hamish?'

'The same way that I know everything about The Holy Conception, Morag told me.'

'Is there a story with it?'

'Naturally.'

'Can I hear it?'

'Morag, Kathleen Helen and another girl were due to leave the convent on the same day in October 1962. A couple of days before they were due to go the three girls posed for some photographs. Immediately after the photographic session Kathleen Helen was summoned on her own to see the Mother Superior. When she arrived at the nun's office there were three other people in attendance: a young man, an older man, who was a giant of a man, and an older woman. The Mother Superior then left the room and left the three visitors and Kathleen Helen alone together. The woman, who was in a wheelchair, did all the talking, the young man said very little and the giant just stood behind the wheelchair and said nothing at all. Kathleen Helen told Morag that the woman was Irish and she thought that the young man might have been Scottish. The woman told Kathleen Helen that she was her elder sister and that the young man was Kathleen Helen's cousin. She also said that Kathleen Helen's father had lived and died in Ireland some years ago but that she had a mother who was still alive and who now lived in France.'

'Did any of them have a name or did anybody say anything about where they were from?'

'No names of people or places of any kind were ever mentioned. Kathleen Helen asked more than once but they wouldn't give any. Apparently the woman chided her for being impatient and said names would be revealed *in good time*. The only thing that she did say when Kathleen Helen challenged her integrity was that she was *a respected lawyer*. She was greatly concerned with telling Kathleen Helen about an old Irish curse, eighty years old at that time, that had been laid against the female line of the family and that Kathleen Helen as a female member of the family was also the subject of this curse and that her life was in danger the minute she left the convent. She said that Kathleen Helen had not been a foundling child at all but had been brought to the convent to escape the curse and because her family had feared for her life all those years ago. So the story had some truth in it after all.'

'And Kathleen Helen believed her?'

'It was a complete bombshell and she was shocked by it all. She told Morag that she didn't know what to believe. She said that she thought the story about the curse was a bit silly, but the bit about the woman being her sister she believed.'

'Why was that?'

'Morag told me that she asked Kathleen Helen exactly the same thing.'

'Did she give Morag an answer?'

'She said that despite the fact that this lady was in her sixties and she herself was only eighteen, their physical resemblance to each other was startling. Kathleen Helen told Morag that she could see that the older woman, upon seeing her, was visibly taken back by that resemblance. Can you imagine how an eighteen-year-old girl must have felt?' He leaned back in his chair and as he did he removed his glasses and cleaned them with a blue handkerchief. 'So that's about most of it,' he said, 'apart from the photograph.' He picked up an envelope from the small table in front of him and handed it to Maxine, 'After our phone conversation yesterday I went out and had a copy of the photograph made for you. I'll keep the original as a memory, I've also written the name on the back of it.'

'What name, didn't you say that no names were given at the meeting?'

'Not at the time of the meeting, this was later.'

'Later?'

'Yes, two days after the girls came out of the convent Morag was staying with the young teacher, Miss Maggie, the one that you know about. Morag was alone in the house when a taxi, with a young man and a young woman in it, pulled up outside Maggie's. The woman got out of the taxi. She was dressed in fine clothes and at first Morag didn't recognise her then she realised that it was Kathleen Helen, she'd come to see Morag. They said their tearful goodbyes again and as they did Kathleen Helen pushed a piece of paper into Morag's hand, there was a name written on it. Then off she went in the car and Morag never saw nor heard of her ever again.'

Maxine slowly extracted the photograph from the envelope and looked upon it. Even though it was a photograph taken in the 1960's it was in stark black and white. It showed three very young, fresh-faced girls all dressed in similar clothes in awkward and contrived pose on a grassed lawn. Maxine's eyes were immediately drawn towards the girl on the right. 'Which one is Morag?' she said tactfully.

'Morag is in the middle, Kathleen Helen is on the right, the other girl is called Justine Joanne, but I don't think that you are interested in her are you?'

Although this was a photograph taken forty years before Maxine had ever set eyes on Helen Day, the physical resemblance between the teenage convent girl and the reclusive older woman was both astounding and conclusive. Maxine thought that Helen Day had aged very well, in fact her body shape had seemed exactly the same as a young, teenage girl as it was as a septuagenarian lady. Maxine could see without a shadow of a doubt that this was a photograph of a young Helen Day and that she and Kathleen Helen were unmistakeably the same person. She turned the photograph over and Hamish Lennox had written in large black capital letters on the back of it, '**KATHLEEN HELEN de HAY**.'

As if in further substantiation that Helen Day and Kathleen Helen de Hay were the same person, it didn't take much of Maxine's applied imagination to realise how *Kathleen Helen de Hay* had translated very easily over the years into *Helen Day*. She mused over the possible name transition: *Kathleen Helen de Hay, Helen de Hay, Helen Day!*

'There is one more thing,' said Hamish. 'After Kathleen Helen came back from the meeting she was obviously very excited, if not to say a little bewildered, and there and then she made Morag write everything down about the meeting. She was most pedantic about the script and insisted that it was word perfect, as far as her recollection went. Only thing was that Kathleen Helen didn't retrieve it and Morag kept this transcript all these years. I've also had a copy made.' He slid another envelope across the table.

As Maxine looked through the window of the train on her journey home, she thought that it had been a month and a day since she had discovered Helen Day's ritualistically murdered body on that soft, May evening in the White House in Winton Kiss. She looked again at the photograph of the fresh-faced convent girl. It saddened her that Kathleen Helen's life should end just over fifty years later in such a premature and cruel way. Now, over two hundred miles away from Winton Kiss, and through evidence from all those years ago, Maxine knew that she and Danny Senetti now had a name to work with. In fact it was more than just a name, it was the beginning of an identity. It was true of course that whilst Hamish Lennox's revelations answered one set of questions about names and identity, they threw up a whole set of others: who was the woman in the wheelchair, who was the young man? Where were they from, what was this story about a curse and, perhaps the biggest one of all, how and why did Kathleen Helen de Hay move from standing on a grass verge in a convent in County Mayo to being Helen Day and ending up being murdered, shot dead in a chair more than fifty years later in Winton Kiss? What was the journey that brought her to that fateful destination?

In summary Maxine Wells thought that some progress had been made but on the other hand she realised that every time a question was answered, that answer conversely threw up a whole host of other questions that weren't.

Chapter 26

An Unplanned Reconciliation

It occurred to Mademoiselle Antoinette Dubois that if she were to continue to have encounters with Mr Dermot de Hay, even though there were long absences between them, then it would probably mean that she was going to have to spend certain amounts of her life stepping on and off steam trains. Once again she found herself so occupied, only this time it was all very different from the last one. For one thing, she wasn't stepping out into the Wexford afternoon sunshine nor was she a young girl, albeit a headstrong one but with little of life's experience and even less of anything that could be described as resource, nor was she there this time with no clarity of purpose.

No, this time she stepped out into the Manchester March evening smog, but in contrast to the Manchester air her mind was crystal clear and just the same as the Manchester businessmen she had heard about, her will was iron-firm. She was now almost thirty years old and an established stage actress who had appeared across Europe. She had also appeared in a successful run of a play in London and she knew the city fairly well. During her time in London she had toured its countryside outskirts a little but she had never travelled before to England's provinces, particularly its northern provinces.

She told herself that this meeting would have a very different outcome than the one in Enniscorthy over ten years ago, where all the rules had been set out by Dermot the man and Antoinette the girl had been little more than an innocent bystander. This time she had demands of her own and she intended to see that they were listened to and furthermore she intended to see that they were met. She wasn't bitter, that would be too strong a description and her personality would not allow bitterness, but she was aggrieved about being separated from her daughter for the last ten years and there was some anger towards the man that she was going to meet, she didn't want it but she couldn't deny it as she considered him responsible for this separation. In pursuant of this she thought that he had treated her with disdain and some cruelty. She was expecting exactly the same from him tonight, only this time she was ready.

From the start the event of the meeting had been one of mutual consent between both Dermot and Antoinette. The venue though had not been and this had caused some disagreement, which almost amounted to a squabble between the two of them. This was before any dialogue had even begun. Both parties were agreed that the meeting place should be neutral, though it seemed that there were differing views of where *neutral* was actually meant to be. Roisin had acted as mediator between the two and the first suggestion had been a meeting in Dublin, suggested by Dermot, whereupon Antoinette more out of devilment than anything else had suggested Paris. Both cities were rejected by each respective recipient, there were some further suggestions of Galway, Toulouse and then Waterford. Eventually, Antoinette had quite simply refused to go anywhere in Ireland and Dermot, as if seemingly in reciprocation, had refused to go anywhere in France. After some wrangling, and some further mediation by Roisin, they both then agreed to meet in England. Antoinette at first would only go to London and that was the only place in England that Dermot wouldn't go to. In his communications through Roisin he had said that he would rather go to *Purgatory*.

In the end an exasperated Roisin had suggested Manchester to which Dermot had readily agreed, as Roisin knew he would, if only so he could resume his acquaintance with his old friend Arthur Finney. Antoinette had hardly ever heard of the place but she did know that Roisin lived and worked there and because of this she reasoned that it must be a pleasant environment, so to progress the matter she had also agreed. After all, she was probably only going to have to spend a couple of days there at the most, it wasn't as if she was going to live there.

Now, as she stepped off the train, she was beginning to regret her acquiescence. People dashed and buzzed all around her. She thought that they all seemed to fall into two extreme categories and that there appeared to be no middle. One category looked prosperous, well fed, well dressed, bathed and groomed, whilst the other category looked bedraggled, unclean, cold and toil-worn. The former seemed as gentry while the latter appeared as beggars and thieves. It wasn't that she minded this in itself, it was just that it made her feel a little unsure of herself and in this strange city, and with her forthcoming meeting, unsure was the last way she needed to be. As well as this a filthy, dirty, green-grey smog hung in the air. It was all around and it gripped the place like some huge clammy hand in an unwashed lace glove and it seemed to be the true master of the city. She had never witnessed anything to compare it to. All the people had scarves and masks pulled across their faces as if they were frightened of breathing in the air of the place that they lived in.

'Miss Dubois, Miss Antoinette Dubois?' a voice asked.

A man moved forward and gently took her valise. He spoke but he had a strange accent, even for an Englishman, and Antoinette couldn't quite hear what he was saying. She did though notice his appearance, she thought to herself how could she not notice, he was a huge man, both in height and in stature, and he had a large black walrus moustache. His appearance was a little fearsome at first glance, but Antoinette looked into his brown eyes and she saw strength, gentleness and intelligence. She knew immediately that he was a man she could trust. She had never met him before but he had been described to her in one of Roisin's letters, she remembered his name now, it was Stanley Oldknow.

'Ah, you did very well to find me Monsieur, amongst all these people.'

'It was your elegance and beauty Ma'am, I was advised to look for your elegance and beauty.'

She thought that as rough-hewn as Stanley seemed he wasn't without a little measure of the old traditional charm.

Stanley led Antoinette along the draughty station platforms and out of the station altogether. There was a waiting taxi and as they both took their seats inside it he spoke again, 'You are booked into the Midland Hotel which is a short drive from here, it is the best hotel in Manchester. Your room is reserved for as long as you wish it to be and your account has been settled in advance. I have been retained by Roisin de Hay and I am to inform you that I am here for you and that I am on your side and nobody else's, that is in the event that sides are taken, which I am further informed that they will not be. Here is my card and you can find me at this address should you need me.'

'Thank you Monsieur Stanley, I am comforted by your allegiance.'

'Mr de Hay will be arriving shortly at the hotel, if he has not already done so, and I have been requested to give you this.' He handed her a small white envelope, she placed it unopened inside her purse.

After about ten minutes they arrived at the Midland Hotel. Stanley ensured that Antoinette was *safe and sound,* as he put it, then he left as quickly as he had arrived. Minutes later, in the safety and comfort of her room, Antoinette sat on her bed and opened the envelope that he had previously given to her. There was a handwritten note inside, it was brief and it read:

Dear Antoinette,

Welcome to Manchester, I hope your journey was a comfortable one. I will meet you in the hotel restaurant at eight. Looking forward to our discussion.

Dermot

She checked the time, it was 5:45pm, she thought that she had time for a little sleep.

At 8:15pm the headwaiter at the Midland Hotel walked in front of Antoinette Dubois as he led her to Dermot de Hay's table. Dermot first noticed her at the restaurant entrance, she was bareheaded save for a black tiara in her blond hair, which glistened in the restaurant lights. She wore a black satin evening dress that clung to her figure as a second skin. Every head in the room, staff and guest, male and female, old and young, turned in her direction as she passed them by. She was a devastating combination of practised poise, theatrical elegance and outstanding natural beauty.

Dermot had thought her beautiful at their first encounter ten years ago, but she had been little more than a young girl then but now, as she walked towards him, she was a woman at the pinnacle of her sexuality and he thought that she was absolutely sensational!

The headwaiter moved the chair so that Antoinette could sit down at the table. This she did, opposite Dermot, and as she did she fixed him with her amber eyes.

'At last,' he said.

'Yes,' she said, giggling a little, 'I think that I fully understand what you mean.'

The headwaiter handed both her and Dermot a menu and after a few minutes silent scrutiny they chose from it. She studied this man across the table. He was ten years older than their last encounter but apart from a few more grey flecks to his otherwise black hair he looked no different. He still exuded an effortless calm authority, she thought that he was still extremely attractive and that he had a sense of virility that came from within. He poured her a glass of red wine. She placed it to her lips and sipped a little. She thought she tasted plum and damson, she took another sip.

'Miss Dubois...' he began.

'Miss Dubois,' she interrupted, 'you called me Antoinette in your letter, now we have reverted to Miss Dubois.'

'Antoinette, I would wish to start off by saying...'

'Monsieur de Hay, no Dermot,' she interrupted again, 'perhaps I would wish to start off by saying this time.'

'Very well Antoinette.'

'My daughter Marguerite, I presume that she is still called Marguerite, you have not changed her name the way you have changed many other things?'

'No, we have not, she always has been Marguerite and always will be.'

'This is what I want Monsieur from this meeting: I want to be in my daughter's life. I don't quite know how, I have not yet worked out any detail. I have been in exile far too long and I am ending this exile from now, that is it.'

'You are right Antoinette, it is the way it should be, I agree.'

'You agree, just this way, after all these years, after all these terms and conditions you placed upon me, treating me the same as one of your bank contracts?'

'I do agree and more. We cannot alter the past but I apologise for the way that I treated you. I had my reasons, it was all to do with my grief over the loss of my son and another matter that stretches back through time. My thinking became twisted but all this seems excuses now, even to myself. I now realise that my behaviour was unkind and cruel and I am sorry, I apologise. Will you help me make amends?'

'This is amazing, I do not know what to say, I was not expecting it. I came here for a fight, I have prepared for a fight, I want a fight, I demand a fight. I have been cheated of my passion.'

'There is no fight here tonight Antoinette, we are on the same side.'

She sipped the rest of her wine and pushed her empty glass towards him for a refill. He filled the glass and waited patiently.

She leaned over the table and kissed him on both cheeks. Then she kissed him on the lips. There were hushed murmurs around the dining room.

The waiters began to arrive with their food and Dermot ordered more wine. They ate and drank and talked until just before midnight as if they were two old-time, long-estranged, newly-reunited lovers.

Just after midnight and completely unexpectedly for either of them the nearly sixty-year-old banker and the nearly thirty-year-old actress did become lovers. It would prove to be the only complete love that either of them would ever find in another person and that love would last for the rest of their lives.

Chapter 27

The Air Raid Warden

A few hours before the late spring evening fell slowly into its wartime darkness, the air raid warden looked down through the large third floor window of the building in the university campus and onto the small quadrangle below.

For two very different reasons, today was to be a very important day in the life of two very different people and he was one of them. The other person, and she was the object of his current attention, was a casually dressed, slim and beautiful, young female student who he watched as she walked easily through the small garden to the other side of the square. His eyes followed her as she moved out through the open campus gates. She crossed the quiet street and passed into the entrance of the building on the other side of the road before finally disappearing from his sight altogether. He was not perturbed by this temporary disappearance for he knew most of what there was to know about this young woman and that included why and where she was going to now and why and where she was going for the remainder of that evening or for that matter for the remainder of her life.

As he approached his fifty-third year the air raid warden's mind was fixed upon the knowledge that most of his adult life had been a story of shortcoming and failure. His achievements in this time had amounted to very little, in fact they had amounted to less than that, in his own eyes they had amounted to nothing and in the eyes of others he felt that he had been a disappointment to everybody. When he thought of the word everybody, it referred to only a small number, but that number was all that mattered: three persons, two dead and one alive, his Great Ancestor, his late father and himself.

He had tried, he knew that, he had tried but he had not succeeded. This disappointment and failure had not been in the traditional sense of material comfort nor did it relate to status or money for he had enough of these to satisfy his own needs and wants. No, Joseph's disappointment was not concerned with the traditional comforts of life, it was all to do with a promise that he had made to his father many years ago. It made no difference that his father was long dead for this promise was inflexible and was cast in the infinite and he could not be unbound from its fetters until he had honoured it. This promise was rooted in the Peasants Decree and that decree had been sourced in the Oath and he had not yet discharged his own obligation to either of these. This obligation was common to both and it was retribution by execution.

He had almost succeeded fourteen years ago in Manchester, in fact he had come very close, with his meticulously planned and daringly executed attempt on the female solicitor, but he had been deflected at the very last moment and when you were on the business of the Oath there was no such measure as *nearly* or *come close,* there was only success or failure and he had *failed* in this attempt. Even worse than this he had almost been caught and apprehended there and then, which would have been disastrous for the future business of the Oath. For this business had to be perpetuated and live on until all the de Hay women were executed and there was no prospect of any more.

The just hand of his Great Ancestor though had intervened on that day and he had not been apprehended, he had escaped. Immediately after his escape he had stayed in the Manchester area and once he had recovered mentally and physically and once he had discovered that Roisin de Hay was not going to die from her wounds he had considered another attempt on her and for a time he had carried out a few covert observations on the hospital that she had been admitted to. In the end though he had decided against it. Total confidence wasn't there and the Oath dictated that executions had to be carried out observing certain conditions and rituals and he couldn't find a way to have a real chance to satisfy these. As well as this, two people had seen him and he was now recognised.

Roisin de Hay, he decided, was too clever and too suspicious and had allies who were just as clever and suspicious as she was, so the whole idea was too risky. In addition to this his failed attempt had received great publicity. This resulted in a *police manhunt*, as the newspapers described it, being launched and although it very quickly came to nothing, as he felt sure it would for he had covered his tracks very well, the whole fiasco unnerved him. The final point came when, during the manhunt story, the newspapers published a pencil drawn sketch of him that bore too much of an uncanny resemblance. At the time he had no idea where this sketch had originated, but it had unnerved him greatly and immediately after its publication he moved quickly out of Manchester and back down to the anonymity of the great numbers of people in crowded London.

The story was circulating even in London, but soon all the fuss stopped and eventually everything returned to normal. That is to say inasmuch as his life could ever be deemed to have any normality, as it was relentlessly dictated to by his commitment to the Oath. He knew that there was at least one other person around that would enable him to honour his promise. He would just have to exercise some patience. He also promised himself that the female solicitor had not escaped retribution entirely, not whilst she was alive. In time she would forget the danger and become less alert and more complacent and then he would revisit the situation. For the time being though he would leave her alone.

After taking two years out, he then turned his attention to the de Hay family in Enniscorthy, Wexford and in particular to the young French import of that family, Marguerite de Hay. At the time of the attempt in Manchester she had still been a child and the Oath forbade any action against children whilst they were such, but of course children do not stay as children forever. This time he had decided steadfastly that he would operate in a very different way. He would apply patience and operate from a distance. He would not present himself in any guise whatsoever until a few minutes before the actual act. Outside information was just as reliable as inside information if it was correct, it was just that it took much longer in the gathering.

Throughout the 1930's he made two trips to Wexford County where he gathered information about Marguerite. It was all done discreetly and without arousing the slightest suspicion of anybody that was close to her. On the second trip he befriended a female servant in the de Hay household and he learnt much from her.

Latterly he had learned that Marguerite's mother, the French born Antoinette Dubois, had returned to the scene after a long absence in France and was now jointly bringing the young Marguerite up with the Grandfather Dermot de Hay. On one occasion Joseph had also observed Dermot and Marguerite's mother alone, initially he was a little surprised at his findings. On this occasion however, he concluded that he knew enough about relationships to know that their relationship was much more intimate than just that of grandfather and mother and that they had something else in common as well as young Marguerite.

So, throughout the years Joseph tracked Marguerite and as he did he learned everything that could be learned about her but this time he did it from a distance, *observation without engagement* he called it.

The years went by and in September 1940 a twenty-three-year-old Marguerite came to Liverpool University to study languages. So close to the situation and informed was he by that time that he even knew that the family had wanted her to study in Manchester so that she could be kept under the watchful eye of her Aunt Roisin. That news had caused him great anxiety and almost thrown him into a panic and he was gratefully relieved when he discovered that Marguerite had decided that she would study in Liverpool instead, so as to decidedly *not* be under the watchful eye of her Aunt Roisin.

He had arrived in Liverpool himself in June 1940 in anticipation of Marguerite's own arrival and in order to establish himself in residence. He had immediately rented a small house close to the faculty of languages and set up his observations from there. Then he had come up with his masterstroke, he had then volunteered as an air raid warden and had been accepted. This official status gave him both opportunity and impunity to walk around the streets of Liverpool at will, particularly at night when everybody else was inside behind blackout measures.

He had quickly made it his business to find out everything that there was to find out about Marguerite's prospective academic course: when the lectures were, where they were, what times they were, information about the tutors, anything. No morsel of information was irrelevant. He even attended some of the lectures himself and he sat in silence several rows behind her in the darkened auditorium. Nobody took any notice for he was just another interested party, another student, a little older than many of them but nevertheless just another student.

In all this time he wrote nothing down, nor did he seek any interviews with his intended victim or anybody close to her apart from the servant girl. He would not leave behind any tell-tale clues, descriptions nor evidence. Everything he needed to learn would be done by looking and listening, there was no need to speak or make note and everything was retained in his head.

He had been there, hidden in open sight on the dockside, when Marguerite had arrived in Liverpool for the first time with her mother, Antoinette Dubois. He had observed, as an aside, how beautiful she was and indeed how beautiful her mother was, like mother, like daughter, he had thought.

He had stayed at the Adelphi Hotel for the two nights that Marguerite and Antoinette had stayed there and dined in the same hotel restaurant. Sitting several tables away from them, he had observed again as an aside that their relationship seemed a little abrasive for a mother and daughter and that there seemed to be much conflict in their interchanges, but then again he remembered that he had never had a mother nor a daughter, so perhaps this was all usual.

On the second night he had misjudged the time and had been forced to pass by their table momentarily. As they looked up at him he had noticed both mother and daughter's unusually coloured amber eyes. He had taken care not to seem interested in their discourse and neither mother and daughter nor any of the other diners took any notice of the anonymous businessman reading his newspaper sat by the window dining solo, why would they?

He had set about finding out everything about Marguerite: where she lived, who her friends were, what her habits were. He even knew what time she arose in the morning and what time she retired at night, his air raid warden's role enabled him to find such information out. Members of the public confided in him, sometimes about others, and on two occasions they had informed on Marguerite telling him that she had not been in the shelter that night. She had been working alone in her house jeopardising the wartime blackout. As an air raid warden it should have been his duty to call on her and remind her of her responsibilities to both herself and her neighbours during the measures. He didn't do this but then his dutiful neglect suited his own purpose for the time being, so he made no such call.

The intervening months between Marguerite's arrival and the current day had been dominated in Liverpool itself by the early events of World War Two in general and by the German Luftwaffe's aerial bombardment of that city in particular. The German air force had given Liverpool more blitzkrieg attention than anywhere else outside London and now, in May 1941, this aerial bombardment was at its zenith. Air raid precautions and plans were in place all over the city. The general population, the authorities and the university were completely preoccupied with these plans and this preoccupation would be used to his advantage.

This time he would not become weakened through over confidence nor give anybody any opportunity to be alerted to his purpose. He was certain that as things remained anybody and everybody save himself was oblivious to that. He thought again of the attempt on Marguerite's aunt, Roisin. He had made everything far too complicated and he had tried to be far too clever. He had allowed his victim far too much time. He had underestimated her and given her too many opportunities for detection and to recruit alliance to her side. He had been too flamboyant with his fine clothes, posh hotels and his assumed airs and graces. He had got himself noticed. He would not make the same mistake with her

274

niece. This time he would give no hint, it would be swift and straightforward, the whole business no more than a few seconds from start to finish. He reminded himself of some of the content of the Peasants Decree, written by his father in the Gresham Hotel, Dublin almost sixty years ago, it had been preached to him and read to him so many times by his father that he knew every letter of it, every emphasis, every nuance, verbatim, perfect:

'...the end will not linger, it will come quickly to them. The adult women will suffer the deed and their end will be ruthless and shocking yet swift and conclusive...'

That indeed is what he would now be, *swift and conclusive.*

There was another reason connected to the Oath that demanded that Marguerite de Hay's execution must be successful and this was yet again another example of his own familial shortcoming. He had failed to persuade his only child and son, Timothy, to follow the teaching of the Oath. The boy had been totally unreceptive to any involvement and this was because he was deeply and completely under the influence of his Spanish born mother. Her influence had been so strong and Joseph had been so desperate for the boy to follow his teaching that he had made the very mistaken decision of taking Timothy's mother into his confidence. He had told her all about the Oath in exactly the same way that his father had told him.

She had no loyalty towards her own husband and at first she seemed to disbelieve him. Then she had declared the whole idea as mad. She had said to him in front of Timothy that something that happened in Ireland all those years ago has nothing to do with us now and that everybody needed to forgive and forget. She had said that she had come to England to escape the killing in her own country and that there should be no more here. Worst of all she had mocked with sarcasm at his endeavours to persuade Timothy to his cause and had undermined his influence as a father, so much and so often and sometimes right there in front of the boy, that he had seen no way out of her outrageous behaviour and he had planned to kill her.

He got as far as contriving a plan for her demise and having his plan in place. His intention was to take her on a Thames river trip and drown her. He was no more than a few days away from its execution when he was completely thwarted. He had returned to the house after a short business trip to find that his wife had disappeared and taken young Timothy with her. When he made some enquiries he discovered that despite her protestations about her *own country* she had gone back to live there and she had taken his son Timothy with her.

She was a Montoya and as such was a member of a large volatile and protective Spanish family, so to follow her and to try and retrieve the boy would have put his own life in jeopardy of loss. There was little he could do, so he just had to accept the situation. The boy's abduction, for that was how he saw it, now made the business and prospects for the Oath much more difficult to execute and continue, for he had been robbed of his natural successor. Despite all this he had been determined that he would find another and for a while he thought that he may have to find another wife as well. This he didn't want to do and it would be a sacrifice as he wasn't comfortable in the company of most women and found living with one in particular an arduous task that brought him no pleasure whatsoever. Yet he would do all of these things if it meant fulfilling his promise to the Oath. Then he reasoned that he may not have to carry out any of these actions after all.

He thought long and hard in an attempt to reconcile this apparent failure with his own conscience. His reasoning was based thus: there were now only two women who rightly bore the name of the Middleman and stood between him and the business of the Oath, Marguerite and Roisin. If you included Dermot de Hay in this collective then there were still only three people who were de Hay's and the Peasants Decree was not concerned with the male line. The Oath was concerned with female progeny and even though Dermot was a man and was excluded, he was in a relationship with Antoinette Dubois. The man by now was almost seventy years of age and the woman in her early forties, both normally long past the age of giving or conceiving children. It was therefore highly improbable, but not impossible, that any children would result from this relationship. Roisin was a little older than Antoinette and as well as this seemed to have no male partner. His own efforts had rendered her wheelchair-bound so the same deduction in relation to having children that applied to Antoinette and Dermot also applied to her.

Marguerite on the other hand was a young woman who could go on to have many children in all kinds of circumstances and they could all be girls and her own children could have children. In theory she could breed a whole new de Hay female dynasty. By the time that they came to adulthood Joseph would be an old man or a dead one and with no successor to carry on the business of the Oath. This realisation filled him with despair and depression.

This was why his attempt on Marguerite must not go the same way as his attempt on her aunt. It must be quick and clean, but most of all it must be successful. Once he had snuffed out Marguerite's potential the de Hay line was virtually finished. Roisin was still a loose end but he could return to her if and when he chose, but now it was vital that he settle Marguerite. Some of the ritual may have to be sacrificed but that was unimportant as long as her end was brought about. As far as the ritual was concerned he had been forced to leave the one remaining derringer out of the errand anyway. Wartime Liverpool was in a panic, everybody was a potential German spy and the authorities, just to be on the safe side, would arrest you and search your property on the strength of nothing more than a piece of street gossip, or something that had been said in the pub or a shop. He just could not afford for the gun to be found so he had taken it back to London and hidden it. There were many ways to kill a person, you didn't have to shoot them. The method on this occasion would have to take second place to the deed but the deed must be absolute and whatever else happens then Marguerite de Hay's life must end – tonight.

Later that evening, as the sounds and the sights of the bombing of Liverpool continued, first year student linguist, Marguerite de Hay settled down alone in the tiny house that she shared with another student. She sat at the large table with the immaculate white tablecloth in the kitchen of her tiny terraced house and thought about her project. This night she would not go to the communal air raid shelter as her housemate had done. This night she had an important project to work on and she would not be intimidated into ignominious refuge by the Luftwaffe's threat or any orders from minor officials.

A few streets away the air raid warden sat at his own table in the kitchen of his tiny terraced house writing a letter. Having finished it he then placed the letter in a plain stamped envelope and addressed it. He went out of his front door and posted the letter in the post-box at the end of the street. He navigated a few more streets and finally arrived at the one that was his destination. He walked slowly down this street towards the small house at the end of it. The sky overhead was alight and noisy from the illumination and sound of gunfire and bomb blasts but the little street itself was eerily in complete darkness. If anybody was at home they sat in that quiet darkness behind blackout blinds, but the air raid warden knew that on this particular night all the occupants of that street, and the other immediate streets, were already in the communal air raid shelter. All the occupants that is except one, for he had particular information that there was one resident who, not for the first time, was defying the blackout!

Even in the darkness of the blackout he knew every crack and undulation in the pavement for he had purposely walked its length and breadth many times before. As he came to the last house at its end he stopped and tapped on the window with his warden's stick. Quietly he said, 'Air raid warden Miss, please let me in.'

The door opened quickly and silently and he stepped inside it. He shut it just as quickly and silently.

'Keep to the blackout Miss.'

Inside the house he stood face to face with a young woman. The man in the air raid warden's uniform knew her to be Marguerite de Hay whereas she only knew him to be the local air raid warden. Continuing the charade he said, 'You know Miss that you are supposed to be in the air raid shelter.'

She sat down without replying, he fixed her with an avuncular look then without saying another word he moved around to the back of the chair. In the space of a few short seconds he grabbed her long hair, pulled her head back and produced a barber's open razor in his right hand which he sliced with force across her neck from left to right. The young woman made a slight gurgling sound then her life's blood gushed and spurted away from her through the gaping wound. He released his hold and let her head fall to the table and as it did the blood turned the white tablecloth crimson red. He stood silently looking down on the life-expired body of this young woman as she lay slumped and motionless across the reddened tablecloth. Her blood was now beginning to drip off the edge of the cloth on the table top and it formed a small pool on the wooden floor below. The open razor, still in his hand, glistened and dripped with the same blood.

He felt no hatred, no malice towards her and in a perverse way he had some feeling for her. For without her he could not have gained the cold satisfaction and relief of a lifetime's obligation that was now discharged. He felt that perhaps now he had made an atonement to his Great Ancestor and to his beloved late father. He wiped the razor clean on the remaining white edge of the tablecloth, washed the blade clean under the tap on the kitchen sink, then opening the palm of his left hand he pulled the gaping blade across it with his right. The blood oozed gently from the self-inflicted wound and he felt a little weakened by the sudden loss, but he also felt cleansed by this almost sacramental action.

Then, without warning, the bomb came. It crashed through the roof of the tiny house, it blew the walls and floors apart and it lifted the air raid warden off his feet. It blew his right leg in one direction and the rest of his body in another as its deadly force catapulted him through the closed window leaving shattered glass, large splinters of wood and fragments of broken slates all around and leaving him as just another bloodied, broken, wartime bombing casualty, lying motionless in the middle of the dark cobbled, wartime Liverpool street.

Chapter 28

The Funeral

Today at 2:15pm was the date and time set for Helen Day's funeral.

After Helen's death, and in the weeks prior to the funeral, both Norford Borough Council and the local police made some enquiries to see if any trace of her family or friends could be found, but all these attempts were unsuccessful. An Internet appeal had been launched by the council and they had also taken out some space in the *Norford Gazette* in a similar vein but not one solitary person had come forward. There was not even anyone to identify the body and eventually Maxine Wells, as the *registered doctor of the deceased,* had been called in to perform that unceremonious task.

In the absence of such familial or friendship connections the funeral itself was therefore a sparse affair indeed. The Reverend Bel read both the sermon and the lesson in the tiny chapel at Norford crematorium. The other mourners were Doctor Maxine Wells, Ms Theresa Rafferty, councillors Karen Spencer and Danny Senetti, a manager from the council's *Cems and Crems* team and an unidentified detective constable despatched as a matter of police routine by Detective Sergeant Lisa Dobbs on a *fishing expedition*, the extent of which was to see and identify any mourners who turned up for the funeral.

The Reverend Bel made a fleeting reference to the circumstances of Helen's death, *taken prematurely from us in lonely and brutal circumstances*. She then went on to explain how no outcome of death was lonely as God was always by our side and then she focussed on what she probably considered to be the positive aspects of Helen's life, a quiet, sensitive, independent person. All in all, the unspoken general consensus was that under the circumstances she gave a respectful and competent sermon.

When the ceremony was over the *Cems and Crems* man stayed behind to lock the doors and after a brief interchange of respectful courtesies in the afternoon summer sunshine, the rest of the mourners and the vicar went their separate ways. All that is except Danny and Maxine who stayed together. Danny had come to the ceremony straight from council business at the town hall and he had travelled into Norford that morning by train. The plan was for Maxine to drive him home to Winton Kiss and as well as this, apart from a telephone conversation that Maxine had initiated when she was just about to board her return train from Edinburgh, it was the first opportunity that they had been able to find to play catch-up on the case.

Now, as they both sat in the little *In and Out* café across the road from the cemetery with their cups of coffee in front of them, Maxine produced the two envelopes given to her previously by Hamish Lennox. Danny took the photograph out of one and the transcript from the other. He studied the photograph for a few seconds then he read the transcript before speaking, 'Not much of a turnout, I knew that she was a reclusive spinster but I thought that there might just be some long lost relatives or friends that would put in an appearance as they often do at funerals, but I suppose by definition reclusive spinsters don't have those kinds of connections.'

'Helen wasn't always a reclusive spinster, in fact as a younger woman she had a child.'

'Really, I didn't know that, son or daughter?'

'I don't know which, I only know about the birth itself from the medical records.'

'What happened to the child?'

'I don't know that either.'

'You would think that perhaps he or she would turn up for their own mother's funeral.'

'Maybe the son or daughter doesn't know she's dead. I asked Helen about her child some years ago. She told me that they had no contact, as I recall the phrase that she used was that they were *completely estranged.*'

Danny turned his attention back to the photograph. He said, 'it really is quite uncanny that somebody can be so recognisable and still look more or less the same after all these years.'

'A lot of it is to do with body shape and bone structure, Helen probably weighed exactly the same when she was seventy as she did when she was seventeen and with the exception of the last couple of months she was blessed with good health for most of her life. I think that she'd had a bit of a problem with drink and drugs some years back and she was a little bit of an occasional binge drinker, but amazingly enough that doesn't show on some people, she was one of those people, and I don't think that she had any other really bad habits.'

'How exactly do us lesser beings stave off the ravages of time and bad habits?'

'You can do certain things that help such as not demolish your recommended weekly alcohol intake in one day, every day, but in the main genetics play a significant part in it as they do with all anatomy.'

Danny didn't know whether the remark was aimed at him or not. He thought that some of it probably was and that it was best to ignore it so he did. He looked at the photograph again, 'Well, she's obviously a lot younger but there's no doubt in my mind, that's definitely Helen Day or should I say Kathleen Helen de Hay.'

'Yes I agree, it's very conclusive.'

'I ran into Superintendent Mathew Showman this morning in the town hall car park. I could tell that he was trying to avoid me but he just couldn't manage it. When I eventually did engage him he seemed more interested in my dirty number plate than a murder and a hit and run. Even with that I'm not sure that he wasn't just trying to divert attention. I asked him about progress on both Kathleen Helen's and Archie's cases. I was very polite and so was he, but he didn't tell me anything. I used the ex-son-in-law bit in relation to Archie's investigation, only I left the *ex* out, but I don't think he knew of the relationship anyway. He kept calling me

Councillor in that sarcastic way that people do when they want you to know that in their view the position stands for nothing and he also gave me all that police jargon stuff that you hear on those TV detective shows, you know, *lines of enquiry, just need a breakthrough.* He used the word *confidential* and the words *sorry I'm not at liberty to say* more times than what he actually did say.'

'What exactly *did* he say?'

'He said it was all confidential and that he wasn't at liberty to say, *Councillor.*'

'Danny!'

'Maxine, what he actually said was irrelevant, it really was, but it translated as we are the police, you're not, so mind your own business and if we had a clue, which we don't have, then it would be nothing to do with you, which with Dim and Dobb on the case is exactly what I expected.'

'Did you tell him what we'd found out?'

'Well, it went through my mind for about a tenth of a second but no I didn't.'

'Do you think that perhaps we should?'

'I think that perhaps we should, but then again we're not going to are we?'

'Whilst we're speaking police jargon, what about withholding information?' she asked.

'I did think about that Maxine, it's just that there might be more to come from Noel and Hamish yet. We don't know, they might just remember something else. If we put Dim and Dob onto O'Malley and they go over there, he'll run out of the county. He'll probably never speak to me again and with what you've told me about Hamish he'll probably do the same. Anyway we're not really withholding information directly connected to the murder enquiry. We know more about Kathleen Helen's previous life, that's true, but up to now we don't know any more about the murder than the police themselves. In fact they'll have access to all that forensic evidence that you're so fond of reminding me about so they should know much more than we do.'

'Why then Danny do I feel that they don't?'

'You feel that way because you've had direct experience of them and you are probably right but let's just leave them to their own devices, they are not bothering us at the moment which suits me fine, so let's concentrate on what we've discovered about Kathleen Helen and progress from there.'

Maxine said, 'alright then, we know that she started life as Kathleen Helen de Hay and that she spent the first eighteen years of her life in the convent. Going off Hamish's account she had family, and they were not a poor or a troubled family, so why would you be in a convent for the first eighteen years of your life in those circumstances?'

'Perhaps because you were the subject of an old Irish curse and your life was in danger so your family hid you away in the convent for your own protection, where they knew nobody would find you or possibly even be aware of your existence.'

'Do you actually believe that stuff about the curse Danny?'

'I don't have to, it wasn't me that put Kathleen Helen in the convent but perhaps somebody believed it. As you have just said, there seems to be no ordinary reason for her to be in there, so perhaps there is an extraordinary one. I don't think we can just dismiss it as an impossibility. I've heard of these curses and oaths before. Most of the time they are nonsense but let's just keep an open mind for the moment. In Albania these curses can just start out with somebody feeling that they've been slighted then it escalates from there, they turn into feuds and involve whole families. Farmers swear these oaths and they can very quickly turn into vendettas and once established they can last for hundreds of years.'

'Danny, we're in a convent in western Ireland not on a farm in Albania. Are you actually trying to say that you believe this curse is connected to Helen Day's death?'

'No Maxine, I'm not, I'm just saying that it might be and that we should keep an open mind about the whole situation.'

'Well, I think that we should take a more logical and grounded approach.'

'What would that be to do with then?'

'It would be to do with Kathleen Helen's visitors at the convent,' she said.

'We don't know that much about them do we?'

'If they were telling the truth we know some important bits and the more we find out about them, then the more we find out about Kathleen Helen.'

'Is there any reason why they shouldn't be telling the truth?'

'No Danny, I can't think of one but let's accept that they were and let's also accept that Kathleen Helen's ear for accents is to be relied upon. We know that the young man was Kathleen Helen's cousin and we think he was Scottish whereas the woman who was her sister was Irish and she was a respected lawyer.'

'Where does this take us to, a young Scotsman, there are thousands of them? And lawyers, how many of them are around, there must be fifty of them in the town hall alone?'

'No Danny, she didn't just say that she was a lawyer, she said that she was a *respected* lawyer, the word respected is important. Read the transcript, Hamish was very insistent that it's a pedantic record.'

Danny looked back at the transcript, 'It does say respected, but why is that word so important?'

'Well, I've no doubt that it was her own perception she was referring to, but it implies that she had a reputation, at least in her own eyes, and if you think that you have a reputation then you have to have had a certain amount of time to establish it, which suggests that she'd been practicing for some years. Kathleen Helen told Morag that this sister was in her sixties when she visited her at the convent so let's guess and say that she'd been practising for thirty years. This meeting in the convent was in 1962 so that would take the lawyer back to say 1932.'

'There must be some kind of register for lawyers so she should be on it.'

'Exactly,' said Maxine, 'so there is a good chance that she's traceable. If only we had a name.'

'I think that we've possibly got half of one Maxine, it is obvious but we shouldn't discard the obvious.'

'Explain.'

'Well, the sister said that Kathleen Helen's father is dead but her mother is alive and lives in France, why would you live in France when your apparent connections are in Ireland?'

'What apparent connections?'

'Your daughter, your late husband.'

'Well, there could be a hundred reasons, lots of people live in France. Maria Wheeler who used to live next door to me now lives in France. She just went to live there three years ago for no apparent reason. She never said why and I didn't ask.'

'Maxine, forget the girl next door and remember we're in 1962, that's over fifty years ago, before either of us were born. Most people in those days hadn't even been on a boat or an aeroplane, they hadn't been outside their own country unless it was to do military service and that was usually just the men. So there wouldn't be a hundred reasons in 1962 why, as the widow of an Irishman and the mother of an Irish girl, you went to live in France. So what would be a really obvious reason?'

'Because you're French?'

'Because you're French,' he repeated, 'exactly, and that's where your home is. We've got this far through a combination of guesswork and assumptions so let's try a few more. If Kathleen Helen's mother is French and her father is Irish, as is the sister, and also given the sister's age and the fact that the father is dead then it's probable that the sisterly connection is on the father's side, so they are probably half-sisters, same father, different mother. That's enough to be going on with, agreed?'

'Agreed.'

'So, on the balance of probability Maxine, just to review, the mother is French, the sister is Irish and so the blood tie for sister is on the paternal side and sister is Kathleen Helen's father's daughter and Kathleen Helen's name is de Hay, therefore it is a sound assumption that fathers names is de Hay and it follows on that so is sisters.' He stopped speaking and thought for a moment before carrying on, 'There is only one thing wrong with that, sister may have married and assumed her husband's name.'

'It would be very unusual that she would be practising as a lawyer in the 1930's as a married woman. In those days you were just not allowed to have such careers if you were a married woman.'

'I didn't know that.'

'Oh yes, my father's mother had to give up being a teacher when she got married. That was back in the 1930's as well, it was either the husband or the career.'

'Your father's mother, what an unusual way to describe somebody, do you mean your grandmother?'

'Well I never actually knew her and anyway she's not...'

'Not what?'

'She's not my grandmother but let's not get side tracked, if you want to delve into my family history then lets save it for another day. Let's give our attention to filling in the blanks on the de Hay family, not the Wells family or the Senetti family, we can do either of those another time.'

He looked a little puzzled by her incomplete answer but then he said, 'So we're probably looking for an unmarried female lawyer practicing in Ireland in or around 1932 called de Hay.'

'No, not exactly,' said Maxine.

'Why not exactly?'

'Well Danny, the name de Hay doesn't sound like an Irish name to me, in fact I hate to muddy the waters but if anything it actually sounds French. We're assuming Kathleen Helen's mother was French, how do we know that Kathleen Helen wasn't given her mother's name which was de Hay and that the sister didn't have a different family name altogether?'

'Maxine, we don't know anything as absolute, we're just guessing remember, but we're undermining our own guesses a bit now and they could just be right. Let's make an assumption and stick with it until we know otherwise. The convent was in Ireland so to all intents and purposes Kathleen Helen was Irish, at least for the first eighteen years of her life. The sister was Irish and even though de Hay does sound French, and probably is of French origin, I think that I've heard that name before in Ireland. I think that it's one of those old Irish-Norman names like the name of that singer, what's he called? The one that sings about not paying the ferryman, and he's Irish. I think that de Hay has got a very good chance of being Kathleen Helen's father's name so it's also got a good chance of being the sister's family name. It's also an unusual name so we should be able to rule it out fairly easily one way or the other. So, as we've said before, we find again that all roads lead to Ireland.'

'Chris de Burgh, that's who you're thinking of. No Danny, not quite all roads, I can agree with you about the name, it could easily be Irish and I can agree with you about the rest, it's just the idea of the sister practising as a lawyer in Ireland around that time that I disagree with. You see there would have been very few female lawyers in Ireland in 1932. It wasn't until 1919 that a sex disqualification removal act was passed in the UK. Before this act women were disqualified from entering what were known as the higher professions and right at the top of this list that they were excluded from were medicine and the law. So they just were not allowed to be doctors or lawyers. In 1932, that's only thirteen years later, this act would have barely taken effect so I doubt if there would have been a hundred female lawyers in the whole of England, that number would have been down to a handful in Ireland if there were any at all.'

'Maxine, how do you know this stuff, where did you learn it from, why did you learn it?'

'Danny, I know it because I'm a woman and I know it because I now work in a profession that less than a hundred years ago my great-grandmother would have been excluded from. Excluded by a law, a law made by men, the purpose of it being to exclude women.'

'Are you sure you're not just exaggerating a little bit?' As soon as these words left his lips he knew that, for the sake of harmony, they shouldn't have done.

'Danny, for a highly intelligent and well educated man your ignorance on the history of women's issues is highly unintelligent and fairly complete.'

'Alright, alright, I submit, but we can't keep living in less enlightened times can we? So for the sake of the present day investigation, or even just for the exercise, can you just jump down off Boadicea's chariot for a minute, you've sacked Colchester and razed it to the ground, they've all surrendered, including me, and the blades that are sticking out from your chariot wheels are getting a little too close to my legs. What I really think you're saying is that we should start looking in England and not Ireland.'

'I think so, yes.'

'Alright, I can accept your reasoning. If you are right, and I rush to add that I think that you are, then there can't have been an abundance of female lawyers called de Hay practicing in the 30's in either England or Ireland so if we can just find one then it is probably the one that we want so let's at least look for her. The problem now is where do we start to look?'

'Well that's not too difficult, the legal profession's forte is keeping records and I would have thought that the names of its lawyers would have to be right at the forefront of those records, this would have to be public knowledge. The lawyers wouldn't have been able to charge those fat fees that they've been charging since the days of the Sophists, if their identities had been kept secret.'

'That's better, its tremendous when you are being creative, but has anybody told you recently that there is an element of cynicism creeping into your nature.'

'If that's true then it's true. Maybe it's the company that I've been keeping lately but, as I was attempting to say, I'll be amazed if there hasn't been a register for lawyers since we had the first lawyer, so there will surely be one for the 1930's. I've got a barrister friend that I was at school with, she has a practice in Manchester. I'll make contact and see if we can be pointed in the right direction.'

'Man or woman?'

'What do you mean, man or woman?'

'You're barrister friend, man or woman?'

'Woman actually.'

'Hmm!'

'What do you mean hmm?'

'Is she married?'

'She has been, why do you ask?'

'No particular reason.'

He grinned.

Chapter 29

Impossible News

It was impossible news and she said so.

The truth of it was that, even though the top medical opinion in the whole county had just confirmed it less than half an hour ago, as she stood outside in the main street of Wexford town the former Mademoiselle Antoinette Dubois, now the present Madame Antoinette de Hay, still could not quite believe it.

With a confident smile and a flamboyant gesture of his hand, Doctor Cathal Michael Costello, MD, as the mahogany and silver inscribed plaque fixed outside to his surgery wall attested, had dismissed his patient's denials, protestations and arguments regarding her own and the prospective father's respective ages. Defending his own diagnosis in the verbose and pompous way that he was known for, and in contradiction to his very Irish sounding name, he had said, in his very English sounding accent, 'I can categorically assure you Madame de Hey that there is absolutely not one shred or element of doubt in this opinion whatsoever. I have performed this very elementary examination on the good women of County Wexford countless times over the last twenty-eight years and not once have I been shown to be wrong. Your symptoms are complete textbook. I appreciate that this situation may have come as surprise news to you but these circumstances have happened to people much older than you and also much older than Mr de Hay.' He paused, but only for a moment, and then added, 'In these chronicles, as far as the world is concerned or even Ireland alone, you are little more than children. Age is a mere number in this lottery, the advancement of it only makes these circumstances less probable, it does not make them impossible, and it is a fact, an irrefutable medical fact Madame de Hay, that you are pregnant!'

Now, as she stood there outside in the street, she went over the whole thing again in her own mind. She was approaching her mid-forties and Dermot was seventy-two. Why then was she pregnant? She had not conceived a child for more than a quarter of a century and he had not fathered one for almost half a century.

She felt upset and bad tempered and as the chauffeur held open the rear door of the car she climbed into the back seat and said as politely as she could manage to say, 'La Maison s'il vous plait.' During the short journey she began to reconcile herself to the news and to think about her situation. She had known in her heart and her body that it was true and in reality for what other reason had she gone to see the English doctor? Her protestations to him had been just that. Whilst she now accepted it, she did not know what she was going to do about it. She did not know what she *could* do about it, except be a mother again. The only thing was that she really didn't want to be one. The path to being Mrs Antoinette de Hay, or Madame de Hay as she was known locally, with her every want provided for, her future assured and only her husband to consider had been hard-travelled, but she now gloried in her hard-earned, new-found status and all she could see in this pregnancy was that it would be a hindrance to it.

She felt no maternal instinct whatsoever, she had long ago concluded that she had none. When she had first returned to Enniscorthy to be involved as a mother with the bringing up of young Marguerite her intentions had been for all the right reasons, but she had quickly tired of the role. She had stayed around to fulfil it, but she had also made long and frequent trips back to France, sometimes alone, several times with Dermot and only once with Marguerite and that was really to satisfy the wishes of her own father who wanted to see his petite-fille Irlandais before he died.

As well as this there had been problems with Marguerite, she had not been the sweet little girl that Antoinette had expected and the older that she got then the more wilful and disobedient she became. Marguerite was used to the indulging ways of her grandfather who obviously worshipped her and had made her the focal point of his life. The granddaughter would not willingly accept the new ideas and disciplines of a newly arrived, foreign and formerly absentee mama. It was as they say, only to be expected, as her mother had been completely out of her life for the first eleven years. Antoinette could not expect to just come back into it as if this was normal behaviour. At first, and for a while, Antoinette had stayed in Enniscorthy because of a responsibility that she felt towards the child and she did have some fondness for the girl.

Then gradually she had resumed her stage career which eventually took her on tour around Europe. After each tour she always returned to Enniscorthy and each time that she did she always tried again to improve her relationship with Marguerite and she always resumed her relationship with Dermot and, despite a significant age gap between them, their relationship was a passionate one.

By 1939 war had broken out in Europe and Marguerite was a young woman, she was naturally becoming restless and frustrated being stuck in the little Wexford town. Whilst Marguerite had sown plans to get away from Enniscorthy temporarily, Antoinette had sown plans to remain in it permanently, but she was not returning to be near Marguerite. She was returning because she wanted to be near Dermot for she had grown to love him deeply and more than anything, or anyone, else. Even now Antoinette was still a head turning beauty and with maturity she had made some realisations about herself. The acting parts that she had once been offered had now dried up and anyway she no longer wanted a career as a stage actress, she had tired of the whole theatrical business. She still longed for France, but for the time being Ireland, with its declared war-neutrality and awful weather, was still much safer than her war-torn home country. She had money of her own so she decided that for the time being she would stay there, at least for the duration of the War. Anyway, Ireland was where Dermot was and she wanted to be with him, although not now on the casual ad-hoc basis of the past. This time she wanted to be with him permanently, officially and legally.

There came about an unspoken mutual acceptance between mother and daughter as both realised that each other's individual plans could be achieved more easily by assisting the other to achieve their own. Marguerite knew that her path out of Enniscorthy would be smoothed if Dermot had Antoinette around and Antoinette knew that her plans for herself and Dermot would more easily come to fruition if Marguerite was not around him. So, a mother and daughter alliance was accidentally formed and it had worked, each had helped the other achieve their ends. Marguerite had gone to study in Liverpool and Antoinette had stayed in Enniscorthy with Dermot.

Even though Marguerite was out of sight and mind and studying in England her influence over her grandfather was not entirely broken, for when Antoinette had tentatively approached the subject of marriage one evening Dermot had responded by saying, 'There would be some in the town that would not countenance such a marriage because of our familial connection.'

Antoinette though had known that it was not really *some in the town* he was referring to but Marguerite who would not want her grandfather to marry her own mother. Dermot had said to Antoinette that she could have anything that she wanted whilst he was alive, all she had to do was ask, and that she would be well provided for when he was dead and gone. Therefore, what was the real point of marriage? It wasn't as if they were going to have children. So, throughout the war this had become the accepted way of their lives. This was not enough for Antoinette and it had caused some furious rows between them.

Then the unthinkable had happened, the bomb blast in Liverpool which had claimed seven victims on the night, two of them fatal and one of these fatalities was Marguerite. Antoinette had been genuinely upset, what mother, distant or otherwise, would not be? She had never even considered Marguerite's death as a remote possibility. Dermot had been grief stricken. His grief had been further intensified when he had learned that because of the devastation caused by the bombing that no trace of Marguerite's body could be found and that her short-lived life could not even be commemorated by a complete funeral.

There was also something else regarding the circumstances surrounding Marguerite's death, something that Antoinette felt that Dermot knew but that he didn't want her to know. A day after the family had heard of Marguerite's death Dermot had received a letter from Liverpool and its content had upset him even more. He had hidden the letter away and Antoinette had not asked him about it. She accepted that if he wished to discuss it then he would do so of his own volition. Eventually she concluded that all that mattered now was that Marguerite was dead and nothing could be done that would bring her back. There were many casualties of this war and they were all somebody's son or daughter, you just had to carry on. She and Dermot were alive and her attentions would be given totally to this. After he had received the letter Dermot had expressed a desire to go to Liverpool but wartime restrictions had prevented him travelling there.

The inevitable passing of time is a progressive healer and so it was that Antoinette and Dermot grew even closer. In the year after Marguerite's death they had married. There were some in Enniscorthy who had frowned upon their union but they were the same people that frowned upon anything that was a little different. Antoinette was referred to in Enniscorthy in a slightly irreverent Irish way as Madame de Hay as opposed to Mrs de Hay but, if anything, this slightly amused her and in her own mind accorded her even higher status. The most important family aspect for both Antoinette and Dermot was that Roisin supported their marriage, as Antoinette knew she would if only because Roisin would support anything that was a little unconventional.

So they had a very small but happy wedding at Saint Brigit's in Wexford Town. In attendance on the day, as well as Dermot and Antoinette, the wedding party consisted of Roisin, Stanley Oldknow and Mr and Mrs Arthur Finney from Manchester as the only other guests.

Since then Antoinette had been happy and she believed Dermot had been too. Everything had been going smoothly until now and now, the irony of it, she was *pregnant*!

As she entered the mansion house she made directly for the drawing room, she could see the door was ajar and Dermot was sat there studying a newspaper. He knew that his wife had been to Wexford that day and he didn't know why but he didn't pry, he never pried.

'It seems as if the war is turning,' he said, looking up from his newspaper.

'I've been into Wexford, I had an appointment there.'

He waited patiently.

'It was with the English doctor.'

'The English doctor Antoinette, are you unwell?'

'No Dermot, I am not unwell, I am pregnant.'

'Antoinette, there must be some error, I am seventy-two years of age.'

'My husband, you are seventy-two but it does not matter if you are one hundred and one. There is no error, I have had all these conversations with the English doctor. Please, I do not wish to have them again with my own husband. It is confirmed beyond doubt, let us just accept it and decide what we are going to do.'

He stood up and crossed the room. He walked over to the sideboard and poured himself a small glass of poteen from a decanter that rested in a silver tray on top of it. He raised the glass to his lips and emptied the contents in one. She had seen him perform this ritual many times before, on the first occasion she had been a young girl of eighteen. She had come to know this behaviour as a ritual that he performed when he was troubled.

'In line with most men of my generation I am ignorant of these things but is it possible to know if this child is a boy or a girl?'

'It is not possible to say.'

'I am seventy-two years of age,' he repeated.

'Yes, but you have just said this, you are not one hundred and I have just said that too, the point here is that you are a strong, fit and virile man even for someone twenty years younger. The English doctor told you this last month after your medical and if nothing else this situation is proof of it.'

'Antoinette, I do not say my age from the point of view of fathering the child, I accept the reality of this, I say it from the point of view of protecting the child.'

'Dermot, protecting the child from what?'

'From being murdered.'

'Murdered, what exactly are you talking about, how many glasses of that poteen have you had?'

He moved over to the table and chairs and sat down, 'Please sit down Antoinette.'

She sat down opposite him.

'Antoinette, do you love me?'

'Yes, more than anything or anybody.'

'Do you trust me? When I say this I don't just mean do you trust my sincerity, I mean do you trust my judgement?'

'Yes I do, you are my husband.'

'Please listen to what I have to say without interruption. Under normal circumstances this would be happy news, but the de Hay family do not live under normal circumstances and have not done so since the eighteen-eighties. The family is cursed, it is the women, the women that bear the de Hay name by birth are all cursed. They are identified then they are watched and when the time comes they are killed in a most cruel and cold way. It doesn't matter where they go, wherever it is, they are found. My two sisters were murdered together, in their own house and on the same night, in Dublin many years ago, there was the attempt on Roisin's life that put her in that wheelchair for the rest of her life and Marguerite was not one of many victims of this war. I have conclusive evidence that she was yet again a victim of this curse.'

'What evidence, what curse?'

'A few days after Marguerite was killed I received a copy of this Peasants Decree. It was postmarked Liverpool and it was written in the same hand as the one I received after Roisin had been attacked.'

'But Roisin survived the attack.'

'She did, but the Man of Insignificance posts these letters in advance of the attacks. What is for sure is that the same person that attacked Roisin murdered Marguerite all those years later, it was part of the reason why I wanted Marguerite under my protection. I wasn't completely convinced by the reality of this curse all those years ago, but I am now, and what good did it do

Marguerite. I convinced myself that all this had gone away and that she would be safe studying in Liverpool, where nobody knew her, but it hasn't gone away, for in the end we were all helpless to protect her.'

'But who is this murderer, this Man of Insignificance? Why has he not been to the gallows or thrown in gaol?'

'We have never been able to find out who he is, he is very resourceful, he is not the same as the rest of us, he follows no rules, only his own, and this curse is passed on from generation to generation.'

'It is incredible.'

'I agree and it really does take some believing at first but it is true, it is written that this Man of Insignificance, as he calls himself, does not harm children nor men. The men become victims in another way in that they are left behind with all the grief and the suffering as their women are slaughtered.'

'What will happen if our child is a boy?'

'Then he will be free from this curse and left unharmed but his daughters will not. If our child is a girl then her life is in danger as soon as she reaches adulthood. When this time comes around you will be much older and I will no longer be strong, fit and virile, that is if I am still alive, which is highly unlikely. We have no other family except Roisin and she is older than you. We may all three be dead. This child will be completely alone in the world. This in itself would be difficult enough but it would be even worse with the curse against you. I wish to defeat this curse and I would be happy to go to my grave knowing that I have done everything that I can to make and keep this child safe if, as I say, she is a girl.'

'You sound as if you have a suggestion.'

'How many people know about the pregnancy?'

'Three, you, me and the English doctor.'

'We must ensure that it stays that way. I will speak with the doctor myself, he will keep the confidence if asked. If nobody is aware that there is a pregnancy then nobody will be looking for a birth and that includes the Man of Insignificance.'

'But soon there will be signs, it will show. People will talk, it will become common knowledge.'

'We will go away before these signs appear. Just you and I, we will go as far from here as we can get. We will go somewhere where nobody knows us, somewhere quiet where there are no boats and no trains. We will be unassuming, we will do nothing to attract attention we will hide our identities.'

'You feel that all this is necessary?'

'I do.'

'Do you have a place in mind?'

'We'll have to stay here in Ireland. Travelling abroad is difficult with this war and would only attract the attention that we are trying to avoid. We're well known here in the south east so we'll go somewhere in the north west, where nobody knows us.'

'Then what?'

'Then we will wait quietly and patiently for the baby to be born and then, when that happens, then we will decide.'

'What will we say to people?'

'We will say that we are going away for a while. We'll say that I have a slight illness, nothing serious but that I need to convalesce for a few months and that we wish to be left alone. That will divert attention away from you. It is quite natural Antoinette, nobody will think anything of it. It won't be forever. When will this baby arrive?'

'The English doctor said I am about three months pregnant.'

'So we have about six months before the baby is born.'

'Yes, when will we go?'

'I will speak to the English doctor today. Once this is done we can make the arrangements.'

Chapter 30

Dotty Speak

The newly valeted, burgundy Mercedes gleamed and sparkled clean, both inside and out, the rear number plate was totally legible, it read *ARC 70*. Senetti had just treated the car to its annual valet. Now he sat inside it listening to *Danny and the Juniors* singing the Doo Wop classic, *At the Hop*. He'd just been to Previtt's chip shop in Malton and he had begun to eat his cheese and onion pie, chips, peas and gravy from a white plastic tray with a blue plastic fork. His phone, which he had placed on the passenger seat, rang and Maxine's name flashed up on his screen so he push-buttoned his car music system into silence placing the half eaten repast on top of the car dashboard, he took the call.

'Hello Danny, its Maxine, where exactly are you?'

Senetti pondered: Why was it he thought, that people who knew you when they called you on your mobile phone from their own mobile phone always asked you that very intrusive question? Rarely did they ask *about* you or *how* you were. For some reason they didn't seem concerned about you as a person, only about your location and its precision, and where really were you likely to be, only one of the places that you almost always were? Some place that was of no interest to anybody whatsoever. Some place that was as routine as the place you had been the last time that they'd called and asked you the same question. Some place such as the car, the office or the house. I mean, who really cared about that? But they seemed to. It wasn't as if you were going to be on top of a mountain, or at the bottom of the ocean and did it matter anyway if you were? What difference did it make to them, or more to the point to what they were going to say to you, if you were either in the library paying your outstanding fines, running the Manchester marathon or stood on your head in the middle of the Memorial Park?

So eventually he said, 'I'm on my mobile phone. Where exactly are you?'

Maxine was getting to know Senetti by now and she thought that this response of his was sourced in one of those typical cynical, almost neurotic, mental soliloquies of his, so she ignored what he had just said and continued with what she had intended to say, 'I'm in the gym, well I'm not now, I've just finished. I think that I've got something on lawyer de Hay. Remember that barrister friend of mine that I told you about? Well, I've just had a conversation with her. Look, I'm still with her, we're having a bit of a reunion. Can you meet me in the coffee shop in an hour at the Barlow Health Club? You've been here haven't you?'

'Who me, the Barlow Health Club?'

'Well, you know where it is don't you?'

'Yes.'

'Well can you meet me?'

'Yes.'

'See you then.'

The call ended so he casually placed his phone back on the passenger seat then he turned his attention back to his unfinished lunch only to realise that the tray had slid off the dashboard and the contents had slithered down the passenger side walnut fascia of his newly cleaned car in one big brown and green mess. He didn't know which he was more perturbed by, the mess to his car or the loss of his lunch. He ignored both anxieties and the lunch and the car took off in the direction of Barlow Health Club.

An hour later both Maxine and Danny were sat down in Beanie's Coffee Shop, at the Barlow Health Club. Maxine said, 'I went into the steam room after my circuit in the gym and who should be sat across from me but Eloise Gilroy, or at least that was the name she went by at school. I think that she's on her second divorce, or perhaps it's even her third by now, so I don't know what she's calling herself these days. Anyway, it's nice to see your old school friends and to keep in touch with their lives, it's a part of your heritage don't you think?'

'Not the ones I went to school with it isn't. Most of my school friends, and I use the term friends loosely, were just a bunch of immoral misfits, they were bad enough as kids and I'd hate to have to be involved with them as adults. Occasionally, about every five years, I run into one of them but so far I've managed to conceal myself, and once when I was denounced face to face, I adopted a policy of complete denial and said that it was a case of mistaken identity on their part. Luckily enough it was Terence Reynolds, and true to form he was under the influence of something or other and I got away with it.'

'I don't really understand that, you mean you don't keep in touch with any of your old school friends?'

'Not a one of them, well no, that's not true there are two of them that I'm still forced to see from time to time, but I'm working on a plan to get rid of at least one of them, both of them if the plan extends to it.'

'You're an odd man Senetti, anyway I cherish my old school friends. As soon as I said the name *de Hay* to Eloise she knew of her. Her full name is Roisin de Hay, apparently she's a legend in female legal circles, at least in Manchester. She was one of the first ever female attorneys in England and possibly the first in Manchester, which is where she practiced throughout her life. The next bit should interest you, she was also a female councillor in Manchester, again one of the first ever.'

'Was she Irish?' he looked straight into Maxine's eyes.

'I asked Eloise and she didn't know for sure, but with the name Roisin I'd say that there was a very good chance wouldn't you?'

'I would Maxine, but we need a bit more than a good chance, does your friend know any more?'

'No, but she knows the next best thing.'

'The next best thing?'

'Somebody who may do.'

'Somebody who *may* do?'

'Danny why do you keep repeating everything back to me?'

'Is it another lawyer?'

301

'No its not, in fact it's another councillor or more to the point an ex-councillor. It's Eloise's grandmother, she served on the council at the same time as Roisin de Hay. Eloise rang her whilst she was here in Beanie's. Her Grandmother is in a nursing home in Norford. I don't think that they appreciated the short notice in the nursing home, but the fact of the matter is that we've got a thirty-minute appointment with her at 3:00pm. That's all we are allowed. Her name is Joyce Gilroy.'

'Right then, shall we go?'

'Oh, and Danny, she's an old lady and her mind isn't quite what it was, and she has good days and bad days, so we might get next to nothing out of this, but even if we don't learn anything just bear it in mind eh, gently, gently.'

Later that afternoon Danny and Maxine stood outside in the afternoon sunshine in the front garden of Glen Ridings Nursing Home. They were debating on whom should visit Mrs Gilroy. Maxine thought that she should go as she was a woman and Danny thought that he should go as he was a councillor. In the end they decided that they would both go, as both these aspects might give them some common ground with the old lady, especially if she was having one of her less lucid days.

'And don't give her one of those councillors' handshakes, in fact don't touch her at all, remember, as I keep saying, she's an old lady.'

'Maxine, why do you keep telling me this as if I've never seen an old lady before? Old ladies are always coming into my council surgery on a Saturday morning. I understand them perfectly, I know exactly what they are talking about and they know exactly what I'm talking about.'

After they'd signed in the visitor's book the smiley young receptionist said to them, 'only half an hour please and please, nothing too taxing.' She escorted them both along a corridor into a large communal sitting room that contained fifty-odd easy chairs, all in rows of five and all facing the same way. At one end of row six sat an elderly gentleman having an afternoon doze and at the end of row ten sat a beautiful old lady, Mrs Joyce Gilroy.

'Joyce,' said the receptionist, 'here are your visitors, two of them, I'll leave you to it shall I?' Then she left the room.

'Maxine,' said Mrs Gilroy, 'it's lovely to see you after all these years. You probably won't remember, but I sometimes picked you up from school with Eloise and now you're a dentist eh, oh well done you!'

'Thank you Mrs Gilroy, can I introduce you to...'

'Oh I know who he is, Inveterate Senetti the blackguard councillor, I am always hearing about him, but I'm not fooled by his nice smile, he's a wolf in cheap clothing he is. I keep up with the local politics, it still interests me after all these years. For some reason I don't seem to get mixed up with the local politics the same as I do with everything else.' All three of them laughed and she patted Maxine gently on the hand, 'I spent thirty-six years on the city council and I can tell you that all councillors are blackguards, at least the male one's are. What other type of person would stand on their feet in the chamber telling everybody else that they know what's best for everybody else? You've got to be a blackguard to even want to do that.' She laughed to herself with impish delight.

It was hard to consider Mrs Gilroy's stature as she sat in her chair with a shawl draped over the lower half of her body, it was over her knees and around her legs, but Danny noticed that she had bright brown eyes and also bright orange coloured hair and her hands gesticulated actively when she spoke. He also noticed that she had the slight scent of alcohol on her breath. She certainly was not the stereotypical image of an old grey lady.

Just then the receptionist returned with a coffee tray. She put the tray down and left the room again, Mrs Gilroy watched her as if to make sure that she had actually gone.

'Sit down both of you,' said Mrs Gilroy. 'You wanted to know about Roisin.'

'None of that stuff for me,' said Mrs Gilroy as Danny looked pointedly at the coffee pot and she produced a small stainless steel hip flask from under her shawl and took a healthy swig.

'Yes, Roisin de Hay. When you were serving on the council did you know another councillor called Roisin de Hay?' asked Maxine.

'I knew her very well, yes. When I first joined the council there weren't many women councillors. I think that there were three of us out of ninety-nine. Roisin was quite a bit older than me, she was an old hand and she looked after me in the early days. I was a little green behind the ears and I suppose that you could say she was a monitor to me. In fact if it hadn't been for her guidance in the early days I would have been up a tree without a paddle.'

'She was a solicitor wasn't she?'

'She was yes, she was one of the first female solicitors and one of the first women councillors, she paved the way for a lot of things to do with women, but I don't really know much about her soliciting, she kept the two separate.'

'Did you know anything about her personally, did you become friends?'

'I suppose we did become friends in the end. We used to attend a lot of council functions together. For a time Roisin and I were the voucher women attendees. No, not the voucher, what do I mean? The token, yes. There were so few of us you see in those days, so I got to know her reasonably well, she wasn't as fierce as everybody thought once you got to know her.'

'Was she Irish?' interrupted Danny.

'Oh yes, she was Irish, it was said that her family were very wealthy.'

'Do you know which part of Ireland?' asked Maxine.

'No, I don't think that I can remember. As I said I get things mixed up. I do remember that there was a famous saying that originated from the place that Roisin came from, something to do with Laurel and Hardy and Captain Hook. I know that Oliver Hardy is hated in the place for all the trouble that he caused when he was over there, shooting and stabbing people.'

Maxine noticed that for some strange reason that mystified her Senetti smiled knowingly at Mrs Gilroy's apparently confused observation.

'Did you know anything about her family in Ireland?' he asked.

I don't know if I'm remembering this right but she used to mention her three sisters. They all used to go down, where was it now, together? Oh yes, the Slaney but I didn't ever meet any of them and I don't know what the Slaney was, some sort of meeting place, a pub perhaps or a park.'

'Did she ever mention any of her sisters' names asked Danny?'

'Yes, I remember all their names there was: Nora, Sarah and Beryl.'

Maxine noticed that for some obscure reason that was a mystery to her Senetti again smiled knowingly at this revelation as if it meant something to him.

'Did she have a husband?' asked Maxine.

'She never married, although she did have a partner for many years but they were very discreet. You were expected to be in those days if you weren't married. You just had to get on with things in life, my mother used to say you've buttered your bread now lie in it.'

'Do you know his name?'

'His first name was Stanley, I can't remember his surname. It was an odd name but I can't remember. She rarely mentioned it. She once said to me that she could never marry because she was be-devilled, do I mean be-devilled? yes be-devilled, that's exactly what Roisin said.'

'Can you remember anything else about the place that she came from in Ireland or her family?' Maxine asked gently.

'The only other thing I can remember is that the man in the mask came from the same place that Roisin did, what was his name now? He was on the TV the other night, no its gone now.'

Both Maxine and Danny looked on kindly and Maxine noticed that once again Senetti smiled knowingly.

Mrs Gilroy addressed Maxine, 'Oh I know about how she came to be in the wheelchair.'

'Was that later on in life?'

'Oh no, she was a young woman, barely thirty years of age.'

'Did she suffer some kind of disability?'

'Well yes she did, that's why she was in the wheelchair, but it was how she got the disability in the first place, it was tragic and unnatural.'

'How did she get it Mrs Gilroy?' Danny asked.

'Well, it happened two or three years before I was born but everybody knew about it, it was in all the newspapers at the time. Even my own parents used to speak about it for years after. My husband was the editor of the *Daily Express*, he said that it would have been headline news if that man hadn't rowed single handed across the Pacific Ocean and taken all the headlines for a whole month. One day he was in America and the next day he was in France. That story took off like a horse on fire.'

'What happened exactly with Roisin?' Danny asked.

'Somebody tried to kill her. In her very own office in Manchester, can you believe that? The newspapers called him the Mad Monk, no not the Mad Monk, the Mad Doctor or something or other. He shot her for no reason at all and then he fled, he escaped, they never caught him. People just didn't get shot in those days, certainly not innocent women. She didn't die but it was no thanks to the Mad Hatter, whoever he was, and as a consequence of the attack she was disabled and in a wheelchair for the rest of her life.'

A moment later Mrs Gilroy appeared to fall silently asleep and shortly afterwards the receptionist reappeared signalling the end of the meeting.

'Well thank you Mrs Gilroy,' said Maxine as both she and Danny smiled at the now sleeping lady.

As they were leaving the old lady woke up and as she did made a *whishing* noise and raised her arm as if in mock swordplay, 'That's him,' she said, 'Zorro.' Yet again Maxine noticed that Senetti smiled knowingly, by now she thought he was beginning to irritate her slightly.

A few minutes later Danny and Maxine sat on a bench in the front garden of Glen Ridings Nursing Home. 'Well, said Maxine, I don't really know what to say about all that. I find it hard to believe that Roisin de Hay had three sisters and not one member of any extended family came to Helen Day's funeral. As for the rest of it, well she did her best I suppose. I have to say that I thought the Zorro bit was funny. At least you were gentle with her, I was impressed.'

'Hmm,' said Danny, 'let's not be too dismissive too soon. The thing with dotty old ladies is that they approach things from a different perspective than the rest of us. The way to approach it I've found is to work around it being half right and half wrong. It takes a while to understand dotty-speak.'

'And are you saying that you do?'

'Well a little yes, but it hasn't happened overnight. You've not met my mother have you, I'll introduce you sometime, she's fluent in it. I've had to learn it over the years so that I can understand what she's talking about.'

'Danny, where is all this going?'

'It's going here Maxine, we either adopt the stance that Mrs Gilroy is a crazy old lady and that we dismiss absolutely everything that she said in there as potty ramblings, or we at least give some of it a little credence and we try to decipher and translate it.'

'Danny, you obviously know something that I don't know.'

'Maxine, you're a highly intelligent and knowledgeable person on many subjects, particularly on women's issues and on your own subjects, but I know much more about at least two subjects, one of them to do with women, that you don't know much about and these two things are relevant here.'

'Go on, amaze me.'

'I can translate crazy old lady speak and I have a reasonable knowledge of Irish history and geography. You see, crazy old ladies aren't really crazy at all, it is just that their language is different, it's called dotty-speak and it works on fragments of memory and flow of consciousness, some of it is accurate and some of it's made up but it all connects, find the connection and you've got the translation. You noticed how Mrs Gilroy mixed her metaphors up with some of her sayings, but we knew what she meant, we didn't dismiss it out of hand, we tried to understand and that's all we have to do here, try to understand, that's the secret of translating dotty-speak.'

'I didn't know that you knew about the workings of the human mind.'

'I know about the workings of dotty-speak, so are you going to give me a fair go?'

'Well I'll try, but it's not easy when you're claiming to have discovered a new language and you are smiling smugly all over the place. Go on, I've got nothing to lose, carry on Sigmund.'

'Do you recall when Mrs Gilroy referred to herself and Roisin as the *voucher attendees*?'

'Yes I do.'

'Well, we both know now that what she really meant to say was the *token female attendees*, yes?'

'Yes.'

'Well would we have known that if she hadn't told us?'

'Probably not.'

'Yet it is quite easy to see how she confused the word voucher with the word token. On their own, both words could have the same meaning but in the context of her sentence they are entirely different.'

'Yes?'

'She was alert to her mistake then and did the translation for us, but what we have to do is understand when she wasn't alert to her mistakes and then we have to do the translation for ourselves.'

'I'll go along with you but I think that I'm a bit of a passenger at the moment.'

'That's fine, just stay with me. Here's another example, but first let me ask you a question to illustrate it.'

'Alright, ask your question.'

'You went to school with Eloise, did she ever mention what her grandfather's occupation was, her grandfather being Mrs Gilroy's husband?'

'Her Grandfather, Danny why would she? She may have done, I don't know, I can't remember.'

'Come on Maxine, this could be important. Just indulge me for a few minutes, *think*.'

'Er, well, the Gilroy family, the men anyway, were all something to do with the newspapers in Manchester. Newspapers were big in Manchester around that time, they used to call Manchester the *Second Fleet Street*. Eloise's dad was a journalist, I think he worked for the Manchester Guardian at one time.'

'There you are you see.'

'Where am I, no I don't see?'

Mrs Gilroy said that her husband was the editor of the *Daily Express,* which I'm fairly sure he wasn't, but he was probably something to do with newspapers and you've just said that he was a journalist for the *Guardian*. She just got the whole thing slightly off track but that's not the same as crazy ramblings.'

'So is there something that we can learn from this?'

'Yes, we can learn from our translation that Roisin de Hay originally comes from County Wexford and that somebody tried to kill her in the summer of 1927.'

'Can we, how?'

'Remember that stuff Mrs Gilroy said about Laurel and Hardy and a famous saying they had when they were in Ireland shooting and stabbing people?'

'Well that's complete nonsense, who ever heard of Laurel and Hardy stabbing or shooting anybody?'

'No Maxine, that's it, it's not complete anything, that's what dotty-speak is, it's incomplete. It's fragments and bits and pieces all put together. Stan Laurel and Oliver Hardy have probably never even been to Ireland let alone stabbed or shot anybody, but another Oliver has, Oliver Cromwell, and he's responsible for plenty of shootings and stabbings and other violations over there in the seventeenth century. Do you remember Mrs Gilroy's reference to Captain Hook?'

'Yes.'

'When Oliver Cromwell was in Ireland he is thought to have coined the phrase, by hook or by crook. You've heard of it?'

'Well yes, it's an old saying, Doctor Tom uses it.'

'Without going into too much detail, Cromwell was referring to two places, Hook Head in County Wexford and Crook Village in County Waterford. Do you remember the bit about Roisin's three sisters and them all going down the Slaney together and their names Nora, Sarah and Beryl?'

'Yes.'

'Well, what Mrs Gilroy was actually referring to were the three sisters that are not three sisters in the sense that they are not female siblings.'

'Danny, you've completely lost me now.'

'There are three major rivers in Ireland and they are known nationally as the Three Sisters. Mrs Gilroy must have spoken about them with Roisin but again she's got herself slightly confused. They flow through various parts of the south east, County Wexford being one of them. The Slaney is another Irish river that flows through Wexford town, in fact Wexford Harbour sits on the River Slaney. The Three Sisters are called the Nore, the Suir and the Barrow. Roisin will have referred to them in conversation with Mrs Gilroy over the years and as the old ladies memory has faded she's forgotten the whole, remembered some and substituted the rest with some of her own parts. Nore, Suir and Barrow translate in dotty-speak to Nora, Sarah and Beryl. Then there is the man in the mask, Zorro.'

'He's a fictitious character surely.'

'He is yes, but there is a strong lobby of literary opinion that even though he is a fictional character that he was based on a real character, an Irish adventurer called William Lamport. And guess what county William Lamport is from?'

'County Wexford?'

'Absolutely correct.'

'Danny, I asked you to amaze me and I have to admit that you have. What of the story about Roisin being shot by the Mad Monk?'

'Well I must admit, I don't know about the Mad Monk, that's stumped me a bit but didn't Hamish Lennox say that the woman that came to visit Kathleen Helen in the convent was in a wheelchair?'

'He did, you're absolutely right.'

'I think that the woman in the wheelchair was Roisin de Hay.'

'So what about the date then, how did you come up with that?'

'Well, you know the man that rowed across the Pacific?'

'I don't know of anybody that's ever done that and if they had it would take a lot longer than one day.'

'Remember it's dotty-speak so it's half right and half wrong. How old do you think Mrs Gilroy is?'

'Mid-eighties maybe.'

'So let's say she was born about when, nineteen-thirty? She said that the shooting incident happened two or three years before she was born so let's say it was in nineteen twenty-seven or twenty-eight. She said that one day he was in America and the next day he was in France. Well if you concentrate on that for a minute, if you crossed from America to France that would be the Atlantic not the Pacific and if you substituted the boat for what, then you'd do it easily in a day.'

'An aeroplane!'

'So what happened around that time was headlines for a month, it would have to be some really ground-breaking, earth-shattering news, the equivalent of us landing on the moon in the sixties?'

Maxine looked up in excitement, 'Charles Lindbergh!' she exclaimed. 'The first person to fly solo across the Atlantic.'

'Charles Lindbergh indeed, the first solo flight across the Atlantic in 1927, on Friday he was in the USA, on Saturday he was in France, so we put all that together and we come up with...'

'Wexford and the summer of 1927!'

'You know Maxine, I think that you're beginning to understand dotty-speak.'

'You know Danny, I think that you're right, I think that I am, after all, it's not rocket salad is it.'

Chapter 31

Sister Bonita and Granddad Joe

As Ward Sister Bonita Maria Montoya Walsh began her mid-afternoon shift at the Royal London Hospital, she looked with maternal endearment at the photograph of her seven-year-old twins that took prominent position upon the desk in her ward office. She missed them greatly and often felt a little guilty at this time of the day about not being around them as much as she wanted to be. She loved her children and she loved her job and she wanted to have both.

Bonita Maria was Spanish born, but had come to England in 1951 to escape from General Franco's dictatorship repressions. She had been accompanied by her young English-born husband, Timothy Walsh. They had been fortunate for such a young couple and despite having no connections in the English capital had established themselves very easily in post-war London. She already spoke good English and she trained successfully as a nurse. His English was fluent and he found work as an engineer with a multi-national company. In nineteen fifty-five she had given birth to twins and her new life was now complete and happiness had seemed assured.

Then, as many in the past who have felt this way about their future know to their detriment, in a short space of time all changed beyond recognition. Three years after the twins arrived tragedy struck when Timothy was killed in an industrial accident. There had been suspected negligence on the part of Timothy's wealthy employers and wishing to avoid any adverse publicity that would come from a well-chronicled court case it had been settled out of court with a large amount of money and a substantial private widow's pension.

She bought an old, large, run-down, four-storey Victorian house in west London and settled down to the life of a young widow, motherhood and house modernisation. In post-war-austerity Britain she had no need, at least financially, to concern herself with the toil of work again. After a year though of being *stuck* at home she felt unfulfilled and frustrated and she yearned to return to nursing. With two young children to look after this was going to be problematic.

For the next three years she tried a succession of nursing posts and children's nannies. The nursing posts were always a resounding success but the nannies were always a resounding failure. It wasn't so much the nannies themselves as the children. The loss of their father at such an early age had had a negative impact upon them and with their mother also absent at work they began to present behavioural problems. In the end and over the same three year period she was forced to leave four nursing posts that she was settled in to resume care of the children, in addition to which she lost no less than ten nannies. The reputation of the children became so bad that she was having great difficulty finding a suitable eleventh. She was more or less resigned to the situation that she was going to have to give up her life's work for some years in order to look after them, at least until they attained some level of independence, when a miracle happened.

One day she had been out in the park with the children when she had been approached very politely by a very well dressed, well spoken, and distinguished looking older gentleman who had a pronounced limp and she knew from her medical training that he carried a false leg. She thought that it was perhaps a legacy from the war, there were many such legacy's about. There was also something a little familiar about him but she couldn't quite fathom what it was. On the first occasion he engaged her in polite conversation and made a fuss of the children and on the second he did exactly the same but for just a little longer. However when she saw him on the third occasion he made a revelation and she made a discovery. He said that his name was Joe and that he was actually the children's paternal grandfather.

Bonita hadn't even known that the children had a paternal grandfather. She had known the children's paternal *grandmother* and had met her on many occasions but she was now dead and nobody else in the family had ever mentioned a grandfather, so Bonita's initial reaction was one of disbelief. Then she realised that what had been familiar about him was his resemblance to her late husband. She asked him a few questions and as a consequence she made a few enquiries and what she got back was that he really *was* the children's paternal grandfather. There had been some disagreement between him and his wife some years ago and his wife had deserted him and gone back to live in Spain, taking her young son with her, Bonita's future husband, Timothy.

Bonita Maria's enquiries also confirmed that Joe was a quiet, honest and unassuming man and that he had also been a war hero who had selflessly saved the lives of others during the Liverpool blitz. She learned that for one particular act of heroism he had been awarded a medal.

She was a little curious to know why he was *persona non grata* as far as her late husband was concerned, but not too curious for she knew enough about families to realise that relationships didn't always run smoothly. She recalled two uncles in Spain who had not acknowledged each other for over forty years because of some apparent disagreement to do with a chicken. To this day there were no family members, and this included the two uncles themselves, who could quite recall any detail of the origin of this rift, but the rift remained.

After this Bonita Maria and Granddad Joe often met in the park and she began to confide in him, particularly about her being unable to reconcile her childcare with her work ambition. He was fit and active, now retired, independent, intelligent, wise and most important of all he got on well with the children and they with him.

Then he made her a proposition, if she wished to return to work he would act as nanny to the children. After all, what could be more natural, he was their grandfather. He didn't want any money, he didn't need it, he had enough of his own. All he wanted was the pleasure of seeing his grandchildren grow up but he did want a couple of rooms in the house so that he could be *in post* and *to hand* as he described it.

There was no doubt that the house was more than big enough to accommodate all of them. So that was what eventually happened and now the situation was as normal. Bonita Maria returned to work, Granddad Joe assumed the role of nanny, the children stopped playing up and they all lived in the large Victorian house, separately but happily together.

At the same time as Ward Sister Bonita Maria Montoya Walsh was beginning her late afternoon shift, ten miles away Granddad Joe waited outside the school gates of the little primary school in the London suburb for the twins. As both children came excitedly through the iron gates to greet him he picked them both up, one in each arm, and kissed them both affectionately on their cheeks. Then he put them down on the footpath and taking them both by the hand he guided them on the short walk to his car. Ensuring that they were secured safely in the rear seats, he settled himself in the driver's seat and drove off on the short journey home.

Arriving at the large Victorian three-storey house a few minutes later he ensured that they changed out of their school clothes and into their play clothes. He had a panoramic view from his living room window of the tiny park that they played in for two hours every night so he had no concerns for their safety. It was still light nights, so he would let them play out for another two hours after which he would bring them inside, ensure that they were fed, bathed and on time for bed in accordance with their mother's wishes. Their mother's wishes were of the utmost importance, this he had learnt from experience. As far as their mother was concerned he would not ostracise her as an enemy, he would recruit and nurture her as a friend. He would tell the children that a mother is the most important person in your life and they in turn would tell their mother what he had said to them about her.

At bedtime he would tell them a story, just the same as any other night, only tonight this story would be different. He had refrained from telling the children this story until now but tonight the time was right to begin it. The story that he would tell tonight would be the story that he would tell to the children for the first time ever. Tonight the story would not be a fairy tale it would be a true story. A story that had been handed down to him about his family, about their family because they were all one and the same. The story that his father, their great-grandfather had told him many years before.

Tonight Granddad Joe would tell his beautiful twins about Ireland in the Great Hunger. He would tell them about the young heroic peasant boy Finbarr Joseph and the vicious, cruel middleman, Padraig de Hay, the Gombeen and about their Great Ancestor and about the Oath and the Peasants Decree and about their responsibility to their family and most importantly about being a Man of Insignificance. He wouldn't tell them the *whole* story tonight, it would be too much for their young heads, he would tell it gradually over the months and years and eventually it would become their story as it had become his.

Their mother was on the late shift at the hospital tonight and wouldn't be home before the children were asleep. He would wait up for her and make her a light supper with the wine that she was fond of and he would play the flamenco music that she favoured so much on the record player. Then he would discuss the children quietly and in a relaxing and respectful way. He would tell her how pleased he was with them and how well they were doing at school. Then he would tell her how important the work was that she was doing at the hospital, and then he would retire and leave her with her tiredness, her wine and her flamenco music. In the morning she would be sleeping, so once again he would look after the children and prepare them for and take them to school.

His grandchildren were now his life and for the rest of it he would live the life of a grandfather. It was unusual because he had never expected things to turn out this way, but now that they had he was going to ensure that *this way* was *his* way.

There were also two other reasons why his grandchildren would now be his life. The first reason was that throughout the years he had never given up on the business of the Oath, nor his surveillance of Roisin de Hay and periodically he had updated himself on her situation. He swore that if an opportunity presented itself then he would finish what he had started many years ago.

The problem was that since the shooting in Manchester she was often in the company of the enquiry agent, Oldknow, the one who had clubbed him to the ground and prevented him from discharging his responsibilities to the Oath. Granddad Joe hated this man so much that he could hardly bear to think of his name let alone say it. He also knew that as well as hating him he feared him. He was no match for him physically and he just didn't have the courage to take him on. He also knew that the enquiry agent was one of the few people who could recognise him as Professor Jeremy Weedon. He had learnt over the years that the sketch that had appeared in the newspapers all those years ago had been drawn by Oldknow himself.

He had also heard that it was said of Oldknow that whilst you thought you were watching somebody else he was actually watching you. This comment alone chilled him but all in all it meant he daren't go near Roisin for wherever she was, the enquiry agent was close by.

So, over the years he had made his observations through third parties inasmuch as he hired his own enquiry agents and kept himself up to date on Roisin by reading their reports. It was fairly easy as she had stayed in the same locations in Manchester throughout her life. In addition to which she was a woman of great routine. He had hoped in the meantime that Stanley Oldknow would die or become incapacitated in some way but so far nothing had happened to him and he seemed indestructible. Joe tried to cover his own tracks as much as possible. He never used the same enquiry agent more than once, he always met them on neutral ground, he used an alias and he always took care to disguise himself in some way. Nevertheless, he knew that there could be some trail back to him for those that were resourceful enough and diligent enough to seek it.

Joe was not a young man anymore, nor was Roisin a young woman, and for many years he had thought that she was the end of the line, that she was the last of the de Hay women. When she was gone the line was finished so he decided that whilst Oldknow was still around he would let nature take its course, it was though important that the story of a Man of Insignificance did not die and his grandchildren were the natural inheritors of this.

The second reason that his grandchildren would now be his life was that shortly after he moved in with them and their mother there had been a development, it had changed everything. About that time he had commissioned a new report, he had met a Manchester agent in Birmingham, a tall cadaverous man named Lionel Crellin. Crellin had given Joe a verbal synopsis of Roisin's activities and then handed him a written report for which Joe had paid him in cash. Returning to London on the train Joe had read the report.

As Crellin had already told him at their meeting Roisin, accompanied by Oldknow, as usual, and a young unidentified man with a Scots accent, had visited Ireland and Crellin had followed them. Apart from the unidentified young man this in itself was not unusual. What was different was that this time they did not go to County Wexford, they went almost as far away from it in Ireland as you could get, they went to County Mayo. The three of them stayed overnight in a small hotel in Castlebar. The following day they visited a convent, The Holy Conception. Two days later, Roisin and the young man went back to the convent. When they came back an hour later they had a young woman with them.

That night Roisin, Oldknow, the young man and the young woman from the convent stayed at the Castlebar Hotel again. Then Joe read some mundane stuff in the report about the young man and the young girl going off in one taxi and Roisin and Oldknow going off in another. He recognised this as something that Oldknow might have implemented. He would have probably taken it as a precaution in case they were being watched and in an attempt to make things more difficult for the observer had decided to create two avenues of pursuit. Crellin could only follow one taxi and he chose to follow the older couple who headed straight for the airport. The young man and the young woman disappeared and Crellin didn't see them again. After that Crellin went back to the convent and he learnt from a workman that the name of the young woman was Kathleen Helen and she had been in the convent since 1944, that's all he could find out about her.

Crellin had given a very detailed description of both Kathleen Helen and the young man. The description of the man meant nothing to Joe but the description of Kathleen Helen meant very much to him. She was described as being approximately five foot eight tall and of extremely thin build. She had blond hair and her face consisted of an oval shape with a small tight mouth and a small straight nose. She seemed to wear her spectacles most of the time but when she removed them it could be clearly seen that her eyes were very unusual, as they appeared to be amber-coloured, almost gold.

Crellin went on to report that in his opinion it should be said it is worthy of mention that even though there appeared to be a large age difference between Roisin and the *convent girl*, the former a woman in her sixties and the latter approximately eighteen years old, there was a strong physical resemblance between the two, as if they are somehow related in family.

As Joe read Crellin's report he realised that the convent girl was a bloodline de Hay. He had no idea where she had come from although it was obvious where she had been for the last seventeen or eighteen years, hiding in the convent in fear of the Peasant's Decree. Now, with her appearance the whole business of the Oath had started again. She and she alone now stood between the propagation of the de Hay seed and the absolute and final execution of the Peasant's Decree.

It would take time for Kathleen Helen and any progeny that she produced to be found and executed, years, maybe even decades. Joe just did not have that time nor was he able anymore for such a task. That was why Joe now needed his grandchildren! Granddad Joe now had two successors and the Peasants Decree would now have two new strong young executioners.

Chapter 32

The Life of Kathleen Helen

From its beginning and original state Kathleen Helen's life had never really been her own to lead. If it had been led at all, it had been led in a chequered way. Upon reflection it seemed to Kathleen Helen herself that her whole life could easily be represented by journey on a chequers board and aspects of this journey could be divided into black and white squares, just like the board itself that the game was played upon.

Taking up many of these squares would be her first eighteen years, which she had spent in the Convent of the Holy Conception in County Mayo. At Concepta's, for this was the name it came to be known by, and contrary to some reports and allegations about some Irish convents, there was no deliberate abuse or cruelty. On the whole the nuns were a disciplined but kindly bunch. The girls were kept in polite but nevertheless total ignorance about their own backgrounds. Seemingly in some way to assist this ignorance the girls were all referred to in the same way, which was by their first two Christian names and in that respect nobody was any different to anybody else. There was Morag Fiona, Justine Anne, Maeve Edna, Brigit Therese, Ambrosine Annette and of course Kathleen Helen and so on. With comings and goings the total number of girls fluctuated slightly but there were around a hundred of them at any given time.

All the girls entered the convent at a very early age and none of them could actually recall where these forenames came from. None of the girls knew if these forenames were their own by birth right or just something that had been allocated to them along the way to satisfy the system. None of the girls had any surnames, or if they did have, they didn't know what they were, and if the nuns themselves actually did know them, then they wouldn't divulge this information.

When she was seven years of age Kathleen Helen had asked after her surname. She had been told by Sister Valerie who had a reputation amongst the girls for being a bit loopy, 'When you're eighteen Kathleen Helen, surnames, if indeed you have one, may then be divulged. Some people of course have two, although why anybody would want a double-barrelled burden I can't think. Until then they are unimportant. For the moment enjoy the freedom that goes with not having one. Forenames are a good thing, nobody ever takes offence against forenames, it's the surnames that cause all the problems, for they identify you as being of somebody else when really you are of yourself. When you are eighteen, that's when all your problems will start, then you will have a surname, but until then you are in here and you don't have any problems and here is where you are, without surnames and without the problems that go with them.'

It was all a bit of a well pronounced and repetitive monologue-type riddle, in the style that the nuns practiced to perfection, but even to a seven-year-old's curious mind the message came home and clear and Kathleen Helen didn't ask about surnames again for a long time. She'd grown up in Concepta's to believe that she'd been a foundling baby, found on the steps of the convent towards the end of the war. Many of the convent girls had come into the convent by that route. There had been a rush of foundlings in 1944, the year that Kathleen Helen had been born, it had all been to do with the war coming to an end. Sister Bernadette had offered this in explanation, but when asked why it should be so, she couldn't or wouldn't explain any further. She would just say, 'Accept it girls for the way that it is.' Then again, she gave this as an answer to many questions.

The convent had been Kathleen Helen's home since then. She had never actually known anywhere else, just the convent. She'd only been outside its huge wooden gates twice in the whole eighteen years. The first time was when she was eleven years of age. She'd contracted appendicitis and had to spend ten days in the cottage hospital. She'd loved her time there, they had all made a fuss of her. All the doctors save one were young men and she'd never seen a young man before, in fact the only men of any age that she had seen were O'Malley at Concepta's, an occasional contractor there and the old grey priest who visited the convent every weekend to hear confessions on Saturday and say Mass and Benediction on Sunday. The young doctors were modern and handsome and they talked to you and smiled at you. There were five of them altogether and she was in awe of all of them.

She was sorry that she was eventually pronounced well and that she had to leave the hospital and go back to the dreary convent where everything stayed the same year on year and nothing ever changed.

The second time she was allowed outside the convent was in the year of her seventeenth birthday, she'd been allowed to go to midnight mass on Christmas Eve with two other girls: Morag Fiona and Justine Anne. The three girls were accompanied by three nuns. One for each, or so it seemed. The little village church had been packed and after the Mass everybody, all the villagers, the three nuns and the three convent girls had stood outside the church talking into the night. It was as if the occasion had evaporated everybody's inhibitions and everyone was equal. Kathleen Helen had not said much, in fact she'd not said anything, she'd been far too shy, but she'd listened to others and she'd loved the occasion, it made her feel so excited that she couldn't help thinking about it for days and weeks after. In the convent there was no excitement, every day was the same, prayers, meals and lessons but with a slight variation on Saturday and a huge variation on Sunday. These variations consisted of no lessons on a Saturday and fewer meals and even more prayers on Sunday.

Kathleen Helen's convent sister was Morag Fiona, they had grown up together, come through the convent system together and they were due to leave Concepta's together. A month before she was due to leave the convent Kathleen Helen had no ideas about her future. She did not know where she was going, nor how she was going to support herself when, or even if, she got there. She had no money of her own and outside the convent she had no home, no friends and not even one family member that she could turn to. Furthermore, as far as she could see she had no prospects of gaining any of these, she was completely alone.

She had sought an audience with the Mother Superior. This audience had offered her no comfort and Mother Superior had offered her the advice, 'Be patient, it is a virtue.' Kathleen Helen considered that for the last seventeen years she had been virtuous enough.

In the ensuing weeks all of Kathleen Helen's material uncertainties and insecurities about life on the outside would be drastically altered. Her emotional and mental anxieties though would be exacerbated. Two days before her leaving date she had been summoned to the Mother Superior's office. In attendance there were three strangers, people that she had never seen nor heard of, nor imagined existed in her life.

She had learned from these strangers that not only did she have one family member, but she had three and they were all alive: a mother, a sister and a cousin. This news was the biggest news that she had ever received in her life. She had also learned of an eighty-year-old curse that she was the subject of. She was informed by the woman who said that she was her sister that the reason that she was placed in the convent was to protect her from this curse.

Once she had left the confines of the convent she had learned that she was a member of an old Irish family, the de Hay family, and that she was Kathleen Helen de Hay, the youngest member of that family. Her father had been Dermot de Hay who was now dead and her mother was Antoinette de Hay. Antoinette de Hay was French, still alive and lived in Paris. So, Kathleen Helen reasoned that she herself, was half French and half Irish.

All of this came as a traumatic shock to her, in the whole of her eighteen years she had been completely oblivious to all of it. When she had taken in all these revelations, and everything had calmed down, she remembered thinking to herself that the most important aspect of all these family revelations wasn't that she had a mother or a sister or a cousin, it wasn't that she came from a wealthy middle-class Irish family who had money, it wasn't that she now had a surname, de Hay, no it wasn't any of these.

The most important discovery to her, the most cherished of all of it was that her name really was Kathleen Helen. It was very important to her that after all these years she'd been living the truth with her own real name.

There was though, in all this excitement and uncertainty surrounding her new found family, the predominant question that had infiltrated her mind and would not go away and that question was: if she had all this family and they weren't ill and they weren't poor and they weren't restricted in any way, then why as a helpless child did she have to grow up, locked and hidden away, in a convent as far away from them as they could geographically place her?

When the very young, and very unworldly, Kathleen Helen paused for a moment to consider the position of the decision makers in a life that was really hers, she realised very quickly that there was an absentee voice in the dialogue, that voice was her own. According to the voices that were in this dialogue, and there were only two, Roisin and Antoinette, her future was all connected to her name, Kathleen Helen de Hay. Not the forename but the surname. So perhaps the *surname hypothesis* of Sister Valerie, all those years ago, was not so loopy after all.

Shortly after leaving Concepta's, and after a very brief stay with her sister Roisin in Manchester, it was decided that Kathleen Helen should go and live with her mother in France. It was said that the language could be a problem but she was young enough and she could learn it. On the one hand it seemed to Kathleen Helen that she should be with her mother, yet on the other it seemed that she was being shunted about and hidden away again by her new found family. Her young cousin had disappeared off the scene altogether and it was blindingly obvious that her sister Roisin didn't want her around in Manchester. In fact Kathleen Helen gained the distinct impression that her own presence around Roisin made the older woman nervous or perhaps, even more dramatic than nervous, it made her feel afraid.

So it was, that precisely sixteen days after leaving Concepta's that Kathleen Helen, travelling by a convoluted route, arrived at her mother's fashionable apartment on the Boulevard Saint Michel in Paris.

It wasn't that Antoinette and Kathleen Helen didn't get on or didn't accommodate each other, in fact the opposite was true for they both made a great effort to get on and did everything that they could to co-operate together, it was just that, apart from there being an almost forty five year age gap between them and apart from the fact that one of them was from an Irish convent background whilst the other was from a French theatrical background, there was just no mother and daughter connection between two very different people who had never in their respective lives been one of either to the other and as far as that feeling was concerned the boat had well and truly sailed. As if in mutual understanding of this situation, within an hour of them meeting each other, Antoinette called her daughter *Kathleen Helen* and Kathleen Helen called her mother *Antoinette*. The words *mother* and *daughter* were never used in their mutual address when talking to each other or about each other for as long as they lived.

As well as this there was the other matter of the eighty-year-old curse. During Kathleen Helen's brief stay in Castlebar, Stanley Oldknow had been convinced that their party was being watched. Although evidence of this did not surface, Kathleen Helen had come to realise very quickly that Stanley Oldknow was a wise man who was not prone to overreaction of any kind, she assessed him as a solid individual and she concluded that any ideas that he had should be respected. This curse though, that Roisin had referred to, had not been mentioned since the meeting in the Mother Superior's room. Although Kathleen Helen was curious about it, she stopped herself from asking at first. However, once she had been in France for a few days she did ask Antoinette about it and she also asked about her father. The occasion came one morning when they were having breakfast together when Kathleen Helen asked, 'Antoinette, what was my father like?'

Antoinette was silent for a moment then she replied, 'He was a very unusual man, in a lot of ways he was very complicated, he wasn't very relaxed in life and he always felt that he had to behave in a certain way. You know how they say that some people are ruled by their heart and others are ruled by their head, well

Dermot was ruled by his conscience. He always tried to do what he believed was right.'

'He was much older than you wasn't he?'

'We were born in different years yes, but that is not important.'

'Did you love him?'

'The first time that I met him I think that in some ways I hated him but later I grew to love him.'

'Why did he put me in the convent?'

'I am almost certain that he thought that he was protecting you.'

'From what, an eighty-year-old curse?'

'Yes.'

'Do you believe in this curse?'

'Your father did and I believed in your father.'

'Well I don't believe in it and I intend to ignore it.'

'Before you ignore it, which is your choice entirely, don't you think that you should know what you are ignoring?'

'If we know about it and we are in danger then why don't we inform the authorities?'

'Kathleen Helen, *we* are not in danger. I am in no danger from this curse. I am not a de Hay by birth right, I am only a de Hay by marriage. I am not threatened in any way by this Peasant's Decree. You are the one that is threatened, you and your children and your children's children.'

'But I do not have any children and I do not intend to have any.'

'You do not have any children and you do not intend to have any yet. You are young and you have views, but often these views change. Situations can appear to be one way and then turn out to be entirely another.'

'If I do have any children, then I won't put them in the convent to waste away their lives. I will look after them as a mother should.'

'When I was your age I was pregnant with my first child and the man who was to be my husband was killed for nothing in a pointless war. My own father was away in the same war and I never knew my mother. I had nobody to protect me, no home, no money, and no friends. I had to give my child up for eleven years. When we were eventually reconciled and as soon as she was a young woman she was murdered by this *Man of Insignificance* as he calls himself. So, at an age when most women are looking forward to their grandchildren, I was denied them and when my husband was an old man and I was no longer a young woman I had another child. We were forced to find a place of protection for her. You would desire to have your eighteen years in the convent back, and I would forfeit all the life I have in front of me for one day with my dead husband. So my life has not been easy, but I have to live it, as you will have to live yours. You can either live it looking back at the convent or looking forward to something better. It is entirely up to you for I will not be around to see most of it. If you ignore this Peasants Decree then you may not live long enough to have much more of it. This is what happened to Marguerite when she was only a few years older than you are now. Is this what you want for yourself, your own life stopped short because of your own ignorance?'

'I thought that Marguerite was killed in a bomb blast.'

'Your father was always suspicious of the incident, he believed it was this Man of Insignificance.'

'What can you tell me of this Peasant's Decree?'

'I have not actually seen any information. Your father kept me out of it, It was his way of protecting me. All information is now with your young cousin Archie who now lives in Manchester. Your father has entrusted it to him, he is the last male member of the family and his connection to the de Hay name is a much broken one and also, as he is a man, he is in no danger. Your father always wanted this madness to stop but he didn't know how to bring it about. As I said, your father didn't want me implicated in any way, but naturally I have gathered some knowledge through time, though this knowledge is fragmented.'

'What is this knowledge?'

'Be patient, a few minutes ago you were going to ignore everything.'

'I have changed my mind.'

'It started with your grandfather Padraig de Hay and his two daughters in 1883. They were murdered, shot dead in Dublin. Found by their own servants on Monday morning. There was a big investigation, the top detectives of the day were involved but the murderer vanished without a trace, nothing was ever discovered. The day after they were found murdered old Padraig received a letter entitled *The Peasant's Decree* and signed by somebody calling himself *A Man of Insignificance*. I personally have not seen this letter but I have been told about it. It foretold of the murders of the two sisters. The writer was on some crusade of vengeance to eliminate the de Hay female line and this is what has been happening since 1883. In 1927 Roisin was attacked and barely escaped with her life and in 1941 Marguerite was killed. On each occasion nobody has even been suspected or apprehended.' She paused momentarily. 'That is four de Hay women attacked or murdered in less than sixty years. This is not something that ignorance will solve. The murderer disappears for years then, when everybody thinks he's disappeared for good, he reappears again. The Decree states that the de Hay women will not be harmed until they reach adulthood, when you passed the age of eighteen you became the next target, and that's why your father put you in the convent, so that this murderer would not know of your existence. He knew that by the time you were eighteen he would be dead and unable to protect you. You and Roisin are the only de Hay women left alive and somebody wants to murder both of you. Whilst you were in Manchester you were in a dangerous situation, you should be safe here.'

'Antoinette, how can somebody who murdered the sisters in 1883, attempt to kill Roisin in 1927, murder Marguerite in 1941 and then murder me in 1962? This person must be the oldest person alive, by my estimation they must be about one hundred years old.'

'Kathleen Helen, you are not asking any questions nor are you making any statements that have not been asked or made before. We do not know the answer. This is all part of the enigma of this situation. Now you know why we don't go to the authorities with this, as they would ask questions similar to the one's that you have just asked and as I said, we can't answer them but we are not making this up, it is real. The question you need to ask, and it is of yourself, do you want to be another victim?'

'What can I do? Stanley said that he thought we were being watched in Ireland so perhaps I am already discovered.'

'Stanley may have been mistaken but you should be safe here in France. As far as we know there is no connection to France. The Man of Insignificance has never been here. Keep away from England and Ireland. You must certainly not go near Roisin in Manchester, she has lived in Manchester for many years and her life will be an open book to this murderer. As well as this your physical similarity to your older sister is too obvious for you not to be recognised. Roisin and I are the only family that you have but we are no longer young women and we will not be around forever. Roisin is still not absolutely safe but she will not produce any children at her age and she has Stanley to protect her. Both she and Stanley have seen the person who attacked her and they would recognise him again. As well as this, nothing has happened to Roisin for thirty-five years so the murderer may have given up on her. He may have even given up altogether. This is the problem, we don't know. This has always been the problem, he knows everything about us but we know nothing about him. You are alone and you are young, despite your denials you could have lots of children. If your existence is known you will be the prime target. This murderer could sit next to you in the café tomorrow and you wouldn't even know it.'

'What shall I do?'

'Stay in France, learn something, work out a plan. The world is becoming a smaller place now and it will become even smaller. There is money available for you to travel or study and when you are twenty-one you will have all you need from your inheritance. Change your identity, oh, and change your name. It is a grand name de Hay, a noble name, an old Irish-Norman name, this is all true, but as such it is conspicuous, this is the problem, select something plainer, something more common, something nondescript, something used by a lot more people than de Hay.'

So it was that in September 1963 Kathleen Helen de Hay came to study at the Paul Cezanne University in Marseilles, only by this time she was Helen Day. While still in Paris with Antoinette she had taken elocution lessons in English to lose her Irish accent, which was now not pronounced but was still recognisable to the discerning ear. She stayed in Marseilles for seven years. Then she followed Adam, a man that she thought she loved, back to San Francisco, USA. The only problem with Adam was that he developed a drug habit and she began to develop one too. She swirled around in the American West Coast's early 70's drug scene for a couple of years.

Then she met Max, he didn't have a drug habit, he was a doctor who tried to cure people that did have one and he tried to cure Adam, but he failed. He succeeded though with Helen, so she left Adam and took up with Max who she really did love. Max was Welsh and when he went back to Wales Helen went with him. Max though had a medical condition, it could be treated but it was life threatening. He didn't try to hide it from Helen, he told her about it from the onset and they both just accepted that unlike most young couples they didn't expect to reach their old age together but that seemed a long way off at the time.

Max became a country doctor and although they never actually married Helen assumed the role of a country doctor's wife. For the first time in her life she thought that she was happy. At the age of thirty-four she discovered that she was having a baby, this only enhanced her happiness.

Two months after the baby was born Max's health deteriorated and after a very short illness he died. Helen had thought that she was prepared for this but she wasn't. She was distraught and at this time in her life she found it difficult to cope. That was when she turned to alcohol. A combination of her heavy drinking and her depression meant that she began to neglect her own child. This came to the attention of the authorities who intervened. She was declared an unfit mother and the child was removed from her care and ultimately placed for adoption.

Helen suffered a breakdown and spent some time in hospital. She did recover and upon her discharge she moved out of rural

Wales and for the next five years lived in a succession of cities, Cardiff, Bristol, London and then Birmingham. In each of them she would live by the same pattern. She would enter into some futile relationship with yet again the same type of man only with a different name. This man of the moment would share Helen's need for alcohol as they drank the years by with each other. Eventually, at the age of forty-one, she left the last man in her life and brought her drinking under some kind of control. She trained as a social worker and worked as one for several years. Then, at the age of fifty-six whilst at work for an adoption agency and completely by chance and without looking for it, she discovered both the identity and the whereabouts of the child that she had given up for adoption all those years ago. As a consequence of this information, and in the grip of high emotional impetuosity, she visited Dublin intent on an introduction and reconciliation with her long lost child. While she was in the Irish capital she began to understand things about her life that she had never understood before. As far as she was concerned she was enlightened by this improved understanding and although she did see her child from a distance she changed her mind irrevocably about any kind of contact.

Shortly after her visit to Dublin she moved permanently to Winton Kiss. Although she had never actually been troubled by the Peasants Decree it was not entirely forgotten and shortly after moving to Winton Kiss as a precaution she armed herself with a gun, which she carried around with her. The cruel irony of it was that the Man of Insignificance would, after all these years, eventually and finally catch up with Kathleen Helen. Just before the last day of her life, her suspicions about The Man of Insignificance were aroused and she posted the note to the only person in the whole world that could be remotely described as a friend. This action though was taken more for the protection of her now grown up child than for the protection of her own life for in truth at seventy years of age she had now become weary of it. By the time of her last day, The Man of Insignificance and his representative danger had slipped to the back of her mind, if she had remained vigilant then she may have lived longer, if she had wanted to. She may even have been reunited with her long lost child, this we will now never know.

At that time and on that final fateful day in Winton Kiss, Kathleen Helen's life, and indeed Helen Day's life, had now occupied the very last black square in the bottom corner before she moved off that chequers board of life, altogether and forever.

Chapter 33

The Missing Murders

Designed by the Devon born Architect, E. Vincent Harris (the E stands for Emanuel) and opened in 1934 by no less a personage than King George V himself, Manchester Central Library, the design of which is very loosely based on the Roman Pantheon, is arguably one of the finest buildings in Manchester. As befits such a building of learning and achievement, it is located next door to Manchester Town Hall, which is arguably *the* finest building in Manchester. The library is also adjacent to the site of the *Peterloo Massacre,* without doubt Manchester's most significant, historical incident which when it happened had international implications that far exceeded that city's boundaries.

These days Manchester's metro link tram service stops every six minutes outside the library's front door and that's how Maxine and Danny, albeit on separate trams, had arrived for their mid-day date. It was where they had both decided that they might just be able to elaborate on Danny's translation of Mrs Gilroy's *dotty-speak.* When Danny arrived Maxine was already in place and was looking through a thick leather bound file marked *MEN, Manchester Evening News, 1927.* She also had a similar file on the table near where she was sitting marked *Manchester Guardian, 1927.*

'What was the date of the Lindbergh crossing?' she asked Danny.

Danny checked on the library computer terminal that rested on the table beside him, 'Left New York on Friday, May 20th, 1927 and arrived in Paris on Saturday, May 21st.'

'Hmm,' said Maxine, 'let's see if there is anything about the shooting on the Saturday.' She scoured the relevant edition but could find nothing. There wasn't any reference to Lindbergh, which wasn't surprising for as Danny pointed out he didn't land in Paris until 22:22 hours and even though he had been expected with feverish anticipation, with the communication systems being the way they were in those days, it would probably have been Sunday before the story had broken completely and internationally.

There was no publication of the Manchester Evening News for Sunday so she checked Monday's edition, which was full of the Lindbergh story. Then she saw it, in a little column tucked away on the bottom right side of page seven, *Female Solicitor in Shooting*. There were little more than a few lines as virtually the whole paper was given up to the solo Atlantic crossing. It did though mention the name of the lady solicitor, *Roisin de Hay*.

'That's it Danny, we've got it, we are on the right track. The shooting itself was actually on the Saturday of the Lindbergh crossing,' she slewed the heavy file around to show him.

'Let's check later on in the week,' said Danny, 'maybe our story gathers momentum as the Lindbergh story peaks and loses it.'

As predicted, he was exactly right, there was more information about the attack with each day. Towards the end of that week the story had reached the front page and related how *Roisin de Hay, a female solicitor originally from Ireland but practicing in Manchester,* had been attacked by one of her clients in her own office for no apparent reason.

Maxine read from the newspaper, *'The police are looking for a man, identified as Professor Jeremy Weedon, AKA Major Jonas Watt, aged 40 years, six feet tall with blue eyes, fair hair, a clear complexion, well dressed and well spoken.'* Then she added, 'Usual stuff about members of the public not approaching him as he's armed and dangerous and there's actually a sketch of him drawn by somebody that the newspaper has printed. Quite a handsome man really, for an assassin that is.'

Danny said, 'that's who Mrs Gilroy was referring to when she said *the mad monk*, what she actually meant to say was *the mad professor*. It's a common descriptive term and another example of dotty-speak.' He sat back in his chair and looked up at the ornate plaster ceiling, 'I was thinking about what Mrs Gilroy said to us about Roisin being be-devilled and what Noel O'Malley said to me in The Dolphin in Crossmolina that night. Noel said that there was a rumour that Kathleen Helen had been hidden away in Concepta's by her family because the female line of the family had a curse placed upon them from the last century. Let's remember that when O'Malley said the last century he was actually referring to the eighteen hundreds.'

'I can see that you're not going to give up on this one Danny, although I must admit I was also thinking about what Mrs Gilroy said about Roisin being *be-devilled*.'

'Oh, so you think that there might be something in it?'

'Well, she was very adamant about that particular word, she questioned it in her own mind then she confirmed it as if she was quoting Roisin. I was just wondering if for be-devilled you can read cursed. Then again, I suppose that you can read anything into anything if you want to.'

Danny said, 'let's not be deflected here Maxine, that's the important thing, let's stick to our story. Just look at two simple facts that we know and that we have established. In 1927 Professor Jeremy Weedon or Major Jonas Watts, or whoever he was, tried to murder Roisin de Hay, fact one. Fact two: in 2014 somebody murdered Helen Day, also known as Kathleen Helen de Hay. Now what do those two victims have in common?'

'They are Irish, they are women and they are both called de Hay, they are both from the same family.'

'Is there anything else we know about the victims, any other links?'

'Well we don't know much more about the victims but there may be something that we know about the murderer.'

'Go on Maxine, but don't throw away the first bit, remember we're linking the victims come what may.'

'We know that one and the same person can't have carried out both those crimes because one was in 1927 and the other was in 2014 and by my mathematics that's eighty-seven years apart.'

'That's true, but what does that actually give us?' Maxine looked thoughtful.

'It gives us Maxine, that there must be two separate murderers, maybe a bit more than that, if the victims are connected then why can't the murderers be connected?'

'Danny, do you remember the date on the mirror in Helen Day's house?'

'Yes.'

'Let's start from there.'

'You are obviously onto something so go on.'

'Danny, it's a bit far-fetched, a bit wild.'

'Maxine, go on.'

'Suppose you lived in Ireland in 1848 and for some reason somebody did you a great wrong, so much so that you wanted to do them wrong in return. So you decided that you'd murder their womenfolk.'

'Carry on.'

'So that's what you did. Only you grew old so you passed the task onto somebody else and they carried on where you left off.'

'I think that you've got something but there's a flaw in the early mathematics.'

'Why is that?'

'Well from 1848 to 1927 that's seventy-nine years and not discounting the fact that you would be very old, all you've actually done in that time is *tried* to kill one person, then it's taken you from 1927 to 2014, that's another eighty-seven years, to murder your first victim. So, putting aside that you are at least one-hundred and sixty-six years of age all you've achieved is two attacks resulting in one injury and one fatality. That's not really very productive and that means, if what O'Malley said is true, then Kathleen Helen was hidden away in the convent for eighteen years because somebody tried unsuccessfully to kill Roisin seventeen years earlier. That's not really grounds for putting someone in a convent for eighteen years, nor is it grounds for a story about a curse or for somebody feeling be-devilled, there's something missing here Maxine, what is it?'

'There is Danny and I know what it is.'

'So do I.'

'What's missing Danny are more murders. There must be more murders between 1848 and Kathleen Helen going in the convent.'

'You know, you're right, that's it. We haven't been looking for them because we didn't know they were there in the first place. If our theory is to be supported then we need to look for women named de Hay that have died in suspicious circumstances between 1848 and 2014 and I think that we can narrow that date down even more. To go from 1848 to 1927 for your first strike is nonsense, in fact it is more than that it is actually an impossibility for one person. As we said, that's a span of seventy-nine years. I think that there must have been some activity in the eighteen hundreds much earlier than nineteen twenty-seven.'

'Are we actually accepting as a held view that there is a connection through the murderer from 1848 to today?'

'Yes we are, what alternative could there be?'

'I'm not sure Danny, I'm just not sure, and I mean how could you actually do that, how could you achieve it?'

'I've been thinking about this.'

'Have you come up with anything?'

'Yes I have, try this Maxine, why are you a doctor?'

'A lot of reasons.'

'There always are, but why did you even consider it in the first place. All those years ago, when you were alone in your bedroom studying for your GCSEs, what made you decide, I think I'll become a Doctor?'

'Probably because my dad was one.'

'And what about his dad?'

'Well yes, he was one too.'

'This is it Maxine, this is the answer, now I know that this is extraordinary but all we've got to do is believe in our own idea.'

'You'll need to explain a bit more Danny.'

'Suppose you were a baker or a fishmonger or a furniture maker, the specific occupation itself doesn't really matter that much. What does matter is this: it is 1848 and your business becomes your life, it is more important than anything to you and you want to make sure that it lives on after you have died. So, you make sure that your son or your daughter or your nephew or your niece even, that bit doesn't matter, carries it on after you. To ensure that they perpetuate your values you bring them into the business at a very early age, and they in turn do the same with their children, so your business and its values survive through the ages. There will always be somebody in your family that won't follow you but there is always at least one that will and that's all you need. It is a type of indoctrination process that really works the same way as religion does, but a good one done for the right reasons and it's how some family businesses survive through the ages.'

'Yeah, I can see that.'

'Well then, using exactly the same principle, suppose instead of your business being a bakery or furniture making your business is actually murder and revenge. All done for the wrong moral reasons yes, but nevertheless you apply the same kind of indoctrination so that your business lives on through the ages.'

'It should be fairly easy Danny, motivating somebody to take over your cake shop, but it's a different proposition getting your son or your nephew to murder somebody that they've never met long after you're dead.'

'It is a different proposition Maxine, of course it is, but the methodology is the same, only the product is different and this has got to be the way it happened, there is no other explanation. It is just because it is so incredible that we don't want to believe it.'

Maxine resumed her scrutiny of the newspaper file. She began turning over the pages. Something attracted her attention, she stopped for a moment then read out aloud, '*Are this family cursed? The attempted murder of Roisin de Hay last week brought back to mind the slaying of the two sisters Clodagh and Siobhan de Hay in Dublin, 44 years ago…*'

'That's it,' said Danny, 'two of the missing murders, does it say when?'

'It doesn't give an exact date but it gives a year, eighteen eighty-three.'

Danny walked over to the window, he slouched against the wall and dug his hands deep into his pockets. Staring out through the glass he said, 'So now, between 1883 and 2014, we've got three murders and an attempted murder, all women, all named de Hay, all Irish and almost certainly all from the same family. That's four, there could even be more.'

Just then Maxine removed her spectacles and massaged her eyelids with her thumb.

'Are you alright Maxine? If you don't mind me saying so, you look a little tired. Not your usual glistening self.'

'It's just work, there is a lot happening at the minute. I could do with a little break, nothing exotic, just a few days in the open air instead of being penned in, in that surgery.'

'Why don't you take a little holiday?'

'I would go away tomorrow for the weekend, but if I am being truthful I'm just too lazy to make the arrangements. If somebody would make them for me then I'd just go. A few days on my own strolling around during the day and reading and listening to the radio in the evening would suit me at this moment.'

'I know just the place, it's a little rustic but it's ideal for both those things, you wouldn't have any arranging to do, your only responsibility would be to get yourself there which is a two hours plus drive and as a bonus it's free of charge.'

'Sounds ideal, where is this haven?'

'I've got a little house in Beaumaris you can have it all to yourself next week if you wish.'

'Do you mean it?'

'Of course I do, I'll get some information and the keys over to you later today. I'll phone Mrs Jenkins and ask her to go over first thing in the morning, give the place an airing, clean bedding, towels and stuff.'

'Oh thank you Danny, that's tremendous, I am really looking forward to it already.'

Just then Danny's phone beeped with a message. He took it out of his pocket and he could see it was a text from Charlotte so he read it, 'Archie has come round, I'm so relieved and he's *asking for you. Can you go and see him tomorrow morning at the Hospital?'*

Danny passed the phone over to Maxine. She scanned the message and said, 'Well that's good news, I must admit he's been out for quite some time now and I was beginning to get a little worried.'

'I'm relieved too, life wouldn't be the same without Archie haranguing me. I'll go and see how he is in the morning as Charlotte suggests.'

'Do you want me to come with you?'

'It might look a bit mercenary if we both go, after all, he's only just come round.'

'I know what you mean.'

'Why don't you take yourself over to Beaumaris tomorrow morning, I'll go and see Archie. I won't say anything about Kathleen Helen if he doesn't, and if he does, and he's got something relevant to contribute to this, then you'll be the first to know. The keys and that information that I promised, I'll post them through your letter-box this evening but promise me that you'll leave first thing in the morning.'

'It's a promise.'

'How are you getting home?'

'Tram and train'

'Mind if I join you?'

Later that evening Danny drove up the lane from Winton Kiss. He passed Maxine's surgery which he observed was closed and in semi-darkness. Stopping outside Maxine's house he noticed her car in the drive. He didn't stay around or call, he just posted his envelope through her letterbox. Then he returned to his car, turned it around and drove back down the hill. On the way back down he stopped outside the Travellers Oak to let the oncoming vehicles pass on the narrow lane.

It was starting to get dark as he looked at the time on his car dashboard, 9:14pm. Through the lighted windows of the small pub he could clearly see Ben Goldstein and Doctor Tom in conversation with an extremely attractive dark woman in a grey dress that Danny half recognised. Doctor Tom then broke away from his company and stepped outside the tiny village pub into the cool summer evening to take a call on his mobile phone. Danny was so close he could hear what Doctor Tom was saying. The caller was Maxine and she was obviously telling her father about her short notice decision concerning the holiday. After the call Doctor Tom went back inside the pub and returned to Ben Goldstein and the unidentified woman in grey. Even from a distance as Danny studied Doctor Tom's body language he concluded that Maxine's father seemed enamoured of this dark beauty. Just at that moment Flora, Ben Goldstein's wife, pulled up outside the pub and went through its front door. When she re-emerged seconds later Ben was with her. She was obviously acting as chauffeur so that Ben could enjoy a summer evening drink in his local.

Danny looked back through the window, Doctor Tom and the woman in grey now seemed in more intimate pose since the departure of Councillor Goldstein. He could see more clearly and as his eyes adjusted to the changing light he now recognised that what he had thought was a grey dress was actually a priest's cassock. Danny now realised the woman was the Reverend Bel, the new vicar at All Saints. Danny didn't know her very well, he wasn't a big churchgoer although he often thought that perhaps he should be. It was unusual he thought to see the vicar in the local pub but then again, why shouldn't she be? He also thought she was an unusual vicar, he had met her on two or three occasions at council gatherings and had been immediately struck by her natural beauty. He remembered one particular function when, despite being in her drab clerical garb, she had outshone all the other women in their finery. She hadn't set out to do it, he could tell that, but she wasn't in ignorance of it either, he could tell that too. She was tall and slender with an absolutely stunning figure that even a cassock couldn't hide. She had flowing chestnut coloured hair and she had the sultry dark looks of a Latino film star. She reminded Danny of that old movie star, the one that had been married to Frank Sinatra, he couldn't think of her name, anyway he was digressing. He'd heard that she had a husband who worked overseas but he'd never seen him and husband or not he could fully understand how Doctor Tom was apparently taken with her.

Whilst he was thinking about Doctor Tom and the beautiful vicar being an odd pairing he thought about Doctor Tom for a minute and studied him through the pub window. In contrast to the unconventional Reverend Bel, Doctor Tom was the epitome of convention, he was wearing a suit and tie even in the pub on a warm summer night. He was short, stocky and dark, the exact opposite of his daughter Maxine. In fact they bore no physical resemblance to each other whatsoever, but that of course was often the case with parents and their offspring. Perhaps, he thought, Maxine took after her mother whom he had never known.

Danny continued down the hill, tomorrow he would go and see Archie but just now he aimed his car for the Black Swan car park. As he locked up his car and put the keys to bed in his trouser pocket for the night he was looking forward to his own summer night drink.

Chapter 34

Archie's Story

It was 9:00am as Danny Senetti, carrying a huge bunch of yellow flowers, entered Ward 1C of Norford Mount Hospital. As he did he saw Archie Hamilton sat up in the second bed on the right. Archie was dressed in silk pyjamas and silk dressing gown. When Archie saw Danny approach he closed the book that he had been reading and put it down on top of the little locker by his bed, 'Danny good to see you, how are you?'

'Archie, how good to see you, and more to the point, how are you after your experience?'

'Well you know, it is all a little strange really. I don't seem to remember that much about it, one minute I was walking along the street, the next I was waking up in the hospital. Apparently I'm lucky to be alive let alone compos mentis.'

'Who actually told you that you were that Archie, compos mentis I mean, not alive?'

'The doctors did Danny, that's who, and in their opinion, and that's the one that carries the vote in here, they say I'm going to be alright, which is quite amazing really, but I'm more than happy to be amazed at my time of life, in fact I'm just happy to be alive at my time of life, especially after that ride.'

'Well that's all good news and news that I for one, and many others, will be very pleased to hear.'

There were two chairs at one side of the hospital bed. Danny sat down on one chair and placed the wrapped flowers on the other.

'How are your investigations going, bring me up to date?'

'What investigations?'

'Your investigations into Kathleen Helen de Hay's murder. That lady that was murdered in Winton Kiss was Kathleen Helen de Hay wasn't she?'

'Archie, you've been asleep for a month, how do you know that I've been investigating anything?'

'See, even in my sleep Danny, I can still keep tabs on you and I know that you've been to Mayo and you've been to my flat and you were there with Doctor Maxine Wells and the doctor has been to Edinburgh, so what other reason could either of you have for doing any one of those things let alone all of them? The important thing is what exactly have you found out?'

'Archie, are you sure that your well enough for this? Perhaps we should just talk about little things until you are feeling better, you know, small talk and stuff, leave the rest until you're up and about, on your feet.'

'Danny, as for you, you don't have any small talk, you've never had any in your life. You think that everything that you talk about is a major issue simply because *you're* talking about it and if it isn't one, then you'll talk it up big until it is. As for me, I'm well enough to speak and I'm well enough to listen and I probably know what you know anyway. So just tell me to start with, is this Helen Day from Winton Kiss one and the same Kathleen Helen de Hay from the Holy Conception convent, County Mayo?'

'If I tell you that Archie will you tell me what you know about all this?'

'Well was she?'

'Yes.'

'I knew it.'

'Archie, where exactly do you fit into all of this?'

'Danny, pour me a glass of water.' There was a tray on top of the little locker with a glass and a bottle of water resting upon it and Danny dutifully obeyed. Archie held the glass in his hand and he took regular sips as he recounted, 'Right, now you need to pay attention as this can get a bit complicated.'

Danny looked at the older man as he began his story.

'My connection to the de Hay family starts back in Ireland in the 1830's and is only by marriage. My great-great-grandmother

Cara who was also Irish, was a young widow when she married an Irishman called Padraig de Hay. Cara already had a young child from her first marriage, this child wasn't Padraig's, she was Sybil and she was my great-grandmother. Sybil was brought up by Padraig from a very early age and took his name, but he was actually her stepfather and she wasn't a de Hay by birth right. If she had been then I probably wouldn't be here now because she would probably have been murdered. This birth right name of de Hay is an important point in this story so bear it in mind at all times Danny.'

He took another sip from the glass, 'Old Padraig came from a place called Enniscorthy in County Wexford. The de Hays go back in history to the Norman invasion of Ireland in the twelfth century. By the time of the late 1840's Ireland was in the grip of a terrible starvation. People were dying of hunger and disease in their droves and those that weren't were getting out of the place as fast as they could get the price of a boat ticket. There were those, as there always will be, that couldn't get the price of a boat ticket and of course there were those, as there always will be, who chose to stay anyway. A million people starved to death and a million fled the place and many that fled the place didn't survive the journey. The death rate was so high for those that travelled to America that the boats that took them were called *coffin ships*. Ireland never got over it, it was a major disaster for mankind. *An Gorta Mor*, the Irish called it, *The Great Hunger*. Ireland at that time was part of the British Empire and England was the richest country in the whole world. The world just couldn't understand how it could happen. It was a bleak time in the histories of both Ireland and England and people have been trying to shift the blame ever since then, even to this day historians hold differing views as to accountability and responsibility.'

Archie paused and Danny could see that he was a little emotional.

'At that time, apart from particular members of the British government, the most reviled people in Ireland were a group of men known as *middlemen*. Every county had such people. Many of these men were Irish themselves, they operated all over the country and many of them swindled and cheated poor vulnerable people out of their lands. Many a peasant and their families were left penniless and destitute and eventually died because of the actions of these middlemen.'

Archie stopped again for a moment and sipped more water. Apart from Archie's family connection, Danny already knew everything that the older man had told him about Ireland but he listened attentively as Archie continued, 'Padraig de Hay was one of these so-called middlemen, and as such he would have had many a man and woman that hated him. As well as Sybil, Padraig had other children, birth children, amongst them were two daughters Clodagh and Siobhan.'

Danny wanted to ask many questions but he remained silent.

'Now we move forward to 1883, An Gorta Mor had been long over. Sybil by now had married an English rail engineer called Albert Hamilton. She had a family and they had settled in Edinburgh. As I said she was only a de Hay by marriage whereas Clodagh and Siobhan were full-blooded birth daughters of Padraig.'

'Archie is that important?'

'Danny, for chrissake, I said it was ten minutes ago, just listen or you'll break my concentration and get me all confused with great this and great-great that. In addition to which, can I just remind you that I've just come out of a coma. Have some respect will you.' He took another sip of water, 'At this time the younger sisters, Clodagh and Siobhan, were unmarried and were both living together in Dublin. Padraig was no longer a middleman, he'd gone into banking and he became respectable and quite wealthy, in fact at one time he was the mayor of Enniscorthy. On October 6, 1883, a good thirty years after the end of the hunger, both Clodagh and Siobhan were murdered in their house in Dublin. They were murdered in a horrible scene in the same room on the same night in a ritualistic way, the room was desecrated and vandalised beyond recognition. Nobody was ever caught or even suspected of it. The day after the murder was discovered Padraig who was still in Enniscorthy received a letter now known as *The Peasant's Decree*. It was thought to be from the murderer and was signed by somebody calling himself, *A Man of Insignificance.'*

'Archie, does anybody have this letter?'

'Danny, I really want you to listen now and don't interrupt, this is part of my life here that is unfolding, I'll answer questions at the end.'

Danny considered himself admonished.

'The Peasant's Decree, was a proclamation.'

'Have you seen it Archie, have you seen it?'

'Danny I have, many times, now if you want to see it, be quiet and for the last time listen, please. One more word from you and I'm going back into the coma for another month.'

Danny held both hands up as if to signify compliance.

'Whoever wrote *The Peasant's Decree* made accusations and assertions against Padraig. These accusations went back in time to *An Gorta Mor*. The other thing that this *Decree* threatened was that all Padraig's adult female line would be executed and that this would continue throughout time until there were none of them left. Now that is more or less what has happened through the years since 1883. The sisters in Dublin in 1883, Roisin de Hay in Manchester in 1927 although she survived the attack, Marguerite de Hay in Liverpool in 1941 and Kathleen Helen de Hay last month in Winton Kiss. A period spanning one hundred and thirty-one years and including four murders and an attempted murder. All de Hay women and all birth descendants of old Paidraig.'

He took more water, 'It is ironic that the de Hay line didn't actually produce a lot of children, at least not for that time and not for Ireland. There were some sons but one of them was killed young in a skirmish in India in the late 1870's and another son was killed, also young, in World War One. However there always seemed to be at least one female de Hay produced and there always seemed to be this *Man of Insignificance* around to kill her.'

'In 1962 I was the last surviving male member of the de Hay family and I was living in Manchester as was Roisin de Hay. Even though, as I said, my connection is by marriage, I was asked by Roisin to accompany her to Mayo to help bring Kathleen Helen out of the convent. It was thought that someone from her own generation would ease the pain if I can put it that way. So I went over to Mayo with Roisin and a man called Stanley Oldknow. That was the first time that I had ever heard of, let alone met, Kathleen Helen de Hay.'

'Can I ask a question Archie?'

'Yes.'

'Who is Marguerite?'

Marguerite is another de Hay female. She was the daughter of Frank de Hay and Antoinette Dubois, she was in her early twenties, she had her whole life in front of her when she was killed in Liverpool during World War Two. At first everybody thought that she was killed by a bomb that fell on her house, but it turned out that she was murdered by this Man of Insignificance.'

'Who is Antoinette Dubois?'

'She was the mother of both Marguerite and Kathleen Helen but Marguerite's father was Frank de Hay and Kathleen Helen's father was *his* father Dermot de Hay.'

'Archie, you're losing me a bit here.'

'Danny, don't worry about the genealogy of it all at this stage, I've got a file for you, and inside it is a complete family tree and history, you can study it later.'

'It's quite a story Archie.'

'You're right, it is and it might not be finished yet, there could be one final episode to come.'

'Why do you say that?'

'There is at least one more potential victim out there, maybe even more than one, and if there is a victim, and if history is anything to go by, then there will also be a *Man of Insignificance* waiting to murder her.'

'Who is this victim?'

'Just be patient Danny and you'll find out. I tried to keep in touch with Kathleen Helen as much as I could after she came out of the convent. We met up once when I was in France and I wrote to her afterwards, when she was at university in Marseilles, but she didn't respond. I had no jurisdiction over her and I had my own family to look after by then and we lost touch. The big thing with Kathleen Helen, as far as I could understand it, was that she could not get over being put in a convent for all those years by her own mother and father. She would have been what we know now as a damaged child, but this was in the 60's and 70's and we didn't understand that as well as we do now. Eventually, she disappeared altogether, I heard that she'd gone to live in America and then I had no news of her for decades, I thought that perhaps she'd died, as we all do. I later found out that in 1979 she'd had a child, a little girl.'

'What happened to the child?'

'In 1980 that child was removed from Kathleen Helen's care by social services in Wales and she was eventually given up for adoption. That little girl will be a woman by now and she is a full-blooded, top-of-the-tree, birth-right de Hay. She may even have children of her own and they are all in danger. Both she and those children are potential victims of this *Man of Insignificance*. We need to find this missing daughter Danny, before he does.'

'Do we know anything about her, where she is, who she is, what she looks like?'

'None of that except the family trait.'

'What trait?'

'The de Hay eyes, all the de Hay women since Antoinette Dubois have amber eyes. It's a female gene thing, it's not unique but it is very unusual. Antoinette Dubois had them, so did Marguerite and so did Kathleen Helen. There is a good chance that her daughter will have them too.'

'Even if we find this woman and her children Archie, it will not resolve this, we can't watch over people all their lives. Maybe this *Man of Insignificance* doesn't know of this missing daughter's existence?'

'He knows Danny, he always knows, he'll find out, he always does, he makes it his business to find out. Why else would he run me over if he thought that Kathleen Helen was the last de Hay? He'd already killed her, so if he thought that she was the last one, why bother with me?'

'Well in that case we need to find him.'

'People have been trying to do that since 1883.'

'We must look at it afresh Archie. So your accident wasn't an accident, you think that it was deliberate?'

'I know it was.'

'You think that it was the same person that murdered Kathleen Helen?'

'Yes.'

'Do you think that it was him?'

'I'm sure that it was.'

'But as you said Archie, you're not a de Hay woman?'

'No, I'm not, and that makes it even more worrying as for the first time he's gone outside the Peasant's Decree. As I said he's trying to stop our investigation because he doesn't want to be discovered and he has some unfinished business with his next victim. So in order to murder her, he'll murder me if necessary.'

'But Archie, nobody knew anything about our investigation. It wasn't even an investigation, at that time it was just a conversation. Until now we've only discussed it for the first and only time on the landing in the town hall on the night of the council meeting. There was only you and I and the usual town hall people, councillors and officers. They'd think nothing of knifing you in the back politically, but in reality we've know them for years, there isn't a murderer between the lot of them, none of them would have the bollocks for it. Ten minutes later, somebody ran you over, how could anybody know what we were talking about? It is just not possible.'

'I don't know Danny, but somebody does know. I don't know how but they've found out.'

'Do you remember anything at all about the accident?'

'Very little.'

'Anything will do.'

'Perhaps there was something but I might have imagined it.'

'Go on Archie, anything is better than nothing which is all we have at the minute, nothing.'

'I can't be sure.'

'Archie, just tell me what it is.'

'It's just that before I lost consciousness I thought that I heard guitar music, but it might have been in my head.'

'What, was it live music?'

'No, it wasn't live, it was a CD or a radio.'

'What kind of guitar music?'

'I don't know, what kind of guitar music do they have?'

'Well all kinds.'

'Such as?'

'Well erm, rock-guitar, folk-guitar, classical-guitar, Spanish-guitar...'

'Spanish guitar, yes that's it, Spanish guitar.'

'Anything else about it?'

'No, nothing.'

'Where's this file you mentioned?'

'In the locker, I asked Charlotte to bring it earlier today. She arrived with it just before you did.'

'Can I get it?'

'Yes, help yourself.'

Danny reached inside the small locker by Archie's bed, he took out a battered grey box file. On the front was a faded adhesive label but the black, block capital writing could easily be made out, it said:

'A MAN OF INSIGNIFICANCE.'

'Danny, there's only a handful of people in history that have seen what's inside this box. Old Padraig de Hay started this file after the murder of the two sisters in 1883. Newspaper reports, photographs, anything considered relevant. It's been passed down the family line through the years and it has been added to, until it got to me. I've studied it a hundred times. Perhaps you might want to look through it, a fresh pair of eyes as you said. If we are going to identify and stop this murderer then the answer, or at least part of the answer, might just be in that file. Be careful with it.'

'I will do.'

'Take care of it, let me have it back, it's a kind of documented doom-laden family heirloom.'

'It's safe with me.'

'One more thing.' He delved into his dressing gown pocket and took out a small business card, 'That's the safe combination in my place and also the password to the computer and here's the keys to the flat. There's some family stuff in the safe, mostly photographs. They might help, I don't know, use what you need. I'll trust you not to look at anything that's private and not connected.'

Danny took the paper and gave a nod.

'Oh, I'd forgotten there's also a gun and some cartridges in that safe. The gun was found in Roisin's office by Stanley Oldknow at the time of her attempted murder. It was never discharged and Stanley thought that it was one of a pair. So if he was right then find the other one, if it still exists, and you find the murderer.'

'Alright, thank you.'

'I'm getting a bit tired now,' said Archie.

'I'll be on my way. I'll be in touch.'

Archie said, 'just one last thing Danny.'

'Sure.'

'Do whatever you can but remember, this new killer is a different one than the first *Man of Insignificance*.'

'Why do you say that Archie?'

'This killer, he's transgressed the code, broken it when he tried to kill me, he's been prepared to go outside The Peasant's Decree, that's not been done before. As you pointed out I'm not a female line de Hay, I'm only a de Hay by marriage and I'm a man. So if he's prepared to kill me, he'll be prepared to kill anybody that interferes with his objectives and that includes you Danny, especially you Danny, you're on his trail and he'll know it, also that partner of yours, Doctor Maxine Wells. Where is she by the way?'

'She's taking a little holiday miles away from here. So she's out of the way at the minute.'

'That's probably a good thing for the moment, one less to worry about.'

Chapter 35

Beaumaris Revisited

On the same day, and at about the same time that Danny Senetti was walking into Norford Mount Hospital with his bunch of yellow flowers to visit Archie Hamilton, Maxine Wells left her home and set off on the journey from Winton Kiss to Danny's house in Gaol Street, Beaumaris. She had been amused the previous evening when she'd collected the envelope from her hallway and upon reading the contents had discovered that the address of the house was actually number one, Gaol Street. Only Danny Senetti, she thought, would have a house with such an address.

Earlier that evening, after her surgery, she had spoken to her partner at the practice, Duncan Wordsworth, and even though it was short notice he'd encouraged her to take the holiday and had been supportive of the whole thing. After she had spoken with Duncan she had gone home, packed a bag and decided to telephone her father who had been in the Travellers Oak with Ben Goldstein at the time. She had explained to him that she was taking a few days off, where she was going and where he could find her, if he really needed her, then that had been that she thought, all arrangements made.

The following morning her silver Mercedes had glided effortlessly up the A55 towards Beaumaris and after an hour and a half she had even allowed herself a twenty-minute coffee and bun refreshment stop. Then she'd continued on her journey and just before midday the silver Mercedes had swept across the Britannia Bridge, over the Menai Strait and onto the isle of Anglesey. Fifteen minutes later it stopped outside number one in

Gaol Street, Beaumaris, Danny Senetti's house. On the journey over she had been thinking of Dr Tom and of Duncan and her patients but now she determined to forget about them all and everybody else in Winton Kiss for a few days.

As she stepped out of her car she looked up at the formidable looking stone built gaol and laughed to herself. The gates of the gaol were open and a few tourists were milling around the entrance. She made a promise to herself that she would take a tour around it, perhaps tomorrow.

Maxine went through the front door of the little house and immediately came face to face with Megan Jenkins. Mrs Jenkins lived at number eight on Gaol Street and as well as being a neighbour she looked after the house for Danny when he was away from it. She was there sorting out the bedding and towels, and freshening the place up. When she saw Maxine she said, 'Oh you're here, I wondered where you'd gone, you'll be Maxine then, Danny rang me yesterday and told me that you were coming over for a while. I'm Megan, I look after the house for Danny when he's not here. I live at number eight, it's just a few doors down the road, if you need anything just come over and ask.'

'Oh, thank you Megan, I'm Maxine, I've just arrived.'

'Oh, so it wasn't you an hour ago?'

'No, I've just arrived. Why, has someone else been here?'

'Oh, I didn't really take any notice of them, I thought that I saw somebody looking at the house. I thought that it was you because it was a woman and I was expecting a woman. It was probably a tourist, they're always walking around looking at the property in town. I've done everything so I'll go now.'

As Megan left Maxine said, 'Once again, thank you very much Megan, I appreciate it.'

Maxine had a quick look around the house. She concluded that the little place, although rustic, was actually quite charming and she immediately felt happy that she had made the decision to come to Beaumaris. Even though she'd been made aware of the address as soon as she'd opened Danny's envelope she didn't actually think that the house would really be on the same street as a gaol and she found the idea very amusing. The sun was shining so she decided that she would take a little stroll around Beaumaris and its environs. First she stood outside the Gaol. Then she walked around the outside of the castle. As she strolled around she looked in the shop windows and actually went inside two shops. She bought a small amount of provisions including two bottles of expensive champagne. She didn't drink from one month to the next at home but on holiday, and in celebration, she was fond of a glass of good champagne and she decided that later today she would be in celebration. Finally she stopped at the bookshop to buy some reading material for the evening. As she stood at the tiny counter to pay for her purchases she looked out through the small window onto the street. She thought for a brief moment that she recognised a person that was standing there although she couldn't think where from. Then, as she glanced away, both the person and the memory were gone. She concluded that she'd imagined it.

After she left the bookshop it was around lunchtime so Maxine thought that she would treat herself to the unaccustomed luxury of a lunch, she would take two hours just as they did on the continent, it was something that she rarely had the opportunity to do at home. She found a small teashop in the centre of Beaumaris with some tables and chairs outside, it overlooked the harbour and she thought that it would be pleasant to sit down in the sunshine, so she sat down at one of the tables and took out one of the books she had just purchased. As she gazed out past the harbour onto the seascape she felt relaxed, comfortable and a world away from Winton Kiss.

A voice broke into her daydream, 'Doctor Wells, is it Doctor Wells?'

Maxine looked up in the direction of the voice and standing before her was a very beautiful, casually dressed lady whom she half recognised, then she realised that it was the woman that she had thought she'd seen through the bookshop window. It was the Reverend Bel from Winton Kiss. The Reverend was out of her clerical garb and dressed in shorts, tee shirt and sandals and out of this sartorial context Maxine hadn't immediately recognised her.

'Well this is a surprise,' said Bel, 'I wasn't expecting to see anybody here from Winton Kiss. I was hoping that I'd escaped the place, oh I'm sorry, I didn't mean to sound hostile or unfriendly.'

'Oh no, I understand exactly what you mean, I feel the same myself. Are you here alone?'

'Yes, completely.'

'Then as you are here, as we both are. I was just about to have some lunch would you care to join me?'

'Thank you, that's very gracious of you. I hope that you won't think me ungracious if I decline. It's just that I've got an appointment in twenty minutes but it would be nice to sit down for ten of them.'

'Please do,' said Maxine, 'there is a condition though.'

'Of course.'

'That you don't mention the word doctor, any of my patients that might be members of your congregation, or Winton Kiss and that you call me Maxine.'

'Agreed Maxine, as long as you agree to my conditions which are that you don't mention the place that we've just said we won't mention, the words vicar, reverend or church or anything that could be seen to resemble them or any members of my congregation that might be one of your patients.'

Both women laughed together and smiled at each other and Bel pulled out a chair and sat down facing Maxine, 'If it's not an intrusive question Maxine, what brings you to Beaumaris?'

'Oh, I'm here purely as a tourist. A friend of mine has a little house on the edge of town and I was offered the loan of it for a few days. So I decided to take an impromptu holiday.'

'There the best ones to take, have you been here long, have you been to Beaumaris before, do you know much about the place? Your friend, is he or she here too?'

Maxine thought that the Reverend asked a lot of questions but she answered patiently and politely, 'I arrived here about half an hour ago. It's my first ever visit, it seems a charming little place but I know absolutely nothing about it. I've been wandering around without taking any notice of where I was going or where I came from. I'm not even sure that I can find the way back to the little house. My friend isn't here, he's not really that sort of a friend.'

'It is a charming place and don't worry finding your way. I'm practically a native here, I know every street in the place. Where exactly is your little house?'

'It's just outside Beaumaris Gaol.'

'That's easy, a ten minute walk from here, back down the main street towards the castle and turn left at the pub then you'll come upon it.'

'Thanks, what brings *you* to Beaumaris?'

'I did some work here when I was first ordained and I just got to love the place. I've still got some friends here and I visit them from time to time although it's true to say that most of them have moved on now.'

'Where are you staying?'

'I've also got a little house here. It's the other side of town to yours. It's a bit of a luxury really, a bit of a holiday home and I keep thinking that I'll sell it but then I think that it's good to have a little bolthole to escape to.'

The waitress came over to the table and Maxine ordered from the menu. Bel glanced down at the bottles of champagne that were resting on the floor encased in their wooden display box, 'Celebrating?'

'Well I suppose, yes, I don't drink normally but I do enjoy a glass of champagne. I thought that I'd do some reading tonight and before I did that I'd have a couple of glasses of champagne. You know, do all those things that I don't do when I'm back in that place that we're not mentioning.'

'Sounds marvellous, I enjoy a glass of good champagne myself.'

'There's just one thing, I've only just thought of it, my friend, the one who owns the house, is not really a champagne person. So there are probably no champagne glasses in the place.'

'Yes champagne is not the same if it's not in a quality glass.'

'Do you know where I can buy some in Beaumaris?'

'Oh don't go to the trouble of searching around for glasses. I've got some crystal flutes that I can lend you.'

'Thank you, tell you what, are you planning anything this evening?'

'No.'

'Why don't you bring them over later and we'll share the bottle. You provide the glasses and I'll provide the champagne.'

'Well are you sure, I got the impression that you came here to be on your own, and what about your reading? I wouldn't want to intrude upon your solitude.'

'Oh no, you won't be, I'll be glad of the company and I can read tomorrow, but only if you want to you understand.'

'Well then that will be lovely.'

'Same conditions apply, no vicars, doctors, patients, churchgoers or mention of that place that we're not mentioning.'

'Absolutely.'

'What time?'

'Seven o'clock suit?'

'Ideal.'

'Number One, Gaol Street, do you know where it is?'

'I do, I'll be there.'

The waitress arrived with Maxine's food.

'I'll leave you in peace to get on with your lunch. I'll see you later.'

Bel got up from the table, smiled and walked off slowly. Maxine watched her as she disappeared into the town. She thought that she seemed a very nice lady, intelligent, good company, and she was looking forward to the evening in prospect.

Chapter 36

The Missing Daughter

If there was one subject that Danny Senetti knew more about than anybody else in the whole world it was his own political constituency and if there was one aspect of his constituency that he was the top expert on to the exclusion of all it was his own constituents.

There was a population of around 12,000 people in his Malton political ward, living in approximately 3,000 dwellings, and there were very few of those dwellings that Senetti didn't know something about. After fourteen years as a locally elected member he had built up a photographic memory bank on *his people* as he called them. There were many whom he knew much about and there were very few of them, unless they were really new to Malton, that he couldn't give you at least some cursory information on. As far as Winton Kiss itself was concerned his knowledge was even more comprehensive and it had got to the point with virtually all the addresses in the village whereupon he could look at them on paper and tell you about the occupants to varying degrees.

He had not forgotten his conversation with Maxine Wells at the early stages of the investigation where they had both agreed that Helen Day's murderer probably lived in the community and had some local or inside knowledge, and also was probably known, or was at least recognisable, to Helen Day herself. The problem with this for Senetti was that the more he thought about his own constituents the more he could not come up with somebody who could even remotely be considered to be a murderer.

As a consequence of his own deliberations, and possibly also as a symptom of his own political vanity about his local knowledge, he had persuaded himself that the murderer must be new to his ward and one of the few constituents that he had no knowledge of. Earlier that morning he had telephoned Christine Harris and asked her to do an exercise for him against the most up to date electoral roll and he was expecting her phone call any time now.

This morning, after he had contacted Christine, he had gone straight to see Archie in hospital and after the hospital he'd gone straight to Archie's flat. As Archie had actually given him the keys to the place, he reasoned that any information that was useful would be there, so he thought that the flat would make the best base from which to work. He now sat in Archie's bedroom cum office in front of Archie's computer. On the desk in front of him were the grey box file and his own complete electoral roll. This was the first time since the start of the investigation that he felt that he had any real information and he felt excited about it.

He made himself a cup of tea and returned to the desk. Something told him, and he knew in his own mind too, that the mystery of the Man of Insignificance was within his grasp and the identity of the murderer of Helen Day was also within his grasp. He also knew that the answers to any present-day happenings, and any future happenings, lay firmly in the past. He took the copy of the de Hay family tree from the box file and studied it. He knew that he needed to be reasonably well informed about the whole of the de Hay family and he held the document in front of him and followed its origins through repeatedly, mentally and in chronological order.

Starting from *old Padraig de Hay*, the middleman himself, to the two young sisters in Dublin, *Clodagh* and *Siobhan*, then to *Dermot* then to *Lieutenant Frank, Antoinette Dubois* and *Councillor Roisin* then *Marguerite*, then *Dermot* and *Antoinette* again and then finally *Kathleen Helen*. All accounted for through the generations, all except one, the final person and the last piece of the puzzle, Kathleen Helen's child, *the missing daughter*. There were others along the way, Archie's great-grandmother, Padraig's first son, and so on but they were an insignificant supporting act he decided. He read the document through again until he was convinced that he had committed it to memory. He now felt confident that he had a fundamental knowledge of the de Hays, when they were, who they were, where they were, what they were. He was satisfied with this but he was also aware that this wealth of knowledge about this family of victims was completely cancelled out by his absolute paucity of knowledge in relation to the murderer and his own connections.

Whilst concentrating on how to improve this state of affairs he found a whiteboard and some markers which he placed upon the desktop and leaned it against the wall. He began to write his own profile on the investigation. He was slightly humoured by his actions and he recalled Maxine's comments about TV detectives but he persevered with the process. First he wrote up the de Hay family tree at the top of the board then he put up the Peasants Decree at the other side of it. After this he worked at it and with what seemed little or no order he made annotations all over the board. The self-imposed rule was: if it came into his head then he wrote it down. Then after a couple of hours of thinking and writing he stopped and stood off his handiwork and stared at it. In particular he looked at the Peasants Decree over and over. If he could find the first *Man of Insignificance* then perhaps he could get a connection through to the present time. The Peasants Decree document was a chilling prophesy, written all those years ago, of that there was no doubt, but he asked himself again what did it tell him that could help him identify the writer, the one who called himself *The Man of Insignificance, t*he man who had started all of this one hundred and thirty-one years ago with the murder of the two sisters in their house in Dublin?

He decided that the document, although dated 6 October, 1883 was reflective from that date and referred to the period *An Gorta Mor* in retrospect. He knew from his own knowledge that this period in Irish history was considered to be from 1845 to 1852 and he also knew, from the de Hay family tree, that Padraig de Hay was born in 1810. He recalled the writing on Helen Day's mirror remembering the date, *1848*. He decided that this year was significant to Helen's murderer and it was also the middle year of *The Great Hunger* so he determined that he would make this year his first reference point and he placed Padraig as aged thirty-eight years at the time of this year.

The Peasants Decree claimed the writer to be '*a younger man still.*' Senetti didn't know how much younger so he placed the writer at nineteen years for no other reason than it was half Padraig's age. He had to start somewhere so he decided that he was looking for a man from Enniscorthy, who was approximately nineteen years old around 1848, step one, he told himself. He wrote this down on his board. Where did he go from here? He knew from the press cuttings that he and Maxine had seen in the library that the professor who had tried to kill Roisin was around forty years of age in 1927 so even if that approximation was a few years either side he would have either been unborn or a young child in 1883. Therefore the writer of the original Peasant's Decree and the professor were obviously two entirely different people. Different he thought, but not unrelated, uncle and nephew maybe, brothers perhaps, possibly even father and son he surmised. Whatever their connection he knew for sure and in his own mind that this was about *family!*

The Professor was actually the only real person on the murderer's side of the equation that anybody had ever set eyes upon in this long saga. Danny had noticed a written document from a man called Stanley Oldknow, he remembered that Archie had mentioned this man and also Mrs Gilroy had referred to Roisin having a partner called Stanley with a *funny other name.* Stanley's document was a ten-page report, most of it confined to information about the Professor and his activities in Manchester at that time. It was meticulously written and left nothing out and Danny thought that Stanley would have been a man of great method and attention to detail. Danny was drawn to a transcript of a conversation between the professor and Roisin de Hay which Stanley had apparently reproduced.

The report informed that Stanley had taken a statement from Roisin who at that time was still in hospital two weeks after the assassination attempt. However, the actual conversation between

Roisin de Hay and the man calling himself Professor Jeremy Weedon had itself taken place on the same day as this attempt, in reality minutes before it. Danny began to study the transcript which was a record of that interchange. Danny thought that as far as the Professor was concerned that he was about to kill Roisin so he may not have been too guarded about what he had told her. Stanley Oldknow had initialized each speaker in turn and he had written his transcript by hand and in italics, it read:

JW. *As we spoke about at our last meeting your family are from County Wexford Miss de Hay, which part of County Wexford?*

RDH. *It's a small town called Enniscorthy.*

JW. *Oh yes, Enniscorthy.*

RDH. *Do you know it Professor?*

JW. *No, strange as it may seem I've travelled to many parts of the world but I've never actually been to Ireland at all. Although I did actually know somebody from Enniscorthy itself.*

RDH. *Oh really, who was that, perhaps I know him too?*

JW. *That's highly unlikely Miss de Hay, he was around a long time ago and he didn't move in the circles that you would have done but for the record his name was Finbarr Joseph.*

RDH. *I don't recognise the name, did he have another name perhaps, what did he do?'*

JW. *Oh he didn't really have another name, not one of any consequence anyway, and he didn't do that much. He just sat there on the ground. On his own little piece of land.*

RDH. *Well, I don't suppose he was doing anybody any harm just sitting there.*

JW. *That's just it you see, I mean you wouldn't think that he was doing anybody any harm, but he was. He was being harmful just by sitting there. Or even if he wasn't, others thought that he was, and that's what counted in those days, what others thought, not what Finbarr thought.*

RDH. Who exactly was Finbarr?

JW. He was a peasant boy in the Great Hunger.

RDH. An Gorta Mor, that was a long time ago.

JW. For many it was, but for some it is just as if it was happening today.

RDH. So what happened to Finbarr?

JW. He had to leave Ireland.

RDH. Where did he go?

JW. Oh he travelled everywhere.

RDH. Did he ever go back to Ireland?

JW. He visited it yes, but he didn't stay there. He was very typical of his generation and over a period of time millions left Ireland and very few ever went back.

RDH. What happened to his family and his little piece of land?

JW. His family died before he left Ireland, that's one of the reasons why he had to leave, he had to grow up without them.

RDH. That's a very sad story Professor, a person's family are most important.

JW. You are right Miss de Hay, your family is of the utmost importance, you must never let your family down and they must never let you down.

RDH. What happened to Finbarr's land?'

JW. Oh, somebody took it off him and he became a man of insignificance.

RDH. That's an unusual way to describe somebody, I don't think that I've ever heard of a person described in such a cruel way before.

JW. Well, it may seem a cruel description, and I suppose that it is, but if you have no land, no family, no money and no country and all that you actually do have is failure and humiliation then how would you describe such a person Miss de Hay?

RDH. Well, surely feelings are important and humiliation is after all a feeling.

JW. Do you speak from personal experience? Forgive my candour but how would you know, when was the last time that you were actually humiliated? I don't mean when did you last make a little mistake or when did you last feel a bit of a fool. I mean when were you so humiliated that you felt that you couldn't face anything and you had to run away from everything?

RDH. I have to say that I've never really felt that way.

Danny, stood up from his chair. He thought of the Professor's words in response to Roisin's question about Finbarr's land:

'... somebody took it off him and he became *a man of Insignificance*.'

The Professor had given Roisin this vital clue, probably unintentionally and unknowingly, but it didn't matter as far as the Professor was concerned, because in a minute or so he was going to kill her, or so he thought. Danny's face drained of colour and he could hear his own heart beating. At that moment everything seemed to go into slow motion and he knew that he had found the identity of the original *Man of Insignificance*, the murderer of the sisters in Dublin all those years ago, it was Finbarr Joseph, but who was Finbarr Joseph?

His phone rang, it was Christine Harris, 'Hello Chris.'

'Councillor, how are you?'

'I'm fine, how you are?'

'Working away.'

'I've checked the newcomers list against the current electoral roll as you asked. I've eliminated the categories that we agreed on.

Three people died between the dates that you gave me. One has been in Strangeways prison for the last six months and one in long term hospital care and there are a few others I've eliminated for reasons which I won't go into. This leaves nineteen people on your list, all newcomers within the last twelve months. I've just emailed the list over to you. So I'll leave it with you now.'

'Thanks Chris, I am truly grateful, there is just one more question I need an answer to.'

'Go on.'

'I need to find somebody that was living in 1848.'

'They will be dead by now.'

'Chris, this is serious.'

'That should be fairly easy, the first national census was in 1801 and they were every ten years so there would be one in 1841 and 1851.'

'This is in the Republic of Ireland.'

'Ah, that's going to be a little more difficult.'

'Is that because of the fire? I wasn't quite sure which census records were destroyed.'

'Amongst others it was the one that you need. There were a few original ones that were preserved and some transcripts were made but I've been down this road before when it comes to Ireland and it is not an easy task. Sometimes it is impossible.'

'Is there any way at all?'

'What exactly do you need to know about this person?'

'Just if he was alive then and anything else that you can find out about him.'

'Have you got an address for him?'

'I've got a location.'

'Is it a secret?'

'No, of course it isn't.'

'Well where is it?'

'It's in Enniscorthy.'

'In County Wexford?'

'Yes.'

'Have you got a name or is that a secret as well?'

'Finbarr Joseph.'

'Finbarr that's quite a well-known Irish name.'

'I know, but is it a popular one, will there be many of them?'

'I don't know the answer to that and I surely don't know it for the eighteen-forties.'

'Joseph, is that a surname or another forename it doesn't sound very Irish for a surname?'

'I don't know, it could be either.'

'So just let me make sure I'm understanding this, you want to know if there was a man called Finbarr Joseph living in Enniscorthy in 1848.'

'Yes.'

'Anything else you know about him.'

Danny thought of the Professor's words to Roisin, 'He had to grow up without them.'

'Now that I think about it a bit more, he is probably more of a boy than a man, or if he is a man a very young one.'

'When you say a boy do you mean a child?'

'Yes, he could be.'

'Have you got a minimum age?'

'No minimum but let's say twenty years of age maximum.'

'So we could be going back to 1828 as his birth year that would make him twenty in 1848.'

'I can't discount it, everything is possible but I think that he's much younger than that.'

'Anything else you can tell me about him that could narrow it down?'

'He's probably a peasant, possibly some sort of farmer.'

'That's not a category Councillor but I will definitely bear it in mind.'

'I suppose it's urgent.'

'Chris, it is urgent and very important or I wouldn't ask. Somebody's life may depend upon this.'

'Are you sure this is council business? Don't answer that.'

'I won't.'

'It will have to be local Irish records, that's the only way I can think of but there is a big important church in Enniscorthy. It might even be a cathedral, yes I think it is, and there is always a chance in

Ireland when you've got a big church, the church kept a lot of records, often more than the government. I know somebody over in Waterford City, that's close to Enniscorthy, who knows about these things, I'll speak to her. Leave it with me for a few hours, I'll come back to you this afternoon even if I've got nothing.'

'Thank you Chris, I really appreciate it.'

'Alright, I'll speak to you then.' She hung up.

Danny sat down in front of Archie's computer, he brought Christine's list of nineteen onto the screen. She had listed them in alphabetical order, the first one was *Addams* and the last one was *Walsh*. He looked through all the names in a cursory way but nothing leapt out at him. This didn't really surprise him as he didn't know what he was looking for anyway. He printed the list off and attached it to his whiteboard. He then highlighted all the men on the list, there were ten of them. Was one of these ten the killer he thought? Was one of these men the person that murdered Helen Day and the same person that tried to kill Archie and was this man the one who would try to kill Kathleen Helen's daughter and who was Kathleen Helen's daughter and where was Kathleen Helen's daughter?

He recalled the night he'd been in Helen's house and he'd asked her why she'd moved to Winton Kiss. Not for the first time he recalled her exact words, she had said: *'All my life I've had to keep my distance, away from the only person in the world that I've come to realise I ever really cared about, the only person that ever meant anything to me. I wasn't going to intrude upon people's lives, no I wouldn't do that. It's much too late for that and it might cause them unhappiness and that's the last thing I'd want but if I can just see them now and again and know that their life has not been unhappy the way mine has then that would mean everything to me.'*

Did Helen Day move to Winton Kiss to be near her daughter? Was Helen Day's daughter in Winton Kiss already? If she was then who was she? Did the killer discover their identities and move himself to Winton Kiss?

As the afternoon drifted by, he puzzled and pondered on all these questions. He thought about Helen again, if she had moved to Winton Kiss to be near the daughter that she'd given up years ago and she wanted to see her, *now and again*, then why did she live the life of a recluse, staying in her house most of the time, never going out? In fact, when was the *now and again* that she had referred to when she actually saw her daughter? All Helen did was sit on the Safeguarding Panel and have an occasional drink in Manchester. How did any of that put her in front of her own daughter? Perhaps she didn't need to be in front of her. Perhaps she was satisfied to see her from a distance. Perhaps her daughter was on the Safeguarding Panel herself. He did a deliberate mental roll call of its members, going through them one by one. Excluding himself and Helen there were nine other people. For one reason or another, gender, age, race and what he already knew about some of them, not one of them was even worthy of candidacy.

The only person that Helen Day had any association with in Winton Kiss was the foster mum, Theresa Rafferty. Was Theresa Rafferty, Helen Day's daughter? She was certainly the right age. If Helen's daughter was born in 1979, as Archie said, then she would be about thirty-five by now and that's roughly what Theresa was, aged about thirty-five. He thought to himself, what did he actually know about Theresa? She wasn't native to Winton Kiss, she'd appeared on the scene about ten years ago which, coincidentally, was about the same time that Helen arrived. Had Helen, after all these years, tracked her own daughter down in Winton Kiss? This was beginning to make a bit of sense to him now. The more he thought about Theresa the more he made parallels with Helen and his own perception of her daughter. She was the right age, Helen had arrived in the village just after Theresa had, she came from Dublin so she was the right nationality. Helen was a social worker, and Theresa was a foster mum. In fact, hadn't Helen been involved in some casework on Theresa's behalf? Helen was a recluse, well Theresa wasn't that but she could easily be described as a private person. Most importantly Theresa was probably the only person that he could think of, apart from himself, who had been in Helen's house. She was also, he recalled, at Helen Day's funeral. So why was she actually there? What was Helen Day to Theresa that she would attend her funeral? Surely you wouldn't just ship up to a stranger's funeral but you would go to your own mother's, even if you were estranged. Was Helen Day Theresa Rafferty's mother? Was Theresa the missing daughter? It was circumstantial, but it all fitted, though somehow he couldn't avoid thinking that he was making it fit. He could contact Theresa directly and ask her. What was to stop him? He knew where she was, he could drive around to her house now and ask her straight, point blank. Was Helen Day your mother? It would take him half an hour at the most. So why didn't he just go and do it? What was actually stopping him? Again, what if Theresa was the missing daughter but she didn't actually know it? He didn't know the answer to that any more than he knew the answer to all the other questions. He looked at his whiteboard again to see if he could find any inspiration from his scrawls and scribbles. The afternoon drifted by into the late part of it.

His phone rang, it was Christine again, 'Hello Councillor.'

'Thanks for ringing back.'

'I've just sent all this detail to you on email but I think that I've got something.'

'Something on Finbarr Joseph?'

'Yeah.'

'Tell me.'

'I've only been able to find one Finbarr Joseph in Enniscorthy in the year that you mentioned. He had quite an unusual surname, it's Breathnach.'

'So, it's Finbarr Joseph Breathnach?'

'That's the name I've got, yes.'

Senetti wrote the name on his board, 'What do we know about him?'

'We know this, his date of birth was 30 September, 1834.'

'Then in 1848 he would have been thirteen or fourteen years of age.'

'Yes, your maths is good.'

'Do we know anything else?'

'Well, I did come across something else but we'd have to make an assumption.'

'Well let's make it.'

'There were six other people around at the same time with the same surname.'

'Same address?'

'There isn't an actual fixed address, not an address as we would know it with a house and number, which would indicate that they were a poor family which fits in with your peasant theory?'

'So what exactly do we know about them?'

'We've got names, dates of birth and in the case of the six, the dates they died.'

'What do you think? It's an unusual surname Christine for them not to be connected.'

'The six other people are a man and five women, four of them very young women, almost girls. The man is described as a *tenant farmer*; the girls were aged between fifteen and twenty-one years-of-age when they died, all in the period from December 1845 to July 1848.'

'Do we know when Finbarr Joseph died?'

'No, there is no recorded date for that.'

'What do you think?'

'I think that as we say, it's an unusual name and they are connected.'

'You think that they are his family?'

'I think that because of their ages it's very probable that the other people are Finbarr's father, his mother and the young girls would be his four sisters. They probably all died in the famine leaving him as the sole survivor then perhaps he left town, or maybe even Ireland altogether, and that's why there is no record of his death. That's the lot, that's all I know, hope that it helps.'

'So Finbarr had a mother and four young sisters, his life would have been dominated by women.'

'Yes, I suppose that's true.'

'Chris, as always you've been very helpful, I really appreciate it. What would I do without you?'

'Right Councillor.'

'Thanks Chris, bye.'

'Finbarr Joseph Breathnach,' Senetti said softly to himself and he looked at the name on his board. Was Finbarr Joseph Breathnach the first *Man of Insignificance*, the killer of the two sisters in Dublin and the original author of the *Peasants Decree*? Senetti thought that he was. Was Helen Day's murderer a descendent of Finbarr Joseph Breathnach, his great-grandson perhaps or his great-great-grandson or even his grandson or at least some family relative? Senetti thought that he was. This was the first time that the name *Breathnach* had made an appearance in this investigation, it was an unusual name, he certainly didn't have any constituents in his ward with the name *Breathnach*, he would have remembered if he had, new or otherwise.

Then, for the first time that day he noticed Archie's safe on the floor and he took out the business card that Archie had written the combination number on. He punched the number in and turned the big key handle and the door groaned open. It was reasonably tidy inside and papers were stacked in some form of order. Something glistened in the corner. He picked it up and brought it out. It was the gun that Archie had mentioned, it was a small gun, a double-barrelled derringer pistol. In his army officer days he'd been both a crack shot and a weapons trainer and he recognised it as a Remington Model 95, over-under, double-barrelled derringer pistol. It was actually now a collector's item. It wasn't loaded but inside the safe he found a small box of cartridges which he also brought out. He thought that the gun must be easily over a hundred years old but it was in perfect condition and as a weapon was absolutely deadly. It was the type of weapon that people who didn't want other people to know that they had a weapon used. There was also a thick brown leather book inside the safe with, *de Hay photos*, written on the front, the obligatory family photo album he thought to himself. He considered that it would be interesting to see what all these people looked like so he brought that out as well. He opened the album at random but he didn't look at it. He put it on the desk then he put the gun and cartridges on top of it.

At that precise moment his mind went back to Finbarr Joseph Breathnach, or at least to the surname part of it, and to Christine's list of nineteen. There was something there that he couldn't quite bring out. There was also something else that was niggling him, it was to do with Archie's comments about *amber eyes* but he couldn't quite get that thought out either. He'd seen amber eyes somewhere and it was recently. Was it Theresa Rafferty at Helen's funeral, did Theresa have amber eyes? He thought that she might have but he couldn't be sure, his mind was all over the place.

He looked at Christine's list again. He knew from his knowledge of Irish history that Irish immigrants to England during the Great Hunger often changed a very Irish sounding name to a more English sounding name. Often these names were just translated from their Irish origin into English, so what was it about *Breathnach* that was on his mind? He browsed around the Internet and discovered that the name Breathnach was originally derived to define *Welshman* and that an anglicized version of this often became *Walsh*. Why did the name Walsh register with him, what was it about that name? Then he recalled Christine's list of *nineteen*, Addams to Walsh. Walsh, the last name on Christine's alphabetically ordered list of nineteen was Walsh!

He snatched the list off the whiteboard and stared at the last name on it. Ysabel Maria Montoya Esmeralda Walsh, the Rectory, All Saints, Winton Kiss. She was the Vicar, the Reverend Bel. She was a woman and he was looking for a man, but why was he looking for a man, who decreed that the killer of Helen Day had to be a man? You didn't need to be a man to shoot somebody in the head. Why can't the killer be a woman?

There was something else too because whilst the name Walsh was English or Irish or Welsh then Ysabel Maria Montoya Esmeralda was decidedly none of these and was without doubt of Spanish extraction. Then he thought of what Archie had said about Spanish guitars. He told himself that he wasn't making all this fit together this time just for the sake of it.

He began to think about the night of the council meeting when he'd been stood on the landing with Archie. There had been one other person on that landing within possible earshot. She was listening to her mobile phone through earphones and he had paid no attention to it at the time. Now he realised that it probably wasn't a mobile phone, it was a listening device. She had overheard every word that he and Archie had uttered. Then she'd followed Archie outside and run him over. The Spanish music that Archie thought he'd imagined was probably from her car music system. That person was Ysabel Maria Montoya Esmeralda Walsh. She'd given the lesson that night at the council meeting. She was a descendent of Finbarr Joseph Breathnach. She was new to the community yet she was at the hub of it. She would know most things that were going on inside it and because of her position she would have no problem gaining access to Helen Day's house.

She was the killer, he knew it. She, was the *Man of Insignificance*.

Finbarr Joseph Breathnach had probably been swindled by the Gombeen, Padraig de Hay, he probably left Ireland as a young boy and he held a severe grievance all those years. Then in 1883 he committed the double murder. His bitterness and anger was such that he ensured his descendants felt the same way and they in turn ensured that their descendants did too. Senetti knew it, just the way he had discussed it with Maxine. The same as any family business, only the business of this family was *murder and revenge*.

What was his next move he asked himself? He could at least establish where Ysabel Walsh was at this moment. He checked the number and rang the rectory, a woman's voice answered, 'All Saints Rectory.'

'Oh hello,' said Danny, 'its Norford Council here, can I speak to Reverend Bel.'

'I'm afraid she's not here at the moment. She's taken a few days off and gone away somewhere.'

'When is she back, where has she gone?'

'She said she'd be back on Monday, as to where she's gone, she doesn't tell me and even if she did I couldn't tell you.'

'It's very important.'

'As I said, I don't know, who is this?'

'Norford Council.'

'Yes, I know, you said that, but who at Norford Council?'

He hung up.

Danny was thinking but his brain wasn't coming up with any kind of plan. There was a killer on the loose and she could be anywhere. He needed to concentrate and as an aside he removed the derringer and cartridge box from on top the album and he began to flick through its content. He was drawn to a page that contained a photograph of a beautiful young girl. She was aged, he thought, about eighteen and she was stood outside on a lawn in front of a lavishly appointed country home. She was smiling on the photograph but Danny thought that the smile was painted and that she looked vulnerable and frightened. There was a handwritten caption underneath that said, *Antoinette Dubois, 1917, outside the mansion house.* He thought that this young girl looked a little familiar to him. Turning the pages of the album he was suddenly *stopped absolutely dead in his tracks*, he was amazed and astounded by his accidental discovery.

His eyes came to linger upon a black and white photograph of a group of people. It was a full-length photograph and the subjects were three men and three women. All the men wore suits and ties and the women wore hats. Danny didn't know much about the fashion of any gender for any era but he guessed the period to be the nineteen-forties. Although the six people were grouped together they were obviously three couples and there were forenames written underneath each individual as they appeared from left to right: *Roisin, Stanley, Antoinette, Dermot, Arthur, Jane.* Underneath the names was a date, *June 1942*, this confirmed Danny's fashion guess. The men wore buttonholes and the women carried flower posies. It was also obvious that it was a wedding photograph. All the subjects were standing save Roisin who sat in a wheelchair. Danny didn't recognise any of the men although their names told him who they were. Neither did he recognise the woman, Jane. However the physical appearance of Roisin was familiar to him. For although he had never met Roisin de Hay he had met Helen Day. He estimated that Roisin would be approaching fifty years of age at the time of the photograph and both she and the Helen Day that he had known were almost a mirror image of the other. It wasn't though the physical similarity between Roisin and Helen that held him in a state of totally unexpected shock, that came from looking at another physical similarity. It was Antoinette Dubois, who he now recognised as the young girl in the photograph on the lawn outside the country house, only this time twenty plus years on she no longer appeared vulnerable and afraid instead she exuded confidence and happiness on what was obviously her wedding day.

He glanced up at his board towards the de Hay family tree and he confirmed to himself that Antoinette de Hay was the birth mother of Kathleen Helen and as such would be the maternal birth grandmother of Kathleen Helen's missing daughter. Kathleen Helen herself had inherited the plain looks of her father, he could see that, but Kathleen Helen's own daughter had inherited the looks and natural beauty of her grandmother Antoinette. This often happened in families, he knew that genes and likeness often skipped a generation, sometimes even more than one. Not only had the granddaughter inherited Antoinette's beauty and likeness, she had inherited every aspect of her grandmother, her smile, her poise, her eyes. It was as if he was looking at a true double of one woman to another and the only thing that separated them was the time span of seventy-two years. The discovery and the knowledge enveloped him like a tidal tsunami. He also knew that even the missing daughter herself did not know who she was and that she was completely unaware of her own identity as far as this was concerned. Then, as if in confirmation of his sensational discovery, he remembered where he'd seen the amber eyes. He'd looked right into them on many occasions as a matter of course and he had not even noticed. He had not even given them a second thought. He now knew why Helen Day had moved to Winton Kiss and how she'd been able to initiate and sustain contact with her own daughter and he now realised that there were only two people alive, himself and the Man of Insignificance, who knew the true identity of that missing daughter who had been taken away from Kathleen Helen, thirty-four years ago, and it shocked him rigid for incredibly it was – *Maxine Wells*.

Once Danny Senetti allowed himself ownership of his revelations about Maxine and Bel. He knew that one was intent on killing the other. He knew too that he knew the whereabouts of one but not the other. What if Bel had discovered that Maxine was in Beaumaris? What if she had gone over there herself?

The little house in Gaol Street would be an ideal place to commit a murder.

How could she have discovered Maxine's whereabouts, was it possible? Maxine didn't decide that she was going herself until yesterday and before that she didn't even know the place existed. Would she have told anybody where she was going? Her partner perhaps, her father certainly. That was it, her father, Doctor Tom. Danny recalled he had seen him in the Traveller's Oak with Bel last night. He thought back to the phone call that he'd overheard between Doctor Tom and Maxine outside the pub. Perhaps Doctor Tom had told Ysabel Walsh, *The Man of Insignificance*, quite innocently of Maxine's whereabouts.

He picked up his phone and dialled Maxine's number, he didn't know what he was going to say to her, he just wanted her to answer, but there was no sound at the other end. Then he remembered – there was no reception in the house in Gaol Street, that was one of the things that he liked about it. He looked at his watch, it was just 5:30pm. He thought that if he drove as fast as he could and didn't get caught in rush hour traffic he could be at the house in Gaol Street for around eight o'clock. He pulled his jacket from the back of the chair then he looked at the derringer and the cartridges on the desk. It had been a long time, going back to his army days, since he had held any kind of weapon in his hand let alone a gun. He made a dash for the door but before he did he picked up the gun and the cartridges.

Chapter 37

Calling All Angels

Maxine Wells had always considered the concept of *family* to be a complicated sketch.

Over the years she had concluded that there was no such thing as a typical one. In pursuant, she had also concluded that there were no two that were the same. She herself had been adopted as an eleven-month-old baby and she considered herself fortunate and privileged to have the upbringing that she'd had. In contrast to some other adopted children she had never been interested in finding out about her birth parents. She did know that her late birth father had been a doctor but that was the complete extent of her knowledge and she wished it to remain that way. She bore her natural parents no negativity of any kind. She quite simply didn't have any feelings for them, nor interest in them, nor in that past situation one way or another. She took a completely pragmatic approach, it was all water under the bridge. She had come to be in life where she had come to be and that was that.

Some years ago when she had reached the age of eighteen she had been visited by two social workers from the Norford council. They had informed her that she was entitled, by statutory requirement, to know the identity of her birth family and also that she was entitled to see her file. She thought it a little cold and cynical that her life should be referred to as a *statutory requirement* and a *file* and she could tell that the social workers had been a little surprised when she had declined their offers on both counts. She thought it to their credit that they didn't do or say anything to try to persuade her one way or another. After the interview they left her some contact details, in the event that she should change her mind, then they left and as far as she knew, the matter was never raised again by anybody and, as far as she was concerned, it was well and truly closed.

As Maxine opened the door to Bel she took the two champagne glasses from Bel's outstretched hands. 'Where you would prefer to sit, lounge or kitchen?' Maxine asked.

'Oh, I'm more of a lounge person myself.'

'Lounge it is then.'

She showed Bel into the lounge then she went into the kitchen and took a bottle of champagne from the fridge. She popped the cork and returned with the opened bottle in one hand and the two champagne flutes in the other. She filled the two glasses and handed one to Bel, then both the women sat in chairs at opposite ends of the small room.

Maxine said, 'I suppose a toast is in order, to Beaumaris,' she said spontaneously and raised her glass.

Bel raised her glass too, 'to Beaumaris, indeed.'

'I've just realised that I don't know your preferred name. In the short time that I've known you, I've only ever known you as the Reverend Bel, which sounds a bit formal for a girls champagne evening.'

'Actually, when it comes to names I'm more blessed, or cursed, than most, depending upon your view, but I've got a few to choose from, my mother was Spanish and my father was English, my full name is Ysabel Maria Esmeralda Montoya Walsh. At school it was all shortened to Bel and that's what it came to be, now my friends call me Bel so please do the same.'

'Bel it is then Bel, I'm Maxine.'

'Well then Maxine, are we still applying our conditions about not mentioning the place that we're not mentioning?'

'I think that we just might have to suspend that clause otherwise we may find that we have nothing to talk about, especially as I was just going to be really inquisitive and ask you about how you are finding life in Winton Kiss and what actually made you come to it in the first place.'

'Oh I'm finding life alright and I came to Winton Kiss in search.'

'In search Bel, have you found what you were in search of?'

'Yes, I believe that I have, were you actually born in Winton Kiss?'

'No I wasn't, a lot of people think that, but I've been here from a very early age.'

'But I heard that your father has been in practice here for many years and his father before him.'

'Yes, that's quite true, there has been a Doctor Wells in the village since 1880 but Doctor Tom is not actually my birth father.'

'Oh, I'm sorry Maxine, I didn't mean to upset or embarrass you by being intrusive.'

'Actually, it's all rather topical as I was just thinking about it before you arrived. I'm not upset or embarrassed so don't concern yourself Bel, it was all a long time ago. I was very young at the time, a baby in fact. I don't keep it a secret but I don't go around proclaiming it either. I was adopted by my parents when I was less than one year old.'

'That's very interesting, do you know who your birth parents are? Do you have any children yourself?'

'No, I don't have any children and as for my own birth parents I understand that my father died a long time ago. I believe that he was also a doctor and I know nothing of my mother and I've now decided to keep it that way. I've never felt curious or even slightly interested in any of it. I did have the opportunity to have some information some years ago. I thought about it for a time but I couldn't work up any natural enthusiasm for the idea, I thought that I would have been forcing the issue so I didn't take it up. As well as that I couldn't really see what good could come out of it but I could see that some harm might. So, I just decided to be satisfied with what I have. I've always been happy to have a wonderful mother and father. The biology doesn't really come into it. What about your family background or is that an intrusive question?'

'Not at all, as I said, my mother was Spanish. I also lost my father at a very early age, he was English, he was killed in an accident at work. My mother, she was a good person and probably a good mother but she was never there, she was an absentee parent. She was a career woman before they had career women. She came to be in charge of a big hospital in London and as I was growing up I didn't see a lot of her. For most of my formative years I was brought up by my paternal grandfather and I owe most of everything to him. He taught me about the value of family and about the responsibility that we all have to our families. That's all members of your family, both past and present, whether they are either dead or alive.'

'I suppose being an ordained priest you mean that in a spiritual way.'

'No, I don't believe that I do.'

'In what way then?'

'Well, as I said, you are responsible for your family and they are responsible for you. If your own Great Ancestor had something bad and evil done to him then as a family member you have a responsibility to settle that situation.'

'Your own great ancestor Bel, who would that be?'

'The people that have come before you in your family, your father, grandfather and his father and before that and as far back as you can go.'

'I am not sure that I fully understand that, how could you have any influence over a situation that occurred say a hundred years ago, it's happened and gone before you were born and all the people involved at that time have long since died. Haven't they?'

'Yes they have, but that's what I meant by all members either dead or alive. It's all to do with your family history.'

'Sometimes the best thing for history is that it is consigned to the past.'

'No, I don't agree with that, it can be consigned to the past but we should learn from it in the present and of course there should always be retribution for wrongdoing.'

'Retribution?'

'Yes, don't you believe in retribution?'

'What exactly do you mean by retribution?'

'Well, exactly what that word means.'

'So very often it means punishment, revenge?'

'Yes, but not just any old punishment, not just any old revenge. It has to be something that has been decreed and also it has to be punishment that is morally right and fully deserved.'

'Sorry, but did you say decreed and morally right punishment, I'm not sure that I understand. You mean such as capital punishment?'

'Yes, I think that there is a case that can be made for capital punishment. If a wrong has been committed, and it is serious enough, but we shouldn't be so quick to push the task onto the government or the state, that is just us abdicating our own responsibility.'

'Who exactly do you mean when you say us?'

'Anybody, you, me, family members. As I said, we all have a responsibility to our families and they do to us.'

'I'm a little surprised that a priest would hold such views. Nevertheless, it's an interesting debate and it brings up some philosophical points but I'm not absolutely sure that I understand your own stance, particularly the bit about your great ancestor.'

'It's a fascinating subject which I believe is greatly ignored, I'll explain a bit more if you want me to.'

Maxine felt that she didn't really want to pursue the conversation but she found herself saying, 'if you wish, but it isn't really necessary.'

'Let's just say that my ancestor, grandfather or great-grandfather, that bit doesn't really matter, had a great wrong done to him by your ancestor and that this wrong caused my ancestor great pain, sorrow and humiliation.'

'What sort of wrong?'

'There are so many wrongs that one person can inflict upon another and the wrong in itself again doesn't really matter that much, but let's say, for the sake of the argument, that your ancestor murdered all my ancestor's family and he stole all his land.'

'Well that's a fairly extreme anecdote. I think that I would agree that these are not very gracious things to do but my ancestor and yours are both presumably dead and we weren't there at that time so we can't know all the peculiar circumstances. So that wrong can't be put right. It is all a bit too late isn't it? So don't we just forgive?'

'No, we don't just forgive, forgiveness is not any part of the answer, closure perhaps but forgiveness no. Forgiveness is too easy and it is a craven way of reconciling no action with our own conscience. The actual wrong act itself cannot be repealed I agree, but that is an entirely different situation than accepting that it can't be put right.'

'How can it be put right?'

'By retribution.'

'Retribution, against whom, they are all dead?'

'Retribution against you as the progeny and surviving member of that family.'

Maxine was beginning to feel very uneasy about the course of this conversation. She considered this point of view to be one that she would not have expected from a woman who was a priest. She thought that she would try and change the subject and she looked out through the window and onto the street in an attempt to find some inspiration that she could deflect the conversation towards. When she returned her gaze she found to her astonishment that the Reverend Bel was holding a small gun in her hand and it was pointed firmly at her.

'Let me tell you about my great-grandfather and your birth great-grandfather, you see they really did know each other all those years ago.'

'I've already said I don't know anything about my birth family.'

'No Doctor, you are misunderstanding the situation, *you* may not know anything about your birth family but *I* know quite a lot about them. In fact I know as much as anybody can know about one family. I've put a lot of research into finding out about them and I've put a lot of research into finding out about you and establishing exactly who you are.'

'Why would you want to do that? What possible interest to you could my background be?'

'Because you're great-grandfather was called Padraig de Hay and mine was called Finbarr Joseph Breathnach and your ancestor really did murder my great-grandfather's family. Oh he didn't do it with his hands but he did it with his cruel, vindictive actions and he murdered them just the same and he really did steal my family's land and now the time for retribution has arrived and you are the only one that's left, therefore you are the last one to pay this retribution. Then, once you are dead my family responsibility has been completely discharged as you are the last of a line. Your great-grandfather was an evil man who committed great sins against defenceless, vulnerable people and somebody has to atone for those sins and that person is you.'

'What person?'

'The person you are Doctor, the real person, not the person that you've been pretending to be all these years, not Doctor Maxine Wells.'

'I am Doctor Maxine Wells.'

'The name that you call yourself doesn't really matter that much. What does matter is who you came from. No, you are not Doctor Maxine Wells, this is really nothing more than an assumed identity. It's very easy to assume an identity but you can never really discard the real identity that comes from your family, you are not Maxine Wells you are Maxine de Hay. Your father was blameless so he is not connected in any way to this situation but your mother was Kathleen Helen de Hay and she was not blameless and neither are you.'

There was a very long pause then Maxine realised exactly who she was dealing with. The whole situation seemed incredible to her and a stream of questions hurled themselves through her mind. She found herself saying, 'You murdered Helen Day didn't you.'

'No, there was no Helen Day, somebody made her up, Helen Day has never existed. It wasn't murder either, I am not a murderer, murderers are criminals, and I am not a criminal. I am an executioner and I executed Kathleen Helen de Hay, not Helen Day. It was retribution for crimes that her family committed against mine, it was retribution that was morally right and justly deserved.'

'You didn't even know Helen Day before you came to Winton Kiss. You didn't even know what kind of person she was.'

'I have been searching for her for many years and it was of no consequence what type of person she was. This responsibility that I have is not person to person, it is history to history. I am concerned with past identity and connection not with present conduct and behaviour. What matters is who you are and where you came from, not what you have become. Just because you become something better or different than your ancestor, that doesn't mean that you can abdicate all responsibility for his wrongs just by dismissing it as all being in the past.'

'Now you want to kill me and we'd not even met before today, you don't even know me.'

'You're a de Hay, you're Maxine de Hay you were born Maxine de Hay, your great-grandfather was Padraig de Hay and mine was Finbarr Joseph Breathnach. That really is the only knowledge that we need. This final act of retribution has been promised since 1848. My great-grandfather executed your great-aunts Siobhan and Clodagh in Dublin. Finbarr's son, my grandfather, failed in his attempt to execute Roisin de Hay but succeeded in executing Marguerite de Hay. All these are ancestors of yours and of mine. I personally executed Kathleen Helen de Hay who was your mother.'

'My mother, Helen Day was my mother!' exclaimed Maxine.

'No, Kathleen Helen de Hay was your mother.'

Maxine's complexion drained but she determined to keep her composure. She did not know a way out of this situation, she could see that Bel's resolve was maniacal but it was also ruthless and determined. Just then Maxine thought that she heard music and then a man's voice start to sing:

> *'Calling all angels, callin' all angels, callin' all angels, oo-ou*
> *There's trouble in paradise*
> *The birds no longer sing*
> *Some devil told my angel a lot of lies*
> *And now my tears are falling*
> *Like raindrops from the sky.'*

It was coming from outside in the street and had filtered through the open lounge window. Maxine turned toward the window. She didn't recognise the singer and she didn't recognise the song but she welcomed the distraction and she recognised the style of music, it was a distinct type of music that she'd only ever heard once before, it was one of Danny Senetti's *Doo wop* tunes. She knew immediately it was intended as a signal from him to her and she read it, it told her he was here in Beaumaris, he was here in Gaol Street. Senetti had somehow worked this all out, but where was he now? She was also concerned for she knew that Bel would have no compunction whatsoever in shooting both her and Senetti. She grappled around in her mind for a solution that would save both their lives. Sub consciously she heard the cellar kitchen door rattle on its latch.

Bel was also distracted by the music and she stood up. As she turned towards the window she let the hand with the derringer fall down to her side.

When the two women again turned away from the window and looked back towards each other, stood framed in the doorway to the kitchen was Danny Senetti. Maxine guessed that he had come in around the back and up through the cellar.

The three of them looked at each other, Senetti held a gun which was identical to the gun that Bel was holding, his arm was outstretched and he had it pointed directly at Bel's head. The barrel tip was no more than four feet away from her, he didn't say a word and in a totally uncharacteristic way remained completely silent. Surprisingly to Maxine he seemed to hold the gun in a comfortable and expert way and he appeared determined, concise and extremely calm. Maxine thought that she had never seen him so unanimated. It was as if in a few short seconds he had already read the situation and knew exactly what was going to happen.

Bel on the other hand seemed in a quandary, un-decisive and agitated by Senetti's sudden and unexpected appearance. Her gun arm wavered and it appeared that she didn't know whether to shoot Maxine or Senetti. She stepped back and as she did she raised the gun slightly and in Maxine's direction, it went off with a crack!

Only it didn't go off, it was Senetti's gun that had fired whilst Bel's remained silent. The murderous priest fell down and over the side of the armchair onto the floor. The bullet had struck her clearly in the middle of her forehead. As her body struck the floor the tiny room shook and reverberated, then it took on a deathly silence. She had been killed in the same way and by the same weapon that had killed Siobhan de Hay in Dublin one hundred and twenty-one years ago. Danny and Maxine looked across the small room at each other, they remained silent. The cause of Senetti's silence was adrenalin and the realisation that he had just shot someone dead whilst Maxine's silence was caused by shock although she didn't know what had shocked her the most, what had just transpired in the last hour or because of the revelation that Helen Day was her birth mother.

Senetti walked over to the front door and opened it wide to let some of the evening summer air in. He thought of all the events of the last two months, of Padraig de Hay and of Finbarr Joseph Breathnach and the consequences of the actions of these two people all those years ago through the generations of two families. He hoped that now it was finished, that it was all over. For some reason his mind went back to Noel O'Malley in Crossmolina and Christina the barmaid in the Dolphin Hotel. By now she would be just serving the little Irishman his third pint of Guinness. Certainly for sure, *tautology*. Senetti realised that that was the word he had been searching for, tautology.

He asked himself how was he going to explain all this to Karen Spencer, what was to become of his chair-ship of the Airport Committee now, and more immediately, and not without a touch of irony that came from the address of his present location, how was he going to keep himself out of gaol? Just then the supremacy of the silence was humbled as the melodious tones of *Johnny Maestro* and the boys from *The Brooklyn Bridge* could be heard belting out from Senetti's car music system. Their musical riffs glided out of the car's open window and wafted along on the warm summer evening, through the welcoming doorway of the little terraced house in Gaol Street and just like some forlorn appeal for heavenly guidance, the lyrics could be heard:

Callin all angels, callin all angels, callin all angels, oo-ou-oo
Then trouble in paradise would be no more...

THE END

FOR NOW...